Massacre Pond

Paul Doiron

Constable • London

CONSTABLE

First published in the USA in 2013 by Minotaur Books,
an imprint of St Martin's Press

This edition published in the UK in 2014 by Constable

A CIP catalogue record for this book
is available from the British Library.

ISBN 978-1-47211-465-5 (paperback)
ISBN 978-1-47211-466-2 (ebook)

Typeset by SX Composing DTP Ltd, Rayleigh, Essex, UK
Printed and bound by CPI Group (UK) Ltd, Croydon, CR0 4YY

Constable
is an imprint of
Constable & Robinson Ltd
100 Victoria Embankment
London EC4Y 0DY

An Hachette UK Company
www.hachette.co.uk

www.constablerobinson.com

For Daniel Lee, who always believed

Nature looked sternly upon me on account of the murder of the moose.

—HENRY DAVID THOREAU

Nature looked warily upon me on account of the murder
of the animal.

—HENRY DAVID THOREAU

I

The first time I laid eyes on Billy Cronk, I thought he was the biggest badass in the Maine woods: six-five, braided blond hair, a tangled mess of a beard. He had arms that could have snapped a two-by-four over his knee for kindling. The night I arrested him for hunting on posted property, I kept my hand close to my pistol, wondering if this wild blue-eyed bruiser would be the death of me.

As a game warden, I'd met more than my share of roadhouse brawlers and die-hard deer poachers, and I understood that most violent men are cowards. Billy Cronk was different. He never doubted his physical prowess and had no need to prove himself against lesser men. He accepted the summons I wrote without forcing me to wrestle him into handcuffs. In fact, he thanked me for it, lowering his eyes out of embarrassment. The more I learned about the man, the more he surprised me.

He'd been a rifleman in Iraq and Afghanistan, and one of his duties had been picking up the pieces of friends blown up by roadside bombs. Back home in Maine, working as a hunting and fishing guide, he'd gutted his share of black bears and hoisted them on a pole for smiling hunters to pose with for photographs. He'd seen coyotes disembowel fleeing deer they'd chased onto frozen lakes, leaving bloody paw prints on the ice. Once, while fly-fishing, he'd watched a school of

bass gulp down a row of ducklings while the mother beat the water with her wings. Billy Cronk understood that nature was as indifferent to the moral sensibilities of twenty-first-century human beings as humans themselves were.

Our friendship had taken us both by surprise, since I was the game warden who'd gotten him fired from his job at the Call of the Wild Game Ranch. At my urging, in exchange for dropping the illegal-hunting charge, he had informed on his asshole boss for various crimes and misdemeanors, the least egregious of which was letting loose a live skunk in the trailer of the district game warden (me). When his employer told Billy to go to hell, the news hit him hard. Despite all the atrocities he had witnessed, there was a surprising innocence about the man, as if he never expected the worst from anyone, and so found himself on the receiving end of one disappointment after another. It was in his makeup to be continually heartbroken.

Billy had avoided me for the first few months after his termination, but we'd kept running into each other on the same trout streams, and eventually we struck up a conversation that revealed we shared a favorite book, an obscure Siberian adventure called *Dersu the Trapper*. I had never taken Billy for the literary type. His first take on me was equally unflattering. In his estimation, I had a stick permanently wedged halfway up my ass. But we were the same age—twenty-six—and loved the North Woods in a way few other people seemed to understand.

The last time I'd visited his house, I'd come upon him stripped to the waist, chopping firewood in the backyard. The glittering late-autumn sunlight made his tanned arms and chest look like they'd been cast in bronze. Billy usually wore his long hair in a braid, but he'd let it loose for the afternoon, and my first impression, when I saw him whaling away with an ax on a

defenseless hunk of oak, was of a Viking marauder driven into a frenzy by vengeful gods.

Every law officer understands the danger of making quick assumptions, but this truism applied to my new friend in spades. His sheer size and resemblance to the Mighty Thor gave him a dangerous aura, especially when you caught sight of the KA-BAR knife strapped to his thigh. In a crowded roadhouse, Billy could reduce the loudest biker to silence just by fixing him with a pale, cold stare. But I had seen tears in those same eyes while he watched his kids chasing each other like puppies around the picnic table and his soft-hipped wife, Aimee, served us Budweiser tall boys.

"I'm a fortunate man, Mike," he'd said.

"Yes, you are."

"Sometimes I forget, though."

"You've got five reminders right there," I said, indicating his wife and children. The blond kids were all under the age of six, dirty-faced, and confusingly similar in appearance. Billy called them the "Cronklets."

"I wish I could do better for them," Billy said in his thick Down East accent. "A man should be able to provide for his family. Something's wrong with him if he can't."

I was between girlfriends myself, and the thought of a family of my own seemed like one of those empty promises doctors offer at the bedsides of dying patients. "There's nothing wrong with you, Billy."

My friend smiled, trying to humor me, but I knew he was unable to accept my assurances.

I couldn't really blame him. I'd grown up poor myself and understood what it was like to feel the constant anxiety of unpaid bills and empty cupboards. Before my mother grew sick of my father's abuse and alcoholism and filed for divorce,

we'd lived a lot like the Cronks—holed up in drafty cabins we couldn't afford to heat, and wearing secondhand clothing scavenged from boxes in church basements. Just that week, I'd seen Aimee Cronk at the supermarket in Machias paying for her groceries with one of those EBT food-stamp cards, and I suspected that Billy might still occasionally poach some deer for the freezer (he and I had our own don't ask, don't tell policy). It had taken him six months to land another job after Joe Brogan fired him.

"How's work going?" I asked as we stood over the sizzling grill, turning venison hamburgers.

"It's different."

I rubbed my newly barbered crew cut. "What do you mean?"

He lowered his voice so Aimee wouldn't hear. "Yesterday, Ms. Morse made me open a package that came in the mail. She thought it might be a pipe bomb or something. I told her we should dip it in the bathtub first, just to be safe."

"What was inside?"

"An old book her friend bought at some auction, paintings of birds by that guy Audubon. It got kind of waterlogged. Ms. Morse threatened to deduct the cost from my paycheck. She pretended she was joking, but you can never tell with her."

I swatted a no-see-um that had alighted behind my ear. "She didn't recognize her friend's handwriting on the package?"

"Ms. Morse said it looked 'suspicious.'"

"I can't say I blame her for being paranoid."

Elizabeth "Betty" Morse had built a log mansion on Sixth Machias Lake on a pine-shaded point where a historic sporting camp had stood for more than a century, and now she required a considerable domestic staff to help run the property. I'm not sure what Billy's official job title was, but he seemed to function as her personal driver, handyman, and forester—his

duties dictated by the needs of the day. Increasingly, he also served as her bodyguard.

Betty Morse needed guarding. She was a former hippie who had started a small business selling dried herbs at farmers' markets. In time, she hired some local women to help produce various types of organic teas, which she peddled to natural-food stores, first in Maine and then around the country. Eventually, she opened a factory somewhere out of state—down south, I think—and began manufacturing herbal health supplements. These pills won the endorsement of Hollywood celebrities, who, in turn, made the brand a hit with a nation of dieting housewives. When EarthMother, Inc., went public, *The Wall Street Journal* said Betty Morse netted half a billion dollars. She gave away some of the money to animal-rights groups and used another chunk to purchase 100,000 acres of Down East timberland, which she'd promptly declared off-limits to loggers, hunters, all-terrain-vehicle riders, fishermen, and snowmobilers. Her intention, she announced, was to donate the land to the federal government to create a new national park where timber wolves and woodland caribou would once again roam free.

The idea hadn't gone over well with my neighbors, many of whom were employed by the woods-products industry and didn't know where to ride their ATVs or shoot their AR-15s now that "Queen Elizabeth" had cordoned off half of Washington County. Morse told them not to worry; she promised a sunny economic future in which they would sell goods and services to crowds of tourists eager to experience a brand-new wilderness within a day's drive of Boston. Her de facto subjects greeted this promise with skepticism, to say the least.

I was doing my best to withhold judgment on the idea, but it wasn't easy staying out of arguments. Elizabeth Morse was

the number-one topic at every diner and bait shop I visited that fall.

The number-two topic was the weird October heat.

No one in Maine could remember an autumn this insufferable. Johnny-jump-ups were jumping up for the third time outside the Washington County courthouse, and the persistence of mosquitoes in the woods behind my cabin seemed less like an annoyance and more like an ominous disruption in the natural order of things. Frustrated moose hunters blamed the seventy-degree heat for the refusal of the big bulls to leave the coolness of the peat bogs and move to the upland clear-cuts, where they could be dispatched (illegally) from the backs of pickup trucks. Even the old cranks down at Day's General Store muttered the words *global warming* without their usual sneers.

Every day, going on patrol in my shirtsleeves and orange hunting vest, I experienced a sense of temporal dislocation. The foliage was fading in the treetops, and yet the sun continued to blaze like a frying pan left too long on the stove. Sooner or later, I knew, we would pay a price for this never-ending Indian summer.

So when Billy Cronk called to say that he'd stumbled on something bad on the Morse property, I figured the bill might finally have come due.

"It's bad, Mike," he told me in a quavering voice I'd never heard from him before. "Wicked bad."

But what I found on Betty Morse's estate was more than bad. It was evil.

2

Billy wouldn't get into details over the phone, but he said he'd meet me at Morse's new gate—the one that blocked access to the south shore of Sixth Machias Lake.

My patrol truck was making a shrill noise that might have been a loose belt or a dying scream—I wasn't sure which. The old GMC was covered with "warden pinstripes" from where bushes had scratched green paint from its sides, and it had a fist-size dent in the middle of the Department of Inland Fisheries and Wildlife logo on the door. I'd put in a request for a new vehicle over the summer but held out little hope of seeing a replacement, not while my own future continued to be in doubt.

For three years, my fellow wardens had been taking bets on my own longevity in the service. In the minds of my superiors, Warden Mike Bowditch was the human equivalent of a grenade with a pulled pin. How, they wondered, can anyone behave so self-destructively without ever actually destructing? Here they'd gone and exiled me to the easternmost county in the United States—a desolate outland where game wardens were hated and oxycodone abuse was epidemic—but still I refused to explode. Instead, I kept doing my job as if I were oblivious to the contempt in which I was held. I had decided that the only way for me ever to be happy was to be true to

my own values. And while I can't say I was the embodiment of joy, I was beginning to understand the emotional rewards that come from living in the moment and doing good work.

Billy had opened Betty Morse's iron gate and was standing beside the new NO HUNTING sign, waiting for me to drive through. He was wearing blue jeans tucked into tall neoprene-sided boots, a Western-style belt with an actual tarantula embedded in the buckle, and a blue Henley pullover that showed off his impressive musculature when he swung the gate shut behind my pickup. The heavy metallic *clang* reminded me of past visits to the state prison and other hopeless places. I felt a growing sense of dread as I rolled down my window.

Glancing in the side mirror, I watched Billy stoop to reset the combination lock and then come striding up alongside the truck. He peered down at me, his eyes flat, his sharp cheekbones shining with perspiration.

"What's going on, Billy?"

"The first one is up here a ways," he said, pointing at the rust-colored road. There were no hardwoods in this part of the forest, only pines, firs, and hemlocks. Over the decades, the trees had shed their needles, forming a soft carpet for any vehicles that might pass beneath them. I saw Billy's blue F250 parked in the shadow of the boughs.

"You want to ride with me?" I asked.

"It would be better if I went ahead." His voice started as a rumble down around his spleen and was as intimidating as the rest of him. "We got some ground to cover, and I ain't sure where we're going to end up."

I waited for him to start his pickup and then tagged along behind his trailer hitch a few miles, wondering what all the mystery was about. Billy had a flair for the dramatic—witness the tarantula belt and the heavy-metal hairstyle—but this

seemed different: a reluctance, or even inability, to put what he'd discovered into words.

Eventually, the road emerged from beneath the evergreens and crossed a meadow overgrown at the edges with poplars, paper birches, and speckled alders. The road was powder-dry from baking in the sunlight, and Billy's tires kicked up a cloud of dust so thick I almost ran into the back of his tail bed when he applied the brakes.

I watched him unfold himself from his Ford—no vehicle made offered enough headroom for my towering friend—and then I unbuckled my shoulder belt.

A dead moose lay in the ragweed ten feet from the road. It was a young bull, a little bigger than a Clydesdale, but with the long, knobby legs of a camel. It had a modest rack of antlers, five feet across or so, and a brownish red coat stuck all over with brambles and wisps of cattail fluff. Green flies buzzed loudly around its open mouth. Its tongue was hanging out like a gray inner organ it had half-expelled from its gut, and its drying eyeballs were coated with an abrasive layer of dust. At first glance, I couldn't see any obvious wounds or dried blood on the carcass. Nor were there any of the telltale signs of the fatal brainworm that often afflicts moose in Maine.

"What do you think?" Billy asked.

I crossed my bare arms, slick with SPF-45. "I'm thinking someone shot it last week during the hunt but didn't bring it down. It might have stumbled around for a few days—and wandered across the road onto Morse's property—before it bled out or the wound got infected. It's not unusual to find a gut-shot moose after the hunt."

"That's what I thought at first."

I squinted to get a better look at the moose's underbelly. "Or it could have gotten paunched by a bigger bull during the rut."

"I thought of that, too."

"But that's not what happened, is it?"

"Nope."

I crouched down beside the moose, scattering the winged insects that had come to lay their eggs in its mucous membranes. A faint odor—like crushed wet acorns—rose from its obscene tongue. I lifted one of the floppy ears and saw a cluster of blood-swollen ticks attached to the underside. During a bad year, like this one, a moose can play host to tens of thousands of parasitic ticks, not to mention the mosquitoes and other biting insects—no-see-ums, black flies, deerflies, and moose flies—that are its constant, lifelong companions. For the thousandth time, I reflected on how much it must suck to be a moose.

"Well, there's no smell of putrescence," I said, "and there are still ticks feeding on the blood, which means it hasn't been dead long enough for the blood to totally dry up. The birds and coyotes haven't been at it yet, either."

"It was alive last night," said Billy. "I drove by here to close the gate, and I would have seen it in my headlights."

"Do you think it might have been a poacher, and you scared him off, either last night or this morning? Before he could take the meat and head, I mean?"

"Nope."

"I guess that means you found something else."

Billy hitched his jeans up on his narrow hips and spat hard into the road. "Yep," he said.

We returned to our trucks and set off again. I had to roll up my window to keep from choking to death on the billowing dust. I put on my expensive new pair of Oakley sunglasses, hoping they would help against the glare, but they didn't.

Whatever this trouble was, I already knew I didn't need it. I'd spent the previous week running myself ragged during

the annual Maine moose hunt. I'd patrolled miles of logging roads and clear-cuts and visited every tagging station within a hundred-mile radius of my cabin. The nonstop action had frayed my nerves. I'd been hoping to spend some time with my friend Charley Stevens hunting partridge and woodcock, or scouting around for chanterelle mushrooms down in the wetlands behind the house. Maybe even read an actual book for once. Now I would have to cancel my plans for the morning—and probably the afternoon and evening, as well.

The dirt road entered a thicket of yellow birches and white pines that someone had logged fifty years ago and then allowed to grow back in anticipation of a future harvest that never came. Every now and then, I caught a reflection of the sun hitting the surface of a half-hidden pond through the trees: a brilliant sparkle that reminded me of light shining on shattered windshield glass. Eastern Maine is beautiful country—not particularly mountainous, but expansive and largely empty of people, with evergreen forests that stretch to the horizons and blue lakes so numerous as to almost defy counting. It was how I always pictured northern Minnesota, around Voyageurs National Park and the Boundary Waters Canoe Area Wilderness. No wonder Queen Elizabeth wanted to protect this magnificent forest forever. Wasn't it for the same reason I'd become a game warden—to guard places like this from reckless human intrusion?

The road branched a couple of times, heading away from the lake into the wilder country of the Machias River watershed. After fifteen minutes of spine-jolting bumps, we came to another treeless meadow. This one was significantly larger and damper than the first. Despite the August-like temperatures, the vegetation was painted with the palette of autumn: sun-faded greens, tarnished golds, and burnt umbers. On one side

of the meadow, a sluggish brown stream flowed out of a pond shaped like a kidney bean. Fallen leaves, red and yellow, drifted on the surface of the water.

As Billy rolled to a stop, I saw two ravens lift up from the puckerbrush, big black birds that beat the air heavily with their wings. One of them called, making a distinctive *quork* sound, to express its displeasure at being interrupted in the middle of its meal. The ravens flapped across the clearing to the exact distance where they would be safe from a man with a shotgun—ravens somehow know these things—and settled together at the top of a tree to await our eventual departure.

I followed Billy through the dying grass. Late damselflies flitted in the air, blue-bodied and faster than thoughts. I felt sweat ooze down my spine beneath the ballistic vest the Warden Service made us wear beneath our olive-drab uniforms.

"The ravens were here when I found them," Billy said quietly, speaking with the hushed tone one uses in a house of worship. "Otherwise, I wouldn't have noticed anything."

I swallowed hard to keep my breakfast from coming up in my throat.

"Those beaks of theirs ain't too sharp," he said, "but they really did a job on the little calf's face."

I took note of the location: seventeen yards from the road.

"You ever seen anything like this before?" Billy whispered.

I shook my head no.

The cow moose had both sets of legs crossed, almost as if someone had posed her that way for a formal portrait, but I knew the big animal had fallen heavily, dropped by a single bullet to the head. The first calf, the baby, lay beside her, with its face torn open by the ravens and the bloody skin peeled away from its mouth. The birds had pecked away at her lips, giving her a perpetual smile that she would wear into eternity.

The other calf—a yearling bull that had the gangling look of a teenager that hadn't grown entirely into his body and now never would—was lying closer to the pond. It had been shot through the eye. The bullet had left a star-shaped hole that you could slide your index finger into all the way to the knuckle.

I would need to dig the slug out of its brain for evidence, I realized. I would need to cut them all open with my knife to find the bullets. The entire family.

I removed my black duty cap and wiped the sweat from my forehead with the back of my arm, but the perspiration just streamed back into my burning eyes. Billy was still speaking, but his words were unintelligible; it was as if I were lying at the bottom of a pool, my ears full of water, while things happened in the world above.

In my imagination, I watched a vehicle creep slowly through the trees under the cover of darkness. I saw the small moose family turn curiously toward the sound of the engine, their eyes glowing green in the handheld spotlight. How long had they been blinded by the intense illumination? Thirty seconds? Less? Enough time for three bullets to be fired in rapid succession. The animals had died so quickly, they'd never even realized they should run.

As Billy's voice rose, I found I could understand his words again. "Whoever shot them didn't even bother to take the meat! He just killed them for the fun of killing, and then he drove off down the lane to shoot another one, like it was a fucking video game. What the hell is this, Mike?"

The sun seared the back of my neck. "It's a serial killing, Billy. I don't know what else you'd call it."

3

The ravens watched us from the edge of the clearing like nosy witnesses lingering at the scene of the crime.

"What did you see?" I heard myself mutter.

I'd recently picked up the alarming habit of thinking out loud. My job meant that I worked alone a lot, patrolling remote places without backup, and sometimes I felt the need to hear a human voice, even if it was only my own. Living in the woods does strange things to lonely men.

I turned in a complete circle beneath the rising sun, trying to get my bearings. The air smelled of pine pitch and stagnant water. There were no hilltops or other landmarks visible, but my internal compass placed us four miles northwest of the gate we'd entered.

"Are we still on Morse's property?" I asked Billy.

"This whole township belongs to Ms. Morse, from Sixth Machias west to Mopang."

"It's all gated?"

"Yep. I supervised the crew that put the gates in over the summer. Ms. Morse wanted someone from the staff on-site during the construction."

"So if this section of woods is blocked off, how was the shooter able to drive in here?"

Billy blinked a couple of times and then lowered his head

to look at my boots, his braid dangling down. "Maybe he walked in."

"That's a long haul in the middle of the night. There wasn't even much of a moon with those clouds."

"We might have missed one of them old Jeep trails when we were installing the gates," he said. "There are so many logging roads to keep track of. Christ, I don't know! Maybe the shooter came in on an ATV. What does it matter?"

"I'm trying to reconstruct the sequence of events. How the killer got in here and his specific movements are important if I hope to solve this case."

"This whole thing pisses me off," Billy said by way of apology.

I pointed in the direction our vehicles had entered the clearing. "From the position of the bodies, I'm thinking it was a truck that came in the same way we did. And I don't think it was just a single shooter who did this."

"Why?"

"Because one of them had to hold the spotlight while the other took his shots."

"Couldn't he have used his high beams?"

I drew an imaginary arc in the air with my hand. "That's what I thought at first, but the angle is wrong, based on the position of the road. Is it possible any of the gates were left unlocked?"

Billy looked down at his boots again. "Nope. No way."

"How can you be sure?"

"That's my job. Ms. Morse is real clear when it comes to rules, and keeping the gates locked is rule number one." He reached back, grabbed his ponytail, and gave it a thoughtful tug. "So you think there were two guys?"

"At least two."

"I guess that makes sense. Jeez, I'd like to get my hands on them sons of bitches."

I shuddered to imagine the punishment my friend would inflict. Over beers one night, he'd told me how he'd seriously injured a man in the pugil-stick-fighting ring at Fort Benning. He'd sent the recruit to the hospital with such a severe head injury, the man was discharged from the army with full medical benefits.

I decided to give my brooding friend some space and walked slowly back toward the road, looking for human footprints in the jimsonweed but finding none but our own. The shooter hadn't even bothered to venture out into the field to review his marksmanship. He had just opened fire from his vehicle and then driven off.

There were truck tracks in the road, but the conditions were too arid and the ground was too hard to grab any prints. I did come across a cigarette butt lying in a tuft of rabbit's foot clover. The filter was white, not tan. A Salem, maybe? Or a Marlboro Light? It had rained two nights earlier, but this cigarette didn't look like it had ever gotten soggy. I returned to my GMC to find an evidence bag.

"Hey, Mike!"

Billy was standing at the edge of the grass. He motioned me toward him emphatically, the way you do with a small child when you come across a frog in a pond. He knelt down to inspect the metal cylinders at his feet.

"Don't pick those up," I said. "There might be fingerprints on them."

He dropped a brass casing onto the ground. "Sorry."

There were four shells, all from a .22 Magnum rifle.

"That's a small caliber to take down a moose," said Billy.

"I wouldn't use my twenty-two on a varmint bigger than a woodchuck."

That was because Billy Cronk didn't take reckless potshots at animals, hoping to get lucky. In his mind, it was a cardinal sin for a hunter to use too small a gun on a living creature. You might miss your kill shot and leave an animal mortally wounded. But I knew plenty of cruel and careless men who didn't worry about the casualties they left behind.

"My dad always used a twenty-two Mag when he was poaching," I said. "He told me that a twenty-two was powerful but quiet. He said it was deadly in the right hands."

"Or the wrong ones," said Billy.

"Or the wrong ones," I agreed.

In addition to his many other sins, my father had been one of the most notorious poachers in the mountains of western Maine, a man who killed deer, moose, and grouse at will, daring ineffectual game wardens to catch him—which they never did. The idea that his only son had become a warden himself either amused or disgusted him. He kept his emotions in a hermetically sealed box that he refused to open in my presence. But even my poacher father had never committed an act this cold-blooded. To steal the life from another creature as if it had zero value, to kill for fun rather than food or self-defense or revenge—even Jack Bowditch would have been nauseated by this meaningless slaughter.

When I surveyed the distant tree line again, I discovered that the ravens had vanished. They must have flown off while I focused on the moose. I remembered that in Norse mythology, the god Odin had two ravens—Thought and Memory—that he sent out each day to collect information. They were his personal spies. In the evening, the black-bearded birds would return to Asgard, perch on Odin's shoulders, and whisper the

world's secrets into his ears. What would they tell the father of gods tonight? I stared at the empty tree where the birds had last perched and tried to make sense of an utterly senseless crime.

Four dead moose, all seemingly killed by the same gun in the same night. What had started this killing spree? And what had ended it?

The realization took hold in my mind.

"There are others," I said.

"What?"

"Whoever did this didn't just stop at four. They were on a joyride, and they were having too much fun. If we keep looking, we'll find more bodies. I'm sure of it."

The image in my head was of redneck punks at a carnival shooting gallery, plinking one target, then the next, until their time was up or they were out of quarters. How many moose could someone shoot in a single night? There was only one way for me to find out.

"I want you to take me everywhere in the area you can remember seeing a moose," I told Billy.

We found two more corpses before noon: a bull and a cow.

The bull was a monster that had survived many hunting seasons in this pathless forest. For nearly a dozen years, judging from his tremendously humped back and the wear on his lower incisors, he had managed to elude hunters who had hoped to mount his head above a fireplace. And then one night, when all the orange-clad humans had departed the woods for another season, this majestic animal had walked face-first into a .22-caliber bullet. His killers hadn't even bothered to take home their thousand-dollar trophy; instead, they'd left those magnificent antlers to be gnawed at by porcupines while the moose's body rotted in the sun.

The cow was just a delicate little thing that most hunters wouldn't even have troubled with. Billy found it within a mile of Morse's new mansion, sprawled at the edge of a grove of northern white cedars that the landscape architects had chopped back to make way for a scenic driveway with a view of the lake. I located two .22 long rifle cartridges and a Salem cigarette filter in the roadside needles.

"That's a different caliber," Billy said. "The other shells were twenty-two Mags."

"Yeah, but there was a Salem with the first moose," I said. "The manner of death is the same, too: an opportunistic shot taken at medium range, probably with the help of a jacklight to blind the animal. This could have been the second man using a different gun."

Billy glanced up the road in the direction of his employer's residence. "The Morses should have heard the shot, this close to the house."

"Maybe they did hear it," I suggested.

"Ms. Morse didn't say anything to me about it."

"Did you talk with her this morning?"

"Not yet. But she would have called if she'd heard gunshots."

"Is she the only one who lives there? Does she have any family?"

He gave me an embarrassed smile. "Yep."

"What does that shit-eating grin mean?"

"Her daughter Briar's been living there since she dropped out of college last May."

"Briar?"

He shrugged as if to suggest the name made no sense to him, either. "Plus, there's her assistant, Leaf," said Billy, "and the housekeeper, Vera; the cook, Meagan; and sometimes Mr. Albee spends the night."

"Who's he, her boyfriend?"

"No, he's helping her with this park thing." A look of alarm widened his blue eyes. "Oh fuck. She's going to blame me for this."

"Why? You didn't shoot the moose."

"She'll say it was my fault somehow for not watching things close enough. Oh fuck, Mike, I'm screwed. I just bought Aimee a new washer. I can't afford to lose my job again!"

"Let's not get ahead of ourselves, Billy," I said. "We need to get a bunch of wardens out here pronto. Each one of the dead moose needs to have its location mapped. Cody Devoe's dog can help us find any spent shell casings I missed, plus whatever other evidence we can scare up. Cigarettes, candy wrappers. And there might still be other animals out there. Basically, I need to call in the whole fucking cavalry."

He lifted his bristling blond eyebrows. "Is there any way you can do it . . . quietly?"

"Billy, this is the worst wildlife crime I've ever heard about— and it's taken place on Betty Morse's property. You don't think we can hide this from her?"

"I guess not."

I patted one of his shoulders, but it was like trying to reassure a boulder. "Let me call my sergeant, and then you and I will go talk to Ms. Morse together."

I rummaged around behind the seat of my truck until I found the rolled-up U.S. Geographic Survey map that showed the quadrangle for Sixth Machias Lake. I tried to spread it open on the griddle-hot hood of my truck, but the edges kept curling back on themselves. The map was only four years old, but it was already terribly out of date, since it failed to show any of Elizabeth Morse's new construction. With a pen, I marked the approximate locations of the six dead animals, but I detected

no obvious pattern, except that whoever had murdered them was obviously familiar enough with the old tote roads to travel through a woodland maze without getting lost or discovered.

I laid out the evidence bags with the shell casings and the cigarette butts in a row beside the map. My division supervisor, Lt. Marc Rivard, was one of those bosses who always tells you to bring them solutions, not problems. His latest bit of managerial wisdom, which he'd taken to quoting frequently in our monthly meetings, was, "Who needs a carrot when you've got a stick?" Rivard had been my warden sergeant until he was suddenly promoted over the summer, after our previous lieutenant was diagnosed with prostate cancer. My new sergeant, Mack McQuarrie, didn't seem to care what I did as long as I didn't rile up the powers in Augusta.

Given Rivard's love of the limelight and the sensational nature of this case—a mass slaughter of animals on the property of the richest and most despised businesswoman in Maine— the lieutenant was certain to take a renewed interest in me. If I didn't handle this investigation by the book, I could expect him to break his proverbial stick across my nonproverbial back.

Based on the initial evidence, I would tell the lieutenant that two guns had been used, suggesting two different shooters. They had left their brass behind, meaning they were unconcerned that their rifles would ever be connected to these crimes (perhaps they'd planned on tossing their guns into the lake). Either that or they were just careless. The relative scarcity of spent shell casings implied that the killers were extraordinary marksmen; they'd barely wasted a bullet bringing down the moose. As far as the cigarette butts went, all I could determine was that one of the guys, at least, smoked menthols, which provide more of a rush than other forms of tobacco, if you don't mind ripping the lining of your lungs to shreds. So he

had a reckless disregard for his own well-being in addition to that of God's creatures.

Christ, I thought, I'm going to need all the help I can get on this case.

I put in a call to Sergeant McQuarrie and reached him at a backwoods butcher shop.

During the fall, moose- and deer-cutting businesses sprang up in the forested corners of the state. Most of the meat cutters were solid citizens, but a few of them viewed Maine's wildlife laws as unnecessary limits on commerce. It behooved game wardens to drop in on these fly-by-night outfits for impromptu investigations. Mack and I had our doubts about the Butcher Brothers of Baileyville.

"Bowditch!" McQuarrie had abused his throat with liquor and tobacco for four and a half decades, and you could hear it in his voice over the phone. "I had a feeling I'd hear from you today. I was hoping it was just heartburn from Peg's chili. What's the rumpus, kid?" Mack spoke like a person who'd learned English by watching Jimmy Cagney movies.

I cut to the chase. "Someone shot up six moose on Elizabeth Morse's private estate."

"Christ on a cracker."

"Yeah," I said. "That about sums it up."

"They take any meat?"

"No. It was just someone riding around and killing things for kicks."

I heard a woman's voice in the background, asking him a question. The line went dead for a second while Mack clamped a hand over the receiver. He came back, his voice overloud against the new sound of a bone saw starting up at the butcher shop. "So where do you want to meet?"

I gave him the directions to the new gate. He told me

he'd be there in half an hour. He added that he was bringing "company." He didn't elaborate.

"The L.T.'s gonna fucking love this," he said, using the division nickname for the lieutenant.

"Are you speaking ironically?"

"You're the college boy. You figure it out."

McQuarrie was my third sergeant in three years as a warden. The first, Kathy Frost, was the best by far: one of the only women in the service, funny, smart, and hard as nails. To this day, she remained among my closest friends, and I wished I could somehow reach across administrative divisions and pull her from the midcoast to eastern Maine to help me with this investigation. My second sergeant was Rivard, and all I could say about that experience was that it had been mercifully brief. McQuarrie didn't strike me as a bad guy, but he was a conventional thinker who tended to follow his young lieutenant's orders and then gripe about them behind his back. I guess that was what happened when you were pushing sixty-three and the finish line was just down the hill.

Billy Cronk was standing above the cow moose with his fists clenched, staring at the carcass the way a person looks into a campfire: mesmerized.

"Billy?"

"I'm trying to think of the assholes I know who might've done this."

"Any names spring to mind?"

"Yeah, the whole fucking phone book. You know how popular Ms. Morse is around here." He glanced at me with his lip twisted into a smile. "I ain't so popular myself now that people know who I'm working for. Aimee's brother won't even talk to me. Kyle works over at Skillens' lumber mill. He says I picked my side and I'm going to have to live with the

23

consequences, like he'd prefer his nephews and niece just went hungry."

I could sympathize with Billy's plight, but I understood his brother-in-law's argument, too. Skillens' was the largest employer in the region, a historic sawmill built in the nineteenth century, when there were still miles of virgin forest in eastern Maine. The company had once owned the land on which we were standing, until hard times had forced it to sell out to Elizabeth Morse. I'd heard Skillens' was losing big money since Morse cut off the supply of quality hardwood. The mood at the mill was that of a deathwatch.

Sometimes life pushes you to make hard choices. People pretend they can spend their whole lives standing on the sidelines, as if taking a stand and not taking a stand are different things, when really they are both ways of choosing. One's just more cowardly than the other. As a game warden, I knew what it was like to be hated for no other reason than my uniform. Billy had made a choice, too, even if he didn't fully understand the ramifications yet.

"Let's go talk with your employer," I said. "It sounds like it might be better if she hears what happened from me."

"It won't help," Billy said.

I had a feeling he might be right.

4

Elizabeth Morse's mansion was like nothing I'd seen before. The descriptions I'd heard around town didn't do it justice.

It had been built in the form of a compound, with a four-story residence overlooking the lake and a cluster of smaller guest cottages, boathouses, and work spaces built around the edges. The main building looked like the sort of grand hotel you might expect to find on the shores of Lake Tahoe. Its foundation was of great gray fieldstones carefully chosen so that all the heavy slabs fitted perfectly together without needing cement. The logs, as long as telephone poles, glowed like new copper in the morning sunlight. Two enormous stone chimneys rose from the steeply pitched roofline, and long balconies perched along the higher floors. There were windows everywhere, tall panels of glass to soak up the sunlight. The mansion had been constructed at the tip of a natural point of land, and it wouldn't have surprised me to learn that nearly every room had a view of Sixth Machias Lake.

We had parked at the top of the bluff in an area reserved for maintenance vehicles. Two identical forest-green Toyota Tacomas seemed to be waiting patiently, like unused toys. Down the hill, closer to the front door, sat a hybrid Toyota Highlander SUV, also forest green, and a shiny new Prius

painted a color that made me think of metallic sand in an atomic desert. The odd vehicle out was a cherry-red BMW Z4 roadster parked at a careless angle in front of one of the guest cottages.

Billy brushed his shirt as if to remove nonexistent crumbs. "I should have called ahead," he said. "Ms. Morse doesn't like surprises."

He gestured toward the entrance. A hand-carved sign hung over the double doors, bearing the inscription MOOSEHORN LODGE.

"Does Mr. Toad live here, too?"

"Lay off, Mike." He pushed the buzzer beside the intercom. "Hello?" he said, bending over the gray box. "Anyone at home? It's Billy."

After a minute or so, the double doors swung open and a smiling gray-bearded man looked out. He had deep laugh lines around his eyes and a ponytail that must have gotten progressively harder to maintain as his hairline had receded over the years. He was wearing an off-white hemp shirt with a groovy tie-dyed necktie, jeans that showed dirt on the knees, and leather sandals.

"Hey, Billy? What's the good word?"

"Not good, Leaf. This is Warden Bowditch. He's here to see Ms. Morse."

I'd pegged the guy as an aging hippie from his outfit and the surfer-dude inflections in his voice. But even I was unprepared when he held out a strong calloused hand and introduced himself as Leaf Woodwind.

"What's going on, man?" he asked. I detected the herbal odor of a certain smokable plant on his clothes.

"A crime was committed on Ms. Morse's property last night," I said.

His bushy eyebrows fell. "Did someone fuck with the gates again?"

"Worse than that," said Billy.

"Dude, you've got to tell me. You know Betty hates surprises."

"I think it would be better if I told her myself," I said.

"Hang on, then. I'll see if I can find her."

He stepped suddenly back into the room and shut the door in our faces.

"Leaf Woodwind," I said, repeating the name for my own pleasure. "What's he—the gardener?"

"He's Ms. Morse's personal assistant. Been with her forever. They used to be partners in her business when she was starting out in Cherryfield. Seems like it must be kind of weird for him, watching her get so rich. But he seems pretty mellow about everything."

"Yeah, I smelled his mellowness."

Minutes passed. Billy had grown quiet and inward again. I had the sense he was already checking the help-wanted ads in his head. I found myself gazing through the screen of pine boughs at the brilliant blue lake. I could hear a boat knocking against a dock somewhere, a rhythmic, relaxing sound.

My momentary sense of calm was disturbed by my cell phone, which gave off a sudden electronic chime that sent a pulse of adrenaline shooting into my bloodstream. The previous winter, I'd been stalked by an extremely dangerous man who called himself "George Magoon," after a legendary Down East poacher, and who seemed to delight in tormenting me. He still sent me taunting messages from across the border in Canada, where he'd fled to escape a murder rap. Every time I heard my phone beep, I expected to find another untraceable threat.

This e-mail was from my mother:

"When one door of happiness closes, another opens, but often we look so long at the closed door that we do not see the one that has been opened for us."
—Helen Keller

Lately, my mom had begun sending me inspirational quotes from famous people without any explanation. We hadn't been close in a very long time—since before the bad business with my father—and I had no idea what she was trying to communicate with these vague aphorisms. My mother spent the warm months in Maine and then moved with my stepfather to a golf-course condo in Naples, Florida, every fall. Beyond that, I knew very little of her whereabouts. She was as elusive as George Magoon in that regard.

The door opened again, and Leaf Woodwind stepped out, shoulders sagging noticeably. "Betty and Briar are out back. I'll take you around."

So we were not going to be given the grand tour after all. Too bad. I was curious to see what half a billion dollars bought you these days. I put away my cell phone and followed.

Woodwind led us along a flagstone path, past raised flower beds set within rock retaining walls. The rhododendrons had flowered and gone by months ago, but someone had brightened things up with an assortment of orange, yellow, and pink mums. Out of the sunlight, you could smell the autumnal odor of rotting vegetation, and the chill brought goose bumps to my exposed arms.

We emerged from the shadows onto an enormous stone patio, roughly the size of a baseball diamond. In the center, two Adirondack chairs flanked a fire pit in which no fire was

burning. Two women were sitting in them, looking down the length of the lake. We seemed to have caught them in the middle of morning tea.

The younger one remained seated, her head turned away, but I had that impression you sometimes get, when you glimpse a stranger for a split second, of youthful attractiveness. I saw bare brown legs, thick dark hair, and a heart-shaped face hidden behind enormous sunglasses.

As we approached, the older of the two arose. Elizabeth Morse didn't remotely resemble an ex-hippie. Instead, she projected an air of aristocratic confidence, as if she'd just stepped off a yacht. She had sun-streaked blonde hair, cut and curled to accentuate an attractive face that reminded me, somehow, of a cat's. She wore no makeup that I could see and minimal jewelry, just a simple gold locket and bangles at the wrist. She wasn't particularly tall or heavy, but she looked solid. Underneath her expensive outfit—sepia-tinted sunglasses, cream linen shirt, shiny brown slacks, open-toed sandals—she still had the physique of someone who rose at dawn to till the earth.

"Good morning, Billy." Her voice was firm, with a faint Brahmin inflection, as if the muscles in her jaw were clenched.

Billy inclined his head. "Hello, Ms. Morse."

"Leaf says we had another incident but that you're being very mysterious about it."

"This is Warden Bowditch. He's with the Department of Inland Fisheries and Wildlife. He can explain it better than me."

"I know what a game warden is." She turned her golden head to me. "People seem to forget that I used to have a homestead in the woods around here. I wasn't always the titan of industry that I am today."

I couldn't stop myself from smiling, but the worried expressions never left the faces of Billy Cronk and Leaf Woodwind.

"You seem to be the only one who gets my sense of humor, Warden," said Elizabeth Morse. "But you're not here for my comedy routine. What's this about? Not good news, obviously."

"No, ma'am," I said. "It's not. This morning, as Mr. Cronk was driving onto your property, he discovered evidence of a pretty heinous crime." I held out my business card with my name, title, and phone number. I felt that she was measuring me from behind those shaded glasses.

"You don't have to sugarcoat things for me, Warden Bowditch. I am tougher than I appear."

"Someone shot a young moose near your Sixth Machias gate."

She removed her sunglasses and let them dangle between her fingers. We locked eyes for a while; hers were almond-shaped and a spectacular shade of hazel. Then she said, "A poacher?"

"No, ma'am."

"What, then? Some sort of vandal?"

"That's what it looks like. The person—or persons— killed the moose for the sake of killing it. So you could call it vandalism."

She waited. "Go on."

"There were five others," I said.

Elizabeth Morse's brilliant eyes softened. I could tell that she was trying to absorb the impact of my words. She blinked several times before looking away. "I see."

It was the young woman who spoke next. "Six moose! Oh my God!"

Billy had mentioned that Morse had a daughter by the odd

name of Briar. I didn't detect much of a resemblance. She was wearing bright red lipstick, and she had painted her toenails red to match. Her sleeveless smock was white—to show off her toned arms—and her shorts were made of some shimmering black material that looked expensive. Around her neck hung an elaborate wooden necklace that made me think of tribal people living in a distant jungle. "I think I'm going to be sick," she said.

When I turned back to Elizabeth Morse, I saw that she had put her sunglasses back on, and I had a sense that it was to conceal from the rest of us whatever emotions she was experiencing. Her voice turned blunt and businesslike again. She had shoved her momentary softness back beneath her rocky exterior. "So how do you plan on investigating this . . . atrocity? I assume there's some sort of protocol."

Yes and no, I wanted to say. The Warden Service was expert at wildlife forensics, but I wasn't sure my organization had dealt with a crime of this magnitude before.

"I'd start by asking if you know who might've had reason to shoot those animals," I said.

She turned to the ponytailed hippie. "Leaf, can you go fetch the folder?" Without pausing for an answer, she returned her attention to me. Her efficient manner suggested she was well practiced at running meetings. "If you're looking for specific names, I can't help you. Most of the people who hate me don't bother to sign their death threats."

"You've received death threats?"

"Does that surprise you?"

"No," I admitted.

"I would like to see the bodies myself," she said.

"Mom," said the younger woman, "that's gross."

"This is my daughter, Briar," said Elizabeth Morse.

I nodded her way. "I'd prefer to get a team of wardens on the scene first."

"I don't understand why I should have to wait," Elizabeth said. "These shootings occurred on property I own and are almost certainly in retaliation for my recent land purchases."

"I'd also prefer to hold off on making assumptions about motives," I said.

"You haven't read my mail, Warden."

Briar Morse rose to her feet. As she stood beside her mother, I could see that they had similarly muscular builds. "You can't keep us from driving on our own land."

I took a deep breath and gave my attention again to the person who most deserved it.

"Ms. Morse," I said. "I'm not trying to prevent your seeing the bodies for some frivolous reason. There's evidence at each of the shootings that might lead us to identify—and prosecute—whoever did this. I don't want a crowd of people contaminating the scenes, because I want very much to punish the perpetrator or perpetrators here."

"What kind of evidence?"

My cell phone rang on my belt. "Excuse me a moment. I need to take this."

I wandered across the patio, holding the phone to my ear. It was McQuarrie. "So we're at the gate," he said. "Where are you, kid?"

I dropped my voice. "I'm up at Morse's house."

"Queen Elizabeth's?"

"I wanted to tell her what happened before she came blundering on the scene."

"How did Her Highness take the news?"

"Not well."

"I got word to the L.T., and he and a bunch of other

wardens are on the way. So you'd better excuse yourself and get your keister down here to let us in the gate. This is going to be the perfect shit storm, Mikey boy. And you don't want to be the one who catches it in the face."

It would not be a new experience, I thought.

"I'll be right there," I said, and hung up. I wondered again who Mack had riding with him today. It could be any of a number of people.

I paused a moment, listening to the soughing of the pines as the winds ruffled their branches. When I turned back to the people on the patio, I found that Leaf Woodwind had returned with a file folder the size of the Manhattan phone book. "Where's the letter we got Friday?" Elizabeth asked him.

"I just printed it."

"Billy," I said. "Mack McQuarrie needs you to open the gate."

"We're coming with you," said Ms. Morse, as if the matter had been settled.

"That's not a good idea—for the reasons I mentioned before."

"Yes, your arguments were very sound and well put, but the fact remains that this is my land."

"Here it is," Leaf said, producing a piece of paper from the stack.

The letter was a photocopy of another document. The original had been printed in one of those generic fonts that are standard on all computers.

You Fucking Bitch—
      You think you can just move in here and buy up our Land and our Heritage! How many good *Maine* people do you plan to put out of work? Do you even

33

care about our families ,or are you only concerned
about baby ducks and bunny rabbits ,you naive tree
hugger? Well ,we have news for you ,you goddam
slut. We don't want your gates. We don't want your
park &we don't want some out of state cunt deciding
she's our queen. You think your money will protect
you? It won't stop us from putting a . 223round
through your ugly face anytime we choose. This is
your Final Warning ,lady. Leave now or leave in a
coffin—*your choice*!

"I thought him calling me 'lady' was amusing," said Morse
with no trace of amusement in her voice. "It was as if he'd run
out of expletives by the end."

I handed the paper back to her. "Have you shared this letter
with the state police?"

"The entire file." She gave me a catlike smile. "So when you
say you'd prefer not to make assumptions about the persons
and motives behind this incident, how certain are you?"

I had a hard time coming up with an answer.

"That's what I thought," she said.

5

We rattled along in a column of vehicles, with Billy leading the way and the Morse women and Leaf Woodwind trailing me in the Highlander. I wondered if I should call ahead to McQuarrie and warn him of the oncoming trouble, but I decided there was no point. The situation was escalating itself without my assistance. I only hoped that Elizabeth Morse would speed past the dead moose—the first one, near the gate—without noticing.

No such luck. As we rumbled past the carcass, I saw Morse's green SUV slow and then stop, and I stepped hard on my brakes. I turned off the engine and hopped out of the vehicle. In my peripheral vision, I saw Billy's truck continue toward the gate. Maybe I could stall them long enough for Mack to ride to my rescue.

Leaf Woodwind and the daughter were content with rolling down their windows to gawk at the body in the weeds. But Morse, true to her reputation, wanted to inspect the carnage firsthand. I caught up to her as she was stepping out of the vehicle.

"Ms. Morse," I said. "It would be better if you stayed away from the scene until we've had a chance to have a closer look around."

I could smell the floral odor of useless organic bug dope on

her skin. "I'd like to say a prayer to mark the departure of this animal's spirit."

Under her all-business demeanor, it was easy to forget that she had once been a hippie.

"Let her see the moose!" Briar said through the backseat window.

"I think it would be best for everyone to remain on the road," I said.

Elizabeth Morse smiled, showing chemically whitened teeth. "Warden Bowditch, you're not really trying to make an enemy of me?"

"You seem to have more than your share of enemies," I said. "Would you really notice another one?"

Instantly, I regretted having spoken my thoughts aloud. I'd been making so many strides in carrying myself professionally over the past year. I was about to apologize, but she cut me off with a short, sudden laugh.

"Aren't you the saucy one." She tilted her head forward to make eye contact with me over the top of her sunglasses. "I take it you don't approve of me or my plans for Moosehorn National Park."

"It's not my job to approve or disapprove of you."

"What happened to the brave teller of truths who was just standing here? You don't like me. Do you?"

I took a deep breath. "Ms. Morse, I don't know you well enough to dislike you."

"That doesn't seem to stop most people."

I was saved from continuing the conversation by the roar of a truck engine behind me.

An unmarked teal GMC patrol truck rolled to a stop about twenty feet from my front bumper. Two people climbed out.

The driver was a stocky warden with a beet-red face and

thick white hair. Even in his sixties, Mack McQuarrie was in no danger of ever going bald. He had other worries, though: melanoma from a life spent outdoors without ever using sunscreen; heart disease from a diet that leaned heavily toward red meat fried in grease; esophageal cancer from daily doses of chewing tobacco and Scotch. Mack was one of those rugged Maine woodsmen who can hike up a mountain in a snowstorm without breaking a sweat but are destined to keel over a month after they retire, dead from one of a dozen predictable and preventable causes.

The person with him was a young woman, and the second I realized who she was, the rest of the world dropped away. It was as if I were looking through a tunnel straight at her face. She had a prominent jaw that wasn't exactly pretty, but the combination of full lips and high cheekbones would have attracted the interest of a fashion photographer if he'd spotted her walking down the street. She was tall and lanky, with long brown hair pulled back tightly from her face and secured by a rubber band. She was wearing cheap sunglasses, oil-spotted jeans tucked into rubber boots, and a khaki shirt with the Inland Fisheries and Wildlife logo stitched over one of her small breasts. I'm not sure how many men's heads she would have turned with no makeup, dressed in ill-fitting clothes, and defiantly not giving a damn about her pinched hair or the sweat stains under her arms. But behind those sunglasses, I knew, were eyes like Chinese jade.

And on her left hand was a diamond engagement ring. From twenty feet away, I saw it glinting in the sun.

"Where's the moose?" asked Stacey Stevens before anyone could exchange greetings. The daughter of my old friend and mentor, retired chief warden pilot Charley Stevens, was never one to waste time on pleasantries.

"Over there," I said.

Mack came straight at us. "You must be Ms. Morse. I'm Sergeant McQuarrie, of the Maine Warden Service." His own voice was always too loud, in part because his hearing was going, but mostly because he liked to use a tone of command with impressionable civilians.

Elizabeth Morse didn't seem impressed. "What did you do with my man Cronk?"

"We left him at the gate to admit the other wardens on the way. We understand multiple animals were slaughtered on your property, Ms. Morse."

Stacey brushed past me, all business. "Which way did you go in, Mike? Never mind. I see your bootprints."

"You're not afraid of *her* disturbing the evidence?" Elizabeth Morse asked me.

"She's a wildlife biologist," McQuarrie said.

I tried not to watch Stacey while I spoke to my sergeant, but my eyes kept drifting. "Ms. Morse wants to have a closer look at the moose," I said, "and I was telling her she needed to wait until we'd done a sweep of the scene."

"You probably don't want to get too close, ma'am. Those animals smell pretty bad alive, and dead's a whole lot worse."

"I used to be a sheep farmer, Sergeant. I know that mammals of all kinds stink."

McQuarrie's face tightened, as if he wasn't sure whether he'd just been insulted. "Warden Bowditch, can you bring me up to speed here?"

He turned his back on Elizabeth Morse and escorted me through the weeds in the direction of Stacey and the moose. I was glad Morse couldn't see me wincing. After all my talk about the sanctity of the crime scene, Mack was acting careless

and cavalier when there might be ejected rifle shells or other important clues around us.

"Jay-sus," he whispered. "She really does think she's the queen of England. So there are six dead critters?"

"I'm betting there are more," I said.

We stood over Stacey, who was down on both knees beside the moose. She'd put on a pair of latex gloves and was poking and prodding the animal's body. I tried to observe her actions from a dispassionate distance, but my heart was beating so loudly, I was surprised they both couldn't hear it.

I'd met Stacey the previous winter, after knowing her parents for years. At the time, I'd been involved with another woman—maybe not the best romantic choice I'd made in my life—and I'd tried to pretend to myself that I was not powerfully attracted to my friends' daughter. The fact that Stacey didn't like me for a variety of reasons, some of them legitimate, didn't help matters. Nor did her engagement to the handsome and well-to-do heir of a local logging company.

"I couldn't find an entry wound," I said.

"There are two, actually," said Stacey. "One behind the mandible—it broke the poor guy's jaw. The other was a missed lung shot. Basically, he bled to death."

"The others were all shot cleanly," I said. "Pretty impressive head shots."

"Multiple shooters," McQuarrie pronounced.

"That's what I was thinking. I found two different-caliber cartridges, too: twenty-two long and twenty-two Mag."

McQuarrie glanced around in the grass, as if suddenly realizing that there might be actual evidence lying about underfoot. "We need to police this whole area."

"A little late for that." It was Elizabeth Morse, who'd wandered up behind us while we'd been focused on the moose.

Mack thrust out his chest. "Ma'am, I asked you to stand back," he boomed.

"Oh, please, gentlemen. Let's cut the bullshit," said Morse. "I followed your own footprints in the weeds, so I can hardly have contaminated anything more than you already have. This animal died because of me, and I have a right to mourn its suffering."

"It doesn't matter anyway," Stacey said. "See that blood trail in the grass there." She gestured with a stained finger at bent goldenrod and steeplebush. "It goes all the way back to that snag of dead firs. You're not going to find any shell casings here, Mack, because this animal was shot somewhere else. He only happened to collapse in this spot."

I'd missed the blood trail, along with the two bullet wounds, in my initial inspection of the moose. And Stacey had found them right off. Why should I have been surprised? Her father, Charley, was the best game warden I'd ever met, an expert tracker and investigator, not to mention a crazy daredevil pilot. I'd had the white-knuckle experience of flying with Stacey before, as well. Father and daughter were alike in many ways.

McQuarrie rubbed his chapped lips and looked at Morse. "What do you mean, it died because of you?"

Her voice sounded like she'd swallowed a bitter piece of fruit. "Some monster couldn't bring himself to take a shot at me, so instead he drove around on my land killing innocent animals. This is an atrocity against nature—but it's also a personal attack against *me*."

"Ms. Morse believes these shootings are an act of retaliation against her proposed national park," I said.

Stacey gave a sudden laugh. "Well, that's pretty obvious."

"I don't appreciate your tone of voice, young lady," Morse said to her.

When Stacey rose to her feet, I saw that she was taller than the other woman. "My tone of voice?"

"Stacey," I warned.

She ignored me, as usual. "Is it news that people around here don't like you, Ms. Morse?" Stacey didn't have a diplomatic bone in her body. "I'm sorry to be the one to break it to you."

McQuarrie stepped between the two women. He was braver than I was in that respect. "The first question to ask, Ms. Morse, is have you recently received threats of a suspicious nature?"

"As opposed to threats of an *unsuspicious* nature?" Elizabeth Morse threw up her arms. "You people really are professionals. Yes, I have received dozens of *suspicious* threats. I just showed the most recent one to Warden Bowditch."

"Ms. Morse has provided copies of all the threatening letters to the state police," I said.

"Those documents might be the appropriate place to begin your investigation," said Elizabeth. "But what do I know? I'm just a naive tree hugger."

Another patrol truck came rumbling up the dirt road, raising a billowing cloud of dust. It was the first time in my life I was glad to see Lt. Marc Rivard.

6

The pickup was an onyx GMC with all the bells and whistles. District wardens like myself mostly drove beaters that we could bang the shit out of on patrol. The higher-ups who worked the desks in Augusta, or spent their days inside one of the five division headquarters around the state, got the fancy unmarked vehicles. Lieutenant Rivard's new Sierra was a gift he'd given himself upon the occasion of his recent promotion.

Marc Rivard was one of the youngest lieutenants in the history of the Maine Warden Service, having risen faster through the ranks than anyone would have deemed possible, thanks to his deft political skills. In the eyes of the Augusta brass, Rivard embodied the four stated values of the service—honor, loyalty, compassion, and trust. But to the men he supervised, he was widely regarded as a grudge-holding prick. If you kissed his ass and laughed at his off-color jokes, he would bestow upon you whatever perks a district lieutenant has to give. If you pissed him off on a regular basis—by answering his questions candidly instead of the way he wanted; or by following your own ethical compass, as opposed to the politically expedient alternative; or simply by embarrassing him or, worse, outshining him in the eyes of the Augusta brass—he would fling you into a distant orbit. My own current position was somewhere out beyond Pluto.

So it was no surprise that Rivard made a beeline for Mack McQuarrie and Elizabeth Morse without tossing a glance in my direction. He removed his signature sunglasses, an act he only performed before rich and powerful people he hoped to charm.

"It's unfortunate to meet you under these circumstances, Ms. Morse," he said, extending a palm. "I'm Marc Rivard, the lieutenant in charge of this division. I want you to know my men are going to work around the clock to find the individuals who did this."

Elizabeth Morse accepted his handshake, but I detected a barb in her reply. "That's very reassuring."

Despite being only half a dozen years older than me, Rivard had a touch of gray around the temples, which gave him a certain gravitas. He also wore a Clark Gable mustache, which three wives, at least, had found dashing. Out of uniform, he looked middle-aged and paunchy, but with his stomach flattened beneath his ballistic vest, he projected a barrel-chested manliness.

He next addressed himself to my sergeant. "Mack, I want to see each of the kill sites myself ASAP."

"You're going to need Bowditch for that," said McQuarrie. "This is his case."

It was the first time Rivard made eye contact with me. Let's just say there was no love in his deep brown gaze. "You were the first on the scene, Bowditch?"

"Yes, sir. Billy Cronk and myself."

"That's Joe Brogan's former guide? The one he fired from Call of the Wild?"

"Mr. Cronk works for me now," said Elizabeth Morse. "He's one of my caretakers."

"So he has access to all this land. That's very interesting."

43

Rivard stroked his mustache with his thumb and forefinger. "Ms. Morse, I'm thinking it might be best for you and me to have a conversation before we go rushing around your woods here."

"I would welcome the opportunity, Lieutenant."

"Mack, get the coordinates for all the kill sites from Bowditch." He returned his sunglasses to their familiar position between his private thoughts and the rest of the world. "That's assuming you wrote them all down," he said to me.

"Yes, sir. I've got latitude and longitude for each of the shooting sites."

"Then I want you to give the sergeant a complete report of what you found, including any evidence you recovered."

I watched Rivard and Morse stroll down the dirt road, heads down, talking like two world leaders at Camp David.

I felt someone standing at my shoulder.

"He really doesn't like you, does he?" whispered Stacey.

"Are you kidding? I'm his fair-haired boy."

As the first officer on the scene, I had the most information about the case, but the lieutenant disliked the power this gave me over him. If he had the coordinates and my full report, he'd no longer need me to direct him around the Morse property on a dead moose safari. I looked hard at McQuarrie. "He's not going to bring me in on this case at all, is he? Even though it happened in my district and I was the responding officer?"

My sergeant was fidgeting like he had a line of fire ants marching up his trouser leg. "It ain't fair, Mikey, but you know it's his call."

There was no point in complaining or arguing the matter, I realized. "You want the shell casings I collected, too?"

"Give me a minute first," said McQuarrie. "I need to use the little boys' room."

After my sergeant had gone off to find a private pine tree, Stacey said, "Mack must have the biggest prostate on the planet. The poor guy has to take a piss every half hour."

Stacey Stevens wasn't the most beautiful woman I'd ever met, or the most emotionally grounded, and God knows she wasn't the nicest. So why did I get all googly-eyed when she was near? I couldn't explain the attraction, except to say that she felt real to me in a way that no other woman had before. Her vices were as familiar to me as her virtues. And it pained me that she didn't feel the same sense of recognition when she looked into my eyes.

She removed the bloody latex gloves she'd been wearing and stuffed them in her pockets. Having spent the morning inspecting butcher shops, she obviously wasn't fazed by a little gore.

"How's your dad doing, by the way?" I asked.

"You should ask him yourself," she said. "He said the two of you were supposed to go partridge hunting before the moose hunt but that you kept canceling on him. He thinks you're two-timing him with some other old geezer."

"I've had a lot of work." The truth was that I'd been afraid of running into Stacey, who lived in a guest cabin on their land, especially in the company of her fiancé.

"That's between you and my dad," she said. "I'd just prefer not to see him disappointed, you know?"

Ornery was the term Charley often used to describe his daughter. He said it with affection, but I knew that Stacey blamed him for the plane accident that had left her mother a paraplegic. Charley had been teaching Ora to fly when they'd crashed. The experience hadn't dissuaded Stacey from getting her pilot's license, though. My working hypothesis was that the reason father and daughter knocked heads so often was

because they were actually so much alike. Her impatience with me seemed like a guilt-by-association deal, because the old bird had taken me under his wing as a fledgling warden.

She stared down at the dead moose. It was drawing a swarm of large and loud blowflies. "What kind of sick bastards would do something like this?"

"I guess it's our job to figure that out," I said. The sun shone off her hair, showing dimensions of subtle color: every strand a different shade of brown. "You were a little rough on Ms. Morse before."

"She doesn't strike me as the delicate type."

"I think all this bothers her a lot more than she lets on."

"She has a soft spot for animals—just not the two-legged variety." Her voice, which was always a little throaty, as if she'd screamed herself hoarse, began to rasp even more. "Her whole scheme for creating a national park is just incredibly condescending. A lot of people around here are really scared about their futures. It's one thing for her to have this . . . vision. It's another for her to toy around with real people's lives."

Why did it surprise me to hear Stacey take this position? She was engaged to Matt Skillen, whose family owned Skillens' Lumber.

And yet I'd also heard Stacey talk in awe over her parents' dinner table about visiting Yellowstone National Park for the first time. At that same meal, I'd listened to her rant about the oil company that had destroyed an entire ecosystem in the Gulf of Mexico. So whose politics was I hearing now? Stacey's, or those of the man she happened to have fallen in love with instead of me?

"I thought you were an environmentalist," I said.

She took a step forward, as if intending to shove me in the chest. "The woman is an opportunist and a hypocrite, Mike.

She made her millions selling herbal supplements—snake oil, basically—but she presents herself as this righteous do-gooder. She says she wants to create this giant ecopreserve, and yet she builds a megamansion right on the edge of it? On top of that, she's given millions to animal-rights groups that hate everything you stand for. Or have you forgotten that she's banned hunting and fishing on her entire property?"

"None of that excuses death threats," I said. "None of it excuses what someone did to these animals."

"I can hate what happened to this moose and still wish Elizabeth Morse would go somewhere else to play Earth Mother. Those ideas aren't mutually incompatible, you know. And how dare you accuse me of justifying the slaughter of six innocent animals?"

"I wasn't accusing you of anything, Stacey."

"Screw you."

Inevitably, McQuarrie chose this moment to return. He came striding back through the wilted goldenrod, straightening his belt beneath his solid stomach. "What did I miss?"

"Nothing," said Stacey as she walked off into the woods.

7

M y pickup looked like it had been beaten with dirty chalk erasers. Mack told me to pull it into the shade of a pine tree so I could debrief him without the two of us roasting like a pair of rotisserie chickens.

I spread the topographic map across the steering wheel and drew a line to show the meandering route Billy and I had followed through the timber to get from one kill site to the next. My sergeant took careful notes as I offered my theory on how the serial killers had used a spotlight to blind the animals before blowing their brains out.

"Except for the last moose, there was just a single shell casing for each of the carcasses, so these guys were pretty good shots," I said. "They might have prior poaching convictions. And their choice of calibers seems unusual. Did you ever bust any night hunters around here who used a twenty-two Mag or a twenty-two long?"

"I've pinched guys using every armament known to man, from peashooters to tommy guns," McQuarrie rasped. Even with the windows rolled down, I could smell the chewing tobacco stuck in his teeth and the vinegary odor leaking from his armpits. "Sure, I've seen a few twenty-twos in my time, but I don't got a suspect's name in my back pocket, if that's what you're asking. I can tell you one thing for sure, though.

In a few years, every poacher we pinch is gonna be carrying one of those military-type AR-15s. Every night-hunting detail is gonna be like going on patrol during the Tet Offensive."

I watched through the dirty windshield as a crowd of wardens gathered in the sunstruck meadow. Another patrol truck drove up and stopped beside the dozen others that had already assembled. I recognized my friend, Warden Specialist Cody Devoe, who traveled everywhere with his German shepherd, Tomahawk. The lieutenant was bringing in the entire division, I realized. In a matter of hours, the field would look like a McDonald's parking lot. Rivard had somehow even managed to persuade Morse and her entourage to return to her house. I saw him shouting and waving, trying to get his men assembled.

On the dash of the truck, McQuarrie had spread out the bags containing the shell casings and cigarette butts I'd collected. "If we're lucky, the lab is gonna find some DNA on these smokes," he said. "AR-15s and DNA tests—the miracles of modern science. It's a brave new world for dinosaurs like me. Except *Tyrannosaurus rex* never knew he was going extinct."

To a man like Mack McQuarrie, who had always lived for his work and could never imagine an identity for himself that didn't include wearing a badge and a sidearm, retiring was just the last stop on the road to the cemetery.

"Did you and Stacey find anything at the Butcher Brothers?" I asked, hoping to change the subject and his mood at the same time.

"Nothing we could nail them on. They had tags for all the meat, and everything matched with the registration book. But those two are shifty all right. And the place was a fucking sty. There were moose legs sticking up out of this fifty-five-gallon drum next to the bay door."

"What was Stacey's take on them?"

He gave me a cockeyed grin. "You're sweet on her. Don't tell me you're not. The girl's a looker, I gotta admit. Smart, too. She charmed old Clay into letting her take a few evidence samples from his taxidermy collection. After his boner went away, it probably dawned on him that they're headed for the forensic lab. You never know what the DNA's gonna show now. Maybe there's a match with a slab of moose steak we pulled out of some night hunter's freezer. I guess we should be grateful for those DNA tests. It'll probably be what cracks this case, too."

So much for changing the subject, I thought.

"I know Rivard is big on forensics," I said, "but my gut tells me there's only a handful of guys around here who fit the profile. A couple of borderline psychos with excellent marksmanship skills and a beef with Elizabeth Morse? If we ask around enough, we're bound to get some good leads. It just seems like old-fashioned police work."

"Old-fashioned police work!" said McQuarrie. "Who are you—Joe Friday? Tracking down the perps is one thing, kid, but you've still got to make a case that stands up in front of a judge and jury."

"Anyone who slaughters six moose on Elizabeth Morse's land is going to crow about it, Mack."

"You willing to bet your career on that?"

I had been on the job only a few years, but I had already learned to stop making absolute predictions about human behavior, especially my own.

"I didn't think so," said McQuarrie.

My phone chimed on my belt, indicating I had another e-mail. It was my mother again:

"Do not anticipate trouble, or worry about what may never happen. Keep in the sunlight."

—Benjamin Franklin

McQuarrie studied my expression. "Something wrong?"

I clicked the delete button and tucked the phone away. "Just my mom."

"It used to be you could never get a signal out here in the boondocks," Mack said. "Then Queen Elizabeth builds her palace by the lake, and suddenly there's a new cell tower in Grand Lake Stream. That dame has got some serious pull."

"Do you think she has a chance of actually creating a new national park here?" I asked. "Every politician in Maine has come out against the idea because it will cost wood-products jobs. They won't even approve a feasibility study. The whole thing seems like a pipe dream."

"You want my honest-to-God opinion?" McQuarrie removed his hat and ran a hand through his unruly hair. "Right now, the politicians don't want to lose the blue-collar vote—the loggers, the papermakers, the guys like you and me who hunt and fish. But we're an endangered species in this state. Most people down south, in the cities and suburbs, they like the idea of a park. Eventually, the city mice are going to outnumber the country mice. And when that happens, you watch how fast those same politicians flip their positions. Morse knows that time is on her side."

"Did anyone ever tell you you're a cynic, Mack?"

"That just means I'm old." He adjusted his black baseball cap atop his head. "Speaking of politicians, it looks like the L.T. is getting ready to address the masses out there. Come on, Mikey. Let's go hear what he's got to say. The man dearly loves to give a speech."

*

We walked through the desiccated field, kicking grasshoppers ahead of us with every step. Here it was, the end of October, and we still had seventy-degree temperatures and a plague of locusts. McQuarrie's talk of end times and extinction must have gotten under my skin.

The lieutenant stood before a semicircle of a dozen or so wardens with his right hand raised in the manner of a politician standing at a podium.

I had first observed Rivard's dramatic tendencies when he was my sergeant. I'd watched him put on a menacing performance to intimidate a high schooler he believed was robbing cabins for drug money. I'd seen him fall flat on his face. But now he was running his own division, with twenty-six men under his command, and had the stage to himself whenever he wanted it. "Not bad for a poor French kid from Lewiston," he liked to say in a Francophone lilt.

"I just got off the phone with the colonel, informing him of the facts on the ground here. He said he believes this is the worst wildlife crime in Maine history. Think about that for a minute." He paused to give us an opportunity for quiet contemplation. "The Warden Service has been around since 1881, and this is the worst wildlife crime on record. Six animals shot and left to rot."

"At least six," I muttered.

To my surprise, the lieutenant heard me. "What's that, Bowditch?"

"We found only six animals this morning," I said. "There may be others out there we haven't found yet."

"That's a good point." His accent tended to make his *th*'s sound like *d*'s and brought a singsong melody to many of his sentences. "We need to do a canvass of this entire township.

For ease of evidence tracking and communication, we're going to assign letters to each of the carcasses." He pointed across the field. "This animal is moose A, the next three are B, C, and D, and so on. We'll be creating a map that shows the kill sites. The initial focus will be on collecting evidence. If you see so much as a candy wrapper, I want it logged and bagged."

I glanced around, looking for Stacey, but she had disappeared into the woods. I had been such an idiot to provoke her—and to what end? I felt like a hormone-addled teenager who had acted out in order to be noticed by the head cheerleader.

"I don't want the fuckers who shot these critters getting off on a technicality because one irresponsible warden"—Rivard focused his polarized gaze at me—"decided some detail wasn't important. This investigation needs to be done by the numbers! We've got a metal detector to sweep each of these sites for lead. Sergeant Polson will be in charge of photographing and videotaping the carcasses. You'd better call your wives and tell them you'll be late for dinner, because we won't be leaving these woods until it's too dark to see."

"What about the other investigations we're pursuing?" asked Cody Devoe. He was a big-boned guy with a perpetual blue stubble on his chin that no razor seemed able to erase.

"This case takes top priority. I expect these killings to receive intense media attention. That is why I am assuming personal command of this case, so everyone understands the seriousness of this matter." Rivard gestured toward a whip-thin warden leaning against the door of an unmarked pickup. "I will be assisted by Warden Investigator Bilodeau."

Bilodeau had closely set eyes, a pointed nose, and a thin-lipped mouth, which I had never once seen in the shape of a smile. He wore his sandy hair cut straight across his forehead. He had a toothpick pressed between his lips.

I didn't know the man well, but I coveted his job. Investigators in the Maine Warden Service were the closest things we had to detectives. They worked undercover, often for months at a time, to break up poaching rings; investigated boating accidents where the evidence didn't quite match up with the testimony of the survivors; pursued all hunting homicides, of which there were still too many, even after the introduction of strict blaze orange and target-identification laws; and otherwise stuck their noses into every suspicious-smelling case that drifted our way. Being a warden investigator was my dream job, but I had zero shot at ever getting it while bureaucrats like Rivard were in a position to deny me promotions.

The lieutenant went on: "All of us are familiar with Elizabeth Morse and her idea for a national park."

Behind me, someone coughed the word *bullshit* into his fist. McQuarrie scowled, but I heard a few chuckles from the peanut gallery.

"I do not want personal politics interfering with this investigation!" said Rivard, thrusting his jaw forward. "Whatever you think of Elizabeth Morse and her scheme, you need to leave those opinions at home. I will serve as the liaison between her estate and this investigation. I have already convinced her to grant us complete access to her employees. We will run a textbook forensic investigation that will result in swift arrests and an ironclad case for the DA to bring to court. That is the pledge I made to Ms. Morse."

There was no way in hell that Rivard had ever considered delegating the liaison job to another warden. This case was a career maker for the lieutenant, his next step on the road to colonel. You could hear his excitement in the raised pitch of his voice.

It hadn't dawned on me until now what an ungodly spectacle

was going to take place in these woods once the media got hold of the story. Elizabeth Morse was already front-page news across Maine, and that was before some psychos started murdering moose outside her mansion. Rivard had probably already called the television stations in Bangor, encouraging them to send out news vans with satellite antennas to broadcast from the scene. The only thing I cared about was busting the men who'd shot these animals, no matter who got the credit. Nothing Rivard was saying gave me confidence that we shared the same priorities.

The lieutenant took a deep breath, as if considering the best way to conclude his stem-winder. "You might not know this," he said. "But in China, they use the same word for *crisis* as they do for *opportunity*. I believe we have an opportunity here to make history as conservation officers. Someday, I expect this investigation will be taught to every recruit at the Advanced Warden Academy. So I am not exaggerating when I say this will be a textbook case." Suddenly, his face broke into a grin that made his mustache wriggle. "OK. That's enough hot air from me. The day is already hot enough, and we have lots of work to do. Bilodeau and I will be meeting with the sergeants now, and they will be responsible for assigning specific duties to each of you. Understood?"

I raised my hand. "Can I ask a question?"

This time, Rivard chose to ignore me. "Make me proud, Wardens," he said.

Cody Devoe came over, with his dog trotting close to his knees. "What question were you going to ask?" he whispered.

"I wondered if he knew the Chinese word for *clusterfuck*."

8

The actual question I'd wanted to ask Rivard was whether he was bringing in a pilot to scout for additional moose kills. Charley Stevens lived just a few townships away. Despite being officially retired from the Warden Service, he was constantly volunteering his aerial assistance on search-and-rescue missions and other details requiring eyes in the sky. Knowing Stacey's dad the way I did, I expected the old bird already had his Cessna gassed up and ready to go. All he needed was a formal invitation from the lieutenant.

I understood that Rivard needed to formulate a plan, but the sun was lobbing itself across the sky, and we weren't any closer to finding the shooters. And where had Stacey disappeared to? I hadn't seen her drive off with anyone.

Cody Devoe's dog sniffed my knee. I bent over and scratched the panting K-9 behind her velveteen ears. "How are you doing, Tomahawk?"

"She doesn't like the heat," Devoe said.

"She's not the only one."

He waved absently at a yellow jacket that was noisily circling his head. "So everyone is saying you were the first one on the scene here."

"Me and Billy Cronk."

"I saw Billy on the way in. I didn't know he was working for Queen Elizabeth. That's an odd couple to be sure."

I straightened up and brushed the dog fur from my hands onto my pants legs. "You shouldn't call her that, Cody."

"Why not?"

"It seems disrespectful."

Devoe shrugged, ceding the point. My friend had the blocky shoulders and heavy brow of a caveman, but he was no Neanderthal. Anyone else might have needled me for defending Elizabeth Morse, but not Cody. "How do you think the shooters got in here anyway?" he said. "There are gates on every access road coming in."

"Billy says he supervised the construction crew who built the gates, and he thinks they might have missed an old tote road or two."

"No way," said Cody. "I used to hunt these woods hard for partridge and woodcock. They didn't miss any roads, so I don't know what Billy's talking about."

I chewed over this nugget of information, unsure whether to swallow it. McQuarrie had stationed Billy at the Sixth Machias gate to let in whatever law-enforcement vehicles arrived on the property. For a moment, I considered hopping in my truck to go press my friend on this point, but I reconsidered when I saw my sergeant coming toward us across the field. Mack's face was as red as a canned tomato, and his uniform was splotched with perspiration.

He whistled with his fingers. "OK, Wardens, time to get to work!"

In his job, McQuarrie supervised six men, only five of whom happened to be present. He gathered us together like a coach assembling his basketball squad before a game. "Here's how it's going to go," he said. "Bayley and Sullivan, you get

moose A. The lieutenant wants you to retrieve whatever lead or bullet fragments you can from the carcass. The site's been pretty trampled, but do a sweep again to see if you can pull anything out of the weeds. Use Polson's metal detector. Devoe, I want you to take your K-9 and see if you can backtrack the moose to the point where he was shot. That's assuming Stacey is right about it not being killed here." He turned his head. "Where is our pretty little biologist?"

"She disappeared," I said.

"What do you mean she disappeared?"

"She wandered off while the rest of us were listening to the lieutenant's rousing speech."

"Hopefully, we won't need to send out a search party." He spat toward the ground and accidentally hit his own boots. "Bard, I want you to drive out to the gate and get a statement from Billy Cronk."

"Shouldn't I be the one to do that?" I asked.

"The L.T. wants Bard to do the interrogation, since you and Cronk are so chummy. Tibbetts, your job is to inspect every gate along the Stud Mill Road. See if anybody's fucked with any of them. We're looking for signs of forced entry. I'm going to take the lieutenant around to the kill sites using Mike's map."

"Doesn't it make more sense for Mike to do that?" asked Cody.

I was relieved that I didn't need to ask the question myself.

"We've got another job for Bowditch." McQuarrie looked me in the eyes and, without blinking, said, "We want you to check out the gravel pits."

"What gravel pits?"

"All the local ones. You're looking for anyplace where these guys might have done some target practice beforehand. Check

around for twenty-two shell casings. If we can get a match on the brass these guys used, we might be able to link their guns to the ones used to kill the moose."

I clenched my molars together to keep from spitting out an expletive.

Again, Cody Devoe did my speaking for me. "Isn't that kind of a shot in the dark, Mack?"

"This case is going to live or die on whatever circumstantial evidence we gather."

The other wardens turned their heads in my direction. For reasons that made no sense at all—beyond the fact that Rivard disliked me—I was being deliberately marginalized from my own case. Even more than that, I was being assigned a task so obviously useless that the insult was plain for anyone to see. The lieutenant *wanted* me to waste my time. His treatment of me was a warning to other wardens who might choose to think for themselves. But instead of telling Mack McQuarrie what he could do with his gravel pits, I turned and walked toward my truck.

"Hey, Bowditch!" said Bard, a classmate of mine from the academy who was widely known to be one of Lieutenant Rivard's pet poodles. "We're not done here."

"Let him go," I heard McQuarrie say. "It's OK."

I noticed the ravens circling high overhead as I drove back toward the gate, small black specks twirling against the deep blue sky. There were two of them again, probably the same two. And I knew they were ravens, because crows do not soar.

Hugin and Munin: those were the names of Odin's ravens.

My Viking friend could have told me as much. But as I passed into the shade of the conifers and peered forward at the closed gate, I saw no one standing guard. Billy Cronk had

deserted his post. How was I supposed to get off the estate, or anyone else get in?

I stopped the truck and left the engine idling while I inspected the hunk of steel blocking my way. The heavy bar was set on a metal post and pivoted open and shut if you unlocked it and gave it a shove. It probably weighed several hundred pounds and looked like something scavenged from an abandoned military installation. Billy had told me that Morse's first gate had been an expensive wooden affair, hand-crafted by an artisan in Bar Harbor, with leaping stags and calling loons engraved in the red cedar surface. It was a thing of beauty until some maniac had driven his truck, kamikaze-style, straight through it one night. Billy had spent the next morning collecting the splintered boards to burn in Morse's lakeside fire pit.

The next gate, she told her caretaker, should be made of iron.

I scanned up and down the pine-needle road but didn't see Billy's blue pickup anywhere. Behind me, the serpentine belt screeched like a migraine. I got out my phone and was on the verge of punching in my friend's number when it occurred to me to give the gate a gentle pull.

It moved.

I put the phone away and pulled with both hands. The gate groaned and swung heavily toward me on its axis. My absent friend had left the damn thing open.

Maybe Morse called him away, I thought. Billy spent his waking hours running fool's errands for the woman. It didn't matter that Rivard had asked him to help protect the integrity of the crime scene, not if Betty Morse had called and commanded him to drive into Grand Lake Stream for a case of Château Margaux. I couldn't think of any other reason he

would have left the gate unlocked, except that his employer had ordered him to do something, and he knew that wardens would need to drive in and out. He was already terrified of losing his job.

Unless the shooters had torn one down, then they had to have driven in through an open gate. But Billy swore that keeping the gates locked was Elizabeth's rule number one at Moosehorn Lodge. You had to think that after all the death threats Morse had received, she would have impressed that point sufficiently on all the people in her circle. There was always the possibility that someone had forgotten, I supposed. McQuarrie had assigned Tibbetts to check the other gates along the Stud Mill Road. Maybe he would discover that one of them had been bulldozed to the ground overnight and that was how the shooters had gained entry to the killing ground.

Meanwhile, I had gravel pits to inspect.

There were at least a dozen in my district alone, deep holes excavated out of the forest to provide crushed rock to make logging roads. People had been using them for target practice for generations. The sheer number of spent .22 casings scattered amid all that sand and bottle glass made my head hurt. Did Rivard honestly expect the forensics guys in Augusta to dust all that brass for prints?

I was fighting a strong urge to drive to Charley Stevens's house outside Grand Lake Stream and ask him to take me aloft in his floatplane. We could fly low over Morse's estate, looking for additional dead moose in the beaver bogs, and I would prove to the lieutenant that I was right about there being additional kill sites.

The only problem was that Rivard *wanted* me to go rogue. By sending me away from the action and giving me a fruitless task, he was hoping to goad me into disobeying a direct order.

Then he would have another complaint against me, another piece of paper to add to my already-fat personnel file. I had never worked for a man I hated before, and the experience was testing me in ways I'd never imagined.

Not long ago, I would have taken his bait, but not this time. For once, I decided, I was going to be a good soldier. I would follow the chain of command even if it drove me crazy. There was one consolation I could cling to in all this, I realized: when Rivard learned that I'd actually carried out his absurd commands, thoroughly and without complaint, it would send his blood pressure through the roof.

I was smiling at the thought when I nearly ran over Stacey Stevens. She was standing in the leafy shadows at the edge of the road with her thumb out. I had to brake hard to keep from clipping her.

"Oh, it's you," she said when she saw my slack-jawed face through the driver's window. Her pants were soaked and brown with mud all the way up to her waist. Her shirttail was hanging out, and there was a crescent of perspiration above her breasts.

"What are you doing out here?"

"Trying to catch a ride."

"Seriously?"

She gave me a sour-lemon expression. "No."

"Then what?"

"Get out of the truck and I'll show you."

I followed her down the gravel road, trying to keep my eyes trained on her shoulders. Under the heavy boughs of the hemlocks and cedars, the air felt wetter and heavier than out in the open sun. Somewhere, off to the side of the road, I heard the musical sound of water tumbling down cascades in a hidden stream. A white-throated sparrow sang in the distance:

a pretty, thin whistle that sounded like *Old Sam Peabody-Peabody-Peabody.*

"Here," Stacey said, pointing at a clump of fallen birch leaves.

It took me a moment to spot the shell casing.

I squatted down and poked at the brass with a twig. It was a .22 Magnum.

"This was where that first moose was shot," she said. "I followed the blood trail from the meadow on Morse's land through a beaver flowage and back through that cedar stand."

"You tracked the blood through a beaver pond?" I asked in amazement.

"Not through the water. The moose stumbled along the edge for a while. And it left some blood on the pondweed out in the middle. You could see it from a certain angle."

"I'm impressed."

She shook her head as if I was being ridiculous and then knelt down beside me. I could smell her perspiration, but it wasn't unpleasant. Not at all.

I smiled at her, but her face was impassive as she rolled up her pant legs above her calf. It was tan and beautifully shaped. I didn't know why she was showing it to me. Then she reached down into the top of her Bogs boot and extracted something black, red, and wriggling. It was a leech, swollen with blood. She nonchalantly flicked it off into the bushes. "Thought I'd missed one," she said, rolling the pants back down over the boot.

"I need to call this in," I said.

"Before you do, I should show you something else."

She motioned me farther down the road. This time, she didn't need to point to get my attention. Approximately ten feet from the shell casing, in a dry ditch that the road makers had carved

to keep the road from washing out in the springtime, lay a crushed red-and-white piece of aluminum. It was a sixteen-ounce beer can.

"Do you think they're connected?" Stacey asked. "The cartridge and this can?"

I didn't answer. I was thinking about the Budweiser tall boy I'd seen on Billy Cronk's picnic table three weeks earlier.

9

My first call was to McQuarrie, alerting him to the .22 cartridge Stacey had found. He told me to hang tight while he sent another warden to "assist."

My second call was to Billy Cronk's cell phone. There was no answer.

I tried his home number and got Aimee on the fifth ring. "Oh, hello, Mike," she said. "Is everything OK?"

"Sure, Aimee. Everything's fine. Why do you ask?"

In the background a child bawled in that unconvincing way they tend to do when acting hurt. "Billy said he was meeting you this morning, and he sounded real upset over the phone—I can always tell—and I haven't heard from him. Now here you are calling the house. It has to do with Ms. Morse, don't it?"

To the unsophisticated eye of the city slicker, Aimee Cronk might have looked like a backwoods stereotype. She tended to giggle easily and blink rarely. Giving birth to four kids had given her the shape of a Mesopotamian fertility goddess. Her outfits were assembled from the aisles of Wal-Mart: white Keds sneakers, ill-fitting mom jeans, flannel shirts, and a scrunchie to hold back her hair when she cooked the kids' Hamburger Helper. But she was a tack-sharp young lady who had the highest emotional IQ of anyone I'd ever met.

"Yeah," she had once told me, "my dad was a drunk. And

so my brothers and me, we got real good at reading his moods wicked quick, 'cause otherwise we might get a slap across the face before we even opened our mouths."

It was no wonder she and Billy had ended up together. The world looked at him and saw only his wild hair and ice-blue eyes and the raw strength of that long body. But Aimee noticed the gentleness in the way her husband stroked a cat, and she saw the faint mist in his eyes when he looked at the sunset lighting up the mountain above their house. If she had graduated from high school, she might've made one hell of a psychologist—or a detective.

"You're right, Aimee," I said. "I am kind of worried about him. Someone shot a bunch of moose last night on the Morse property and Billy feels responsible somehow. He's worried Ms. Morse might blame him." There seemed no reason to withhold this information, since her husband shared everything with her, as best I could tell. "He was supposed to be waiting for some wardens at the Sixth Machias Gate, but when I went by just now, I didn't see his truck. I thought maybe Ms. Morse had sent him on an errand."

"Nah, that ain't it." The child's crying petered out, diminished to a few poorly delivered sobs. And then Aimee Cronk said, "It's more likely he's gone for a drive. That's what he does when he's wrestling with something and ain't sure what to do."

"If you hear from him soon, can you have him call me on my cell?"

"I definitely will do that."

"I'm sorry if I've gotten you worrying about him, too, Aimee."

"Worrying never helped me none, so I just avoid it," she said. "Besides, I got three loads of laundry to do, and there's an apple pie in the oven."

*

McQuarrie sent Jeremy Bard to photograph and collect the spent shell casing. He was Rivard's favorite among my sergeant's men: a rookie even younger than me, but with that hard-core attitude you often see in new cops. He wore his hair in a "high and tight" buzz cut and lifted weights twice a day. His neck was thicker than his head.

"You didn't touch it?" His suspicious tone implied I had.

"The shell is lying where Stacey first spotted it."

"It is," she confirmed.

He scanned the leaf litter and clumped sand along the roadside, squinted into the alders beyond. The bushes were all tangled in shadows. "Hmm."

"There's probably another shell along here somewhere," I said.

He had close-set gray eyes. "Why do you say that?"

"Moose A was shot twice," I said. "In the jaw and the lungs. Two shots, two shells."

"The shooter could have picked up his brass."

"That doesn't seem to be his modus operandi."

Bard stared at me.

"Method of operation," I said. "Do you want me to help you search these alders or not?"

"You're supposed to be checking out gravel pits," he said.

"The pits will still be there an hour from now."

"No, I'll find it." Locating the brass on his own had become a point of pride now, and there was no reasoning with him.

"Good luck, then."

"Aren't you forgetting something?" Stacey asked me, pointing behind us. "There's a Bud pounder can ten feet down the road there."

In truth, I had forgotten about the beer can—probably

67

because I didn't want to contemplate its association in my mind with Billy Cronk.

Bard frowned at me. "Anything else you forgot to mention?"

"You know what I know, Bard."

"Have fun in the pits," he said, grinning at his own joke.

I gave Stacey a vague smile and tried to keep all emotion out of my voice. "Do you need a lift back to McQuarrie? Because I can give you one—if you want."

She worked a kink out of her neck forcefully with one hand. "Shit, I didn't think about that part. Mack's going to be busy for a while now, which means I'm stranded here. I don't suppose you're headed toward Wesley. I need to pick up my truck."

"I could be," I said. "Come on."

She followed me back to my dusty, battered GMC but hesitated at the door. "I'm not quite dry," she said, touching the back of her pants. "I'm going to get mud all over the passenger seat. The inside of your truck is going to smell like the bog I just waded through."

"I don't mind," I said.

"What's that noise?" she asked.

"I think it's my serpentine belt."

"Can't you tighten it?"

"It comes and goes."

"Matt's been having the same problem. Must be a GMC thing."

The police radio burped and mumbled. I hit the wipers, hoping to clear away some of the dust. When that didn't work, I tried spraying some wiper fluid but succeeded only in smearing mud across the windshield, which made it impossible to see through it for several frightening seconds. I kept up a steady stream of blue fluid until the glass became

somewhat transparent again. Stacey didn't seem to notice my alarm.

"What did you think of the Butcher Brothers?" I asked, hoping to start a conversation that wouldn't end in an argument.

It was as if she'd been half-asleep. "Huh?"

"Clay and Scott Butcher."

"Those guys are real pieces of work. They had tags for every moose and deer hanging up in their coolers, but I know they must get in some poached animals, too. They were a little *too* relaxed about our visit, if you know what I mean."

"I'm afraid I don't."

"Like they knew we weren't going to find anything on the premises. They let us take some samples, like it was no big deal. The other butchers Mack and I visited—they were scared and suspicious as hell."

"Around here, game wardens come in right below politicians and used-car salesmen on the trust scale."

"Wildlife biologists don't score much higher. If you're driving a state or federal vehicle, you're considered an automatic asshole."

"You don't have to tell me," I said. "Someone let a skunk loose in my trailer last winter."

"Yeah, I remember that. You really stank that morning in my dad's plane. Did you ever catch the jerks who did it?"

"It was Joe Brogan, the guy who used to own Call of the Wild Game Ranch."

"My dad told me the ranch was for sale." She kept massaging her sore neck. "I wonder what Brogan's up to these days. Rivard's probably going to want to check him out. A disgruntled ex–hunting guide—sounds like a suspect to me."

"In Rivard's book, everyone is a potential suspect."

"What's his problem with you anyway? I can guess, but I want to hear your version."

The little jab she'd given me stung, but I didn't let it show. "I was involved with the sister of that drug dealer who fell through the ice on the Machias River. She had a pretty serious substance-abuse problem of her own, it turned out. But the real reason is that I solved a homicide everyone thought had already been solved, and Rivard didn't like me getting the credit. I'm just focused on doing my job these days. I'm not going to let myself get dragged into Warden Service politics."

She gave a sharp laugh, which caused me to glance her way. "So you've turned over a new leaf? No more troublemaking? Or pissing off everybody you work with?"

"Something like that."

"I'll believe it when I see it."

I turned my head back to look at the road. "Where do you want me to drop you?"

"Skillens' Lumber," she said.

For some reason, I'd had a suspicion we were headed to her fiancé's place of business.

The Skillen family had been original settlers in northern Washington County, during a time when virgin forests blanketed the land as far as the eye could see and Passamaquoddy Indians, dwelling in seasonal camps along the St. Croix River, speared salmon as they leaped free of the tumbling falls. Amos and Harlan Skillen opened their first small stave mill in 1879 on the East Machias. The brothers cut the pines with axes and crosscut saws, and they filed their blades by lantern light.

Flash forward a century and the Skillen Lumber Company was the seat of a small woodland empire. The family owned forty thousand acres of its own forests in Washington and

Hancock counties and bought logs from another hundred contractors to mill at their plant in Wesley. Five generations of Skillens had outfitted their factory with state-of-the-art machinery: debarkers and chippers, circular sawmills equipped with band resaws, planer mills, kilns, and bark processors. Each year, the company planted twenty thousand balsams to harvest as Christmas trees when the saplings reached five feet in height. In the fall, before the first snows, it sent forth dozens of "tippers"—men and women who ranged through the woodlots to snap the tips off fir boughs to weave into holiday wreaths and ship to market in Boston and New York. In a part of the world where the only other industry was commercial fishing—which itself seemed to be suffering the first stages of a fatal decline—the Skillens employed hundreds of people and were seen by all accounts deservedly as benign feudal lords.

Then came the collapse. In his rush to grow the company, Merritt Skillen, the current CEO, had overcut his own lands, just as his outside suppliers discovered it was more profitable to send their logs across the border to Canadian mills. Repeated spruce budworm infestations laid waste to the Skillens' young Christmas trees. The mechanization that had seemed so wondrous a decade earlier soon led to layoffs. Men who had gone straight from high school in Calais to jobs with six-figure salaries found themselves being handed pink slips on Friday mornings. They woke up in late middle age to discover that their services were no longer needed and, furthermore, that the decades they had spent working the debarker had prepared them for absolutely nothing else in life.

Merritt Skillen began cutting select parcels to the bone and then selling them off for quick cash to keep his line running and his trucks rolling, hoping to save what jobs he could. It

was this same stubbled land—acres that had once been the heart of a logging empire—that Elizabeth Morse had snatched up for a song. The shell-shocked Skillens had no idea what hit them the morning Betty Morse called a press conference to announce that she had acquired not just most of their land but also that of their neighbors and planned to donate it all to the U.S. Department of the Interior to create what she hoped would be called Moosehorn National Park.

I had never met Merritt Skillen, but I'd seen him interviewed on television and had once caught sight of him across the room at the Crawford Lake Club. In the dim light of the restaurant, with his face illuminated from below by a flickering candle, he looked careworn and haunted. He was still handsome, with a straight nose, a forceful jaw, and a crown of silver hair. Somehow, though, his regal bearing seemed to make him an even more tragic character, and I thought of a fallen king out of Shakespeare, wandering, adrift in his former kingdom.

His son, Matt Skillen, I knew better. He was, after all, Stacey's fiancé. Recently, he had become the public face of the company, appearing in television ads to promote Skillen Lumber's commitment to clean energy and its new line of pinewood homes—the initiative the family hoped would save its business. He was as good-looking as his old man, but with none of the desperate sadness. On TV he came across as magnetic, well-spoken, and genuine: the kind of bright young businessman the entire state of Maine was rooting for these days.

The mill complex was hidden from the road by a castle wall of evergreens. All that was visible was the sign—SKILLEN LUMBER COMPANY: SINCE 1879—and the plume of white smoke feathering up from somewhere in the trees beyond. We

drove down the long, wooded lane, wide enough so that two logging trucks could pass each other, one carrying logs in, the other carrying boards out. Even with my squealing engine, I could hear the loud industrial rumbling of machines ahead.

Eventually, we came to a gatehouse, where an old man in bifocals sat on a stool with a book of crossword puzzles. "Afternoon, Warden. What seems to be the trouble?"

In Washington County, no visit from the local game warden was ever assumed to be less than worrisome. "No trouble," I said.

Stacey leaned across my body to wave. "Hey, Earl," she said.

The old guard sat up straighter. "Hello, young lady. I didn't see you in there."

"We're just picking up my car."

"Go ahead, go ahead. I don't know if the boys are done detailing it, though. I'll tell Matt you're here."

The guard pushed a button, which caused the gate to roll back ahead of us, retreating on squeaky wheels inside the high wire fence that surrounded the mill. We pulled into the enormous parking lot, which was notable for two things: the relative scarcity of vehicles and the weeds pushing through the cracked asphalt. Mountains of unprocessed logs were piled ahead of us, like wooden bulwarks meant to thwart an attacking army. Behind them rose the buildings of the mill—tall and largely windowless gray structures that seemed large enough to contain a fleet of 747s. The air smelled acridly of burning wood. A red light blinked atop the fuming smokestack that towered over everything in that vaguely menacing way industrial structures do.

I turned the wheel to avoid a forklift carrying an impossibly high stack of pine boards toward the section of the complex where the processed lumber was waiting to be carried away.

The mill might have been a shadow of its former self, but there was considerable activity: forklifts darting back and forth, men entering and exiting the buildings in hard hats, a crane lifting logs from the back of an eighteen-wheeler to drop onto the pile. The place was as busy as an anthill.

"Is that my car?" Stacey said. "I wouldn't even recognize it."

I followed her line of vision to a Subaru Outback that looked newly washed and waxed. The metal surfaces had been polished to a mirrorlike brightness. It was parked at the edge of the lot, away from the hustle and bustle.

I parked beside the wagon and she climbed out. She gazed toward the open bay of one of the buildings expectantly. There was an enormous smile on her face.

"I guess I'll get going, then," I said. I was eager to depart before Matt Skillen appeared on the scene.

"Thanks for the ride." She bent over again to push her head through the window. "You really do need to call my dad. It would make his day to hear from you." She straightened up again. "Here comes Matt."

Now I had no choice but to stay. I watched a slender young man advance across the parking lot. He had an easy gait, the way natural athletes do, and to look at him, you could imagine that he'd excelled in college track and field. His hair was black and wavy, and he was wearing a white T-shirt with some sort of red-and-blue logo on it, faded jeans, and fawn-colored work boots.

A small boy, maybe eight years old, dark-skinned, and wearing the same T-shirt, trailed along behind him.

"Hey, Beautiful," Matt said to Stacey Stevens.

"My car looks incredible!"

"Do you like it? The guys just finished detailing it." He turned to the little boy, who had the flat features of the Central

American migrants who came to work in the Maine blueberry barrens, and said, "*Diga hola a Stacey, Tomás.*"

"*Hola,*" said the boy. The logo on the T-shirt they were both wearing read BIG BROTHERS, BIG SISTERS OF WASHINGTON COUNTY.

Stacey crouched down so she was at the child's eye level and held his small brown hands in hers. "Hello, Tomás. Did you have a fun camping trip?"

"*Sí.*" His voice was so soft, I could barely hear it.

"We roasted marshmallows and told ghost stories," said Matt with a smile. "Tomas even got to swim because the water was still so warm. It was pretty crazy, though, with only four adults and thirty kids. I was up all night taking them back and forth to the outhouse."

"I'm sorry I had to work, or I would've gone with you," said Stacey.

"Maybe next time." Skillen suddenly seemed to notice my presence inside the truck. He peered through the open window at me. He had long eyelashes that would have made his face seem feminine if not for the strength of his stubbled jaw. "Who's that in there?"

"It's Mike Bowditch," she said.

"How are you doing, Matt?" I said.

"I'm good, Mike." He straightened up and leaned his body close to his fiancée's. "I thought you were going out with McQuarrie today," he said, a hint of confusion in his voice.

"I got waylaid."

His nose twitched. "What's that smell?"

"I'll explain later." She flicked her eyes in Tomás's direction to indicate the story wasn't appropriate for all age levels.

"I'm going to hit the road," I said.

Stacey leaned back in through the open window. "Thanks

again for the ride. And I'm serious that you'd better call my dad. If you don't, you and I are going to have a problem, Warden."

"Understood," I said, shifting the truck back into drive.

I watched the two of them in the rearview mirror as they walked around the glimmering Outback, admiring its renewed beauty. The little boy held Stacey's hand. Then I looked down at the passenger seat. Just as Stacey had warned me, she'd left a wet, muddy imprint there in the shape of her ass.

IO

By late October, the sun sets early in Maine. It takes a more southerly trajectory across the sky than it does during the summer. If you happen to find yourself standing in a shadowy north-facing place—a gravel pit, say, surrounded by high walls of pebbles and sand—you might find yourself needing a flashlight by four in the afternoon.

It was my third pit of the day, and I had already collected hundreds of shell casings and cigarette butts. Along the way, I'd discovered ripped bags of trash, plundered by raccoons that had eaten everything except the dirty diapers; a putrid gut pile that had once been the inner organs of a deer before a poacher carved them out; weather-stained paper targets in the shape of human torsos stapled to splintered pieces of wood; thousands of cigarette butts; crushed beer and soda cans; and more used condoms than I cared to count.

I found shell casings from every caliber of firearm known to man amid the litter: a lot of .30-06s, Remington .223s, the two popular Winchester loads—.270s and .308s—but also plenty of handgun shells: .45s and 9×19 mm Parabellums, .380 ACPs like the kind I used in my off-duty Walther PPKS, .40 Smith & Wessons, .357s (both Magnums and SIGs), and more than a few .38s fired from snub-nosed revolvers. Not to mention all the red, yellow, blue, and green shotgun shells. The .22 casings

alone were beyond belief. Gravel pits were the places many Mainers learned to shoot, and the guns that beginners used tended toward easy-kicking .22s, either rifles or handguns.

The work had been hard and hot in the direct sunlight. Then the sun dipped below the edge of the cliff, and it was as if someone had opened a refrigerator door behind me. I shivered and reached for the SureFire flashlight I carried on my belt.

I was down on my hands and knees, bagging and tagging yet another assortment of brass shells while carefully avoiding the shards of broken glass that had already sliced a hole in my knee, when I heard my call numbers come over the police radio. I'd left the windows rolled down to clear the fetid bog smell from my truck, but also so I could listen to life happening back in the real world. I'd never expected to hear myself called to a 10–32.

There is a movement across the nation in law-enforcement and emergency-response circles to dispense with the confusing jargon of ten codes in favor of what is called "plain language." The campaign was yet another outcome of the terrorist attacks of September 11, 2001, when police and firemen rushed to the smoldering towers from far-flung locales and found themselves unable to communicate with one another because, it turned out, different communities in the tristate area used different ten codes. This commonsense movement to speak normally over the radio had not yet reached the easternmost county in the United States, where I lived. Washington County always seemed to be at the ass end of every fad.

10–32: person with a weapon.

I just about leaped into the patrol truck. "Twenty-two fifty-eight," I said into the mic.

"Twenty-two fifty-eight," answered the deep-voiced Washington County dispatcher. "Ten-thirty-two in progress at

Twelve Jerusalem Road. Shots have been fired. What's your twenty?"

"I'm about ten minutes away."

"Then you're the nearest unit, Mike. Be advised that state police and sheriff's deputies are on the way."

"Ten-four," I said.

I unlocked the Mossberg 590Al from the rack behind my head and set the heavy shotgun on the floor mat. I knew the man who lived at the house on Jerusalem Road. Every law-enforcement officer in the county did, and we'd all made wagers on when this day of reckoning would finally come. If things went as badly as I feared they might, I would need every round in my service weapon and every shell in my shotgun before the night was done.

Karl Keith Khristian had been born Wilbur Williams on an island in Penobscot Bay. He came from a long line of lobstermen, many of whom spent their entire lives within a hundred miles of their home ports. Unless they served in the military, they often went decades without encountering a person of another race. In my own life, I have learned that there is a fine line between innocence and ignorance. Some of the native islanders I met were the most open and accepting people on the planet. Others were, inexplicably, the most hardened bigots you'd ever want to meet. All you need to know about Wilbur Williams is that he left the island his ancestors had settled eight generations earlier when one of his neighbors adopted two Cambodian girls.

By the time he ended up in the deep woods of Washington County, he had legally changed his name to Khristian and acquired an arsenal capable of repelling any urban refugees from the coming race war, the goose-stepping United Nations

troops that were sure to follow, and the zombie apocalypse that would cap the whole thing off. When it came to doomsday prophecies, KKK was an equal-opportunity paranoid. He was a bald gnome of a man with sun-damaged skin and a permanent squint that suggested irritable bowel syndrome or an undiagnosed need for reading glasses.

According to Washington County's longtime sheriff, Roberta Rhine, Khristian's devolution from harmless backwoods crank to potential serial shooter was complete the day we elected our first black president. She'd told us to keep a close watch on the old buzzard. My patrols took me frequently past his personal compound. Khristian lived alone in a tiny house, along with his three rottweilers, but the actual residence was hidden behind a plank fence topped with spirals of razor wire. He used the fence as a billboard to promote various political and religious sentiments:

SOVEREIGN CITIZEN OF THE U.S.A!

WE HAVE AFRICAN LIONS IN THE ZOOS AND A LYING
AFRICAN IN THE WHITE HOUSE

WARNING TO BURGLARS: THIS HOUSE IS GUARDED BY A
SHOTGUN THREE DAYS A WEEK. GUESS WHICH DAYS?

The sheriff had told me that Khristian kept an underground bunker beneath his house, a combination survival shelter and shooting range. "Some day," Rhine said, "I'm afraid he's going to have a massive coronary on his way to Cigarette City, and we're going to find the bodies of fifteen missing prostitutes down there."

I didn't think she was joking.

My own encounters with the man had been fleeting, since Khristian was one of many firearms enthusiasts who had no interest whatsoever in hunting. I had seen him behind the wheel of his camouflage-painted Dodge Ram, his small head barely visible behind the wheel, and he had scowled at me a few times in the supermarket. But I had read his venomous letters in the *Machias Valley News Observer*, and I seemed to recall that he had spewed considerable bile over Elizabeth Morse and her proposed national park. Coincidence that this 10–32 call would come tonight? It didn't seem likely.

The forest flashed by my windows in a green blur. My heart was pumped so full of blood, it made my ribs ache. I tried to control my breathing and prepare myself mentally for a range of possible scenarios, from an armed standoff (likely) to a peaceful surrender (fat chance).

What I found on Jerusalem Road was the last thing I would have expected. In the failing light, I saw Billy Cronk's truck parked before Karl Khristian's gate. My friend stood beside it, his hands loose at his side, as still as a statue. Above the wall loomed a man with a rifle. Khristian must have constructed elevated walkways so that he could patrol his fenced property from a great height: the better to assassinate the blue-helmeted storm troopers.

Before I could even report to dispatch that I had arrived on the scene, I heard a gunshot and saw a spray of sand at my friend's feet. Billy didn't even flinch. He seemed utterly unafraid. Inside the walls, ferocious-sounding dogs were barking. I grabbed the Mossberg and threw open the door, using it as a body shield as I drew a bead on Khristian's vulture head.

"Get down on the ground!" KKK was screaming in a shrill, scratchy voice.

"Police!" I said. "Drop the weapon, Khristian!"

Billy remained motionless: a six-foot-five-inch target.

"Get down on the motherfucking ground," the little man screeched, "or I'll blow your nut sack off!"

I had the shotgun sling wrapped around my left hand to steady it and was using the edge of the door to hold the barrel still. "I said, 'Drop the weapon!'"

Khristian's rifle wavered. "He's a trespasser!"

"If you shoot him, Khristian, I swear to God I am going to shoot you next! Put the rifle down."

"Castle doctrine! Castle doctrine!"

The castle doctrine, or the defense of habitation law, holds that a home owner has the right to use deadly force against an intruder without becoming liable to prosecution.

"He's the one who did it, Mike," said Billy in a calm voice. He hadn't turned his head since I had arrived, so I didn't know how the hell he knew it was me, unless he'd recognized my voice. "He shot the moose."

"Goddamned liar!"

"I'm not going to say this again," I said. "Put the rifle down, Khristian!"

Suddenly, the bald head disappeared. One second, he was there; the next, he was gone.

Oh shit. I could only imagine the secret holes in Khristian's walls where he could aim a gun at an intruder. My spinning blue lights made me feel as if I were watching these surreal events unfold from inside a kaleidoscope.

"Billy, I want you to get down on the ground."

"He's not going to shoot me, Mike."

"Yeah, well, I might shoot you if you don't listen to me." I scanned the fence, looking for any sign of movement behind it, anything to indicate KKK's intentions.

"He's the one who killed those moose," said Billy.

"At the moment, that's not my concern. Just get down on the ground so we can both get the hell out of here. I don't want to tell Aimee I watched you get shot."

His wife's name seemed to touch a nerve. His head dipped, and he dropped to his knees in the sand. His braid swung back and forth along his shoulders.

"All the way down," I said.

"Sorry, Mike. This is as far as I go."

My truck belt wouldn't stop shrieking. Inside the fence, the dogs continued their hoarse and horrible barking. I could easily imagine KKK opening his gate and unleashing his hellhounds on my friend and me.

"Goddamn it, Billy."

"I'm not afraid of that kook."

"Khristian!" I shouted. "I need you to step out here!"

From somewhere on the opposite side of the fence came a shout: "I claim castle doctrine!"

"That law doesn't apply after a police officer is on the scene," I said. "Just get your ass outside and tell me what happened."

The next noise was that of a man yelling at a dog, followed by a canine squeal, as if it had been kicked. Then the fence gate slid open wide enough for a man to slip through the gap. KKK stepped out with a black AR-15 carbine on a sling over his shoulder. He seemed even shorter than I remembered, a beardless Rumpelstiltskin.

I trained my ghost-ring sights on his torso in case he did something stupid. "Put the rifle down, Karl," I said.

"I am a sovereign citizen with the right to bear arms guaranteed by the Second Amendment."

"You're a gutless coward who shot six defenseless animals," said Billy.

Khristian's whole body seemed to quiver like a metronome that had been struck. "Liar!"

"Billy," I said, "I would appreciate you shutting the fuck up now."

Behind me, I heard the faint sound of approaching sirens. KKK squinted and cocked his head like a suspicious bird. Billy took the arrival of another police officer on the scene as a sign that he could now rise to his feet.

Khristian disagreed. "Get back on the ground!"

Two things happened next that seemed simultaneous: the old man swung the assault weapon off his shoulder as if to bring the barrel up again, and Billy Cronk sprang forward like a jungle cat. He must have covered twenty feet in a single second, because by the time I had stepped out from behind my truck door, he had thrown KKK to the ground. I came running up, aiming the shotgun at both of them, shouting for Billy to stop. Dust drifted around their struggling bodies in the headlights of my vehicle. I feared that Khristian might manage to get a shot off from the AR or produce a hidden pistol to blast a hole through my friend's mighty heart.

I needn't have worried. By the time I cleared the distance, Billy Cronk had the sovereign citizen pinned to the ground, flattened beneath the weight of his long body and with both of the man's spindly arms splayed out to the sides.

"You piece of shit," Billy snarled. "I ought to break both your arms."

"Get off me! Get off me!" The old man could barely wheeze out the words under Cronk's crushing weight.

The approaching siren had grown shrill, and I heard the roar of a V-8 engine and pebbles scattering beneath skidding wheels. I kept my Mossberg trained on both bodies.

"Let him go, Billy," I said.

"Not until he says he did it."

"Didn't do a goddamn thing," KKK hissed.

I heard a car door open and someone come running up. When I finally turned my head, I found myself blinded by my own headlights.

"What the hell is going on here?" said a woman with a deep, gruff voice.

I didn't need to see her long, handsome face or black ponytail to know who she was.

"He attacked me," wheezed KKK.

"I wasn't talking to you, Wilbur," said Roberta Rhine. "I was addressing Warden Bowditch."

By blinking repeatedly, I had managed to clear my vision, and I now saw Washington County's chief law-enforcement officer standing at my shoulder, holding a pistol at her side. She was wearing shorts and flip-flops and a chambray shirt thrown on over a white tee. Her hair was wet and loose, as if she'd just stepped from the shower.

"I've got it under control, Sheriff," I said.

"It sure looks that way."

She kicked Billy's leg with her painted toes. "Get off him, Cronk."

"I think you should check him for concealed weapons first," said Billy. "I feel something underneath me, and it ain't his boner."

The sheriff looked at me. "Warden?"

I slung the Mossberg over my shoulder and crouched down beside the two men. Billy released Khristian's limbs one at a time in order for me to remove first the Bushmaster AR-15, which was trapped under the old man's bony shoulder, then a Colt 1911 holstered inside his pants and a pocket Glock secured to his left ankle. I placed all three firearms on the hood

of my shuddering pickup. Then I watched Billy Cronk rise from the ground, lifting his adversary along with him. He held Khristian aloft by both arms, as if the other man was one of his children and this was a game, but there was no smile on my friend's handsome face, just naked contempt.

"Let him go, Billy," I said.

KKK dropped to earth and fell hard on his bony ass.

Rhine inhaled deeply and blew out a breath. "Bowditch, can you tell me what I just witnessed?"

"Sheriff," I said, "I have no idea."

II

One of Rhine's deputies arrived next, a new hire I didn't recognize, followed by a local state trooper whom I knew all too well. Earlier that year, he had taken my statement after I chased a suspected murderer across a frozen lake. I had ended up fighting for my life in icy water while my quarry swam to safety. The state police officer's name was Belanger, and he was nearly as tall as Billy Cronk, with a chin you could break your fist on.

"I had a report of a man with a gun," he said from beneath the tilted brim of his blue Smokey the Bear hat.

"We're still trying to sort it out," the sheriff told him.

Her deputy had taken custody of Karl Khristian while she and I got Billy Cronk's side of the story.

Inside the compound, the rottweilers continued their frightful racket.

Rhine gathered up her wet hair and twisted it into a ponytail while she interrogated Billy. "So you drove here because you deduced Mr. Khristian was the man who'd shot those moose on the Morse estate?"

"Yes, ma'am."

"And how did you arrive at this conclusion?"

"I always figured Karl was the one who took out Ms. Morse's first gate, the nice cedar one," said my friend. "I never

had no proof of it, but the day after it happened, I saw him drive by while I was cleaning up the broken wood, and then afterward he used to give me this smirk whenever I'd see him at the True Value hardware."

"A smirk," said Rhine.

"Yeah, like he had a secret that was burning him up inside."

"That's your proof?" I said.

"I also got to thinking about his letters to the newspaper and how he's such a good shot and all. That's what people say anyway. I heard he showed up at the Wa-Co Fish and Game Club when they were having a shooting match. He wasn't a member or anything, but he came because they was offering cash prizes, and he walked away with five hundred bucks."

"Why didn't you tell me any of this?" I asked. "Why did you drive over here on your own and nearly get yourself shot?"

Billy shrugged. "I knew he'd just deny it if a warden asked him. I thought maybe I could trick it out of him."

The sheriff gave me the special look law-enforcement officers reserve for situations when we find ourselves confronted by an act of pure boneheadedness on the part of a civilian.

"So what happened when you arrived?" Rhine continued.

"I banged on his gate a few times until he finally came out to his—what do you call it?—his parapet."

"That's one word for it, I suppose," said the sheriff.

Billy began scratching his beard the way he always did when he began to spin a yarn. "He asked me what I wanted, and I just started bullshitting with him at first, asked him if he was interested in selling that camouflage truck of his, 'cause I'd always admired the paint job he'd done on it. He couldn't figure out if I was pulling his pud at first and said it weren't for sale. And then I said it was too bad, 'cause I was hoping to get some red cedar toothpicks out of the grille. That's when

he realized I knew he'd knocked down Ms. Morse's gate. He told me to get lost or he'd sic them dogs on me. I said he'd done some fine shooting last night, some of the best I'd ever seen, even in the military. I really laid on the butter thick, figuring that he couldn't help himself and would accept the compliment."

"And how did he respond?" Rhine asked.

"Like he didn't know what I was talking about." Billy stared down at me with a knitted brow. "But I know he did it, Mike. I feel in my bones it was him."

"That's not exactly evidence we can act on," I said. "We can't just turn over his house looking for twenty-two rifles based on your hunch. We need probable cause to get a search warrant."

"It ain't a hunch."

Rhine tapped my shoulder. "Warden, can I have a word with you? Trooper, why don't you keep Mr. Cronk company for a few minutes."

She and I retreated back to the hood of her cruiser, a white Crown Victoria. She was a tall woman, somewhere in her late fifties. She dyed her hair raven black and had a penchant for turquoise jewelry. Some people assumed that she had Indian blood, but my own guess was that it was more of a Southwestern-style thing.

"I was surprised to see you," I said. "I thought you lived down on the coast in Machiasport."

"Lauren and I have a camp on Syslodobsis Lake," she said. "I was swimming when she called me from the porch. I'm still wearing my bathing suit under this getup."

As parochial as Washington County could seem at times, its people showed frequent outbursts of open-mindedness. With few exceptions, they had shown themselves to be welcoming

to the Mexican and Central American immigrant workers who arrived each summer to rake blueberries from the barrens. And they had elected an openly gay woman as their sheriff not once, but four times.

"What's your take on this?" she asked me.

"When I pulled up, I saw Khristian fire a shot in the ground at Billy's feet."

"Go on."

"I told Khristian to put down the weapon. He said Billy was trespassing and claimed the castle doctrine as justification. Eventually, I persuaded him to come outside, where Billy tackled him."

"Did you try to prevent Cronk from assaulting him?"

"I wouldn't term it 'assault,' but no, I didn't have a chance to act." A question occurred to me suddenly. "Who called in the ten-thirty-two?"

"Neighbor down the right-of-way. I guess she drove by with a minivan full of kids and groceries. Can you imagine living next door to that fruitcake?" She brought both of her long hands to the lower half of her face and held them there for a while. "So we've got Cronk on a trespassing charge, and Wilbur on recklessly discharging a firearm, at the least. My instinct here is to take them both down to the jail to cool off overnight."

My heart sank. Billy was about to lose his job. In seeking to impress his employer, he had probably just bull-rushed himself out of her good graces. That was my sense of how Elizabeth Morse would react to this news anyway.

"I could follow Cronk back to his home instead," I said. "I think he's learned his lesson."

"You're more forgiving than I am." Rhine focused her steady gaze on me. "I've been on the phone with Rivard a few times

today. That moose massacre sounds like some pretty bad shit. I offered my department's assistance, but I think your lieutenant wants to keep this one for himself. I take it you saw the dead animals?"

"Billy Cronk and I were the ones who found them this morning."

She nodded, as if this disclosure confirmed a suspicion. "Do you think he's right about KKK being the shooter?"

I considered the question carefully for the first time. "If he was, he had help. The animals were jacklighted, and two different guns were used: a twenty-two Magnum and a twenty-two long rifle. The evidence suggests two shooters. And Khristian doesn't strike me as the sort of guy who pals around with a buddy."

"I told Rivard that he'd better solve this case quick or we're both in for a long, hard fall."

"What did he say to that?"

"Let's just say your lieutenant doesn't lack confidence."

I kept my mouth shut.

"There's been another 'Magoon' sighting," she said out of nowhere. She was referring to the man who had stalked me the previous winter, the prime suspect in the murder of a local drug dealer. He had escaped across the border into New Brunswick before Rhine and the state police could close a net around him. He'd left me to drown in a hole in the ice on a frozen lake.

"Where?" I asked, as if the information barely interested me at all.

"The Gaspé Peninsula in Quebec. The first sighting was in northern Ontario. The second one took place outside Montreal. What does that tell you?"

"He's coming back."

"I don't suppose you've heard from your ex-girlfriend lately."

The sheriff was referring to Jamie Sewall, a recovering alcoholic and drug addict who had fallen off the wagon while in my arms. She had never technically been my girlfriend, but we'd had a brief physical relationship, and I had formed a connection with her strange, disturbed son, Lucas. Over the course of the summer, I had done my best to forget about both of them.

"No, ma'am," I said.

"Her house is still on the market. Nothing ever sells up here unless it's right on the water. I know people who cut their asking price in half, and all they hear are crickets. There are no jobs, and if Elizabeth Morse gets her way, there will be even fewer." She sighed. "Anyway, it wouldn't surprise me if Miss Sewall reappears someday, as well. This place is like the Hotel California. You can check out any time you'd like . . . You know the rest."

"Yes, ma'am. So you're arresting Billy?"

"Do you have a problem with that?"

I studied the back of my friend's blond head, knowing how baffled and hurt he would be to find himself in handcuffs. He'd driven over here on a foolish quest to expose a dangerous criminal and win back a job he feared was slipping from his grasp. Now he was facing a trespassing charge instead. "No, ma'am," I said.

"Good."

"Do you mind if I get his truck keys first? Billy can't afford the cost of having it impounded. I'll make sure it gets home."

The sheriff chewed her lower lip, considering the request. "Go right ahead. The DA will want your report on this incident as soon as possible."

"I understand."

While Rhine went to interrogate Khristian, I steadied

myself and walked back over to where Cronk and Trooper Belanger were shooting the shit. Outwardly, the wild man and the straight-arrow cop would seem to have had nothing in common, but both men, it turned out, had done tours in Iraq. Billy had even managed to get a laugh out of the stone-faced state police officer. I always marveled at how disarming my scary-looking friend could be.

"Can I have a word with him?" I asked the trooper.

"Sure," said Belanger. "I need to call in anyway."

I waited for him to get out of earshot before I laid into Billy. "You stupid son of a bitch. Rhine is arresting you on a criminal trespass charge. You're going to jail, Billy."

His mouth fell open. "Why? All I did was knock on his gate."

"And refuse to leave when he ordered you to. That's trespassing. I don't think the DA will actually prosecute you for it, but you're going to spend the night behind bars."

"But Khristian is the one who shot the moose!"

"Rhine doesn't care about that," I said. "All she cares about is getting a message through your thick Scandinavian skull."

"I'm Dutch, not Scandinavian."

"Whatever. The point is that I can't help you here. I tried, but she's not going to budge." I wanted to throw up my arms. "Jesus, Billy, what am I supposed to tell Aimee?"

His eyes glistened. "Tell her I'm sorry. She's used to me fucking up. It won't come as no surprise."

"Do you want me to talk to Elizabeth Morse for you?"

"Would you?"

I hadn't expected him to say yes. I had no idea what I might say to the rich woman. "Of course."

At that moment, the sheriff returned. "That was a pleasant experience. Wilbur was as cooperative as I'd expected. And I

think the man must eat onion sandwiches for dinner. Are we ready to go here?"

"Almost." I turned to Billy. "Give me your truck keys. The least I can do is save you the cost of having the wrecker tow it away."

He reached into his jeans pockets and produced the keys. They were attached to the actual foot of a rabbit that I was certain he had shot one winter while hunting with his former employer's beagles.

"You're a good friend, Mike," he said.

I watched Trooper Belanger fasten the handcuffs on him, wondering what I would tell Elizabeth Morse, and thinking that Billy Cronk might be the unluckiest person I had ever met.

12

I took a deep breath before knocking on Aimee Cronk's door. She had turned on the porch light in preparation for her husband's return home, and a gauzy cloud of insects was swirling about the sconce. People think moths are attracted to man-made sources of illumination because they mistake them for the moon, but the truth is, scientists have no clue why they hurl themselves against white-hot lightbulbs. Their senseless suicidal behavior is an unsolved mystery.

Through the thin clapboard walls of the house came the clamor of children fighting, and a television was turned up way too loud in some back room, playing a Disney song. I had to knock hard to make my presence known.

There was a crispness in the night air, but it was nothing like the usual cold that comes to Maine in late October, and this mass of self-immolating insects was yet another reminder of how crazy this Indian summer had been. I'd grabbed a wool jacket from behind my seat, but now I found myself too warm. With these wide swings in temperature, it was impossible to ever feel comfortable.

At last, a small, platinum-blond boy answered the door. There was a smear of tomato sauce on his chin and dribbles down the front of his Red Sox T-shirt. He looked up at me with ice-blue eyes that announced to the world who his biological father was.

"Hello, Ethan," I said, "is your mommy here?"

"I'm Logan."

"Can you get your mommy for me, Logan?"

When the Cronklet slammed the door in my face, I nearly lost my nose. I heard the scrabbling sound of children's feet and then a woman's commanding voice issuing orders. The door opened carefully, and Aimee peeked out. She was a soft, pale woman with pink skin that burned easily in the sun and ginger-colored hair held in place by a purple scrunchie. Without a single prompt from me, she asked, "What has he done now?"

"The sheriff arrested him for trespassing on Karl Khristian's property."

"Billy must have thought he killed those moose," she stated.

"How did you know that?"

"Why else would he go to that freak's house?" She glanced over her shoulder into the bright, warm, spaghetti-smelling house and then back again into the dark evening with a look of resignation. "Hang on for a minute while I call the neighbor girl to look after the kids. I want to get a sweater, too."

Sitting side by side with Aimee in my patrol truck, I explained the situation to her, omitting the detail about her husband nearly getting his head blown to pieces. The dashboard gave off a faint greenish glow. Aimee had her arms crossed above her heavy breasts, but not because she was cold.

"You won't be able to bail Billy out," I said. "The sheriff wants to keep him overnight to send him a message."

"Good luck with that," she said. "She could hit him over the head with a log, and she still wouldn't get what she was after. He's like a dog that way."

The words sounded bitter, but her tone was matter-of-fact, as if she understood her husband's natural cluelessness and

accepted it as part of who he was. I knew that Billy loved her, heart and soul, and this moment helped me see why.

"How much do you think the bail will be?" she asked.

"I'm not sure. Five hundred dollars. Maybe more."

"Shoot."

I tried to remember the bottom line on my last bank statement. Unlike a lot of Maine wardens who worked other jobs in their free time or owned their own small businesses to make ends meet, I subsisted entirely off my government paycheck. Given my problems with the top brass, it seemed wise not to divert my focus. "I could loan you a little money if you need it."

"We'll see," she said. "But thank you for the offer. He's going to be out of work again, so we've got that to consider, too."

"You don't know Morse will fire him."

She gave me a look down the length of her freckled nose: now I was the one being stupid.

"Thanks for coming to get me, Mike," she said as we neared Khristian's darkened compound. "I don't know that we could have paid the impound fee on top of the bail."

"Billy says you're a saint, Aimee."

She rolled her eyes. "I ain't no saint. I'm just used to him is all."

Driving home alone, I thought about the women I had dated in my life: the giggly girls in high school; Jill, my freshman-year crush at Colby, who broke my heart when she slept with my roommate; and then Sarah, long-suffering Sarah. The dynamics of that relationship had resembled those of the Cronks' marriage—I was reckless, remote, never giving a thought to the future, or to her emotional needs—but unlike Sarah, Aimee had somehow come to terms with her husband's incurable

maleness. I didn't blame Sarah for leaving me; she wanted and deserved better. But I still wondered what it was about me that failed to inspire the kind of unconditional love that I saw between Billy and Aimee, or Charley and Ora Stevens. I hadn't even been able to rescue Jamie Sewall from herself.

This self-pitying line of thought led, inevitably, to Stacey. Aimee hadn't commented on the swamp smell lingering inside my truck, but I was acutely aware of it as proof that the woman I loved had recently sat only inches away from me. And she had barely acknowledged my presence the entire time. What was the fundamental flaw in my makeup that kept her at a distance? What did Matt Skillen have that I didn't? Besides ambition, dark good looks, a seven-figure trust fund, and a seemingly carefree love of life?

I pulled the truck up in front of my cabin, expecting, as I always did, to find it vandalized in some imaginative new way. When I'd first been transferred to Washington County, I'd been an object of mirth and derision. Once, I had found a coyote skin nailed to my door. I'd had the tires of my old Jeep slashed, as well as those of the vintage Ford Bronco I was hoping to restore. Crank calls still woke me up at night.

In Down East Maine, game wardens had been reviled for more than a century, and I couldn't tell whether the hatred that was directed at me was part of a generalized phenomenon or something more personal. I had started my stint in the district as a hard-ass in the mode of Marc Rivard or his protégé, Bard, but over the past months I had changed course. Since vinegar wasn't working, I decided to try honey instead. I presented myself as a figure of trust. I hoped the word would get out that Mike Bowditch was no fool but that he wasn't an asshole, either.

And yet still the crank calls continued.

When I saw I had three messages on my home voice mail, I automatically assumed one would be a hang-up call. But none of them was.

The first call was from McQuarrie. "Where are ya, kid? I tried your cell, but you must have it off. I was expecting a report by now. The L.T.'s wondering where you are and what you've been up to, and that ain't good. He's scheduled a regional strategy meeting at the field office in Whitneyville for tomorrow at seven A.M."

The second call was from my stepfather. "Mike, it's Neil. I'm not sure if this is the best number to reach you at. I'm afraid I misplaced the one for your cell. You probably don't have the greatest coverage up there in the sticks anyway. Look, when you get a few minutes, can you give me a call back at my office? Hope you're well, son."

Son? Neil never called me that.

The third call was the most surprising. "Warden Bowditch, this is Betty Morse. I have a question for you about this man, Lieutenant Rivard. Here is the number for my direct line."

I pulled the pen from my uniform pocket as fast as I could.

As much as I wanted to call Elizabeth Morse back, I knew McQuarrie would have my hide if I didn't report in first. I was about to return his call, when my stomach made a plaintive moan. Except for a couple of crushed granola bars that I had found in the console of my truck, I hadn't eaten since breakfast. When I was investigating a case, I often got so wrapped up in my thoughts that I forgot to feed myself.

I sat down at the plank table in my kitchen with a ham sandwich and a glass of milk that was right on the edge of going sour. As I ate, I looked around at my new digs with an unfamiliar sense of contentment.

Ever since I was a boy, I had always wanted to live in an

actual log cabin. It wasn't the lap of luxury by any means, but I was doing my best to make it comfortable. The cast-iron woodstove threw out a lot of heat. I kept a pailful of well water on the rust-ringed top to keep the air from baking everything I owned. It would steam when I got a good fire going.

I'd even tried my hand at decoration. I'd hung deer antlers on the wall. At the antiques store in Ellsworth, I'd found some framed maps of Washington County from the days when river drivers still drove logs down the flooded Machias River to the sea. And I'd spread an actual bearskin rug that I had won in a Warden Service fund-raising raffle in front of the stove in case I ever found a woman who wanted to get naked on it.

I wasn't sure if my efforts at interior design made the place look like an underfunded logging museum or a Bugaboo Creek steakhouse. In either case, it was home, and I liked it.

The phone rang before I could finish three bites. It was Sergeant McQuarrie again. "Where the hell were ya, kid?"

"I was just about to call you."

He made a horsey snorting sound that suggested he wasn't convinced. "So what's this about Billy Cronk and KKK?"

"I'm sorry, Mack, but I just got back from taking Billy's wife to retrieve his pickup. I knew the Cronks couldn't afford the impound fee on top of the bail. I was trying to do a good deed."

"Just give me the lowdown, Saint Michael."

My sergeant listened without interruption while I recounted the events of the tedious afternoon and the explosive evening. Every once in a while, I heard him spit tobacco juice into a metal cup. I ended my narration with a third apology for not reporting in to him faster, although I knew plenty of wardens who spoke to their sergeants once a week at best. They weren't investigating the worst wildlife crime in Maine history, however.

"Khristian was already on the L.T.'s list of suspects," McQuarrie said.

"I have my doubts about him as the perp here."

He spat again into his cup. "Of course you do."

"There were at least two shooters. And Karl Khristian seems like a lone-wolf type to me."

"Don't fall in love with your theories. Besides, it's Bilodeau's job to crack this case, not yours. All we need from you is to gather evidence—and report in. Understood?"

I took a sip of my half-curdled milk. "So what else did you guys find today? Were there other kill sites?"

McQuarrie laughed until he started coughing. "Frost was right. You really are a nosey parker. You'll hear about it at the briefing tomorrow morning. I suggest you arrive early—and bring doughnuts."

It would take more than a box of crullers to win my way into the lieutenant's good graces.

Rivard had always resented my ambition. "If you want to play detective," he'd once told me, "you should join the state police." But what was this case if not a criminal investigation? By all rights, it should have been mine to solve, not Bilodeau's. As the district warden who'd found the bodies, I should at least have been partnered with the investigator. The fact that I was determined to apprehend the shooters—that I was driven by a sense of duty—shouldn't have been scorned by my lieutenant or laughed off by my sergeant. I might have meddled in cases outside my jurisdiction in the past, but that wasn't the situation here, not by a long shot. Rivard could take the investigation out of my hands, but he couldn't stop me from giving a damn.

I realized that I'd forgotten to tell Mack about the call from Elizabeth Morse. Until I spoke with her and learned what she wanted, it was probably just as well. I could imagine Rivard

hitting the roof when he heard that the queen had reached out to me.

I tried the number she'd given me and got one of those automated female voices that instruct you to leave a message at the tone.

"Ms. Morse," I said. "This is Warden Bowditch returning your call. I'm in for the night if you'd like to try me again, or you can reach me anytime on my cell phone." I recited the ten-digit number. "I'm sure Lieutenant Rivard can answer any questions you might have about the investigation into the shooting. But I would like to talk with you about another matter, concerning Billy Cronk, when you have a chance. I look forward to speaking with you."

That night, I lay awake, waiting for the phone to ring and wondering how to explain Billy's reckless confrontation with Karl Khristian, or the irrational fear of losing his job that had motivated him to take such reckless actions. I needn't have worried, because Betty Morse never called me back.

13

The Maine Department of Inland Fisheries and Wildlife kept a field office on Route 1A outside Machias. It was little more than a farmhouse with an attached garage and barn. All of the structures were painted green, like just about everything else the department owned, and this morning the buildings were surrounded by a fleet of pickups, many of them green. Rivard had commandeered the place to serve as the headquarters of his moose-massacre investigation.

At McQuarrie's suggestion, I had stopped at the Dunkin' Donuts in East Machias and purchased three dozen doughnuts at my own expense. I entered the already-packed house, expecting to be greeted as a hero. Instead, I found my colleagues chewing on Dunkin' Munchkins and pouring cups of coffee from a Box O' Joe. It seemed that Warden Bard had been a step ahead of me this morning.

In normal times, the field office was used by fisheries biologists who were trying, in vain, to bring Atlantic salmon back to the Down East rivers from which they had mysteriously vanished over the course of my lifetime. There were a hundred explanations why the salmon had gone away—global warming, acid rain, overfishing. All anyone could say for sure was that the effort to restore them had been fruitless. I couldn't imagine spending my life devoted to a lost cause, but the department

biologists and biotechs must not have thought in those bleak terms. I saw two of the "fish heads" laughing and eagerly eating doughnuts in the back of the room.

As I set the surplus pastries on a table, someone clapped me on the shoulder. "Hello there!" came a familiar voice.

I turned, to find myself looking down at an old man with a lantern jaw and bright green eyes.

"Charley!" I said, shaking his strong hand.

"I looked across the room just now and said, 'Who's that stranger over there with the chocolate éclairs?'"

"I know," I said. "I've been meaning to stop by, but one thing keeps leading to another. The moose hunt this year ran me ragged."

"A warden's work is never done."

"I thought that saying referred to women."

"Them, too." He clapped me on the shoulder again, hard enough to leave a red mark.

Charley Stevens kept himself in great shape for a man of his advanced years. He had a farmer's build: flat stomach, muscled forearms, and an unbreakable back. Women I knew, even young women, considered him unconventionally handsome. He had eyes the color of sea ice, and his big face was creased with laugh lines around the eyes and mouth. Every two weeks, his wife, Ora, barbered his stiff white hair with big scissors out in the yard. She was in a wheelchair, so Charley would sit on the ground, his legs folded like a yogi's. This morning, he was wearing a crisp white T-shirt tucked into green Dickies.

"I know Ora would love to cook you dinner some evening," he said. "The mushrooms haven't been great this fall, but we have lots dried, and I've shot a fair number of black ducks. The door's always open, as they say, and Nimrod and I are at

your disposal should you ever want to send a few woodcock to their eternal rest."

Listening to him, I couldn't remember why I had been dodging his invitations. "I'd like that."

"Then it's a date."

"Once these killings are solved," I said. "What are you doing here?"

"Stacey told me Rivard was planning a powwow, so I decided to invite myself over and see if I could make myself useful."

I didn't see his daughter in the crowd. "Is she here?"

"She's got the day off. Matt's taking her out on Passamaquoddy Bay on his dad's picnic boat."

"Oh."

Someone whistled. It was McQuarrie, calling the room to order. "All right, we've got a lot of ground to cover this morning, so let's stop with the yapping."

Rivard stepped forward. Despite the long day and night in the woods, he had seemingly found time to get his hair cut and his mustache trimmed. He looked like a man who expected to be interviewed on television. "Good morning," he said. "I have some news before we begin. This morning, Ms. Morse informed me that she is offering a reward of ten thousand dollars for information that leads to the arrest and successful prosecution of anyone involved in the shootings."

A warden behind me—it might have been Bayley—whistled when the lieutenant announced the dollar figure and said, "If I catch the bastards, do I get to keep the reward?"

"Settle down!" said McQuarrie, quieting the laughs.

"The purpose of this meeting is to plot strategy," said Rivard. "So far, we have managed to collect very little in the way of hard evidence from the kill sites. Mack, can you run down the list of what we've found?"

"Yes, sir."

There was almost nothing new in the inventory beyond the items I had personally discovered: ten shell casings from a .22 Magnum, three from a .22 long rifle; four .22 bullets and one fragment recovered from the bodies; three cigarette butts (Salems); two candy wrappers (Starburst and Tastetations); one empty sixteen-ounce can of Budweiser located outside the Morse property; one empty bottle of Miller Genuine Draft, found in the same vicinity. That was it.

"Last night, we transported all these items to the Maine State Crime Lab in Augusta," said McQuarrie. "The techs are dusting what they can for prints. We should get those results soon. It's going to take longer to see what DNA evidence we can pull off those cigarettes."

So they hadn't found additional kill sites. Had they even looked? I fought down the desire to raise my hand and ask.

"We also collected insect samples," said Warden Investigator Bilodeau in a near whisper. He had a toothpick tucked in the corner of his mouth again.

"That's right," said McQuarrie. "We collected some bugs to help us determine the time of death for each animal. There's a professor over at UNH who's a specialist in that stuff, and he agreed to take a look."

The whip-thin investigator continued, so softly that we all leaned toward him to hear. "The evidence so far points to all the moose being killed the night before last—based on rate of decomposition and residual core body temperatures."

"What this means," said Rivard, "is that we haven't caught any breaks so far. We might get lucky with the prints or the DNA, but we can't bank on it. The crime lab ballistics guys should be able to narrow down the firearms we're looking for." He took a sip of coffee to smooth his throat. "Continue, Sergeant."

"Last night," said Mack, "I put Sullivan and Bard on a detail on the road outside Morse's Sixth Machias gate, figuring the shooters might come back for sloppy seconds. Bard, you want to tell everyone what you found?"

My muscle-bound rival took the opportunity to puff out his already-thick chest. "We stopped three vehicles on the public road," he said, reading from a Rite in the Rain notebook. "A 2001 Subaru Outback registered to a Peter Wyman of Baileyville, who was the driver. He consented to a search of the car, but there was no evidence he had been engaged in hunting activities. The second vehicle was a 2005 Ford Ranger registered to Alice Dade of Grand Lake Stream. It contained two juveniles, a boy and girl. The boy produced a driver's license identifying him as Scott Dade. He said he was the owner's son, which we confirmed. The girl had no identification in her purse."

"She had a packet of rubbers, though," said Warden Sullivan with a leering grin.

Half the room laughed; the rest of us fidgeted and looked at the walls. Beside me, Charley voiced his displeasure with a grunt.

"There was no evidence of hunting activities," continued Bard when the laughter had died down. "The third vehicle was a 2008 Toyota Tacoma driven by Chubby LeClair."

I heard murmurs from those around me.

Chubby LeClair was a fleshy fellow who lived in an Airstream camper in the woods. For years, he had passed himself off as a Passamaquoddy, claiming he was one-quarter Indian on his dead father's side, until the tribal elders managed to pick enough holes in his story to determine that he was just another white opportunist who liked to wear his hair long and collect checks from the Feds. The tribal manager

had him evicted from his rent-free brick house overlooking Big Lake and drove him off the reservation and into the wilds of Plantation No. 21. Despite the counterweighing genetic evidence (Chub had reddish hair and gray eyes), he continued to proclaim his Passamaquoddy heritage. He remained popular with the teenagers in the area, who knew him as a dealer in choice weed. It was said he traded blow jobs—from girls *and* boys—for blunts.

The Warden Service knew him as an incorrigible poacher who would be caught jacking a deer one season, lose his hunting license for a while, and then be caught again the moment he got his license back. Chubby seemed constitutionally incapable of obeying a law or taking a hint. I had busted him in August when I saw him drive down the road with a doe's foot sticking out of his passenger window. He had responded to the summons I'd written with big smiles and "No hard feelings," and the next thing I knew, he had decided I was now his friend. It wasn't unusual for him to call me to ask where the bass were biting.

"I don't suppose Chub had a twenty-two on him?" someone asked.

"Just a twenty-gauge Remington," said Bard, "and enough grouse feathers inside the cab of his truck to stuff a pillow. I confiscated the firearm and wrote him up for hunting without a license. The fat fuck was smiling the whole time, like I was giving him an ice-cream cone."

"That's just Chub," said a warden across the room.

"We would have dragged his fat ass to jail," continued Bard, "but we didn't want to leave our position beside the road."

"Let's get back on track here," said Rivard. "One of my goals for this meeting is to develop a list of potential suspects that Bilodeau can pursue while we continue our search of the

Morse property. LeClair is one name." He lifted his chin in my direction. "Karl Khristian and Billy Cronk are two more. Warden Bowditch, I understand that you had an interesting evening at Mr. Khristian's house. We'd all like to hear your account of the events."

I felt like a daydreaming kid who had just been called upon in class. "Sure, Lieutenant." I set down my coffee cup on a bookcase. "I was the first officer on the scene of that ten-thirty-two."

Rivard couldn't resist the dig. "You seem to be the first officer at the scene a lot these days."

"Just lucky, I guess."

It wasn't meant to be a joke, but I heard chuckles.

With all ears in the room turned in my direction, I told the story of collecting evidence at the gravel pits when I heard the call come over the police radio. I described in detail what had happened when I arrived at the armed compound: KKK shooting into the dirt at Billy's feet, the words I'd used to persuade the sovereign citizen to emerge from inside his castle walls, how my friend had quickly disarmed the little man, and the arrival of the sheriff and other officers on the scene.

"As far as I know, they're both still in jail," I said. "But I don't see the point in adding Billy Cronk's name to the list of suspects."

Warden Investigator Bilodeau made his presence known again. He had a habit of slithering out of sight for minutes at a time and reemerging only when you'd forgotten about him. "He is a convicted poacher, and he knows the combination to the gates," he said in his papery whisper. "You said he touched at least one of the casings, as if to deliberately leave his prints on it. That suggests he was worried about being linked to the shells and was looking to have an explanation."

"I think he was just being careless," I said. "Billy's like that."

"We have testimony from Morse's other employees that Cronk regularly complains about his job," said Bilodeau. "And his eagerness to focus attention away from himself and onto Khristian might be considered suspicious."

"You're drawing the wrong conclusions," I said. "Billy is desperate to keep his job. He's worried that Morse will fire him for negligence."

"He can stop worrying," said Rivard.

My heart dropped down around my liver. "She fired him?"

"I suggested it was unwise to keep him around under a cloud of suspicion."

"There was no reason for you to do that, Lieutenant," I said.

The crowd parted as the L.T. moved toward me. "What did you just say?"

"Billy Cronk's a good guy."

"That's your opinion."

"Yes, sir. It is."

The room itself was already sweltering, with all the bodies packed inside, and now the temperature had seemingly risen ten degrees higher. "I want names," barked the lieutenant. "Who else is on our shitlist? Who else do we know with a beef against Elizabeth Morse? I've asked McQuarrie to cross-check our MOSES database against the people who wrote letters to the newspapers complaining about her national park. Later today, I'm meeting with Zanadakis of the Maine State Police. He's investigating the death threats she has received."

Beside me, Charley cleared his throat. "May I make a suggestion?"

"Stevens," said Rivard. "I didn't see you there in the back. How nice of you to join us this morning."

My pilot friend offered a friendly smile. "I figured you might need my airplane to look for other kill sites and such."

"We have our own pilot," the lieutenant said.

"Yes, sir. But their salaries and gas money come out of the division budget. I'm just an unpaid old geezer who's happy to help."

Mack leaned close to Rivard and said something into his ear. "All right," said the lieutenant to the old pilot. "Talk to Sergeant McQuarrie and me after the meeting, and we'll discuss it."

I raised my hand. "I'd like to volunteer to go up with Charley, Lieutenant."

"That's good of you to volunteer, Bowditch," said Rivard. "But we have something else we'd like you to work on today."

14

The sun burned through my windshield as if through a magnifying glass and made the steering wheel too hot to touch. I tried flipping down the visor, but it did no good. When I rolled down the windows to let cooler air inside, a logging truck rumbled past, and the cab filled with choking dust. I didn't have enough gas to run the air conditioning all morning and afternoon while I waited for hunters to appear.

Rivard had stationed me at a checkpoint on a private logging road still owned by the Skillen family, in the heavily cut timber to the northeast of Morse's vast property. My assignment was to inspect rifles and collect bullets. The hope was that the men who'd killed the moose were still skulking around in the backwoods. Maybe they were camped somewhere on the nearby Public Reserved Lands, or maybe they were locals who spent their Saturdays prowling the forest, taking potshots at squirrels. I did a quick calculation and factored the odds of the shooters actually appearing at my checkpoint as somewhere less than zero. Whenever a vehicle approached (which was seldom), I was tempted to cry out, "Halt! Who goes there?"

The first vehicle I stopped held a party of upland bird hunters being led by a guide I knew from Weatherby's Sporting Lodge in Grand Lake Stream. Jeff Jordan was an athletic, middle-aged guy driving a rugged white SUV. His passengers—

two men and a woman—were dressed in khaki and orange clothing. A Brittany spaniel was riding in a dog crate in the back of the vehicle.

The guide rolled down the window as I approached. "What's going on, Mike?"

"Hey, Jeff," I said. "Had any luck this morning?"

He had a copper-wire beard and was wearing a blaze orange ball cap. "We're just heading out."

"How's the season been for you so far?"

"Better than last year. The birds like this warm weather."

"What's going on here?" asked the man in the passenger seat. He was an older gentleman with a thick head of silver hair. He was wearing yellow shooting glasses, which disguised his identity. It took me a moment to realize that he was Merritt Skillen, the father of Stacey's fiancé and the owner of the local lumber mill.

I addressed Jeff Jordan. "I don't suppose you or your passengers have a twenty-two in the vehicle."

"Who shoots woodcock with a twenty-two?" asked the man in the backseat. He had heavy thighs and a thick Texas accent, and was seated beside a handsome older woman with frosted hair.

"I've got a twenty-two pistol in the glove compartment," said Jordan.

"I know this might sound strange," I said, "but would you mind giving me one of your bullets?"

Merritt Skillen lowered his voice. It was an impressive baritone that matched his aristocratic demeanor. "I'd like to know what this is about, Warden."

Jordan studied my deadpan expression. "This has something to do with those moose shootings, doesn't it?"

"What moose shootings?" asked the wife in a twangy

accent. She leaned between the front seat, so I could see her heavily made-up face.

I ignored her. "We're collecting twenty-two rounds, looking for a match. It's nothing personal."

Jordan chewed on his lower lip for a while. Then he reached across Merritt's broad chest and opened the glove compartment. He ejected the magazine of a .22 Ruger and handed it to me so I could remove a cartridge. "Be my guest."

I put on a pair of latex gloves from the case on my belt. "Thanks."

"I'm doing this because I appreciate your honesty," he said, "but I kind of resent the request."

I kept my mouth shut and thumbed a cartridge from the magazine and tucked it into my shirt pocket, being careful not to smear whatever fingerprints might be on the brass. The forensics lab would dust it and then fire it into a synthetic target so they could compare the lead to the bullets we had dug out of the bodies of the moose.

"Whatever in the world is this about?" asked the wife.

"We're investigating a wildlife crime in the area," I said.

"Well, that's no explanation at all!"

"You're not being particularly courteous, Warden," said Merritt Skillen.

"I apologize for the inconvenience, Mr. Skillen. As I said, we're checking every vehicle that comes through here."

The old man turned in his seat to address the couple behind him. I wondered if they were friends or business associates of his from down south. "I've never been stopped like this in all my years living in this area."

"So everyone around here with a gun is a suspect?" asked Jeff Jordan as I handed him back his pistol magazine.

"I wouldn't go that far," I said, but the words felt like a lie

when I heard them aloud. "If you're after woodcock, there's an alder thicket about two miles south of here where I flushed a bunch of birds last week. You'll see the covert after you cross that new bridge over Sandy Stream." I tapped the brim of my black hat. "Good luck on your hunt, folks. Nice seeing you, Jeff, and thanks again."

I watched them drive off, trailing a glittery cloud of dust behind their wheels.

Jeff Jordan was one of the most ethical outdoorsmen I knew. Now his name would be added to Rivard's "shitlist" merely because he owned a .22 and had been good enough to give me a bullet. The interchange had left me feeling vaguely sick to my stomach. I debated tossing the bullet into the weeds but decided against it.

My BlackBerry chimed as I returned to my truck. It was yet another bizarre e-mail from my mom:

"It is easier to be wise for others than for ourselves."
—*François de La Rochefoucauld*

I was certain that my mother had no clue who François de La Rochefoucauld even was. What the hell was going on with her?

It was then that I remembered my stepfather's voice mail from the night before. Neil Turner and I had never been particularly close. He was a careful, emotionally reserved man: a rare specimen of WASP that seemed to have gone extinct everywhere during the 1960s except at select yachting clubs, upscale boarding schools, and certain northeastern Episcopal congregations. My hero worship of my estranged father hadn't made it any easier for us to create a bond during my teenage years, and once I'd gone away to college at Colby,

Neil had given up trying. But I had come to see my stepfather as a fundamentally decent man who deserved some sort of medal for bringing my perpetually unsatisfied mother as much happiness as he could.

I didn't want to call him now, not when a pickup full of hunters might come roaring past at any moment, but these weird messages from my mom, coupled with Neil's out-of-the-blue voice mail, were beginning to make me worry.

By the end of the afternoon, I had collected exactly three more .22 cartridges and been told to go to hell twice.

The day wasn't a total loss: I had written up a summons for a hunter who had too many woodcock in his possession and another to a kid who had mistaken a protected spruce grouse for the more common ruffed grouse. When I told him the fine for shooting a "fool hen" was five hundred dollars, he looked like he might drive off a bridge. Part of me wanted to confiscate the bird and let him off with a warning, but I had resolved to begin living my life according to the Warden Service manual. And so I wrote the kid up.

Out of boredom, I phoned McQuarrie, and he informed me that Charley Stevens had located another kill site, a cow moose shot to death along the southern edge of Morse's property. The animal had been found a hundred yards from the road, hidden behind a swale of young birches and poplars. Like moose A, it had staggered into the underbrush before the blood had drained from its enormous heart. Wardens were on the scene now, examining it for evidence.

"How are things going?" Mack asked.

"The shooters haven't come by yet, but I'm sure they will any second."

My sergeant took a moment to respond. "It might not feel

this way, kid, but you're earning points here. Every hour you spend eating shit counts in your favor with the brass. The L.T. needs to know he can trust you to do your job."

"I've done my job for two years," I said. "You know my conviction rate, Mack. None of those guys Rivard has working the case has a better one."

"Yeah, but you also have this . . . reputation. Look, I can see that you're trying here. You might be a smarty-pants college boy, but I know you've got some grit in you. Let me keep working on the L.T. He'll come around eventually. Why don't you head down to the HQ and turn in the bullets you collected?"

The dashboard clock came on as I started the engine. I had lost nearly ten hours of my life manning that checkpoint. The realization made me gun my engine as I headed toward the village of Grand Lake Stream. I didn't care about the rocks banging against my truck's undercarriage or the damage inflicted to my already-worn shock absorbers. All I wanted was to beat the long shadows that signaled the end of another day in the woods.

Grand Lake Stream was a village of sporting camps and tidy little houses built along a swift-flowing river of the same name. The stream was famous for its landlocked salmon, which dropped down out of West Grand Lake in the autumn when it came time to spawn. Ted Williams had fished the Hatchery Pool, and so had Dwight Eisenhower. Their photographs hung in places of honor on the wooden walls of Weatherby's beside taxidermied fish—salmon, trout, and bass—so fantastically huge, it was hard to believe they were real.

I crossed the bridge over the stream and saw a crowd of fly anglers upstream at the Dam Pool. Combat fishing had never been my thing, so I tended to avoid the river during its more popular months, but I never crossed that bridge without feeling

a desperate desire to pull on the waders and cast a Black Ghost out into the current.

The store at the crossroads constituted the beginning and end of the village's commercial district. It served the multiple roles of pizzeria, fly tackle shop, hardware store, gas pump, tagging station, and gossip hub. If you wanted to know what was going on anywhere in the woods of northern Washington County, it paid to shoot the shit at the Pine Tree Store.

I gassed up my vehicle and then went inside to order a meatball sandwich. The blonde behind the counter tried to pull some information out of me concerning the moose shootings— the massacre was the talk of the town—but I refused to bite. I politely paid for my dinner and headed back outside to the parking lot, feeling proud of my professional restraint (I had a tendency to blab too much to blondes), only to find a very fat man leaning against the door of my truck.

He must have weighed close to three hundred pounds. His face was like a ball of bread dough before it has been rolled flat. Tiny gray eyes were pressed into the soft flesh, and a wispy red goatee decorated the topmost of several chins. The beard was the same color as his long hair. The big man had hitched his size fifty-something jeans halfway up his enormous belly with the help of suspenders, and he wore a faded black T-shirt over B-cup breasts. The shirt bore the words PASSAMAQUODDY INDIAN DAYS 2011, framed by two eagle feathers.

"You've got to help me, Mike!" said Chubby LeClair in a huffy, heavy-breathing voice I recognized from his frequent phone calls. "They think I killed them moose."

"Did you?"

"Heck no! My people believe moose are, like, sacred omens. The elders say that if you dream of a moose, you'll live a long time."

"The Passamaquoddy tribal manager says you're not a real Indian."

"He can't see into my heart. The blood flowing through my veins is totally *wolamewiw*. It's authentic, man, one hundred percent."

I had heard Chubby's bullshit before, but I'd never seen him in such a sweaty state of agitation. I worried for the heart beating beneath all that blubber. "So what happened?"

"Bard busted me last night for driving in the woods. I was driving my uncle's truck, and there was a shotgun I didn't know about stashed behind the seat. But he said I was hunting without a license, because there were some feathers in the bed. I told him the truck wasn't mine and the gun wasn't mine, but he wrote me up anyhow. Then, today, he came to my crib, man, my *wikuwam*. He asked if he could search it, and I said, 'Sure, man. Be my guest, right? You know I never got nothing to hide.' Dude didn't tell me he was going to trash the place!"

"He trashed it?"

"Yeah! Said he didn't need a warrant if I gave my permission. He kept asking where I kept my twenty-twos. I told him I don't own any guns because, you know, I'm a peaceful person."

"Chubby," I said. "I busted you with a rifle this summer, remember?"

"That was my cousin's gun, like I told you. I don't even know what that gun was doing in my truck."

"There was also a dead doe sticking out your window," I reminded him.

"I was transporting it for my cousin. Doing him a favor and all. I'm too softhearted. That's my problem."

My own theory was that Chubby LeClair kept his arsenal in a footlocker buried somewhere beneath the matted leaves around his camper. God only knew where he hid his marijuana

stash. The Maine Drug Enforcement Agency had sent a K-9 team to sniff around the property on two occasions, without finding so much as a single roach.

I motioned him aside so I could get into my truck. "I don't know what to tell you, Chub. You have a history of poaching, and we're investigating all possible leads. It makes sense that Warden Bard would want to talk with you."

"He didn't have to trash my *wikuwam,* though! It ain't right; it just ain't right."

"I'll talk to Bard about it." I wasn't sure what I would say to him. For all I knew, Bard had cause to give Chubby a hard time, and it wasn't cool for one warden to question another's methods.

"Thanks, man. I owe you." His small eyes were moist.

As I drove off, I glanced into the rearview mirror and saw the fat man leaning against the gas pump for support. I worried it might tip over from his considerable weight. Chubby was clearly distressed, and I wondered if Bard might have been onto something after all.

15

I ate my dinner at the boat launch on West Grand Lake. I pulled in, the nose of my vehicle facing the water, and thought about the windmills being built along the ridgeline of Stetson Mountain far to the north. From this distance, I couldn't see the red lights of the turbines, but I knew if I motored up the lake, they would come into view.

For some reason, the wind farm made me think about Elizabeth Morse and her national park. The land she had purchased included many leased camps, just like the one Charley and Ora had once owned on Flagstaff Pond. My friends had been evicted from their beloved cottage by a Canadian timber company, and now the same thing was happening to people in Washington and Hancock counties. One of Morse's first actions as the new landlady had been to cancel the existing leases, forcing the people who owned those lakeside cabins to relocate the buildings or simply abandon them to the elements. Morse had been quoted by a conservative blogger as saying she wanted to remove "the human cancer" from the landscape and allow it to revert back to wilderness. You can imagine how well that offhand comment had gone over at the Pine Tree Store.

Maybe Stacey was right about her, I thought. Morse had made her millions peddling worthless herbal remedies to

consumers desperate to lose weight. She promised cleaner colons and healthier livers, smoother skin and renewed sexual vigor. Did it make her less of a snake-oil saleswoman if she believed her own fantasies?

I thought about her cryptic message from the previous evening. What could she possibly have wanted to ask me about? It couldn't have been important, since she hadn't called again. By now, I figured, Billy Cronk would have made bail. He would also have learned that he was without a job. Such a bombshell would inevitably awaken my friend's powerful thirst. I might need to do a sweep of the local roadhouses before bed.

The light above the hills had turned salmon-colored. I crumpled up the wax-paper sandwich wrapper and dusted the bread crumbs from the front of my shirt. I didn't want to keep Mack waiting at the field office. The four measly bullets I had collected were sure to be the crucial pieces of evidence Warden Investigator Bilodeau needed to crack this case once and for all.

I was driving down the Milford Road, headed back toward Route 1 and what constituted real civilization in this part of the world, when I saw headlights approaching fast in my rearview mirror. A car came tearing up the road behind me and then went shooting past, scattering fallen leaves into the ditches. It was a cherry-red BMW Z4 roadster, and I estimated its speed at seventy miles per hour. The woman behind the wheel was seemingly unaware that my truck's flashing lights signified I was a law-enforcement officer who wanted her to stop.

I stepped hard on the gas and hoped my engine had enough power to keep this chase from becoming a total embarrassment. For a while, it looked like the Z4 was going to leave me in the dust. Then the driver must have finally noticed

the pursuit lights in her mirror. She slammed on the brakes so hard, I was afraid my own forward momentum would flatten the convertible against my grille. Somehow, we both managed to come to a halt without a collision.

I hopped out of the patrol truck and strode up alongside the expensive sports car, the nerves in my neck and arms buzzing as if touched by an electrical charge. The young woman behind the wheel had a leopard-spotted scarf wrapped around her dark hair to keep it from whipping in her face, and despite the lateness of the hour, she was still wearing giant sunglasses, which might have concealed her identity if I hadn't already known who she was.

"Officer, thank God you're here," said Briar Morse, breathing hard. "Someone was just chasing me!"

My first thought was that she had made up the story to get out of a speeding ticket. But then I noticed that her hands were shaking when she removed her sunglasses, and her brown eyes were wide with what sure looked like panic. Briar Morse was either genuinely terrified or she was ready for her acting debut on the Broadway stage.

"Who was chasing you, Miss Morse?" I asked.

"I don't know." Her voice wasn't as flat and commanding as her mother's, but it wasn't her most feminine attribute, either. "Someone in a pickup truck."

"What color was it?"

"I'm not sure. Dark?"

That narrowed it down to several thousand vehicles, including most of the patrol trucks owned by the Maine Warden Service. "Why don't you step out of the vehicle and tell me what happened."

She unbuckled the chest strap and opened the door. She was wearing a sheer white blouse over a scoop-necked brown

top that showed her considerable cleavage, khaki short shorts, and Roman sandals. Her exposed skin—of which there was so much—was deeply tanned. She had an oval face that was pretty more because of her youth and vitality than because of the underlying structure of the bones. The hair gathered beneath the scarf was very dark and very thick.

Briar peered down the road in the direction of the village, as if expecting to see two headlights waiting in the distance. But there was nothing there except the forest, slowly darkening beneath an indigo sky streaked with lavender clouds.

"Why don't you start from the beginning," I said.

"I went for a drive."

"Where?"

"Nowhere in particular," she said. "I like to drive, and there isn't much to do up here except swim and lie around in the sun. And seeing all those wardens on our land was getting me down. I just wanted to get away from all that *death*, you know?"

I nodded, trying to follow her lurching thoughts. "When did you notice this dark truck?"

"As I was driving past the store. Maybe it was parked there? I'm not sure. I drove past, and it crept out behind me. It was moving slowly at first—hanging back, you know? But for some reason, I got this bad feeling about it."

"Why?"

"It just seemed to be following me. I thought maybe it was one of your Warden trucks headed back from my mom's place again. I decided to pull over and let it pass, but instead it stopped, too. That was when I started getting scared. I didn't know what to do, so I made a turn down this road, and it turned right behind me. I made this big loop back to the main road, and it kept following me the whole time! Finally, I

decided just to gun it and see if I could get to that Indian police station out on Route One."

"I don't suppose you got a license-plate number," I said.

"No. It had its high beams on—that was another weird thing—and it blinded me to look in my rearview mirror. It had kind of a whiny engine."

"And you couldn't tell what color it was?"

"Green maybe? Or blue? It was too dark for me to tell."

I had been watching Briar as she told her story, and I couldn't tell if her anxious body language—the fidgeting from foot to foot, the lack of eye contact—was the result of genuine fear or merely the stress most people experience when telling an elaborate lie. There was a quiver in her voice that made me feel she was frightened and needed protection. I had always been susceptible to this particular impulse in myself and tried to be on guard against pretty girls who showed too much cleavage and knew how to manipulate gullible men into doing their bidding.

"I'm going to let you go with a warning," I said. "But if you see a truck following you again, you should call nine-one-one instead of trying to outrun it. There are lots of deer along this road, and you could have hit one or wrapped your vehicle around a tree."

Suddenly, she reached out and grabbed my forearm with both of her hands. She locked her dark eyes on mine. "You're not going to leave me here?"

"What do you want me to do?"

"Follow me back to my mom's place. The truck stopped back there, and I'll have to drive past it again to get to the north gate."

This might all have been an act she was putting on, just a game she was playing to break up the boredom of being in the

middle of nowhere. But I could feel her soft hands shaking, and I decided to err on the safe side. At worst, she would have some fun at my expense, and it would cost me an extra half hour of time on the road tonight.

"All right," I said.

Her eyes filled with sudden tears, which gleamed in the headlights of my truck and made me feel cynical for having doubted her intentions. "Thank you so, so much," she said.

The northern gate to Elizabeth Morse's property was located off the gravel logging road that ran from Grand Lake Stream through fifty-five miles of unbroken timberland all the way to the Penobscot River above Bangor. The Stud Mill Road closed during the winter and stayed closed through the depths of mud season, but the rest of the year it served as a tire-slashing superhighway to the wildest country in eastern Maine. Wardens often came across stranded motorists who had underestimated the road's ability to incapacitate the sturdiest vehicles. It was not a thoroughfare to travel alone, especially after dark.

Briar drove slowly along the abrasive surface, her caution making me think the road had inflicted a few flat tires in the past. We had passed without incident through Grand Lake Stream, encountering no creepy trucks; just a wagonful of fly fishermen moving from one pool to another and a white van returning with bird hunters to one of the sporting camps along the lake. When we hit the gravel road, I kept my distance from the roadster's taillights in order to avoid the bombardment of rocks the spinning wheels launched into the air.

It took longer than I had expected to reach Morse's northeast gate. This was a different way onto the property than the Sixth Machias entrance, where I had met Billy Cronk two mornings

ago. Technically, we were in Bard's district here. I was out of my territory in many ways, I realized.

There was a car waiting on the other side of the heavy steel gate. I saw its headlights snap on as we approached, and the silhouette of a man advanced to open the lock and admit Morse's wayward daughter. I stopped my pickup and remained idling in place, waiting for Briar to drive through. As she did, the headlights lit up the man, and I saw that it was Leaf Woodwind. The hippie had his hair in its signature ponytail and was wearing cutoff denim shorts, flip-flops, and a faded blue T-shirt with the symbol for anarchy emblazoned on the front. I would have figured Leaf to be more of a peace symbol type of guy, but that showed just how little I understood these people.

After the roadster had entered the grounds, Leaf pushed the gate shut and bent over to turn the dials on the combination lock. He straightened up and looked in my direction, shielding his bespectacled eyes against the glare of my lights. I saw Briar come up behind him and say something into his ear, and then the two of them came strolling toward me. I turned the volume down on the police radio and unrolled my dusty window.

"Evening, Warden," Leaf said.

"Hello, Mr. Woodwind."

"Call me Leaf. Briar called us at the house to tell us what happened. Thank you for coming to her rescue."

Again I detected the unmistakable odor of marijuana on his person. Under the circumstances, I didn't feel like giving him a hard time. I could imagine Rivard's displeasure at learning I had arrested Morse's personal assistant on a misdemeanor drug-possession charge.

"I didn't really do anything," I said.

"Yes, you did," said Briar with a surprising insistence. "You totally saved me."

"We're not the most popular people in this neck of the woods," said Leaf, scratching his salt-and-pepper beard. "Sometimes Briar forgets that."

"Why shouldn't I be able to drive where I want?" she said. "It's a free country."

The hippie placed his arm around her shoulders and gave her a hug. "Honey, you need to read that Noam Chomsky book I gave you."

"He's so self-righteous and boring."

"Briar dropped out of Bennington last spring," Leaf explained, "so we're all doing what we can to continue her education."

"Bill and Melinda Gates have done more good in the world than Noam Chomsky ever will," said Briar. "Just look at Africa. That's where Mom should be spending her money."

At this hour, I didn't want to get drawn into a debate over the role of philanthropy in a political world. I found a business card in the console between the front seats and handed it to Briar. "If someone threatens you again, you should try nine-one-one first, but don't hesitate to call me, too."

She gave me a smile and held the card between two fingers over her breasts. For a moment, I thought she was going to tuck it into her bra, but the gesture was only meant to make me look. "Do I have to wait that long to call you?"

I laughed. "You two have a good evening." I had little doubt that Leaf, at least, intended to do so.

"You, too, Warden," said the hippie. "You, too."

As they walked side by side back to their waiting cars, I noticed that they were exactly the same height.

16

Shortly before dawn, I awoke to a bloodcurdling scream. I swung my legs off the bed and sat upright. For a few disoriented seconds, I sat there, heart racing, trying to recall the nightmare that had shattered my sleep. Then I heard the scream again in the woods outside my cabin. It sounded like a woman. I grabbed the flashlight that I kept in the dust beneath my futon and ran out of the bedroom in my undershorts.

I had locked my firearms in the safe for the night, so I grabbed the only weapon in view, which just happened to be the hatchet beside the woodpile, and I went leaping through the front door and down the steps into the darkness. In less than a minute, I'd gone from a deep, dreamless sleep to a state of high alert. My hand was shaking from the adrenaline, causing the flashlight beam to jump along the pine-needle floor of the forest.

"Hello?"

The night was still. The air had the tangy, almost pungent aroma that is the smell of autumn in the North Woods. I heard in the distance the ecstatic warble of a purple finch that had risen to greet the sun, which would soon be pushing pink light above the horizon. I sprinted around the back of the cabin to the steep, wooded hillside where chanterelle mushrooms appeared in orange clusters after rainstorms. I shined the

light back and forth, high and low. To another human being, I would have looked like a crazy man, running around in his underwear, brandishing an ax and shouting at the dark.

But there were no other human beings present, only a fisher and the snowshoe hare it had just killed.

It was the hare I'd heard screaming. When they are injured, rabbits make a noise like a child being murdered. I'd heard the sound often enough over the years, and if I'd been fully awake, I would have known instantly what it was. This one's brown fur had already started to turn white in spots. Despite the balmy temperatures, it was growing out a pale winter coat that would have allowed it to hide amid the inevitable snowbanks. Instead, the white splotches had given the hare away as it tried to vanish into the lingering greenery. The poor thing had never stood a chance.

I watched the fisher grab the lifeless hare by the neck and trot away into the darkness. Trappers sometimes call them fisher cats, but they are actually weasels on steroids. Weighing in at a deceptively light ten pounds, they are ferocious and fearless critters—brown of coat, with devil-pointed ears and shaggy tails—that feast on porcupines, which they flip onto their backs to attack the soft underbellies. Fishers are usually the culprits behind the disappearance of neighborhood house cats. I had even found a lynx skull once with two fang marks that must have pierced the brain; a biologist friend told me those mortal injuries had been inflicted by a fisher.

Later, I would remember the scream of that luckless rabbit and wonder if it was a portent of the bad things that were to come. I had to remind myself that nature doesn't send us omens to warn us of all the calamities we bring upon ourselves.

I couldn't fall back to sleep. I lay flat on the bed, with the

screen window open above my head and the curtain fluttering in the warm breeze. I watched the green fabric billow out like a sail and then be sucked back against the mesh when the gust had passed. The air had the evergreen smell of a Christmas wreath.

After a while, I got up and made myself a cup of instant coffee. I took it outside and sat on the porch in my underwear and listened to the forest waking up around me, the finch still singing his hopeful tune, joined by a chattering red squirrel, a flock of cooing mourning doves, and all of it backed by the sighing sound the wind made in the tops of the hemlocks and tamaracks. I was never happier, never more my best self, than when I was in the woods.

I had been that way as a boy, as well, which had made my mother's decision to divorce my dad and leave the woods so much harder to accept when I was nine. Nothing about the suburbs had appealed to me: not the chemically green lawns or the backyard cookouts with neighbors you invited out of politeness rather than real friendship, and certainly not the three-floor McMansions with so many rooms the owners didn't even know what to put in them. I'd spent my teenage years running to the last wild places in town the developers hadn't yet destroyed. But my mother seemed to be happy living in Scarborough, a stone's throw from the beach. Today I would call her and ask what was going on between her and Neil. What was up with all the inspirational messages? And why had Neil phoned my house for perhaps the first time ever?

At precisely eight A.M., my cell phone rang. The display read UNKNOWN. I answered the call anyway.

"Warden Bowditch, this is Elizabeth Morse."

The sound of her voice made me self-conscious that I was standing there half-naked. "Hello, Ms. Morse. Good morning."

"I understand that you rescued my daughter from some trouble last night."

"I wouldn't go that far."

"She seems to think it was significant." She paused. "I'd like you to come to my house this morning."

I set the empty coffee cup down on the bureau. "Um. Why?"

"I have some questions for you about the progress—or lack thereof—in this investigation. It was what I wanted to speak with you about the other night."

"Ma'am," I said. "You really should be talking to Lieutenant Rivard."

"I've been talking to him. Now I would like to talk to you."

"I'll need to clear this with him."

"All right," she said, and I sensed that she was handing off the phone to someone else.

"Just get over here, Bowditch," said Marc Rivard, sounding as pissed off as a person can be without totally blowing his lid.

An hour later, I pulled up to the gate that allowed entry onto Morse's woodland estate from the south. Again, the gatekeeper was Leaf Woodwind. He was wearing the same outfit he'd had on the previous evening—anarchy T-shirt, cutoffs, and flip-flops—although he had added a floppy wide-brimmed hat to the ensemble. He must have left the Toyota Prius parked back at the log mansion.

"I like to go for a walk in the morning," he said as he climbed into my passenger seat. Behind his glasses, his eyes were threaded with pink lines. "There's something so beautiful about first light—it's like the color of magic."

I glanced at him through my Oakleys, wondering how high he was flying. "That's an interesting way of describing it."

"Back in Vietnam, in the mornings, this mist would rise off

the rice paddies. The sun would catch it just this certain way, and it would shimmer, you know, like ghosts dancing."

"You were in the war?" For some reason, this news surprised me. He seemed like such a peacenik. Then again, I supposed that a lot of the back-to-the-landers had been men whose faith in the modern world had been shattered by mechanized warfare.

"Ninth Infantry," he said. "The 'brown water navy.' "

"My dad was in the Seventy-fifth Ranger Regiment."

"He's dead, isn't he?" asked Leaf.

"Why do you say that?"

"I can hear it in your voice, man."

We drove past the place where Moose A had dropped dead in the withering weeds. The carcass seemed to be gone, whether removed by wardens or picked apart by ravens and coyotes, I had no idea. I studied the roadside, but I was thinking that Leaf Woodwind was a more perceptive and complicated man than the smiling stoner he appeared to be at first glance.

Rivard's spiffy black GMC was parked outside Morse's front door in the open area she reserved for guests. This time, rather than parking around the corner with the hired help, I pulled in beside Briar's expensive convertible. Mine wasn't the only vehicle out of place: a dented and scraped blue Subaru Outback was also parked here.

As we approached the entrance, I again gazed up at the MOOSEHORN LODGE sign over the door, this time wondering how Morse could reconcile her desire to create this ostentatious log castle in the woods with a campaign to remove other human habitations from the area. Her yearning to experience wilderness seemed to end at her own doorstep.

Leaf punched a coded number into a console beside the double doors, and I heard the very clear sound of a lock clicking

open. Then he twisted one of the knobs and led me inside. We entered a vast, airy foyer that reminded me, in its openness and the random placement of chairs and couches, of the lobby at the El Tovar Hotel on the edge of the Grand Canyon. The log walls gleamed with new varnish, and the flagstone floor showed no sign yet of the inevitable scuffing you get from boots tracking abrasive winter sand inside. A spectacular chandelier hung overhead, like a leafless tree turned upside down, with bulbs at the tips of the branches, although there was no need this morning for artificial illumination, not with the shafts of golden sunlight falling from the high windows.

"They're in the kitchen," said Leaf.

I followed him past a broad set of stairs leading up to the second story, down a hall hung with paintings by Maine artists whose names I recognized—Hartley and Fitzgerald and Welliver—and finally into a bright kitchen bigger than my entire cabin, where Elizabeth Morse stood at a stove, frying tofu, while Lieutenant Rivard drank tea from a stoneware mug and conversed with a jug-eared man whose face seemed vaguely familiar.

"I'm just making breakfast," Betty Morse said. She wore an apron over a chambray shirt and jeans that had been patched with squares of patterned red fabric. I noticed she was barefoot. "I'm making my signature tofu scramble with curried spinach."

"Thank you," I said. "I've already eaten. But I'd love some coffee."

"Leaf, pour the warden a cup of tea."

The hippie happily obliged.

Rivard glared at me over the rim of his mug. "Bowditch," he said by way of a growled greeting.

"You haven't met my partner in crime," said Morse, turning from the stove. "Dexter, introduce yourself."

The jug-eared man grinned and held out an overly large hand for me to shake. Everything about him seemed out of proportion. His chin was too small and his cheekbones were too wide; his shoulders were too broad and his legs were too short. His dark blond hair seemed beset by cowlicks. There was something almost endearingly grotesque about his appearance, as if he had been drawn by a small child. He was wearing a red-and-black flannel shirt over faded Levi jeans, the legs of which were tucked into well-worn Bean boots. "Dexter Albee," he said.

"Dexter is with the Thoreau Initiative. He's the one who sold me on the idea of creating a park."

"Betty, that's a fib," he said.

"How so? You've been running around the state for a decade with this idea, getting nowhere. I'm just your sugar momma."

Albee flashed a smile that made his exaggerated features seem even more so. "You were at the very first meeting of the initiative in Concord. And I still have the check you wrote, so don't deny you were a pioneer."

Morse scooped the mushy tofu onto three stoneware plates and carried them to the butcher-block table beside the windows. "All right," she said, untying her apron and draping it over the back of a hand-crafted chair. "I am a pioneer, as well as a crackpot, nutcase, tree hugger, bitch, flatlander, queen, and what else, Leaf?"

"One of the letters accused you of being a hermaphrodite," said the hippie.

She sat down heavily at the table without waiting for her guests. "I think he said I had a cock where my cunt should be." She picked up a fork and pointed the tines at Rivard. "Why mince words? Right, Lieutenant? When someone wants to kill you, it doesn't pay to soft-pedal the truth."

Rivard and I remained standing while the others began to eat.

"What about Briar?" Leaf asked.

"She finished a bottle of wine after we went to bed. We won't see her till noon." Morse raised her eyes from her plate and locked them on mine. I had forgotten what an interesting shade they were, green, with flecks like polished pieces of amber. "I'm guessing by now you're wondering why you're here, Warden Bowditch."

"Yes, ma'am."

"Tell him, Lieutenant."

"Charley Stevens has located three more kill sites, bringing the total of dead moose we've found now to ten."

"Jesus," I said.

Elizabeth frowned. "You're leaving something out, Lieutenant."

"Ms. Morse has asked that you be assigned as her personal liaison for the duration of the investigation into the moose killings." Rivard said this with all the joy of a man telling his wife he'd just lost their nest egg at a Las Vegas casino.

"Why me?"

"The lieutenant has more important things to do than 'handle' me," said Morse. "Two days have gone by, and my understanding is that you don't have a single plausible suspect—"

"That's not entirely accurate," said Rivard, smoothing his mustache.

"A single plausible suspect," repeated Morse, "with the possible exception of my own former caretaker, whose motive still seems a bit unclear to me."

"If you don't believe Billy shot those moose, then why did you fire him?" I asked.

Morse leaned back in her chair and showed her pearly teeth. "There you go, Lieutenant. When I told you I wanted your people to be more candid, that's exactly what I had in mind. You're not afraid of me, are you, Warden Bowditch? You don't worry about sugarcoating your opinions for my delicate ears."

My eyes darted to Rivard's scowling expression and back. "No, ma'am," I said.

"I fired Billy Cronk because he can't do his job if he's in jail. And frankly, if there's a chance he *did* have something to do with the murder of those moose, then having a violent man around my family is a risk I see no point in taking." She lifted a forkful of tofu to her mouth and swallowed. "Besides, he lied to me about his criminal record."

I felt an urge to stand up for my friend, but the firmness in Morse's voice told me that she didn't back down from many decisions. "I'm not sure what being your liaison entails," I said.

"You'll be in communication with the investigative team throughout the day," Rivard told me. "You'll also be the point of contact between Ms. Morse and the state police, since they're cross-checking the death threats she received against our MOSES database of convicted poachers, and following a parallel investigation on that front. They're hoping to bring stalking or terrorizing charges, as well."

"Should I just stay here all day?"

"Is there somewhere else you need to be?"

"No, sir."

The lieutenant picked up his hat. "In that case, I am going to head back to the field office."

"Thank you for coming over, Lieutenant," said Morse. "Do you need someone to show you out?"

"I think I can find my way." He nodded at the people seated

at the table but pointedly avoided looking in my direction, and then he disappeared down the hall.

I caught up with him as he was opening the front door. "Lieutenant! Can I have a word?"

"What is it, Bowditch?"

"How much do you want me to tell her?"

"As little as possible—although I doubt she'll accept that. She didn't accept it from me." He stepped out into the sun.

"I didn't ask for this," I said.

"I know," said Rivard, reaching in his pocket for a tin of chewing tobacco. "That's what pisses me off."

17

After the lieutenant left, I wandered back into the kitchen. Leaf had already wolfed down his tofu and started on the doughnuts that had been sitting on the counter. It was dangerous to stand between a plate of junk food and a man with the munchies.

He held up a curved piece of doughnut. "Want one? They're gluten-free."

"My cook uses almond flour on account of Briar's allergies," said Morse.

"No, thank you."

Morse gave me that sly catlike smile of hers. "You have excellent manners, but they don't seem to get in the way of you voicing an opinion. And I don't get the sense that you, unlike some of your colleagues, have an issue with strong women."

I thought of the confident women I'd known in my life—my former supervisor, Sgt. Kathy Frost; Sheriff Rhine; my strange and inscrutable mother. "No, ma'am."

Dexter Albee was watching me carefully, as if he had seen Morse engage in this cat-and-mouse game with other people before and already knew what would happen to the mouse. I remembered having seen him quoted in a number of newspaper articles about the proposed Moosehorn National Park. He had an office near the Maine state capital, where he was a

registered lobbyist and conservative punching bag. Given the general disdain in which Elizabeth Morse and the Thoreau Initiative were held, I admired Albee's courage in being the spokesman for such an unpopular cause.

"I want you to tell me what's going on with your investigation," she said.

"I haven't been privy to all aspects of the case," I said. "I've kind of been on the periphery."

"That's undoubtedly why the lieutenant agreed to station you here. You don't know enough to spill any of the important beans. So in that case, what can you tell me?"

I braced myself against the granite counter. "We're operating under the theory that there were at least two shooters, based upon the different-caliber bullet cartridges we recovered. We also found some cigarette butts and candy wrappers at the kill sites. The state police forensic lab in Augusta is testing everything for fingerprints and DNA. The fingerprint matches should come back soon—if there are any matches—but the DNA tests can take weeks."

"Was the lieutenant being straight with me when he said you had a list of suspects?"

"There is a list," I said.

She leaned an elbow on the table and brought her hand to her face in contemplation. "And what have you been doing since I last saw you?"

"I have been searching the local gravel pits, looking for spent cartridges that might match the ones we found on your property. If we knew where the killers practiced, we'd have another potential clue to identifying them. I also spent some time checking the rifles of local hunters, trying to find a match with the bullets used to slaughter the moose."

"And did you?"

I shifted my weight from one foot to the other. "That remains to be seen."

"What's your confidence level in the investigation?"

"My confidence level?"

"How much faith do you have in the men overseeing the case? Rivard and that weaselly one?"

"The Warden Service has an exemplary track record in solving shootings like these."

"That's not what I asked."

"I know, ma'am."

Her mouth dropped open. She looked at Albee with her jaw hanging loose, and then she let out a belly laugh. "Very diplomatic! Dexter, you should recruit this young man to come work for you. We could use someone with his silver tongue in Augusta."

"My guess is that the warden isn't a Moosehorn supporter, Betty," said Dexter Albee.

"That's because he hasn't heard your sales pitch." She stood up from the table. "Why don't you take him into the great room while Leaf and I do the dishes. I'll be in to join you in a few minutes."

Elizabeth Morse had a way of framing all her suggestions as commands. Is her forcefulness a result of being rich, I wondered, or is it an innate quality that enabled her to rise from a hardscrabble farm to the corporate boardrooms she now frequents?

Whatever the answer was, I found myself blindly following Albee through a formal dining room that could have comfortably seated the New England Patriots' fifty-three-man roster and into an immense open area where the ceiling shot up past second- and third-floor walkways to distant dark rafters. The great room held not one fireplace, but two, and was walled

entirely with glass overlooking Sixth Machias Lake. Looking out the windows, I saw far green mountains and bottle-blue waves rippling across miles of open water. The light inside the room had a shifting, aqueous quality from the reflection of the lake below.

In front of one of the fieldstone hearths, an easel was set up with a chart showing eastern Maine; a red line delineated Morse's extensive property holdings. She really did own the northern halves of Hancock and Washington counties, I realized. There were folding chairs arranged in front of the easel, as if Morse had recently compelled a dozen of her unwitting houseguests to listen to Dexter Albee's promotional pitch.

He tugged on one of his puppet ears and said, "You don't really want to hear this."

"Actually, I'm kind of curious."

From reading the Bangor paper, I was familiar with the broad-brush description of the proposal, but I hadn't spent hours immersing myself in the details. Maybe boning up on the specifics would give me some insight into the twisted mind-set of the men who had slaughtered the moose. I was also trapped in the house for the rest of the day, so what else did I have to do?

He motioned for me to take a seat, but I shook my head and remained standing.

Albee spread out his arms, as if pantomiming a welcome to a sizable crowd. His voice projected across the room. "'Primeval, untamed, and forever untamable Nature.' Those were the words Henry David Thoreau used to describe the Maine woods after his 1846 expedition to the summit of Katahdin. At the time of Thoreau's three visits to Maine, most of the North Woods was public, a resource owned entirely by

the people of the state. But by the time of his death, in 1862, this 'collective commons' had been destroyed. Shortsighted Maine politicians had sold off all the land or granted deeds to private interests. And so began the taming of nature, and the loss of one of America's crown jewels.

"Thoreau believed that wild places such as the ones he found in northern Maine should be set aside as national preserves, and over the decades efforts were made to secure large-scale protection for the North Woods. In 1933, Maine's then governor, Louis Brann, put forward the idea of establishing a million-acre 'Roosevelt National Park' in northern Maine. Four years later, Congressman Ralph Brewster proposed the creation of a four-hundred-thousand-acre 'Katahdin National Park,' with the backing of both the Appalachian Trail Conference and the Millinocket Chamber of Commerce. Alas, both these efforts failed, and it was only through the personal vision, determination, and philanthropy of a former governor, Percival Baxter, that Katahdin itself was spared. Today the 'forever wild' preserve Baxter created out of his own funds and which he donated in its entirety to the citizens of Maine— two-hundred-thousand-acre Baxter State Park—stands as a testament to what one brave individual can accomplish in the face of well-financed corporate opposition.

"Now, after decades during which the surrounding woods have been clear-cut and despoiled, developed without regard to the natural movement of wildlife across the landscape, or without any effort to maintain the scenic beauty of one of the nation's last unpeopled places, there finally comes a successor. Maine entrepreneur, philanthropist, and mother Elizabeth Morse has accepted the challenge thrown down by Percival Baxter to take personal action to protect the North Woods. She stands ready to donate one hundred thousand acres of

her own land to the citizens of the United States to create its newest national park, Moosehorn, here on the eastern edge of our great nation."

I found my eyes drifting toward the sparkling lake and imagined the spell his words must cast on the powerful people Morse invited to sit by her fires.

Albee continued his well-practiced speech. "Moosehorn National Park will be a place of verdant pine and spruce forests, multicolor hardwoods that blaze with foliage in the autumn, boreal bogs brightened by lady slippers and swamp loosestrife, crystalline lakes, and rolling mountains unbroken by cell towers or other man-made structures. It will be a safe haven for fish and animals, not just the salmon and moose and eagles that already live here but also the cougars, timber wolves, and woodland caribou that were cruelly extirpated from these remote forests. People weary of twenty-first-century noise and overpopulation—the artificial condition we call 'civilization'— will find solitude here and experience the spiritual rebirth that comes from meeting nature in its primeval state. Moosehorn will be a time capsule containing the hopes and dreams of—"

Above my head, someone began to clap. "Preach it, Pastor Albee!"

Dexter frowned at the second-floor walkway. "Hello, Briar."

I craned my neck and found myself looking straight up the oversize T-shirt she wore as a nightie. Out of reflex, I turned my eyes to the floor.

"I never get tired of hearing your sermons," she said. "Who are you trying to convert to the cause this morning?"

I heard a creaking noise that sounded as if she was leaning over the polished log bannister for a look at the top of my head. I raised my face so she could see it.

"Hi, Briar."

She had her mother's superwhite smile. Her loose hair was hanging down. "Mike! I didn't realize it was you. What are you doing here?"

"Your mother has asked Warden Bowditch to be her contact with the investigation," said Albee.

"Really? That's so awesome."

I heard the slapping of bare feet on the floor above and then quick steps as she came prancing down the stairs. She entered the room with her luxuriant brown hair all a mess and her eyes still a little unfocused, as if she'd just awakened from an enchanted slumber that had lasted for years. Her T-shirt was pink and had a slogan on it: SAVE DARFUR: DON'T JUST LOOK AWAY. STOP GENOCIDE NOW. It barely covered the tops of her suntanned thighs. Briar Morse was clearly not self-conscious about showing off her body.

"So, has Dexter persuaded you to join the cult?"

Albee gave a polite smile. "Briar has been forced to hear my presentation on more than a few occasions."

"Have you gotten to the part about how it's never going to happen in a million years?"

"I was curious about the process," I said. "Everything I've heard suggests you need to get votes from politicians who are opposed to removing so much timberland from the tax rolls."

"I usually save that part for the end," he said. "The first thing you need to keep in mind is that this is almost always a long road. It took twenty-six *years* to create the Grand Canyon National Park. Today, we can't imagine anyone not wanting to protect the Grand Canyon, but a hundred years ago there was still a contentious debate around setting that land aside. It's the same dynamic here at Moosehorn. Our task is to persuade people that these lands are investments and that the returns will be accumulated not just by future generations

but by those in the existing communities surrounding this area. Tourists spend eleven *billion* dollars a year in park gateway towns like Bar Harbor and West Yellowstone. Critics of our plan cite the loss of hundreds of woods-products jobs, but they don't mention the three thousand jobs Acadia National Park has created seventy miles from here on the coast."

"You still haven't explained the process," I said.

He grinned as if I had caught him with his hand in the cookie jar. "There are two ways that a parcel of land can become a national park. The first is when Congress asks the Department of the Interior, which oversees the National Park Service, to conduct a special resource study to evaluate the site's boundaries and budget. The NPS then sends a report back to Congress, which can choose to accept or ignore its recommendations."

"My understanding is that the state's entire delegation is on record opposing your plan," I said.

"A teensy problem," said Briar.

"There's also another way to do this," said Albee. "Under the 1906 Antiquities Act, the President can confer national-monument status on an area by executive order. That's how Teddy Roosevelt created Grand Canyon National Monument. In the past two decades, six new national parks have been designated, and most of them were national monuments first. The exception—which is closer to the model we're following here—is Voyageurs, in Minnesota, which was also created through the acquisition of private land."

"In either case, it seems to me you need to win over public opinion," I said. "I can't imagine the President is just going to ride roughshod over local politicians and voter sentiment."

"That's not necessarily the case," said Albee. "Most presidents wait until the lame-duck period of their presidencies

to designate national monuments. They have their eyes on their place in history at that stage and not on the next election, and thus are more willing to assert their privileges. But you're right: it absolutely helps to have a groundswell of support from the populace. That's why this moose massacre might ultimately be a good thing."

I could feel my face flushing with blood. "Excuse me?"

Albee held up his hands to show his peaceful intentions. "It's horrific, inexcusable—don't get me wrong," he said. "The perpetrators need to be prosecuted to the fullest extent of the law. But a violent incident like this can create a backlash of sympathy. I'm not sure if you've been following the news, Warden, but because of Betty's celebrity, this is now a national story. The shootings have cast the opponents of our proposal in a highly negative light. The Maine papers have all come out with editorials reconsidering the opposition to Moosehorn, and Betty has been invited to New York tomorrow to appear on three of the morning TV shows. From a public-relations stand-point, the slaughter of those ten animals might actually be—"

"Dexter, that's enough." Elizabeth Morse stood in the door leading to the kitchen.

Political animal that he was, Albee instantly sensed the waves of anger coming off his patron. "Betty, I'm just trying to point out the silver lining to this horrible event."

She ignored him and looked straight into my eyes. "Mr. Albee's passion is his most endearing quality, but sometimes he lets it get the better of him."

"My apologies," said Albee.

Elizabeth pivoted toward her daughter. "Good morning, Sleeping Beauty. It's so nice of you to join us."

"You didn't tell me you were having Mike assigned to the case."

"How could I tell you when you were passed out with an empty wine bottle?"

"Someone tried to kill me, Mom!"

"So you said." It sounded like Elizabeth wasn't as quick to believe her daughter as Leaf or I had been. "How about putting on a robe? I'm sure Warden Bowditch doesn't mind the peep show, but I would prefer it if you acted with more maturity around my guests."

Briar pinched the top of her nightgown closed. "Leaf says you used to be like this cool free spirit when you were my age. What happened to you?"

"I became a mother," Elizabeth said. "Warden, I'd like to speak with you alone out on the patio if you have a few minutes."

Again, the suggestion was a command. "Yes, ma'am."

Briar leaned over and kissed my cheek for no apparent reason. My face grew warm again.

"Knock it off, Briar," her mother said.

Briar made a *harrumphing* noise that didn't exactly demonstrate the maturity her mother wished for her, and then she turned on her bare heels and scurried upstairs.

"Betty, I really didn't mean anything," said Albee with a flutter in his voice and an expression that seemed to be growing more and more nervous by the second.

"Yes, you did," she said, exiting the room.

I gave the jug-eared man a curt nod by way of a farewell, thinking that I needed to phone Rivard and tell him to check out Dexter Albee's whereabouts on the night of the moose massacre.

18

We stopped briefly in the kitchen to pick up two mugs containing EarthMother herbal tea and then proceeded through a sliding door onto the immense flagstone patio beside the lake. The air was heavy and muggy, and a translucent haze hung along the distant hills. It could have been the dog days of summer. The morning was already too hot for tea.

Elizabeth Morse didn't speak until she had settled herself into one of the two Adirondack chairs flanking the extinguished fire pit. She waved a hand at me to indicate I should do the same. It felt awkward. I was a law-enforcement officer, in uniform and on duty, and not some vacationer here to enjoy the view.

"When I die, I intend to donate this house to serve as the park's welcome center," she said. "I had it designed with that purpose in mind."

"It's certainly spectacular."

"Albee didn't shoot those animals," she said.

I didn't inform Elizabeth Morse that she had an uncanny habit of reading my mind. "That's good to hear."

"He was giving a presentation at a house party in Cumberland Foreside, near Portland. You can ask the hosts."

Greater Portland was approximately five hours away by car.

Since I doubted that Albee had spent the night at the home of Morse's potential backers, he might easily have driven to Washington County after the party had ended. Given that the moose might well have been shot between midnight and dawn, his alibi didn't amount to much.

"So what was your reaction to the proposal?" Morse asked me after a long pause.

"It's ambitious," I said.

"That's true, but you don't support the idea. I can always tell a skeptic."

"I know a lot of good people who work in the forest industry," I said. "You're not going to retrain them to run bed-and-breakfasts and souvenir shops. Maybe someday all the good economic benefits you talk about will happen, but a generation is going to struggle in the meantime."

"What else?"

"I'm a game warden, Ms. Morse. I know it's not politically correct. But hunting and trapping and fishing mean something to me. They're part of our heritage here in Maine and important activities in my own life."

She leaned forward in her chair. "Last week was the moose hunt, wasn't it?"

"In this zone, it was. The moose hunt happens during different weeks in September and October around the state."

"How many dead moose did you see?"

I thought back to my patrols during that long, hot week; the many times the agent at the tagging station had called to tell me a big bull had just come in on a trailer; the occasions when I had happened on a party of hunters field-dressing an animal in the woods.

"I'm not sure," I said, "but I know they tagged twenty-three at Day's General Store."

"Yes, I saw several being weighed as we drove by. They were lifted on a chain by their hind legs over that pole contraption they have set up there. All of them had been gutted beforehand, and there was a pool of blood on the ground. People were taking pictures. It was a grotesque spectacle." She set her mug down on the arm of the chair. "The question I have for you is, how was that any different from what happened on my property?"

"The hunters who shot the moose didn't just leave them to rot," I said. "They're going to eat the meat. In many cases, these men and their families are poor, and they are going to save hundreds of dollars in food bills. Nothing is going to waste."

She waved her hand, and I saw that her fingernails were newly polished. "You pretend it's all a utilitarian enterprise. What's that word hunters always use? The deer *harvest*? That's a cozy term for mass murder, in my opinion." Her throaty voice began to rise in pitch. "But you're deliberately ignoring the key similarity between the 'legal' hunters who gleefully pose for photographs with their trophies and the hunters who shot the moose on my land."

"Which is what, ma'am?" I tried to keep the personal insult I was feeling out of my voice.

"The enthusiasm. The joy of killing another living thing. You hunters can pretend you're engaged in some noble tradition that softhearted city people will never understand. But the truth is, you get a kick out of inflicting death, and I find that repugnant."

I had heard this argument many times before when I was in college, and I had usually answered that *Homo sapiens* evolved as a species of hunters. It wasn't some cultural artifact we would morally relinquish, the way we had slavery or leaving old people on ice floes. Hunting was woven into the strands

of our DNA. It was the reason we had incisor teeth. Man is a meat eater—and always will be.

But I was already tired of debating with Elizabeth Morse, when what I wanted to be doing was searching for the men who had killed those animals. And the fact that I was stuck here, seemingly for the sole purpose of entertaining this wealthy woman's whims, made me feel even more like a useless plaything.

"Then you and I disagree," I said.

"Where did you grow up?" she asked me. "You don't remind me of the other wardens I've met."

"In what way?"

"You talk the same talk—about your proud outdoor heritage, et cetera—but it's as if you're pretending somehow. You don't have much of a Maine accent, and your speech is different, not quite so folksy."

"I don't understand what you mean," I said.

"The wardens I've met are always using words like *critters* to describe animals. It's like you come from a very different background to your sergeant and lieutenant. Where did you go to college?"

I paused before I answered. "Colby."

"And what did you major in?"

"I was a history major." I felt peeved that she had identified some special quality that separated me from my colleagues.

"My daughter was studying dance and theater at Bennington. Now she tells me she wants to work for my foundation. She wants to use my money to help 'people instead of animals,' she says. Her latest fixation is curing typhoid fever in Zambia and Zimbabwe. I notice you don't wear a wedding ring."

This woman took a lot of liberties. "No, ma'am."

"I think Briar likes you."

"She's a lovely young woman," I said.

She leaned back in her Adirondack chair and brought her hand to her chin. She studied me with those perceptive hazel eyes. "I've decided to raise the reward I'm offering to twenty thousand dollars. What do you think about that?"

"That's a lot of money."

"Not to me, it's not," she said. "The question is whether it's enough money to achieve the outcome I desire."

"In this part of the world, I would say it is."

"Good, then perhaps you can help me get the word out through whatever channels you use for these things."

"We have a program called Operation Game Thief."

She made an amused noise in the back of her throat. "Another euphemism."

"I'm sorry?"

"*Game*. As in something you play." She rose from the chair and stood in a place where the sun was shining directly behind her, surrounding her silhouette with a celestial aura. "Dexter mentioned that I'm flying to New York today. I have some meetings, and I'm going to tape segments with the network morning shows tomorrow about the shootings. I'd thought of having you appear with me on TV—you are articulate and photogenic—but I have a feeling the idea would give your Lieutenant Rivard a fit. And I don't get the sense that you enjoy the limelight."

Nor would I enjoy being used as a prop to advance your park proposal, I thought.

"I don't think the Maine Warden Service wants me to be its official spokesman," I said, rising to my feet. "But I could check with the corporal down in Augusta who handles information requests. Perhaps he would be available to go with you."

"It was just a fleeting idea I had. Now I should go pack

153

some things. You're free to stay or go. I'll give you a call when I need you again."

And with that, I was dismissed. In Queen Elizabeth's eyes, I was just another servant. I was beginning to understand Billy's resentments.

"Have a safe trip," I said.

"And good luck with your investigation. By the way, do you know what Thoreau's last word was?"

"I'm afraid I don't."

"It was *moose*. I'm coming to see that as an auspicious omen for me."

I put a call into the Augusta headquarters and told the corporal who handled the media for the Warden Service about Elizabeth Morse's twenty-thousand-dollar reward. He whistled when I told him the sum. It would be the largest amount of money ever offered through Operation Game Thief, he said.

The comment made me reflect on Morse's wordplay: *game,* as in a wild animal killed by hunters; *game,* as in a childish form of recreation. I didn't want to think too hard on the point she had been trying to make.

Leaf Woodwind escorted me to the Sixth Machias gate. He sat in my passenger seat, reeking so much of marijuana, it seemed like almost a deliberate attempt to taunt me. After riding with him for a few minutes, however, I concluded that the old hippie was just heedless of how obviously drugged he was.

"So you guys really don't have any leads on this thing?" he asked.

"We have a few."

"Man, I hope you do, because Betty isn't the most patient person on the planet."

I looked at him out of the side of my sunglasses, keeping my head facing the road. "I heard you used to be her business partner."

"Yeah, I was. Back in the eighties." He stroked his beard softly, as if it were a pet he'd owned a long time. "But I never really saw it that way, you know? To me, it was more like we were together and the business stuff was just something we did to pass the time."

"I can't really picture Elizabeth Morse as a back-to-the-lander."

He had a laugh that was more of a deep-throated giggle. "Betty was always more of a pretend hippie. The first time I saw her, she was standing next to this overheating VW Super Beetle, with her hair all in crazy curls, wearing this peasant dress. I asked her where she was heading, and she said nowhere. She was just this restless young thing exploring the Maine countryside. So I gave her a ride, and we ended up back at the shack where I was living, and Betty thought it was the coolest place in the world. She had read the Nearings, you know? She had all these fantasies of eating only food she grew herself and living the good life. She moved in with me that night. I was a bit older than her so I couldn't believe my luck. I didn't realize she was this rich kid from Boston."

Like most cannabis aficionados I had met, Leaf was a talkative character. I let him ramble.

"I had this herb garden back then," he continued. "And I used to dry and sell my stuff at various farmers' markets—parsley, sage, rosemary, and thyme, as the song goes. But one day, Betty heard two guys at the next stall talking about medicinal plants, and she suddenly got all interested in growing milk thistle and chickweed and nettle leaf. She started making tinctures and extracts and teas. I thought it was kind of fun at first,

experimenting, but Betty was all business from the start. She got one of our artist friends to draw up the EarthMother logo to put on the packages. Then she took over a barn down the road and hired these local women to help her brew everything. The next thing I knew, she was driving all over New England to co-ops and head shops to sell her herbal products. I don't know why it surprised me when she told me she wanted to move out of the shack to a real farm, where she could have a bigger operation. But I wasn't interested in moving, and so she asked me to sign a paper giving up my rights to the business, and I did because it was always her thing and not mine, and we peacefully parted ways. Eight months later, she sent me a letter telling me she'd had a baby girl she'd named Briar."

"Briar's your daughter?"

"Betty's never told me for sure, and I've never asked. We were into free love, man. What can I say?"

I didn't have a clue how to respond to this. "Isn't that strange for all of you? Briar doesn't want to know who her father is?"

He pushed his glasses back higher on the bridge of his nose. "I'd say that anyone who has Betty Morse for a mom doesn't need another parent. I think that's how they both feel. But looking at Briar does make me smile, I have to say."

We passed the dry meadow where we'd found the first moose. A small flock of migrating sparrows that was feeding along the roadside took off, each bird flying away in its own crazy direction. When I'd first driven onto Elizabeth Morse's woodland estate, I'd had the feeling of entering a different world. Now it seemed like more of an alternate universe.

"After all that," I said, "how did you ever end up working as her personal assistant?"

"I got busted for growing dope—it was a game warden pilot who spotted my little plantation, actually—and then the

IRS took my shack for nonpayment of taxes. Betty somehow heard I was in trouble, and she asked if I wanted a job, and I didn't have a whole lot of options, you know?"

His muscles had tensed up when he mentioned being arrested for marijuana cultivation, and for the first time during this conversation, I remembered that he'd been a soldier in the Mekong Delta long ago. I wondered what roiling emotions the harmless old stoner might be keeping at bay through regular hits from the bong. Leaf had been Elizabeth's business partner, but now he was merely her assistant. He was seemingly Briar's father, but Morse had denied bestowing that status on him, as well. I couldn't imagine how the man lived with himself.

"If you had kept your share of the business, you could have been rich," I said.

"That's true. But I've never needed a whole lot to be happy."

We entered the thick stand of evergreens, then a minute later rolled to a stop in front of the Sixth Machias gate. As he reached for the door handle, I couldn't help but ask, "The situation doesn't make you feel bitter at all?"

"Sometimes, yeah, it does."

"How do you deal with it?"

Leaf Woodwind shook his head and giggled again, as if the answer were staring me in the face. "I get high, man. I get high."

19

With the rest of my afternoon free, I decided to pay a visit to the home of Billy Cronk. I figured I would give myself a couple of hours before I alerted anyone that I had been temporarily dismissed as Elizabeth Morse's personal liaison. And I wanted to have a frank talk with my friend about his strange behavior over the past forty-eight hours.

On the way, I stopped to use the outhouse at the rest area where Route 9 crossed over the babbling East Machias River. Given what a beautiful day it was, I would have expected to see picnickers at the raised grills and red cedar tables, but there was only a single vehicle in the paved lot: a black Sierra Denali. The truck was brand-new, recently washed and waxed. I didn't recognize the plate number, but I had a vague sense of having seen the expensive pickup around town. The driver was probably fishing on the river. I decided to have a look at him.

Wardens spend a lot of our time spying on people. If your intention is to catch someone taking too many trout, there is no better substitute than watching him from behind a bush. The anglers we arrest—or "pinch"—for these misdemeanor offenses complain that our methods are sneaky and unfair, but most law-enforcement officers aren't prone to worrying whether the ends justify the means.

I made a semicircle away from the river and then back again,

heading for an upstream pool where fishermen liked to dunk worms. Whirlygig samaras spun down from the sugar maples on their rotary blades: the seeds of future giants.

Eventually, I heard voices and spotted a flash of movement through the alders that hugged the riverbank. I crept close to the water, getting lower and lower as I went, until I was crawling on my hands and knees through the puckerbrush.

Out in the river, a man was trying to teach a very small boy how to cast a fly line. My first thought was that it was a father and son. Both were dark-haired and on the skinny side. The man wore a fishing vest and khaki waders; the boy was dressed in a white T-shirt and bathing trunks, and he was having a hard time managing the long fly rod. His fluorescent yellow line just flopped on his head when he tried to throw it forward into the current.

"*No trate de forzarlo, Tomás,*" the man said.

It was Matt Skillen and his "little brother," I realized.

"*No puedo hacerlo,*" said the boy.

My college Spanish had gotten rusty, but I didn't need a translator to understand that the kid was feeling frustrated.

"Watch me," said Skillen in English. He took the rod from the boy's hand and executed a beautiful roll cast that fully extended the leader and dropped a bushy dry fly in the eddy behind a boulder. Just as the fly hit the water, a fish rose to bite it. I knew at once that it was a brook trout because of the glimpse of orange I saw on its underbelly, and I knew that it was big.

Skillen set the hook and then handed the rod back to the boy, who seemed reluctant to take it. "Reel it in, Tomás! Keep the line tight!"

Tomás had a hard time keeping the tip of the rod up and working the reel. I was certain that the trout would escape,

but Skillen leaned over and guided the boy's hands, almost the way a father would teach a young child to pedal a bicycle. The man was doing all the work, but the boy was the one laughing.

After a few minutes of playing the fish, Skillen maneuvered the trout into the net. It was a beautiful male brookie, more than a foot long, with an impressively hooked jaw. Skillen unhooked the fly from the fish's lip and lifted the dripping net for the boy to see.

"Wow, Tomás! Look how beautiful he is. Your first fish on a fly rod. We need to take it home to show your mama."

"*Pero lo agarro.*"

"No, no," Skillen said, putting the fish into an old-fashioned wicker creel. "You caught this one. I just helped. Come on, let's see if we can catch an even bigger one."

On the boy's face was the biggest smile I'd ever seen.

I could have made my presence known to them; I could have congratulated Tomás on his magnificent trout. But the scene seemed so private, I felt almost embarrassed to be watching, especially from behind a bush. Tomás would never forget this moment. My own father had never taught me how to fish like this. Never once had he shown me such patience and kindness. And so, as much as I wanted to resent Matt Skillen for being the man Stacey had chosen over me, I found myself unable to dislike him.

As quietly as I could, I crept away through the alders and left the two of them alone on the sun-spangled river.

When I arrived at Billy's house, I found Aimee stringing wet sheets along a clothesline between two trees. The Cronklets were nowhere in sight, but Billy and Aimee seemed to worry less about their children's safety than did parents in more urbanized areas. At first, I had viewed the Cronks' approach

to parenting as something like negligence, but over time, I had watched the eldest boy carrying the youngest girl up and down stairs, seen a younger child chastising his twin for climbing atop the picnic table when he'd clearly been told not to, and I'd realized that childcare was more of an art than a science, and that I should be careful about making judgments on a subject I knew nothing about.

"Hey, Mike," Aimee said, pushing a red strand of hair out of her eyes and gripping the clothesline with her other hand, as if for support. "Billy's taken his bow and gone turkey hunting."

"That answers one of my questions," I said. "How long was he in jail?"

"The sheriff let him out yesterday morning. I think she was only holding him overnight to make a point. But she's the law, so whatever. Billy's still facing a trespassing charge."

"The DA isn't charging him with assault on Khristian?"

"Threatened to," she said, "but everyone seems to agree it was more like self-defense than Billy kicking the shit out of that old dwarf."

I glanced around at the second-growth forest that clustered at the edges of the Cronks' dooryard. The oaks had held on to their tattered brown leaves, but the limbs of the maples, birches, and beeches had mostly been stripped bare by the autumn winds. An old skidder trail led up through the woods to an overgrown field where I knew Billy liked to hunt.

"Is he up that way?" I asked.

"Yep," she said. "But you won't find him unless he wants to be found."

I started off around the house, feeling the Indian summer heat on my neck, wondering when it would finally break. By the time Moosehorn National Park ever received its official designation, Elizabeth Morse's dreams of creating a

sanctuary for boreal flora and fauna would be foiled by global warming. Instead of observing woodland caribou and timber wolves in their natural habitat, visitors would see feral pigs and opossums; rather than wandering beneath the boughs of hemlocks and jack pine, they would pass through sapling thickets of dogwoods and blue ash. The scorching weather might or might not be a harbinger of climate change, but it was definitely turning my thoughts in morbid directions.

As I came around the corner, I heard the shouted voices of children, overloud, as kids always are. Then, all at once, they fell silent. I raised my shaded eyes at an ancient red oak in which Billy had constructed a ramshackle tree house, with irregularly carved windows and a dangerous-looking ladder that would undoubtedly snap beneath the weight of an adult. Several blond heads poked out through the haphazard windows and doors. The kids were all gathered inside like a nest of raccoons, and like baby animals, they knew to be quiet when an unknown presence approached.

"Hey, guys," I said.

The Cronklets watched me silently. As soon as I had passed by up the hill, the urchins resumed their raucous play.

Billy had cut wood from his hillside lot the previous winter and brought it down the skidder trail. The machinery had flattened the alders and poplars that had been threatening to overtake the path, but the resilient little trees had spent the summer rebounding, and so I had to push through some scratchy vegetation in places. The fallen leaves on the ground—a pattern of red and silver—reminded me of a Persian carpet. Every now and then, I came across one of Billy's big boot prints, but I knew that his wife was right that he could vanish into the foliage whenever he chose. My friend wasn't as expert a woodsman as my father—no one

was—but I always learned a trick or two whenever I followed him into the forest.

Aimee said he was bow hunting for wild turkeys, which meant he was probably decked out in full camo. Most turkey hunters liked to set up decoys and then settle down to call the birds into shooting range. Billy preferred to stalk them, which was a pretty good way to get yourself shot by another hunter, in my opinion. My friend scoffed at the dangers.

"If I don't spot another hunter before he can take a crack at me, then I deserve to die," he'd said.

After wandering aimlessly along the trail for a while, I decided to make things easy on myself and stood in place and started hollering his name at the top of my lungs.

Billy appeared after a few minutes, carrying his bow over one arm, and with a dead jake turkey slung over the other.

"That's another stupid thing to do," I said.

He removed the camouflage hat and face mask he had been wearing. "What is?"

"Toting a dead turkey on your back. There are crazy hunters who will see a flash of what looks like a moving bird and open fire."

"I'll take my chances." His pale irises were even more humorless than that night at Khristian's. "What do you want?"

"You're not going to thank me for helping Aimee pick up your truck?"

"Thank you."

"The last time I saw you, you were telling me what a good friend I was. What the hell happened?"

"I spent a night in jail."

He lowered the turkey to the ground. It was a simultaneously handsome and disgusting creature; its iridescent brown feathers shined in the sunlight as if oiled, but its bald, misshapen head

had blotches of venous blue and arterial red that made me think of a diseased old man.

"Well, I just spent the day with your former employer," I said. "Rivard made me Betty Morse's personal liaison with the moose investigation."

"Did you talk to her about me getting my job back?"

"Frankly, I think you're better off that she fired you."

"Tell that to the power company when they come to cut off our electricity." He ran his hand across his tanned, sweaty face. His beard needed trimming. "I'm sorry I'm in such a piss-poor mood. I just can't see the bright side of anything today."

"Well, you bagged a turkey," I said.

He grunted and came very near to smiling. "Yeah, I guess."

"So what's going on with you, Billy? You've been acting really strange ever since the morning we found those moose. McQuarrie asked you to stay at the gate, but instead you took off for God knows where without telling anyone. The next thing I know, you're outside Karl Khristian's bunker, daring him to shoot you. What gives?"

"I didn't want to lose my job," he said. "I figured if I helped crack the case quick, I would be a hero."

I wanted to believe him, but the explanation seemed forced. "There's something else. Stacey Stevens backtracked the first moose to the spot where it was shot. It turns out it was killed *outside* the gate, and right nearby was an empty Bud pounder."

"So?"

"Bud pounders are what you drink. The forensic guys are going to dust that can for fingerprints. They're not going to find your prints, I hope."

He clapped his hand to his shining forehead again. "They might. I litter sometimes. Cans fall out of the back of my truck. It sure as shit doesn't mean I shot any of them moose."

"Billy, they already have your prints on one of the shell casings," I said.

"I picked that up by accident!"

"Rivard is hell-bent on hanging someone for these killings, and because you have a poaching conviction, your name is near the top of his list."

"God fucking damn it!"

For the first time since the night we'd met, I felt nervous around Billy Cronk. I had to prevent my hand from drifting down to my service weapon. "You need to tell me you didn't have anything to do with what happened on Morse's property that night," I said.

"You don't trust me?"

"That's not an answer."

He spun around in a complete circle, nearly stomping on the head of the bird. "I can't believe you'd accuse me of that, Mike."

It wasn't lost on me that he was evading the simple question I had asked. But instead of helping him to open up to me, my approach seemed to be having the opposite effect and was antagonizing him. I decided to change tactics.

"Betty Morse is offering a twenty-thousand-dollar reward for information that leads to the arrest and conviction of the person or persons who killed the moose," I said.

He became suddenly still. "No shit?"

"No shit," I said.

"Do you think she'd give me the money if I was the one who provided the information?" he asked.

"I don't see why not—as long as you weren't involved with the crime."

He glared at me with a hardness that did nothing to dispel my worries. "You should talk to gun dealers."

"We have been. Cody Devoe has been making the rounds of the local stores, asking if they sold any twenty-twos lately."

Billy shook his head. "I mean the private dealers, the ones who sell under the table. When I worked for Call of the Wild, we bought some used guns from these two guys named Pelkey and Beam. They work with my brother-in-law over at Skillen's, but they've got a sideline dealing guns for cash."

"Lots of people do around here," I said. "Besides, two nights ago, you were convinced Karl Khristian was the shooter."

"I've been thinking what you said about it being two guys. That fucker KKK doesn't have a friend in the world."

"Where do these Pelkey and Beam guys live?" I asked.

"Talmadge," he said. "They live together."

"Together?" I held up two fingers, one twisted around the other. "As in together?"

"Some chick lives with them, too. But who knows what they all do behind closed doors."

"So what made you think of them in particular?" I asked.

"I went with Joe Brogan to their trailer a couple of times to try out some deer rifles. We wanted to get some cheap thirty-thirties and thirty-aught-sixes—you know, big-caliber rifles for guests who weren't the best shots and could use the extra stopping power. The weird thing was, this Pelkey guy kept trying to talk us into buying twenty-two Mags instead. He said it was more of a challenge using the smaller caliber. Brogan told him our clients were challenged enough without using squirrel guns."

"What're their full names?"

"Todd Pelkey and Lewis Beam. Will I get the reward if it turns out to be them?"

I thought about how to answer his question honestly, knowing the consequences of being truthful here. In the end, I

decided that, however cagey he was being with me, Billy Cronk was my friend, and I wasn't going to lie to him. "If it's just your bringing forward their names, I'm guessing it would be no."

He nodded but didn't speak.

"Don't do anything stupid, Billy," I said.

He reached down and grabbed the turkey by its long scaly legs. As he passed, I caught a whiff of the dead jake. I had forgotten how much turkeys stink.

"Where are you going?" I called after him.

"I've got to tag this bird down at Day's store before Aimee can cook it," he said. "Don't want any game wardens to accuse me of poaching it!"

The odor of the dead bird left a bad taste in my mouth.

20

When I got back to my truck, I called McQuarrie to get instructions on what I should do next. He told me to go home. For all Rivard's bold talk about putting his entire division on this case 24/7, I guessed that certain budgetary realities were taking hold. Wardens could volunteer their time to assist on a particularly heinous investigation, but as government employees, we were protected against being coerced into "donating" our services for days on end. Under the Garcia law, we would need to be compensated for all this overtime.

"Do you know Todd Pelkey and Lewis Beam?" I asked McQuarrie.

"Yeah," he said. "Met them in the woods around Talmadge a few times. Pretty good hunters. They both bag multiple deer each season. Why?"

"I think we should add their names to the list."

"Is this a hunch, or have you got proof of something?"

"Their names came up in a conversation I had today," I said. "Can you check them out on MOSES?" That was the computer system the Department of Inland Fisheries and Wildlife uses to keep its records about the individuals we come into contact with during the course of our work. It isn't a criminal records database, although it does include hunting and fishing infractions.

"I'll give the tip to Bilodeau to check out," said McQuarrie. "If he finds anything interesting, we'll let you know."

I'd been hoping to get immediate information, but my sergeant's answer contained clear, if unstated, instructions to me: stay focused on your own assigned duties and leave the investigation to the investigators.

I took his advice and headed home.

As I drove, I found myself having an internal argument with an imaginary version of Elizabeth Morse. She'd found a tender spot when she'd said that I was unlike my fellow wardens in some essential way—that I seemed to be pretending.

I grew up in the woods, lady, I told the out-of-focus blonde image in my head.

Just until you were nine, she replied, somehow having access to the facts of my life. *You really grew up in suburbia.*

Yes, but even when we lived in Scarborough, I hunted and fished. I got my junior hunting license when I was twelve years old and shot my first deer when I turned sixteen. I would have taken one earlier if I'd had an adult willing to accompany me.

But you didn't. Your father was up in the woods of western Maine, and the only sports your stepfather was interested in were tennis and golf.

My dad taught me to shoot a twenty-two in a gravel pit when I was eight years old. He took me out with him on his trap line. . . .

He took you out one time.

I watched him butcher the deer he brought home each season.

But he never took you hunting with him.

I was too young.

Basically, you had to teach yourself everything. You present yourself as having been this impoverished child from the North Woods, but you spent your entire adolescence in an upscale town of green lawns and new subdivisions. So who are you, really? The modern-day Huck Finn or the straight-A student from Scarborough High School?

I can't be both?

There's a division in your personality that everyone can see. It's why you disobey the commands of your superiors and why your fellow officers don't fully trust you. They sense your essential insecurity.

I know exactly who I am, Ms. Morse.

You don't sound very convincing when you say that, Warden Bowditch, said the imaginary woman with the catlike smile.

My cell phone rang as I was pulling into my dooryard. The number was blocked. Elizabeth Morse again? I thought.

"He came back again, Mike!" said Chubby LeClair.

The late-afternoon sun was slanting through the pine boughs outside my cabin. I watched a red squirrel scamper across the mossy roof like a burglar looking for a way to sneak inside. All I wanted to do was grab a beer from the fridge and sit down on the porch and enjoy a quiet moment. The day had left me in a bad place. "Who did, Chub?"

"That other warden, Bard. He came back and asked if he could search inside my camper again. I'd just gotten everything picked up from before. I told him I wasn't *awskassu*, that I didn't want to make trouble. But I wasn't going to let him in again without a warrant. He told me that sounded like I had something to hide."

How had I become the confessor and therapist to this drug-dealing con artist? I took off my sunglasses and rested

them on the dusty dashboard. I needed to rub my eyes. "Well, do you?"

"What do you mean?"

"You're a convicted criminal with a history of poaching. There's a reason we're looking at you for those shootings."

"I thought you and me were *witapiyal*." He seemed to be having a hard time drawing a breath, but then again, the overweight man always sounded as if he had a bank safe resting on his chest.

"Knock off the Passamaquoddy act, Chub."

"I thought we were friends."

"We're not friends," I said. "I don't even like you."

"Why are you being this way, man?"

"Because you have no regard for the law, and the word around Washington County is that you trade drugs to teenagers for sexual favors. For all I know, Bard is right and you did kill those moose."

"I didn't, man." He was definitely hyperventilating now. "I've done some bad things. You're right. But I've got a big heart. Ask anyone."

The squirrel had disappeared. Had it found a gap between the shingles? That was all I needed. Red squirrels were known to chew on electrical wires. Half the house fires in the area seemed to have been started by arsonist rodents. "What is it you want from me?"

"Call him, man. Tell Bard to stop harassing me." His tone had turned babyish, as if he was on the edge of tears. "I can't take it. I'm going through a rough patch, you know? It's like a very, very bad time for me."

"I'm not going to do that," I said.

"But he's outside the house!"

"What?"

"He's been sitting there in his truck for the past hour, just sitting and watching my windows. I'm afraid to go out there."

Leave it to Bard to make me feel sorry for a blubbering pedophile. But the last thing I was going to do was call up another warden, especially one in the good graces of the lieutenant, and tell him to cut out bullying a prime suspect in the worst wildlife crime in Maine history. My reputation didn't need another nail in the coffin I had nearly finished building.

"I'm sorry, Chub," I said, "but I can't help you here. If you have a problem with Bard, call the Maine Warden Service in Augusta and report him for misconduct."

He gave one last sob before he hung up the phone.

I had spent the first two and a half years of my career as an insubordinate troublemaker. McQuarrie had told me my life would get better if I'd just start being a team player and did everything by the book. At the moment, I couldn't say that approach was exactly working for me, either.

When I opened the door, I heard the scratching sound of tiny claws digging into wood and caught sight of a furry tail slipping through a crack between the fireplace and the ceiling. A hole had been chewed through the loaf of bread I'd left on the counter beside the sink, and there were hard black pellets of squirrel shit on the kitchen table. I'd have to get the ladder out and climb up onto the roof in the failing light and attempt some emergency repairs. I needed to act quickly to stop this infestation.

But first I got a Molson out of the refrigerator and opened it using the Leatherman multitool I wore on my belt. I'd gone through a period after the end of my relationship with Sarah when I had worried about my alcohol consumption, so I

had stopped drinking altogether, but I had started having an occasional beer again over the winter and had managed to keep my life (and my drinking) under control.

I noticed a new message waiting on my answering machine. "Were you ever going to call me back?" My stepfather, Neil Turner, rarely sounded enraged, but his voice was as superheated as any time I could remember. "I know we haven't been close for a while, but I think you owe me the courtesy of returning my phone calls, especially where your mother is concerned. Call me at the office, call me at home, or call me on my cell. But please, Michael, just call me today." And he left the three numbers at which he could be reached.

My stepfather was right. It had been rude of me not to call him back, no matter how preoccupied I'd been with the moose investigation. It was almost as if I had been eager to forget about him. Why was Neil so worried about my mom? I hadn't received any of her inspirational e-mails all day, I realized. Now the fact that she'd fallen silent sent a shiver through my central nervous system.

I set the beer down and called my stepfather back on his cell. "Neil? It's Mike."

"Oh," he said with formality. "Hello. Thanks for calling. Can you hold on a minute?"

I had the sense that he was leaving one room and entering another. When he came back on the line, he was whispering, but there was consternation in his voice. "I'd expected you to call sooner."

"I've been working a pretty big case."

"Oh?"

"You've probably heard about it. Ten moose were killed on Elizabeth Morse's land in Washington County. It's been all over the news."

"I must have missed it," he said. "I've had other things on my mind."

"It's the worst wildlife crime in Maine history."

"I'm sure it is," he said.

He was going to make me ask, I realized. I took a swig of beer for courage. "Neil, what's going on with Mom?"

"She has something she'd like to speak with you about."

"What is it?"

"It would be better if she told you herself. Can you come down here tomorrow?"

"Can't she just tell me over the phone?"

"It would be best if you came to the house."

"I'm working this major investigation," I said. "I'm not sure I can get away."

He paused a long time, as if counting to ten. "I think this takes precedence."

"Now you've got me worried. I can drive down tonight if it's that important."

"Tomorrow morning would be best. I haven't told her that I've been in contact with you. We'll look for you around nine o'clock, all right?"

Living in Greater Portland with few reasons to venture north except to ski, Neil had no idea how big Maine was: roughly the size of all the other New England states combined. He seemed to have no clue that I was practically based in Canada here and facing a four-and-a-half-hour drive to get to Scarborough.

"All right," I said. "But I wish you'd tell me what this is about."

"We'll see you at nine, Mike."

By the time I'd hung up the phone, I had given up any idea of climbing onto the roof to prevent any more incursions by

the local squirrels. I wasn't sure what excuse I would give Rivard about taking a personal day in the middle of his career-making investigation, but with Morse away in New York, the lieutenant probably wouldn't care about my whereabouts. I didn't imagine I would be missed.

21

The next morning, I awoke before dawn, dressed myself in jeans and a flannel shirt, and began the long drive in darkness to the suburban town I had spent years trying to escape.

My 1970 Ford Bronco was as mulish on the road as my patrol truck. I'd purchased it from a classified ad I'd seen in *Uncle Henry's Weekly Swap or Sell It Guide*. The guy who'd sold it to me said he'd brought it up from Jacksonville himself, where it had spent the previous four decades sheltered from the elements inside grandma's barn, rarely ever venturing out onto the smooth, unsalted highways of North Florida. At first glance, the vintage truck was a thing of beauty: full cab, original green-and-white paint job, uncut rear fenders. It drove well at first, too, although it took a while to get used to the "three on the tree" shift. Only slowly did the vehicle reveal its hidden flaws: its balky transmission, which had already needed to be replaced, its desperate thirst for coolant, and, worst of all, its alarming tendency to develop rust spots that appeared, seemingly overnight, like acne on a teenager's face. I'd bought the Bronco as a treat to myself, but it had become the gift that kept on taking.

My journey took me along Route 9, nicknamed "the Airline" for its ridge-back views of peat bogs and pine woods, through

the Bangor "metropolitan" area, where my division was head-quartered, and then south along four-lane I–95, which was the closest thing we had in Maine to a superhighway. I listened to music the whole way—classic rock—to keep my mind off my mother's mysterious condition, and also because I needed a mental break from Elizabeth Morse and her dead moose. I pulled into my stepfather's driveway at nine o'clock sharp.

Landscapers were busy in the yard. One of the men was chasing leaves off the wide lawn with a hose attached to an enormous blow-drying contraption he wore strapped to his back. Another was furiously raking and bagging the leaves to take away to an undisclosed location. As a teenager, I had been responsible for these same sweaty tasks.

Returning to my parents' cul-de-sac after having spent nearly three years living in assorted backwoods shacks, trailers, and cabins, I felt like a stranger in a strange land. I had forsaken the world my mother had fought so hard to give me. Was it any wonder we had drifted apart?

The person who opened the door was someone I scarcely recognized. My mother's beauty had been her defining trait. As a dark-haired, dark-eyed young woman, she had turned heads every time we entered a restaurant or store together. My teenage friends had joked about her desirability in a lascivious way that had nearly brought us to blows on occasion. Now she stood in front of me with hollow eyes and a grayish tone to her skin. Her hair looked brittle and badly dyed. Always skinny, she had lost pounds her petite body could not afford to lose.

"Hello, Michael," she said.

I was afraid to embrace her, until she held her arms out. It was like hugging a bag of sticks. "Mom, what happened?"

"I'm not doing too well," she said, hanging on tight.

"Are you sick?"

When she backed away, I saw her eyes gleaming with tears, but she was fighting to maintain a brave smile. She was wearing a fancy pink tracksuit made out of some soft synthetic material. At the base of her throat hung a gold crucifix, the symbol of her abiding faith. My mother still attended Mass weekly. "I thought we could take a drive."

I looked past her into the house. "Where's Neil?"

"I sent him away when he told me you were coming here. I wanted to visit with you alone. He's at his office in Portland for the morning." She picked up a puffy down coat that looked too heavy for a day that was already warm. I helped her get her arms into the sleeves, as I always did. My mom had taught me good manners as a boy because, she said, "Women prefer gentlemen." I'd wondered how she reconciled this statement with her marriage to my rakish father.

"I thought we might go to the beach," she said.

"Sure, Mom. Whatever you'd like."

"Do you need to use the bathroom?"

"No. I'm fine."

In fact, I did need to use it, but I was desperate to learn the nature of my mother's illness. I walked her out to the Bronco and opened the passenger door. She looked at the truck with amusement.

"This is new," she said, reaching for a pair of Gucci sunglasses in her coat pocket.

"Actually, it's pretty old."

It was a very short drive to the water. My parents lived in a newish neighborhood at the throat of Prouts Neck. You could smell the sea from their back porch, and at night in the summer, salt fogs would drift in from the invisible, unheard ocean. The painter Winslow Homer had immortalized the rocky cliffs at the end of the peninsula, a mile or so away. Between his studio

and my parents' development was a strip of sand and marsh through which passed a single slow-moving road. Scarborough Beach drew lines of traffic during the hottest days of the year. The summer we'd moved in with Neil, my mom and I had gone there nearly every day, she to brown her body in the sun and celebrate the miraculous new life she'd made for herself, I to sneak glances at the half-naked girls whose existence I was suddenly recognizing.

"Do you remember when we used to do this?" she asked.

"You'd make me get up early so we could be sure to get a parking space."

"You liked to sleep."

"I was a teenager, Mom." I shifted into second. "So what's wrong with you?"

"I want to wait to talk until we get to the beach."

The lot filled up fast in the summer, but with Columbus Day behind us, and it being midweek, we had no trouble parking, although there were more people than I had expected. We had to park in the outermost of the two lots. An older couple was getting into a Volvo station wagon beside us.

"Good morning," said my mother.

"Good morning," said the woman. "You won't be needing that coat."

"It's a bluebird day," said the man.

As we walked away, heading across the sand toward the little gatehouse where you paid your admittance fee in the summer, my mother whispered, "I don't know what that means. Is it because the sky is very blue?"

"I've always assumed so."

There was a dirt road that led from the outer lot across a bridge that spanned the brackish pond. We paused, as we always did, to take in the view. Herring gulls floated at the far

end, white specks against the blue-brown water. The pond was edged by spartina grass and a towering invasive plant called phragmites, which one day would probably take over the entire place. The rangers who maintained the park kept spraying it with poison, chopping it back, and burning the roots, but still the weed returned, undead, intent upon its conquest.

"What was the story you told me about this pond?" my mom asked.

"There was a massacre here," I said. "Nineteen English settlers were ambushed by Indians during King William's War. There's a plaque near the beach with the details. The story around school was that the Indians threw the hacked-up bodies into the pond. Kids said that on moonlit nights, you could see the white faces of the dead men beneath the surface of the water. My friends and I used to sneak down here at night to look for them, but we never saw anything."

I hadn't thought about Massacre Pond in years. Now I feared the name was going to stick in my head all afternoon: an unwelcome echo of the very different massacre I was investigating hundreds of miles to the north.

"That's a horrible story," she said. "They should change the pond's name. What's the point in remembering something so awful so many years later?"

"Some people think it's important to remember history," I said.

"I've never seen the point of it." She continued on toward the beach.

We passed through the inner lot to the boardwalk, which climbed over a ridge of grassy sand dunes. My mom paused to remove her shoes, but I kept my Bean boots laced. We could hear the crashing waves before we could see them. Except for the dead grass, you could have fooled yourself into thinking it

was the height of summer. The warm air smelled of brine.

The beach was busy for an autumn day. A number of people had spread out blankets and put up umbrellas and those tentlike beach shelters that enable you to hide from the sun. There were young kids splashing around at the surf line, although no one was actually swimming. The water was too cold and the surf was too high. Enormous whitecaps were racing in at a southeasterly angle to the beach. The waves would build and build until they came to the drop-off; they would seem to pause for half a second, and you could see into the translucent water as if through green glass, and then they would crash down with a loud *boom*. I remembered reading online about a hurricane that had passed close to Bermuda without making landfall. These waves had traveled a very long way to get here.

"I hope those parents are keeping an eye on those little kids," my mom said. "The ocean looks dangerous today."

"The waves are from a storm down south," I said. "There's a high-surf warning for the Maine coast."

"Is it supposed to come this way?"

"No."

"That explains why so many people are here. Everyone likes to see the big waves." She spread out her arms, her sneakers dangling from one hand, and tipped her head back into the sun. She looked a little unsteady. "This used to be my favorite place in the world."

I remembered her saying so. This beach seemed to represent the place where she could stop running from the past. It was here that she finally escaped her childhood as the youngest daughter of a Franco-American mill worker, her impoverished and abusive marriage to my father, and the gypsy years afterward, during which she had worked as a bar waitress and

office temp. Marrying Neil, a partner at one of the biggest law firms in the state, she felt she had won some kind of lottery. Later, like most lottery winners, she would conclude that the prize wasn't all it had promised to be. But that first summer in Scarborough, she had been happier than I'd ever seen her before.

"Why have you been sending me those quotations?" I asked.

She turned to face me. "I think you know."

"No," I said. "I don't."

"I have cancer, Michael."

Even before I had gotten that first voice mail from Neil or seen her wan face this morning, some part of me had sensed that she was in danger. And yet, for reasons I didn't understand, I had refused to admit this knowledge into my consciousness. I went out of my way to avoid thinking about her. "What kind?"

"Ovarian. Stage three."

I had a hard time speaking. "Is that bad?"

"There are four stages."

"When did you find out? What can they do? Can they operate?"

She dropped her sneakers to the sand and reached out for my hands. "Neil and I have been back and forth to Boston all week. The doctors say I have two tumors the size of golf balls, one next to my spleen, the other near my stomach."

"Can't they just remove them?" I heard my younger, teenaged self in the pitch of my voice.

"No."

"What are they going to do, then?"

"I start chemo tomorrow. I forget the names of the drugs. Neil could tell you if you're interested."

"I *am* interested," I said. "I want to know everything about this."

"Knowing doesn't help." She let go of my hands suddenly and lunged at me, wrapping her frail arms around my chest and pinning herself to it. "This is the punishment I get."

"Mom, Mom." She was so much shorter than me. I found myself looking down at the gray roots in her dyed hair. I rubbed her back. "Why do you deserve to be punished?"

"For killing that baby."

At the end of her marriage to my father, my mom had left me with some kindly neighbors and disappeared for a couple of days. When she returned to our backwoods shack, she seemed unusually weepy. She would break into tears while doing dishes at the sink or hanging laundry on the clothesline that ran from the side of the house to a moose maple at the edge of the dooryard. She'd never come out and said what she'd done, but over the years I had deciphered the cryptic comments she'd made, and I deduced that my mother—my practicing Catholic mother who still said the rosary each morning—had felt so despairing of life with my father that she'd had an abortion.

"You didn't bring this on yourself," I whispered in her ear. "You're a good person. God wouldn't do that to you."

"I'm not a good person." She was crying now. "You might have had a brother or sister, Michael."

I stroked her hair, warm from the October sun. "I had you."

"Then why did you go away? Why did you disappear from my life? Everything I did was for you."

I found myself unable to answer the question. Saying that we wanted different things seemed too simple. After years of living in trailers and shopping for day-old bread at the Nissen bakery outlet in Skowhegan, she'd found herself suddenly rich—by her standards, if not Elizabeth Morse's—and married to a gentle, handsome man who didn't get drunk while he cleaned his guns at the kitchen table. But I had found myself

unable to exorcise my father's spirit so easily. I missed my early life in the deep woods. And I needed to go back.

I hadn't felt as though my mom cared. She had been disappointed in my decision to become a game warden—she made her feelings clear enough on that point—but she seemed content with her tennis friends and her vacations with Neil to Paris and Rome. She'd never made me feel that in my long silences I was denying her anything valuable.

A young woman, the mother of two small children, was watching us from a blanket nearby. You could see the curiosity and concern on her face. When I caught her eye, she looked away at her little boy and called his name out of reflex: "Matty, come here!" He must have been two years old. He was naked, his pink flesh speckled with sand.

"Do you want to walk along the beach?" I asked.

She let go of me and wiped her eyes with her coat sleeve. "Neil said you were working on a big investigation. Don't you have somewhere you need to be?"

"Right here," I said.

22

I spent the rest of the day with my mother. We walked on the sunstruck beach until she began to feel tired, and then I drove her home to have lunch. She prepared a turkey sandwich for me but made nothing for herself, then sat across from me on the sunporch while I ate. Later, I would feel the sting of a sunburn along my unprotected neck and cheeks, but I was oblivious to the damage that distant star was doing to my body.

In the afternoon, my mom asked if she could take a nap. Except for her weariness and the gaunt look about her, I had noticed no signs of serious illness. She didn't rush to the bathroom or display any symptoms of physical pain in my presence. I told her it would be fine if she slept, that I would stay until she awoke again. This made her smile.

While my mother curled up with a blanket on her enormous bed, more than twice the size of my own stained futon back at the cabin, I peeked inside my former room. They had cleaned out my bed and desk, removed all traces of me except for a few dozen of my old books, which they had left on the shelves. I studied the titles along the spines, remembering the days when I used to rush home to pitch myself headlong across the bed to read the new paperback my mom had bought for me. I found *The Adventures of Sherlock Holmes* and the collected works of Edgar Allan Poe, *The Hobbit,* and the Hatchet series I had

loved so much as a boy. There were other novels from the later years of my adolescence, too: *A Farewell to Arms, Red Harvest,* and *A River Runs Through It.*

The title that caught my eye, though, was a moldy history of Scarborough I had picked up at a used-book sale. I turned to the chapter on the founding of the town in the seventeenth century and thumbed through the water-warped pages until I found the section I was looking for:

By October 1676, Scarborough, a town with three settlements of more than 100 houses and 1,000 head of cattle, had been destroyed, some of its people killed, and others taken captive by Indians. These inhabitants tried repeatedly to rebuild but peace with the Indians was impossible. In 1690, the town was abandoned due to Indian uprisings, with inhabitants going to Portsmouth and other settlements farther south.

The second settlement of Scarborough is regarded as dating from 1702. A fort was erected on the western shore of Garrison Cove, Prouts Neck. Other stockades were at Spurwink and Blue Point. The Hunnewell House was known as the "outpost for the defense of Black Point." The Indian fighter, Richard Hunnewell, and eighteen other men were killed in 1703 at Massacre Pond. This incident took place after peace negotiations had been made with the Indians.

There was nothing here about the men having been mutilated by tomahawks or the corpses tossed into the muddy waters to bloat and rot. There was no mention of ghosts. If Massacre Pond was haunted, it was only in my imagination.

I hadn't attached any special meaning to this passage

before. But places like Massacre Pond proved that my new hometown wasn't as boring as it seemed; it had a mysterious history worth getting to know. As a child recently uprooted from his past, I had been desperate to find a place where I could belong again, and this blood-soaked landscape captured my morbid imagination. Elizabeth Morse had been right about me, I realized. I had lived just as many years on the fogbound marshes as I had in the wooded foothills. I was my mother's son, perhaps even more than my father's. Why had I spent so long trying to deny it?

After a while, I wandered back out into the kitchen to get a glass of milk. Fastened by magnets to the sleek Sub-Zero refrigerator was a picture and a clipping. The photograph was three years old and showed me with my arm around Sarah Harris. She looked blonde and beautiful in the snapshot, and I remembered the winter's day it had been taken, the last visit we had paid as a couple to this house. I used to feel a pang whenever I stumbled across a picture of Sarah, but now I was surprised to realize that the first image to jump into my head was of Stacey riding beside me in my patrol truck.

The clipping came from the *Portland Press Herald*. It was just a scrap of yellowing newsprint.

MAINE WARDEN SERVICE ACADEMY GRADUATES FIVE

VASSALBORO, Maine—Five new Maine game wardens graduated on May 22 from the Maine Warden Service Advanced Academy in Vassalboro. The training first includes attending the Maine Criminal Justice Academy for the Basic Law Enforcement Training Program to become certified as police officers. Then, game wardens attend the Advanced Warden Academy to continue with specialized training and learn skills pertaining to

enforcement of recreational vehicles, crash investigations, search and rescue, public relations, and many other essential skills related to game warden work.

Graduating were Jenn Scott, assigned to Bucksport; Jeremy Bard, assigned to Princeton; Patrick Flynn, assigned to Sanford; Jason LaMontagne, assigned to Caribou; and Mike Bowditch, assigned to Sennebec.

I'd had no clue my mom had even marked this momentous occasion in my life. She and Neil had been traveling in California and were unable to attend the graduation ceremony, but she had belatedly sent me a card with a check for a hundred dollars inside. And yet she had kept this clipping pinned to her expensive fridge for the past three years. My mother had always shown an amazing capacity to surprise the hell out of me.

The only thing I knew about ovarian cancer was that it was one of the scariest ones. If surgeons couldn't remove the tumors, then how did they hope to treat her? The thought of chemotherapy being able to shrink two growths the size of golf balls seemed like an empty hope. Was my mom really going to die?

Out on the porch again with my glass of milk, I checked the messages and e-mail on my cell phone. The only item of importance was a text from my former supervisor, Sgt. Kathy Frost, asking if I'd caught Elizabeth Morse's appearance on the *Today* show that morning:

That woman is a force of nature! By the end of the interview, she'd even sold me on her cockamamie park. Heard through the grapevine that Rivard has made you her sheepdog. Good luck with that. How are things going

in the wilds of Down East Maine, Grasshopper? I worry when you go into your silent running mode.

Kathy knew me pretty well, I had to admit.

My cell phone rang as I was tucking it back into my pants pocket. "Hello?"

"Bowditch?" It was a woman's stern voice. "Where are you?"

"Sheriff Rhine?"

"Rivard told me that he'd embedded you with the Morse family."

"It was at her request. She seems to enjoy debating with me. What's going on?"

"Someone shot up her house last night while no one was home. Broke most of the windows facing the lake. I figure he was in a boat out on the water. I'm not sure if he knew that the house was unoccupied. It was like a scene out of one of the *Godfather* movies."

"Who called it in?"

"The housekeeper. She arrived this afternoon to get the place ready. I can't believe they didn't have a security system installed, but then nothing that woman does surprises me anymore. Morse and her entourage are due back from NYC this evening. I thought you might want to come over and take a look at the carnage."

"Who's handling the investigation into this shooting?"

"The staties. Given the death threats she's received, we all agreed it would be best if they took point here."

"Michael?" My mother stood at the sliding door, rubbing her sunken eyes.

"I'm still here." I smiled to reassure her. "But I'm on the phone with the Washington County sheriff."

"Bowditch?" said the sheriff.

"Sorry," I told Roberta Rhine. "I'm taking a personal day. I'm at my mom's place in Scarborough, but I can be back in Wa-Co in four hours or so."

"That might be wise. Something tells me the queen is going to be ready to chop some heads. Call me when you get here, and we'll send someone down to get you."

Always abrupt, the sheriff signed off without so much as a good bye. I stood up from the glass-topped table and jammed the BlackBerry into the front pocket of my jeans. "Sorry about that."

"Is anything wrong?" my mother asked.

"Some idiot shot up Elizabeth Morse's windows last night."

"Was she home?"

"She was in Manhattan, filming the *Today* show."

"So you know her, then? I've always wondered . . . is she as attractive in person as she looks in photographs?"

My mom had a tendency to judge people entirely on their surface appearance. She had disapproved of my Rubenesque high-school girlfriend for that reason alone. I'd grown used to this flaw in her character, even if it still drove me bananas. "She's a handsome woman." I decided not to mention that her daughter was also attractive, lest it give my mother ideas. "You couldn't sleep more? It seems you should be resting."

"I was having bad dreams about haunted ponds." She stepped aside so I could place my empty glass in the dishwasher. "So you need to leave, then?"

"I'm afraid so. When do you expect Neil to get home? I don't want to leave you alone."

"He's waiting for me to call him. I'll be all right, Michael."

"I feel like the three of us should talk," I said. "We need to make a plan."

She laughed and some of the old light came back into her eyes. "Father Campbell says, 'If you want to see God laugh, tell him your plans.'"

"I think that's a quote from John Lennon," I said. "Why don't you plan on my calling tonight. I'd like to talk with you again before you go to Boston."

"Sounds like a plan," she said with a dry chuckle.

She walked me outside to the Bronco. We embraced for a long time in the driveway, neither of us saying anything. "Are you sure you're going to be all right here by yourself?" I asked.

"I've been alone more than you think," she said, kissing me on the cheek with her cracked lips.

I didn't think she was making an existential statement. But she had spent days alone during her first marriage, tending to me as a baby while my dad went off on a bender or one of his weeklong deer hunts. And then there were the years when she was a single mother in Portland, working two jobs to pay the rent on our third-floor walk-up. I'd also detected a lack of intimacy in her marriage to Neil; the two of them rarely touched each other in my presence. At no time had I ever thought about her loneliness or how I might help assuage it. I felt like the shittiest son on the planet.

Driving back through the spreading subdivisions of Scarborough, I saw kids skateboarding along a paved sidewalk where once there had been an overgrown field at the edge of a second-growth forest. I had shot my second deer there, amid the alders and sumac, using a twelve-gauge that left a bruise on my shoulder when I fired it. Even then, I had been aware of the new houses crowding in on my hunting grounds and felt a sense of anger at what I stood to lose when the bulldozers and builders began their inevitable work.

Was this the same anger that had driven someone to fire

his rifle through Morse's plate-glass windows? Instead of developing her woodland holdings, she had banished all hunters from the hardwood ridges and cedar swamps where they and their ancestors had hunted for more than a century, and the result was the same. I rolled down the window, because the Bronco lacked air conditioning, and let the warm wind swirl about the cab, tickling my ears and sending gasoline receipts fluttering like moths.

First there had been the anonymous death threats against Elizabeth Morse. Then came the attack on her cedar gate. Afterward, two men had sneaked onto the property to slaughter ten defenseless animals in an act of bloody vandalism that horrified even Maine's most hardened game wardens. Were they the same men who had chased Briar Morse along the dark roads outside Grand Lake Stream? Now someone had fired a barrage into the house itself. Had the waterborne sniper known the mansion was vacant for the night, or had he hoped to hurt the residents, whom he believed to be inside? Laying out the chronology like this, it was hard to escape the fact that the violence was escalating. I had a bad feeling that I knew what the next step would be.

23

I didn't bother stopping at my cabin to change into my uniform or swap the Bronco for my patrol truck. Instead, I drove in street clothes directly to the Sixth Machias gate and arrived as the afternoon was fading to evening. As I rolled to a stop on the soft pine needles, I saw a black SUV in the deepening shadows on the other side. A broad-chested man in dark glasses climbed out of the vehicle and moved with surprising speed toward my Bronco. The first thing I noticed about him was his shaved head, which was glistening with perspiration. He wore a loose black shirt with epaulets and black cargo pants over combat-style boots. The military bearing and the untucked shirt made me think he almost certainly had a handgun hidden inside the waistband of his pants.

I didn't notice the radio receiver in his ear until he was standing beside my window. His breath smelled of wintergreen chewing gum.

"Can I help you, sir?" he asked.

"I'm Mike Bowditch, with the Maine Warden Service, here to see Sheriff Rhine."

"Identification?"

I produced my warden ID from my wallet and handed it to Elizabeth's new security guard. He took an exaggerated amount of time to compare my photograph to my face.

Without another word, he passed the card back to me and unlocked the gate. He motioned me through impatiently, as if I were holding up a long line of vehicles.

As I continued on to the log mansion, I wondered where Morse had picked up the thug; he definitely wasn't a local. It made me curious what other developments I'd missed over the past twenty-four hours. A bank of clouds hung above the western horizon like a distant gray wall. Two birds were soaring up high: my pair of ravens.

Moosehorn Lodge had been overrun with vehicles. Parked in the circular drive outside the double doors were three Washington County sheriff's cruisers, an unmarked blue Ford Interceptor that almost certainly belonged to a state police detective, a silver GMC Sierra that was the property of the Maine Warden Service, an obsidian SUV that looked like it had been driven straight from a dealer's showroom, and a mechanic's van with the words STONECOAST SECURITY stenciled on the side. I noticed a man on a ladder installing a camera on a tree trunk, the lens focused on the entrance to the building. I nodded to him as I got out of the Bronco, but he ignored me and continued with his work.

Briar answered the door. "Oh, it's you," she said with a broad smile that showed off her perfect teeth.

She was wearing a purple Bennington T-shirt that was as tight as another layer of skin, denim cutoffs, and no shoes. Her dark hair was wet, as if she'd just come from the shower or swimming in the lake, and she was trying to knot it up so the long strands stayed out of her face.

"I heard someone shot up the place," I said.

"The windows overlooking the lake are all shattered. There are bullet holes everywhere."

I could hear a jumble of voices down the hall; it sounded

like the Morses were having a dinner party.

"It's a good thing you weren't home at the time," I said.

"I'm not sure why we even came back from New York. It's pretty obvious we're not wanted around here. But you know how stubborn my mom is. Nothing's going to scare her off or change her mind. Hey, you're out of uniform."

"I had the day off."

She pinched the fabric of my flannel shirt and gave me a playful look. "I think I prefer the uniform."

She gave a girly laugh that reminded me how young she was, and then she turned and headed toward the sunlit rooms within. I followed her.

In the kitchen, we found Elizabeth Morse, Leaf Woodwind, and Dexter Albee. Another man, a stranger whose head was also shaved, stood in the doorway leading to the formal dining room. He had thin lips, a boxer's flat nose, and cold gray eyes that had probably looked out across more than one Middle Eastern battlefield. A coil ran from his ear down his neck. He wore a tight black T-shirt over his muscular torso and snug blue jeans that made me wonder where he was hiding his pistol.

"Hello," I said to the group.

"Briar, put on some shoes," said Elizabeth Morse. "There's broken glass everywhere."

Her daughter let out an exasperated breath, as if it were a ridiculous request. The windows in this room were all intact. The light streaming through the curtains had softened with the gathering clouds, giving everyone's face a sickly cast.

"You're turning this place into a prison," said Briar.

"Don't be so melodramatic," replied her mother. "Nice of you to join us, Warden. You seem to be in mufti today."

"I was in southern Maine, visiting my mother."

"She must appreciate having such a devoted son." The jab

195

seemed intended for Briar. "You missed all the excitement, in any case. Some nutcase decided to open fire on the lodge last night, as I'm sure you've heard. It seems we are now under siege. I decided to call for reinforcements. Warden Bowditch, this is Jack Spense. He's my new security consultant."

The name seemed vaguely familiar. Maybe I had seen it on a book jacket. He nearly crushed my metacarpals when we shook hands.

"Nice to meet you," he said in a tough-guy tone that didn't seem at all sincere.

"I met your new guard at the gate," I said. "And I noticed you were installing cameras around the property."

"How long have I been telling you to do that, Betty?" asked jug-eared Dexter Albee. "There are some real idiots in this part of the state."

And talk like that is unlikely to persuade them to support your national park, I thought.

Leaf was moping by himself at the kitchen table; he scratched his beard and stared out at the lake. Having his house invaded by the police had thrown the old hippie into a funk. He seemed to be counting the minutes until he could get high again.

"Better late than never," said Morse. "Mr. Spense is an expert in—what's the term you used? Threat assessments? He specializes in providing security to multinational corporations and high-profile individuals."

"Which celebrities have you worked for?" asked Briar.

His smile was so thin as to be almost imperceptible. "I can't reveal the names of my other clients, Miss Morse."

"But you've been a bodyguard to lots of famous singers and actors, right?"

Elizabeth shook her head. "Briar, leave the poor man alone. It's bad enough that we dragged him to the wilds of Maine."

She stepped around the granite island and took hold of my biceps in a familiar way, which surprised me. "We should let Warden Bowditch consult with his colleagues. He has better things to do than listen to my daughter prattle on about her celebrity crushes."

She just about pushed me through the door.

The first thing I noticed was the smell of the lake, that pleasant fishy smell. It floated down the hall on a gust of tepid air.

The great room, where Albee had given me his national park spiel, looked like a hurricane had hit it. Except for a few knifelike shards projecting from the sills, the windows were almost completely gone. Broken glass lay everywhere underfoot, in jagged plates and sparkling fragments. The housekeeper would be finding bits of crushed glass embedded in the furniture and carpets for the next decade.

My entrance interrupted a conversation between Sheriff Rhine and a dark-eyed, dark-skinned man in a sharkskin suit. I'd first met Detective Lieutenant Zanadakis, of the Maine State Police, the previous winter, when he interviewed me about a drug dealer I'd found frozen to death in a peat bog. The detective had interrogated me for a couple of hours on the presumption that I'd omitted some crucial details in my written report. I'd just caught him in midsentence.

"I don't think the shooter ever left his boat," he told the sheriff.

"Why do you say that?" asked Rhine.

"The evidence techs haven't found any brass on the shore."

"Looks like they'll need to do some diving, then." Rhine flicked her coal-black eyes in my direction. She looked more professional than at our last encounter, outside KKK's compound, having swapped her bathing suit for a neat

khaki uniform. Her sheriff's badge was clipped to her shining black belt. "Hello, Bowditch."

"Sheriff," I said. "Lieutenant."

"The question is whether he knew the house was empty," continued Zanadakis. I might have been a dog that had wandered into the room, as far as the detective was concerned. "It's the difference between aggravated criminal mischief and attempted murder."

"Either way, I'm fine with you running the show here," said Rhine. "We'll need to bring in Rivard, though, at least until we rule out a connection to those moose shootings."

"Why isn't he here?" The detective had some sort of paste or gel in his hair that made it look wet.

"He's down in Augusta briefing the colonel and the commissioner on the investigation." The sheriff swung her broad shoulders around so that she was facing me. "What do you think, Bowditch? Connection or no connection?"

"I'd just be guessing," I said.

"You were the one who pointed us in the right direction with the Randall Cates murder. And you were the first warden on the scene of this moose massacre. What does your gut tell you?"

I studied the walls, which were pockmarked with dozens of bullet holes. The rounds had chipped both fireplaces and dug holes in the sofa and chairs. I couldn't imagine how Morse could restore this room to its former glory. Nor could I imagine living here and looking at the scars of the shooting every day as a reminder that someone had tried to murder you.

"It's a different rifle," I said. "The moose were killed with twenty-twos, probably bolt-action. This was a semiauto."

"We've determined that much," said Zanadakis.

"I don't think it's the same shooters," I said.

"Why?" he asked.

"There's a carelessness about this." I waved my hand at the bullet-riddled logs. "The person who shot up the house didn't know if anyone was home or not. There might have been a child sleeping here—or someone with a gun who could have returned fire. This guy just wanted to cause mayhem and didn't seem to contemplate the consequences. The men who shot the moose were very deliberate. They sneaked onto the property. They used twenty-twos because they're quiet. They went about their business and slipped away into the night."

"They left their brass behind," said Zanadakis. "I'd say that qualifies as carelessness."

"But there were no fingerprints—except for Billy Cronk's—found on the shell casings. That means they wore gloves."

The detective removed a notebook from his jacket pocket. "Who's this Billy Cronk?"

"The former caretaker," said Rhine.

A sharp pain knifed through my heart. The last thing I'd wanted was to incriminate my hapless friend.

Zanadakis scribbled something on his notepad. "We're going to need to get a statement from this Cronk about where he was last night."

"You don't have a problem with that?" the sheriff asked me.

There was no accusation buried in the question; instead, it felt as if Rhine wanted me to examine my assumptions for bias.

"We need to follow the evidence wherever it leads us," I said.

Roberta Rhine nodded and gestured toward the shattered windows. "Warden Investigator Bilodeau is out there somewhere. He said he wants a word with you."

24

Outside, I found two of Rhine's evidence technicians digging bullets out of the log walls. One of them trained a flashlight on the side of the building while the other extracted the lead fragments with pliers and dropped them into a bag.

The space beneath the pine was webbed with shadows, and my eyes had trouble focusing as I left the flagstone porch and walked down to the water. The sun had sunk inside the clouds along the horizon, turning them navy blue and leaving streaks of orange and gold in the western sky. The light would be gone very soon.

I walked to the end of the dock and gazed back up at the house. All of the windows were lighted, and there were no signs of anything being wrong. From the outside at least, Moosehorn Lodge appeared, as it probably did most evenings, as a bright and happy place, untouched by violence.

I tilted my head back and spotted a star. I was pretty sure it was Vega. Charley had been teaching me the constellations before I'd realized I was infatuated with his daughter. It hadn't struck me how much I missed my old friend until today.

My mother's diagnosis ached in my head like a hangover. Even when I'd been speaking with Rhine and Zanadakis, I'd been aware of the dull, throbbing pain. I needed to see Charley. I needed to talk through these feelings of dread and regret.

Behind me, there was a sudden loud splash in the water, which nearly caused me to jump out of my boots. I peered at the inky surface and saw a dark shape moving toward the dock. Was it a loon? A beaver?

It was Warden Investigator Bilodeau.

He reached a bare arm up at me and said in that soft, papery voice of his, "Can you give me a hand?"

I grabbed his slick wrist and pulled. The skinny investigator emerged from the lake wearing nothing but a soaked pair of white briefs.

"What were you doing out there?" I asked.

Bilodeau stood, dripping, on the planks and pushed his wet bangs back off his forehead. His rib cage reminded me of a starving child's. "Take a look at this," he said, opening his palm. He seemed to have nothing but a handful of mud until he pushed the dirt away to reveal two metal shell casings. "Found these about fifty feet out," he said.

"Do you think that's where the shooter anchored his boat?"

"Not sure he anchored. Probably just floated while he shot at the house. But yeah, that's where he was."

I reached into my pocket for the small flashlight I kept on my key ring. I shined the beam into his open hand. "Those are two-thirty-threes," I said. "They came from an AR-15."

"Looks like it." He began to shiver. He clenched his fist shut around the cartridges and rubbed his free hand along his wet chest to warm himself. Half-naked, he reminded me even more of a weasel than he did fully dressed.

"What did you do with your clothes?"

"They're down there at the base of the dock."

I'd walked right past his neatly folded uniform and gun belt without even noticing them.

While Bilodeau pulled on his pants, I tried to engage him in conversation. "Have you had any breaks in the case?"

"Aside from these shells, you mean?"

"You think they're connected, then—the moose killings and this shooting?"

He poked his head through the neck of his T-shirt. "What do you think?"

Bilodeau had been a warden for two decades and an investigator for half that time. He had a reputation as a man who pushed hard—sometimes too hard—for a conviction. I knew he'd been reprimanded for going undercover to entrap a well-liked local fishing guide for taking a single undersize salmon.

A half-forgotten memory came back to me. "Did McQuarrie talk with you about two guys named Pelkey and Beam?"

"They didn't do it."

"How can you be so certain?"

"Neither's got a record. They're good guys. Nonpolitical. Don't even hunt on Morse's land, so there's no motive. I went up to see them, just to be sure. I was there last night at ten, when this happened."

"How do you know it happened at ten o'clock?"

"Some kids were camping illegally down the lake," he said. "They heard the rifle. Thought it might be fireworks. Then they heard about the shooting today down at the Pine Tree Store. Told the owner. He called me."

"Shouldn't you tell Rhine and Zanadakis?"

He fastened on his bullet-resistant vest over his T-shirt and secured it with Velcro straps. "Already did."

"Would it bother you if I talked with Pelkey and Beam?"

"Why?" He paused as he was buttoning his shirt.

"If they're such hotshot deer hunters, it seems like I should

make their acquaintance before the season opens. I'm still new around here, and I'm trying to meet everyone who might be able to give me information. Maybe they see stuff in the woods I should know about."

"They live in Bard's district." His voice was so soft, I sometimes wondered if his larynx was damaged.

"They still seem like guys I should meet."

He shrugged his bony shoulders and continued tucking his olive shirt into his olive pants.

"If the lieutenant asks, you'll tell him I got your permission?" I said. "I don't want to be accused of interfering with your investigation."

The warden investigator stared at me with his closely set eyes, but he didn't say another word as he strapped on his gun belt.

Jack Spense's thuggish associate let me out through the gate. I couldn't blame Elizabeth Morse for bringing in muscle, but my thoughts ran along the same grooved track as Briar's. The Morses' continuing presence at Moosehorn Lodge seemed like an unnecessary provocation. Elizabeth might have viewed a retreat as a show of weakness, but discretion often looks that way to proud and stubborn people.

I removed the cell phone from my pocket and hit the speed dial for Charley Stevens. His wife, Ora, answered.

"Mike, it's so nice to hear your voice," she said.

"I'm sorry I haven't been around. I was busy with the moose hunt, and then there were these shootings on the Morse property."

"I was a game warden's wife for thirty years. You don't need to tell me what the falls are like."

"How are you, Ora?"

"I'm well. Thank you for asking. Charley's been building me a new porch, one that's easier to navigate."

"I'll have to come see it," I said.

"Would you like to have dinner with us tomorrow? Charley would be so happy to see you."

"I can't make any promises," I said. "I never know when I might be called away."

"We understand. Perhaps you can let us know in the afternoon."

"Is Charley there?"

"He's over at the stream, fishing. You know how that man hates to be indoors. He's like a barn cat that way."

I told her that I would do my best to get there for dinner. When I asked if I could bring anything, she laughed at the ridiculousness of my offer. I couldn't imagine spending my life in a wheelchair and maintaining my optimism and high spirits. Joy was already an elusive enough emotion for me as it was.

The squirrels had thrown a party in my cabin. They had knocked over a lamp and chewed holes in a granola bar I'd forgotten to put in the bread box. There were pellets of squirrel shit on the counters and table and in the sink, where one of them had nibbled the rotting food scraps in the strainer. Most people don't realize that squirrels will eat anything, even baby birds. Those adorable fluffy-tailed rodents can be ferocious little killers.

I sat down at my Toughbook computer and sent a short message to McQuarrie, updating him on my off-duty visit with the Morses and requesting new instructions. Bilodeau would be filing a formal report on the shooting incident. I wondered how his interviews were going, which suspects might have

risen to the top of his shitlist. Being excluded from my own case burned me more than I cared to admit.

I should have been fired for insubordination and incompetence on numerous occasions in the past, and only the protection of Sgt. Kathy Frost and Lt. Timothy Malcomb had saved my skin. What virtues my previous supervisors had seen in me was a mystery—not just to Rivard but also, increasingly, to myself. At what point do you admit that maybe you're not the right man for the job?

I thought about that surprising newspaper clipping I discovered on my mom's refrigerator. She had reacted to my decision to become a warden with such bafflement. I'd always believed that her confusion came from not understanding the essence of my being. Maybe I hadn't given her enough credit. It was possible she'd seen the mismatch between my rule-bending personality and the duties of a law-enforcement officer and had worried that I was only fooling myself. Mothers see things like that in their children. Whatever her reservations, though, she'd still been proud of me. I couldn't get my head around that concept. My trip to Scarborough had pulled the rug out from under me in so many ways.

Neil answered the phone when I called. "Your mother's asleep," he said. "She told me that you spent the day here."

"I'm sorry I missed you."

He paused, as if measuring his response. "I don't think you realize how much your absence from her life has hurt her. You are her only child. There's a bond between you I can't begin to understand. Love isn't something to be pushed aside, Mike."

"I thought she had plenty of other things going on—you, her friends, tennis."

"All she ever talks about is you."

The words caught in my throat. "How bad is her cancer?"

"Inoperable. The doctors are going to use Taxotere and carboplatin to try to shrink the tumors. Basically, they are going into control mode."

"Isn't there anything they can do for her?"

"We've already gotten three opinions." He lowered his voice, as if he feared waking her. "What are the chances you can take a leave of absence in order to spend more time with her right now?"

"I need to check the union handbook," I said. "I think I can take some of my sick time."

"I suggest you do so."

"There's this case I'm on, though. I can't leave until we've caught the guys."

"That's what I thought you'd say," said my stepfather.

25

That night it rained. I lay awake listening to the drops pattering on the roof. The wind in the pines made a moaning sound that made me think of an injured animal.

Insomnia hadn't been a problem for me since I'd become a game warden. There's nothing like spending long hours in extreme weather conditions to help you sleep. Sarah used to say that I would start snoring before my head even hit the pillow. That night, though, I tossed and turned. It felt like I was trying to sleep on a bed of surgical needles.

An hour before dawn, I gave up trying to sleep and took a hot shower. There were rust stains around the drain and a layer of yellowish film coating the plastic walls. I wrapped a towel around myself and went looking for some Comet. No matter how much I scrubbed, the stains wouldn't come out. I perspired so much, I had to take another shower.

McQuarrie called as I was making coffee. "How was your day off?"

"It was fine." I couldn't bring myself to broach the subject of my mother's cancer.

"Have you been reading the papers?"

"No. Why?"

"Our dead moose have made the front page three days running. Rivard is spending most of his time talking to

reporters. It doesn't help that Queen Elizabeth is on national TV."

"Bilodeau didn't tell me anything about his investigation," I said. "That guy's about as talkative as a potted plant. Have there been any breaks?"

"Nothing to write home about—although Bilodeau seems to think those AR shells he found are a big deal. Rivard wants us to put the screws to the guys on his shitlist today. He's sick of tap-dancing for reporters."

"Great," I said. "What do you need me to do?"

"Head back over to Morse's place and hold her hand for a while."

"Come on, Mack!"

"The best thing you can do right now is stay out of the limelight," he said. "The less the L.T. hears your name, the better. After this thing is over, all he'll remember is that you followed his orders."

"Will he authorize a new patrol truck for me?"

"In your dreams, kiddo."

In the night, the wind had ripped many of the last leaves from the treetops and flung them, almost contemptuously, to the ground, where they continued to glow—red and yellow—like embers from a drowning campfire. The air had a fresh, clean smell, as if newly washed. Water pooled in the hoofprints of a moose that had passed silently in the night.

The best chance I had of catching Pelkey and Beam at home, I figured, was to get there before they left for work at the mill. The address I'd found for them was on an unpaved road in the blink-and-you-miss-it town of Talmadge, just north of Indian Township. The warden there was my classmate from the academy and Chubby LeClair's archnemesis, Jeremy Bard.

Wardens routinely patrol one another's districts; we take our colleagues' calls on their days off and sometimes team up to work deer decoys together or prowl around the woods looking for night hunters. Bard and I had joined forces only half a dozen times. Most recently, we'd done a boat patrol together on Big Lake and had barely exchanged five words. Afterward, he must have said something to the lieutenant, because I hadn't been asked to cover for him again. The message couldn't have been clearer: Bard didn't want me messing around his district.

I hadn't been lying to Bilodeau about my motives in wanting to meet Pelkey and Beam, not entirely. If they were the four-season sportsmen everyone said they were, then it was worth my while to make their acquaintance, since the essence of my job consisted of persuading neighbors to rat one another out over various Title 12 infractions. The more people you knew, the more potential snitches you had calling you up to report that their hated neighbors had just bagged a doe out of season. Grudges, gossip, and backwoods feuds were the currencies of the game warden's trade.

In Talmadge, I left the paved surface of Route 1 and turned onto a branching series of dirt roads that got narrower and narrower the farther into the woods I drove. The experience was like following a river upstream until you found the tiny tributary at its head. The forest here was mostly deciduous: maples clutching their last handfuls of red and gold leaves, bonelike birches already stripped of their color, and gnarled old oaks with tattered brown foliage.

The GPS on my dash guided me into the dooryard of an ancient mobile home that had the appearance of having been tossed there, like Dorothy's house from *The Wizard of Oz,* by a passing tornado. It had flesh-colored metal walls and a flat roof on which snow must have accumulated fast in the winter.

There were three vehicles parked out front: two brand-new pickups—identical jet-black Nissan Titans with cardboard dealer's plates—and a little red Chevy Cavalier that was overdue for its appointment at the junkyard.

How had these rednecks managed to buy snazzy new pickups when half the men they worked with were losing their jobs? What kind of spendthrifts were these guys? And where did they get their money?

Even before I could get out of my truck, I saw one of the blankets hanging over the windows being peeled back, and I got a quick glimpse of a human face before the improvised curtain dropped down again. A moment later, the door swung open and a man stepped onto the porch. He had loose brown hair that feathered down the back of his neck and one of those stubble beards guys in their twenties sometimes sport. He looked fit and flat-stomached and was wearing a canvas shirt, blue jeans cinched tightly around his waist with a big-buckled belt, and camel-colored work boots. In his hand was an aluminum coffee mug with a Big Bucks of Maine emblem.

"Good morning," he said.

I put on my friendliest face. "Good morning."

"What's going on?" He had a thick Maine accent.

"Are you Todd Pelkey?" I knew he had to be one or the other, and he looked like a Pelkey.

"Yessuh."

"I'm Mike Bowditch, the warden down in District Fifty-eight. I sometimes patrol this area, and I wanted to introduce myself."

He eyed me as he took a sip of coffee. "I thought Jeremy Bard was covering this territory. Did something happen to him?" He pronounced Jeremy as *germy*.

"Sometimes we cover each other's districts, and I figured I should get the lay of the land up here."

Another man stepped onto the porch. He was even taller than his friend and had close-cropped platinum hair that looked white in the weak sunlight. From the back, you might have mistaken him for a much older man. There was a pink scar across his chin that looked painful. He was dressed in the very same outfit as his buddy. "Ain't we the popular ones suddenly?" he said.

"You must be Beam."

"That's right," he said. "So you're not here about them moose? We already spoke to that investigator about them."

"This is just a social call. I'm making the rounds before the deer season gets under way."

"What did you say your name was again?" Beam asked.

"Bowditch."

"Oh, yeah," said Pelkey. "We heard about you."

That was no surprise. My name had been in the newspapers enough over the past few years, although Pelkey and Beam didn't strike me as the sort of guys who spent their Sunday mornings doing the *New York Times* crossword puzzle. More likely, they'd heard about me through the back channel of information that flows from one hunter to another when a new warden is transferred to the area.

A tiny young woman appeared in the doorway behind the two men, clutching a flannel robe tightly around her throat. She had mousy brown hair and wore oversize glasses, but with enough makeup that she could pass for pretty in this neck of the woods. "They already talked to a warden about them moose!"

"Go inside, Tiffany," said Beam with a growl.

"Why are they coming around here all of a sudden?" she

asked. I had a feeling that the nervous girl might be my best source of information if I could get her alone. It might just be a matter of circling back to the trailer after her two boyfriends left for work.

"They're just talking to everyone with a hunting license," said Pelkey. "Ain't that what's going on, Warden Bowditch?"

"I'm not even here about that," I said.

"That's right," said Pelkey, who seemed to be the wilier of the two. "This is a social call."

"I heard you guys were quite the deer slayers," I said. "Where do you hunt?"

"All over," said Beam. His expression was the dictionary definition of deadpan.

"Have you gotten any deer with your bows yet this fall?" I asked.

"A few," said Beam.

"You're welcome to have a look at the freezer," said Pelkey, cocking one eyebrow.

"I don't want him tearing up my house," said Tiffany. "I just vacuumed in there."

"Shut up, Tiffany," said Beam.

No one seemed to be buying the bullshit I was selling this morning. "You should have Jeremy take you around," said Pelkey. "He can show you all the stomping grounds."

"That's right," I said. "Bard's from this area, isn't he?"

"Woodland High School," said Pelkey with a handsome smile. "Class of '03. Go, Dragons."

It was unusual, but not unprecedented, for a warden to be stationed in the district where he'd grown up. The plus side was that you knew the territory and the players; the downside was that you were frequently in the awkward position of having to give tickets to your friends and family members.

"The three of us go way back," said Beam with a smirk. I wasn't sure if it was an insinuation or a threat.

Pelkey finished off the coffee in his mug. "How's things down in your district? I heard you got a lot of poachers running wild down that way."

"Everyone says your district is totally polluted," said Beam. He and his buddy seemed to have a Mutt and Jeff act going.

"The poaching hasn't been bad so far this fall," I said. "Except for what happened to those moose on Elizabeth Morse's land."

"We heard all about that from that investigator," said Pelkey. "Sounds wicked cold-blooded if you ask me. You wardens got any suspects?"

"A few."

"But you ain't here to talk to us about that, right?" Pelkey dumped the dregs of his coffee on the ground. "Hey, Lew, we'd better get to work. Don't want to be late, or old man Skillen will have our hides."

Beam gave a grunt that signaled he agreed.

Pelkey turned to Tiffany. "Give me some sugar, baby."

He held her by both shoulders and kissed her hard on the lips. I watched with fascination and disgust as, a moment later, Lew Beam did the same thing. Anyone who thinks that country people are the salt of the earth needs to go on patrol with a game warden.

"Bye, baby," the pale-haired man said to her.

"Bye."

"Come on, Warden," said Pelkey, offering me another of his dashing smiles. "We'll ride out with you."

I glanced at the dense, wet mass of alders and sumac that surrounded the property. "Maybe I'll poke around a bit farther up the road."

Pelkey set the mug down on the porch railing and came down the steps, jingling his keys in his hand. "There's nothing up there 'cept an old pit."

McQuarrie had ordered me to inspect the area gravel pits for spent .22 shells. Reason suggested I should check it out. If I caught any flak for driving up to Talmadge, I could argue that I'd merely been following my sergeant's instructions to leave no pit unsearched.

"You have a good day, Warden," said Pelkey, climbing into one of the Nissans.

Beam merely scowled at me as he started up his own vehicle. He pushed the gas pedal to make it growl.

I had to move my patrol truck for the men to get out. I waited for them to drive off down the muddy road, but instead they idled their engines. I turned the wheel and began creeping farther up the rutted lane in the direction of the gravel pit they had so helpfully mentioned. I gazed in the rearview mirror, wondering if they might come after me: a sure sign they were afraid of what I might find in the pit. Both trucks headed, however, in the opposite direction.

The road beyond the trailer was a mess. It was like driving up a streambed. Rocks the size of footballs scraped the undercarriage of my pickup, and the ruts from the freshets were deep enough that I worried my wheels would get stuck. There is nothing more embarrassing to a Maine game warden than having to call for roadside assistance in the back of beyond. I decided to walk the rest of the way.

There were a pair of ATV tracks in the wet sand. I hadn't spotted four-wheelers in the dooryard of the trailer, but just about everyone in Washington County seemed to own one of those machines, and I was willing to bet money that these prints belonged to my two new friends. I had a feeling

they would lead me where I wanted to go, and they did.

The gravel pit hadn't been used in a long time; you could tell from the spiky weeds and bushes pushing up from the bottom. It was shaped like a large amphitheater, with sloping walls that were fringed at the top with a row of young pines. Someone had decided the place would make a convenient dump. There were a few of those big wooden spools that power companies use for electrical wire, along with an assortment of junked appliances, a wheel-less and burned-out Monte Carlo that was now rusting into the landscape (it looked almost sculptural), and numerous bags of trash that had been well plundered by the resident raccoons, coyotes, and foxes.

Near the back of the pit was an improvised shooting range. Someone had propped up a piece of plywood against the gravel wall and stapled various paper targets, which had largely rotted away or been shredded into bits by gunfire. But you could tell from the groupings of the holes that this was a destination for shooters.

I probably spent the better part of an hour scouting for shell casings beneath the fog-shrouded sky. Just as in the previous pits I had inspected, I found rounds from a wide variety of firearms—everything from little .32 ACP handguns to big .30-30s that could have taken down a charging bull moose with one shot. What puzzled me was what I didn't find. Although there were .22 shells aplenty, there were no .22 long rifle or .22 Magnum shells. The odds alone should have dictated that I would find a few.

So intent was I on my work that I didn't hear Jeremy Bard creep up behind me. One minute I was bent over, picking up casings from a pile of pebbles; the next a shadow appeared beside me, and I straightened up with a start.

"What are you doing here?" He had the flattened face of a

bulldog and a barrel chest that could probably have benched four hundred pounds with ease.

"I didn't hear you," I said.

"You weren't supposed to. What's going on? I got a call you were poking around up here."

"I wanted to meet Pelkey and Beam before opening day. Billy Cronk told me they were worth getting to know."

"What else did he tell you?"

"Hey," I said. "I'm not trying to step on your toes here."

"Too fucking late for that." He crossed his powerful forearms. "I know what you're doing, Bowditch. You're bored with the job Rivard gave you, and now you're trying to get in on the investigation by interrogating Pelkey and Beam. You just can't follow an order, can you?"

"One of my 'jobs' has been hanging out in gravel pits, looking for shell casings."

A muscle in his thick neck twitched. "That's not why you're here, and we both know it."

"I already cleared this with Bilodeau," I said. "He didn't have a problem with me coming out here."

"Yeah, well, I have a problem with it. This is my district, and I don't want you harassing people here."

"I wouldn't call the conversation I had with Pelkey and Beam harassment."

"That's not what my cousin says."

"Your cousin?"

"Tiffany."

So that was how Bard knew I was here. Tiffany hadn't wasted any time getting on the phone with her warden cousin. "It doesn't bother you, her shacking up with those two lowlifes?"

He took another step closer. One more and he could have thrown a punch. "That's my family you're talking about now."

"All right," I said. "I'll get out of your hair. But maybe you can do me a favor."

The request seemed to amuse him. "Why should I do you a favor?"

"I'm getting calls from Chubby LeClair," I said. "He says you're basically stalking him."

"The fat ass is at the top of our shitlist."

"I'm not defending him. I just don't like getting his phone calls every day. He seems to be having a nervous breakdown. If you're going to make a case, you'd better do it fast, because he's going to have a heart attack before you can bring charges."

"Is that all?"

"Yeah," I said. "That's all."

Bard followed me back to our trucks, and we drove out together. He rode my bumper, as if to literally push me out of his district. I thought he might tailgate me all the way to Route 1, but instead he stopped at his cousin's trailer, while I continued south down the branching roads. I wasn't sure what I'd just learned in Talmadge, but the experience wasn't sitting well in my stomach.

26

It made sense for me to enter the Morse estate from the north, rather than circling around to the Sixth Machias gate at the edge of my own district. I left the main drag in Indian Township and drove eight miles into the woods. The little village of Grand Lake Stream was jammed, as usual, with late-season salmon fishermen. Guys in waders and vests were hanging around outside the Pine Tree Store, laughing and sipping coffee, and I saw fly anglers packed shoulder-to-shoulder when I crossed the little bridge over the gin-clear river.

At Morse's north gate, there was no security guard waiting, although I noticed a new video camera twenty feet up a red pine, focused on the entrance. I put the squealing truck into park and called Elizabeth's personal number.

A man answered. "Yes?"

"Hello," I said. "I'm calling for Elizabeth Morse. Is this the right number?"

"Who is this?"

"Mike Bowditch, with the Maine Warden Service."

"This is Spense. What can I do for you, Warden?"

"I'm at the north gate," I said. "Ms. Morse is expecting me."

"Hold on, please."

The security consultant put me on hold for five minutes. My whining truck belt seemed worse than ever this morning. When

I turned the engine off, the sensation was similar to having a bad tooth pulled—a sudden sense of physical relief. I rolled down the window and breathed in that moldering late-autumn smell the forest gets as fallen leaves begin to decompose on the ground. The thermometer on my dashboard said it was sixty-five degrees.

By now, Neil and my mom would be in Boston. My mother would be in a dressing gown, or maybe pajamas, getting ready to receive her first dose of the powerful drugs that might or might not kill the malignant tumors growing near her womb. She might already have the needle jammed into the vein of her thin arm. I could imagine the fear my mom was feeling. It was as if our nervous systems were connected across those hundreds of miles.

"Warden Bowditch?" It was Elizabeth Morse now; those aristocratic inflections were unmistakable.

"Good morning, Ms. Morse."

"I won't be needing you today."

She seemed incapable of speaking to me except as a master addressing a servant. "Are you sure? I can make myself inconspicuous."

"I have construction crews beginning work to repair the house, and I'm going to be preoccupied overseeing them." I heard a saw start up in the background. "Frankly, I'd prefer it if you were out looking for whoever did this, rather than just sitting around my lake house, flirting with my daughter and drinking tea. Mr. Spense is not particularly impressed with the caliber of your investigation so far. It's been five days since you found those moose, and you haven't made a single arrest."

Rivard's instructions to me had been to share as little information about the case as possible, but I knew her impatience would rise as the days went on without a break

in the case. Now that she had an internationally renowned security specialist whispering in her ear, even I was falling out of favor. Having her new mansion strafed with semiautomatic-rifle fire probably hadn't helped.

"We're continuing to narrow the list of suspects, and Warden Investigator Bilodeau has some strong leads based upon evidence he collected last night from your property." I had no idea if any of this was true, but I was certain that it was the sort of goulash Rivard would have wanted me to dish up for her.

"What about my reward? Have you received any tips?"

"Yes, ma'am. We've received a number of promising calls." This, too, was bullshit.

"Don't patronize me, please," she said. "I know that Lieutenant Rivard thinks I'm some rich bitch who's used to getting her way and needs to be 'handled.' He's not entirely wrong about that. But someone shot up *my house* two nights ago. Tell your lieutenant that if I don't get a call from him soon telling me that you have a suspect in custody, my next national interview is going to include a comparison of your organization with the Keystone Kops. Have I made myself clear?"

"Crystal clear," I said.

The problem with being the messenger, I realized, is that sometimes you get shot.

I decided to drive back into Grand Lake Stream and grab a cup of coffee while I plotted my next move. What was I going to tell McQuarrie about my encounters with Jeremy Bard and Elizabeth Morse? I was astonished to find a familiar teal-colored GMC Sierra parked outside the Pine Tree Store and the man himself sitting at one of the picnic tables with a newspaper spread across the wet tabletop. It was as if, by

thinking about him, I had conjured the sergeant out of thin air.

His face was even redder than usual. He had removed his black baseball hat. His swirl of white hair reminded me of meringue. "I thought you were supposed to be standing guard over at the queen's palace," he said, sounding as dry-mouthed as a man crawling through the desert.

"She released me from her service for the day." I peered at the newsprint as I sat down across from him on a bench dampened by the rain. "What's in the paper?"

Mack took a sip from a Styrofoam cup filled with steaming black coffee. "You don't want to know."

"Yeah, I do."

He showed me the front page of the *Bangor Daily News*. The headline couldn't have been much bigger:

SNIPER TARGETS HOME OF ELIZABETH MORSE
No One Injured in Nighttime Attack

An accompanying photograph, taken from the lake, showed Moosehorn Lodge on its piney point, but no signs of damage were evident. My guess was that it was a file photo the editors had used in a pinch.

"And then there's this one," said Mack, pointing to a smaller article beneath the lead item:

STILL NO LEADS IN MOOSE MASSACRE
Wardens Continue to Seek Answers

"Has the lieutenant seen this?" I asked.

"We just got off the phone. I think he broke one of my eardrums."

"What do the stories say?"

"Basically, that we're all a bunch of fuckups. The L.T. keeps saying we expect to make an arrest 'imminently.' But after five days without a bust, the reporters are starting to smell the horse manure. There's a twenty-thousand-dollar reward out there, and we can't make a case? How do you think that's playing in the governor's office?"

"So we're not getting anything good from Operation Game Thief?"

McQuarrie removed a tin of chewing tobacco from his shirt pocket and unscrewed the lid. He pinched out a few brown threads and tucked them inside his cheek. "We're getting a shitload of calls, but nothing useful so far. That kind of money always brings out the crazies. Yesterday I was on the phone with a psychic from California! She said she was in touch spiritually with the souls of our dearly departed moose."

"What about the evidence we collected at the kill sites?"

"No DNA matches on the cigarettes. No prints on the candy wrappers. None of those twenty-two shells you collected were worth a damn, either, by the way."

I tried not to think of the hours I'd spent on my hands and knees collecting them. "Bilodeau seemed to be excited about the shell casings and bullets he collected at Morse's house."

"Bill's got some trick up his sleeve, same as always. But who knows? Maybe this time he's cracked it."

"You don't sound very confident, Mack."

Using both hands, he wadded up the newspaper into a softball-size projectile and hurled it at the top of the nearest garbage can. He missed by a mile. "There goes my second career with the Celtics," he said. "I'm probably gonna need a new job after next week."

"So what do you want me to do today?" I asked. "I can run down some of those OGT calls."

"Maybe," he said. "The L.T.'s talking about having another strategy session tomorrow. He wants to bring in the state police, which shows you how desperate he is. He's got Tibbetts at a checkpoint way the fuck out on the Stud Mill Road, like that's going to do anything. Devoe's been hanging around gun shops, trying to see who bought twenty-twos recently. Bayley and Sullivan are visiting the local sporting camps *for the second time*. As if the guides are suddenly going to remember they had a couple of sports last week boasting about slaughtering moose."

McQuarrie had a reputation as a company man; he might crack wise occasionally about the lieutenant or some of the other officers up the chain of command, but he never displayed any lack of confidence in the decision-making ability of his superiors. What I was witnessing from him—this outburst of exasperation—was surprising, if not completely shocking.

I hesitated before asking my next question. "What about Bard?"

"He's doing a surveillance detail on Chubby LeClair."

"Yeah, I know. Chubby's been calling me, bitching about him. I'm not sure how he got the idea we were friends. Have you talked with Jeremy recently?"

He spit tobacco juice into his half-filled coffee cup. "Just before you got here. Why?"

So Bard hadn't told Mack about my trip to Talmadge or our confrontation in the gravel pit. That seemed strange. It went completely against my sense of the man as a whining kiss-ass. "I was just wondering."

"Speaking of friends," said McQuarrie, "the lab guys found your buddy Cronk's prints on a can of Budweiser in the road where Moose A was shot. Bilodeau's been out to see him a few times. You talk to Billy recently?"

"Couple of days ago," I said. "He asked me if he was eligible to receive Morse's twenty grand if he helps catch the guys who shot the moose."

"That's all we need—a mountain-man vigilante." The sergeant's knees made a creaking sound as he rose to his feet. "If you want to make yourself useful, keep an eye on him. Billy Cronk on the rampage is a scary thought."

27

Mack told me to "go do warden stuff" for the rest of the day. If Morse changed her mind and decided she needed me, I should drive over to Moosehorn Lodge and seek to calm the troubled waters. Otherwise, I should patrol my district and catch up on the calls that had come in while I'd been preoccupied with the moose massacre.

A woman with a heavy New York accent had reported an injured bald eagle in the backyard of her waterfront estate in East Machias. I drove over to have a look. It turned out to be a seagull, which took off on two strong wings when I approached. Two guys were fishing illegally on Mopang Stream, which had closed for the season on the first of the month. I wrote them summonses and confiscated the two brook trout they had caught on jigs. The fish were beautiful: fat and orange-bellied, with hooked jaws and brilliant yellow dots along the sides. Another woman—a wizened lady in Dennysville, whose house smelled of cigarettes and gin—had a problem with a saw-whet owl that had flown down her open chimney and taken roost atop a bookcase. After chasing the bird around the house for half an hour, breaking a Hummel figurine in the process, I managed to capture it in my stinky salmon net. The little owl, which was no bigger than a pigeon, seemed no worse for wear, but I put it in a box and drove it to

the house of the local wildlife rehabilitator. He inspected the bird's primary and secondary flight feathers, found no signs of damage, and tossed the bird into the sky above my head. It winged away, making a direct line for Dennysville, as if intent upon returning to its roost atop the bookcase.

Out of curiosity, I made a detour past Karl Khristian's walled compound. He'd hoisted a new Confederate flag on a pole—an ironic choice for a man whose ancestors had almost certainly fought for the Union—but otherwise I saw nothing noteworthy at the castle. The bald little man seemed to have gone into his bunker.

Late in the day, I called Mack one more time, telling him I was headed over to Charley and Ora's house for dinner. "So we're on tomorrow for another strategy meeting at the IF&W field office at eight," he said. "The L.T. wants to go back down the suspect list one more time. By the way, he's ripshit about an interview Maine Public Radio did with Queen Elizabeth's new chief of security. He doesn't say nice things about our investigative efforts. Don't be surprised if Rivard unloads his anger on all of us."

Nothing the lieutenant did or said surprised me anymore. I wasn't sure if I'd grown a thicker skin or was past the point of caring. This time, I didn't intend to bring doughnuts.

When I'd first met them, Charley and Ora Stevens lived in the western Maine mountains in a lakeside house that reminded me of a woodcutter's cabin in a medieval German folktale. They'd owned their cottage for thirty-odd years, but in an arrangement unique to the Maine North Woods, the land beneath their home had been leased from the Atlantic Pulp & Paper company. When a new corporation—Wendigo Timber—purchased the property, along with thousands of surrounding

acres of forestland, it evicted the Stevenses and their neighbors in order to build expensive waterfront developments they could market as vacation homes to wealthy out-of-staters.

Charley and Ora had fled east, to a pond near Grand Lake Stream, where they'd found a ramshackle home they could repair and a big-enough boathouse to store both Charley's motorized Grand Laker canoe and, more importantly, his Cessna 172 Skyhawk. They'd spent a year fixing up the rambling red building before Elizabeth Morse breezed into Washington County, announced she was canceling leases on the lake properties she'd just bought, and began talking up her grandiose plan for a new national park. Charley and Ora must have felt a disorienting sense of déjà vu. Fortunately for them, they'd made certain to buy the land this time, along with the house. Not all their neighbors on Little Wabassus Lake had been so wise.

After searching all day for a way through the ashen clouds, the sun had finally made its escape, just in time for dusk. It hung above the tops of the old-growth pines that surrounded the Stevenses' house, as round and orange as a Halloween pumpkin. I'd turned on my headlights to see beneath the trees in the failing light. When I snapped them off, the woods became suddenly dark and gloomy. A slight chill was rising from the still-damp pine needles that carpeted the forest floor.

As I climbed out of the truck, I glanced at the guest cabin Charley had weatherized for Stacey. The windows were dark, and her Subaru was gone, leaving a rectangular dry patch where it had been parked on the leaves. I doubted that a woman as independent as Stacey relished living with her parents. But decent rentals were hard to come by in this part of the world, as evidenced by my own rodent-infested cabin.

There was a handicapped-accessible van parked beside

Charley's Ford Ranger and a ramp leading up to the front of the building. I rapped at the door, feeling that familiar sense of homecoming I always experienced when I visited the Stevenses. The old couple had taken me under their wings during the lowest point in my life. They'd fed me and counseled me and given me hope. Standing on their welcome mat, I couldn't remember why I'd stopped visiting them.

After a minute or so, the door opened and I found myself looking down at the radiant face of Ora Stevens. She was seated, as always, in her wheelchair: a beautiful woman with Scandinavian cheekbones, snow-white hair brushed back from her face, and eyes as green as her daughter's. She reached out with both hands for mine.

"Oh, Mike," she said. "It's so nice to see you."

I bent down to kiss her warm cheek. "Thanks for inviting me, Ora. I'm sorry I kept canceling our dinners."

She was wearing a patterned Icelandic-style sweater that I was sure she'd knit herself, and white denim pants and tennis shoes. "You don't need to apologize. Charley is out with Nimrod collecting mushrooms for dinner, and he told me to send you after him. Otherwise, he'll be out there till the owls go to sleep."

I glanced off into the gathering gloom. "How will I find him?"

"Just walk south along the tote road. He'll hear you coming."

"I guess I will see you soon, then."

As I turned away from the glowing doorway, she called after me. "Mike?"

"Yes."

"Stacey will be joining us. I hope that's OK."

The knot that formed in my throat made it hard to get the words out. "That's great."

The emerald light that came suddenly into Ora's eyes told me that she understood exactly what I felt for her daughter.

The last minutes of daylight are my second-favorite time to be in the woods—right after the first minutes of daylight. In the morning, there is an atmosphere of expectancy. Finches and sparrows begin to sing in the darkness, as if summoning the sun to appear. Then the first beams of light begin to filter through the evergreens, strands of gold amid the green, and the sudden warmth causes a mist to rise in the places where the sun touches the ground. Every leaf and blade of grass is wet with dew, and you emerge from the woods into a shocking brightness, with your pants soaked to the knees and a chorus of birdsong in your ears.

But at dusk, the shadows move. The sun sinks down into the treetops and then slides along the trunks until you are only catching furtive glimpses of it through the understory. The wind, if it was blowing throughout the day, might suddenly die completely, and a stillness surrounds you that makes every stray sound—every acorn dropping, every chipmunk peep— seem overly loud. The birds go quiet. Sometimes you'll hear a distant crashing that makes your heart stop; a buck has caught your scent and gone leaping off into the brush before you can spot the white flag of his tail.

I followed the tote road south along the shore of Little Wabassus Lake. Alders and poplars and birches were growing up from the old ruts, and the weeds were as high as my knees. Wilting ferns curled like witches' toes. Loggers hadn't used the trail in many years. The tips of the low bushes showed signs of having been chewed recently by deer. In a few weeks, Charley would be hunting here with that lever-action Marlin he'd owned forever.

As Ora predicted, her husband surprised the hell out of me by suddenly stepping out from between two spruces, right into my path. "You surely make a racket," he said.

"That's because I wasn't trying to sneak up on you."

He was dressed entirely in green, except for his Bean boots and moose-leather belt, and on his long head was perched a green cap with the red logo of the Department of Inland Fisheries and Wildlife. In one big hand he was carrying a mesh bag already stuffed with mushrooms. A hatchet hung from a looped rope he'd tied to his belt. The look on his craggy face was one of unalloyed happiness.

"It's always good to practice creeping along," he said. "You need to put your heel down first and then your toe. Try to push the leaves down softly instead of crushing them flat."

"You sound like the last of the Mohicans."

"I'm the last of something all right." He clapped me hard on the shoulder, his traditional greeting. "It's good to see you, young feller."

I pointed at the mesh bag. "I seem to have missed the mushroom hunt. What have you got there?"

He loosened the drawstring and opened the top of the sack. The gloom made it hard to see anything inside beyond a few bright orange bulbs. "The rain brought out a bunch of these buggers," he said. "I found some chanterelles and a few matsutakes down in that stand of old hemlocks along Curtis Cove. There were some nice hedgehogs in those birches up along the hillside above the house. But I've been saving a real beauty for you. I wanted you to see it in its natural habitat before I went at it with the hatchet."

"Now you've got my interest." I glanced around into the dense underbrush. "Where's Nimrod?"

"Probably on a bird somewhere. He ran off this morning in

the pouring rain. When I finally found him, he was shivering, soaking wet, and pointing at the sorriest-looking woodcock I'd ever set eyes on. That fool dog had probably been there for four hours, waiting for me to show up with a shotgun."

He motioned for me to follow him down the logging road. I paused a second to listen. Sure enough, he moved among the leaves and fallen branches without making the slightest sound.

"So I've been getting daily updates on your moose case," he said in that offhand way he had of broaching important subjects.

"You probably know more about it than I do."

"Sounds like Rivard has his head firmly wedged up his rectum."

"No comment."

"McQuarrie tells me that Bilodeau is chasing his own tail again, too. How that man became an investigator, I will never decipher. He doesn't have the brains to pound sand into a rat hole." He hitched up his pants, which were getting loose from the weight of the hatchet. "Why pick on that Chubby LeClair feller? He's more of your opportunistic-type poacher, one of those hotheads with no impulse control. He sees a deer and shoots it."

"The other guy they're looking at is Karl Khristian."

"You mean Wilbur? Oh, he's a dangerous character and a crack shot to boot. That melee at Morse's lodge sounds like his handiwork. A moose massacre, though? I'm having a hard time connecting the dots there, so to speak."

"Do you know two men named Pelkey and Beam?"

"They sound like two folksingers. No, I haven't had the pleasure."

"Billy Cronk says they're expert deer killers. I'm not

supposed to be investigating anything, but I went to see them out in Talmadge, and I got a definite vibe."

"In what way?"

"They didn't seem surprised to see me."

He veered off the path into a stand of red maples that clung to a steep cut bank to our left. "Your friend Cronk is an interesting case."

I had to scramble, grabbing branches and pulling myself against gravity, to follow him up the hillside. "How so?"

"Billy's a good woodsman," he said. "Handy with a rifle. Knows those woods like nobody's business. Has a key to the gate. Left his fingerprints in some inconvenient places. And McQuarrie says he's been acting squirrelly since the morning you found the first moose."

"That's because he was afraid Morse would fire him," I said. "With good reason, it turns out. Whatever's up with Billy, it has nothing to do with him shooting those moose. I mean, I suppose he could have done it and then called me over, pretending to have been the first person on the scene. But that's not the man I know."

"In that case, I trust your judgment."

I stopped in my tracks. "Since when?"

Charley had a laugh that seemed to start down in his belly. "I guess I should say I *mostly* trust your judgment. You made a few boneheaded calls when you were a green warden, but you're older and wiser now. Older anyway."

"I don't know, Charley," I said. "I'm not sure I'm even cut out for this job anymore."

"Who says that? Rivard?" He scowled. "The colonel made a mistake promoting that man, and I told him so at the time. He'll get his just desserts. You wait and see. Men like that always do."

"I always feel like I'm swimming upstream with him."

"That just makes you a trout."

"I'm serious, Charley."

"Your problem is you're a free thinker," he said. "Now, most law-enforcement officers lack imagination. That's not a bad thing when you're patrolling a beat. You don't want cops who get bored too easily. But investigators need to be a little crazy, on account of the general weirdness of humanity. A normal person tries to apply logic to every unexplained event. A good investigator, though, he knows that sometimes the best way to solve a mystery is to let go of everything he *thinks* he knows." He stopped and pointed at a rotting stump. "Take this mushroom, for example."

At the base of a moldering hunk of wood, the remnants of a formerly impressive tree, was a bulbous brown fungus the size and shape of a brain. "What is it?"

"Hen of the woods," he said. "Some folks call it a ram's head or sheep's head. That fungus there—if I drove it down to one of those fancy restaurants in Portland, I could probably sell it for three hundred bucks."

"Jesus."

"And it ain't even the biggest hen I've found."

"I think you might consider a new line of work in your retirement," I said.

"Who says I'm retired? The thing about these hens is that you almost always find them around red oaks. Sometimes you might see one under a black locust. But what do you see around you here?" He gestured at the nearly leafless trees around me.

"These are maples," I said.

"Red maples," he said. "This mushroom has no business being up here. It's supposed to be in a stand of oaks, down on

wet ground. Instead, it's up on this sandy hillside, where no forager would ever think to look for it."

"So this is supposed to be a metaphor about solving mysteries? Isn't the point that you got lucky when you stumbled on it?"

"Not exactly," he said with a wink. "See, the thing of it is, that stump used to belong to an oak. She was a big beauty that blew down years ago when I was a young warden in this district. Crashed right down onto the tote road, blocking traffic. The Skillens crew had a devil of a time hauling it out of these woods. I happened to remember that giant tree when I was out poking around, so I scrambled up here, and what do you know? There's a baby hen."

"It still seems to me like you lucked out," I said.

"Call it luck, then. I guess my point is that if I were following a guidebook, instead of thinking about my early days as a young warden, I would've strolled past this beauty. Instead, I let my imagination wander and it brought me somewhere I never would've explored otherwise. I only found it because I stopped looking where I was supposed to."

I scratched a new mosquito bite on my neck. "I'm not sure I'm persuaded."

"That won't stop you from eating it, though, I bet." He grinned. "Stand back a way while I give her a whack with this tomahawk."

I stood aside while Charley chopped the mushroom free from its stalk. It had lobes that reminded me a little of feathers on a grouse, which was probably how the fungus got its name. He let me heft it in my hand, and it weighed a lot more than I'd expected. Then he eased it into his mesh sack, rearranging the smaller mushrooms to keep from damaging them. "The Boss is making a pasta dish with wild mushrooms," he said,

using his pet name for Ora. "But there's more than enough to feed a Marine platoon, so I guess I'll be drying some of these for the winter."

As we clambered back down onto the tote road, I noticed how dark everything had gotten. The lichen on the boulders seemed luminescent in the half-light, and the hairy cap moss seemed to give off a spectral glow. If you looked up, you could see the gap between the trees on both sides of the road, but the bushes around us seemed to be closing in, and I found myself experiencing an unexpected sensation of claustrophobia. I loved being in the woods at night and never felt the slightest anxiety. It took me a minute to allow my mother's gaunt face back into my thoughts.

I felt something brush past my head, flying in the same direction as we were going, back along the tote road beside the lake.

"Here they come," whispered Charley.

"Bats?"

"Stand still a minute."

The bats came in waves, just a few at first, zipping around my head and shoulders, using their amazing powers of echolocation to avoid colliding with one another and us. But I could feel the delicate tips of their wings inches from my skin, and I could hear their thinly pitched sonar squeaks. I don't know how long it lasted or how many flew by us—hundreds, thousands—but it was like being surrounded and engulfed by a living, sentient cloud. The fear left me, replaced by an upwelling sense of wonder in my chest. I had an impulse to spread out my arms, wishing the bats might somehow lift me up and carry me off to some secret place only they knew about. Then, just like that, they were gone, and Charley and I were standing silently side by side on the benighted road.

"Happens every evening around this time," he said in a hushed tone like one you'd use in church. "They fly up the lake, following this path in the woods, and then out over the water. Don't have a clue where they go, but it's a rare thrill to be standing here when they come past you in the dark."

"That was amazing," I said.

"It breaks my heart every fall when they migrate. I stand here waiting for them to come, but they've moved on. Ora says the first night without the bats is the official start of autumn around here."

It was in that moment that I decided to tell Charley Stevens about my mother.

28

He didn't press me for details. Charley's preferred method of counseling was to let me say what I had to say, and if he thought I was being shortsighted or unreasonable, he might give me a gentle, usually humorous prod to remind me how irrational I was being. But what do you say to a man whose mother is dying, especially when it is clear that there are no longer any questions left to be asked, when the finality of the situation is all that remains? My friend, who had witnessed so many deaths, knew that all you could offer was condolences and the comfort of a listening ear.

After a few minutes, his German short-haired pointer, Nimrod, emerged from the undergrowth, his coat stuck all over with burrs and bits of leaves. Lacking a real tail, the dog wagged the whole back half of his body.

"I wonder if he found a bird." I pulled a burdock from between his floppy ears.

"I'd thought of bringing my shotgun with me," Charley said. "But I've killed more than a few partridge this fall, and mushrooming is a quieter pursuit."

"Can you do me a favor?"

"Of course, son."

"Don't tell Ora about my mom until after I've gone home tonight. I'm not sure I can tell it one more time."

"She'll sense there's something worrying you," he said. "The woman's got a special insight into the human heart."

"I just don't want to talk about it right now, especially around . . ."

I didn't have to say his daughter's name.

I saw the shadow of his head nod and then felt the reassuring weight of his hand on my shoulder as we walked back to the house in the dark.

As we approached the Stevenses' glowing home, I saw a porch light on outside the little guest cabin beside the water. Two vehicles were pulled up in front: a newly detailed Subaru Outback with a kayak roof rack and a black GMC Denali that I recognized as Matt Skillen's. I hadn't expected to feel any lower after my confession to Charley, but I found myself dropping through an emotional trapdoor.

At the top of the wheelchair ramp, Charley stomped his feet a few times to kick loose whatever mud had stuck to his boots, and I did the same. He opened the door, and we entered what was essentially a single enormous room that combined the kitchen, dining area, and seating area with a set of chairs arranged around the fireplace. Everything was a little lower to the ground than in a typical home, the countertops, the doorknobs: a concession to Ora's wheelchair.

She was in the kitchen, peering into an oven, from which I caught the cinnamon and nutmeg smell of an apple pie.

"You're back early," she said, giving us a radiant smile.

"You know I can't stand to be away from you, Boss," Charley said, bending down to kiss her cheek.

"What did you find today?"

He patted my shoulder. "Aside from this lost soul? I found quite the treasure trove of fungi." He emptied the dirty

mushrooms into the sink. Ora had to raise her body in the chair to get a good look at everything. "Chanterelles, hedgehogs, matsutakes, and this whopper of a hen."

"Oh, Charley," she said. "Those are beautiful."

He glanced farther into the room with a furrowed brow. There was a fire crackling in the fireplace. It threw flickering yellow light on the metal surfaces of the lamps and chairs. "So it looks like we have an extra guest for dinner," he said.

"Stacey invited Matt."

Charley pulled off his hat and hung it from a deer-hoof coatrack I recognized from their former cabin. His short white hair stuck up in all directions. "Where are those two?"

"Down by the lake, watching the sunset." She wheeled herself to the refrigerator and pulled it open with her strong forearms. "Would you like something to drink, Mike? I made some sun tea, but we also have milk and orange juice and beer."

I accepted a glass of tea—I was still on duty—but my throat ached for a beer.

"So where's this new porch?" I asked. "Ora told me you were building her something special, Charley."

"Come have a look-see." He stepped behind his wife's wheelchair without her having said a word and pushed her across the carefully swept floor. Ora seemed not to mind having Charley do things for her—push her chair, fetch fallen objects from the floor—that other paraplegics might have felt undercut their independence. Their relationship seemed not to involve any second-guessing.

The new porch was actually two connected porches— one half was screened and roofed, the other was open to the elements. "The bugs here are worse than back home," said Ora, which was how she still referred to their lost property on

Flagstaff Pond. "And I wanted to put plastic up and create a sort of greenhouse here in the wintertime."

I inspected the joinery, as if I knew a thing or two about carpentry beyond how to hammer a nail. I was about to say something meaningless about the impressiveness of Charley's work, when we heard a woman's laugh down the hill and then the creak of footsteps on the zigzagging ramp that climbed from the lakefront up to the new porch. A moment later, Stacey slid open the screen door and stepped into the sheltered half of the porch, followed by her fiancé.

She was wearing jeans and a bone-colored thermal pullover that showed what a string bean she was. She usually dressed in mannish clothing: a quirk that had given rise to some rumors about her sexuality when she'd first joined the department. I'd never once seen her in a skirt, I realized. But she had inherited her mom's natural prettiness, which needed no help from mascara or lipstick to make her face look feminine.

Matt Skillen was dressed as if he'd just come from celebrating casual Friday at the office: crisp pink oxford shirt, open at the throat; unwrinkled chinos; wingtips. He, too, looked slim and athletic; you could picture them as one of those couples who run 10K races together on Saturday mornings. His hair was thick and wavy, as if he took pride in it and liked to leave it a little long. He was holding an open bottle of Grolsch beer.

"Hello," said Stacey with a polite smile, neither friendly nor forced.

Skillen held out his hand, which was rougher than I would have expected. "Hi, Mike. Good to see you. I heard you were joining us for dinner."

I had been under the impression it was the other way around.

"Did you see the bats?" Ora asked her daughter.

"Not tonight," said Stacey. "I think we were too late."

"Your dad and I ran into them coming up the tote road," I said. "That was quite an experience, to be surrounded by them like that."

"Tomás was telling me that in his village in Mexico there are vampire bats," said Skillen.

"It's so good of you to mentor him the way you do," said Ora. "Those migrant families have such hard lives."

"When you see the living conditions at those camps, it just turns your stomach," said Skillen. "I've been really lucky in my life, and I think it's important for someone in my position to help people who haven't had the same breaks."

If I hadn't seen him fishing with the boy on Grand Lake Stream, I probably would have rolled my eyes at this high-minded speech. But Skillen actually seemed to care about the boy. I found myself both respecting his altruism and resenting it as yet another reason for Stacey to prefer him to me.

"Those farmworkers must be headed back south soon," Charley said.

Skillen took a sip from his beer bottle. "Most of them have left already for Florida, but Tomás's family stayed for the apple harvest."

"He asked if he could join us for dinner," said Stacey.

"I don't think Tomás quite grasps the concept of date night," said Skillen, wrapping his arm around his fiancée's shoulders.

Ora peered at her daughter's chest. "Is that a new necklace, dear?"

Stacey smiled and clutched at the black pendant. It looked like a piece of stone carved into the shape of a raven with outstretched wings. "Isn't it gorgeous? Matt bought it for me in Belfast." She turned to her fiancé. "How did you know to get me a raven?"

"The day we met, you told me they were your favorite

birds," he said. "I also brought you some good beer, Charley. There's a store that sells imported varieties in Augusta."

"Matt was testifying in front of the Land Use Regulation Commission today," said Stacey, fondling the necklace.

That explained the business attire. "My dad and I also met with some legislators and lobbyists to discuss how we can promote woods products in Maine," he said. "We need to do a better job of messaging if we're facing a radical with the deep pockets of Betty Morse. I wish she'd invest her millions into helping out the poor people in this county instead of creating a wildlife sanctuary no one wants. So many people are suffering around here, and she's totally oblivious to their desperation."

Ora held up both hands. "Please, can we not get into that subject until *after* dinner?"

"You say that," said her daughter with a smile, "but I know the only reason you invited Mike over here was to quiz him about Elizabeth and Briar Morse, what they wear around the mansion, and whether they're as elegant in person as they look in photos."

"That's not the only reason," said Charley, pulling on his nose.

"Well, you know what a gossip she is."

"Stacey!" Ora said.

Skillen gave me a wink, for some reason. "My dad suggested that the solution to all our problems would be for me to marry Briar Morse."

Stacey pushed herself away from his chest with mock violence. "And what did you say to that?"

He gave her a handsome grin. "I told him airheads aren't my type."

"She's not an airhead," I said.

Everyone looked at me, as if the statement was meant to be

the start of a longer defense of Briar's intellectual capabilities, instead of just a reflexive act of chivalry on my part.

"Actually," I said, "she's got a pretty wry sense of humor. They both do."

Again, they all waited for me.

"So what's for dinner?" I asked, as if I didn't already know the answer to that question.

During the meal—pasta with wild mushrooms and a buttery sauce—I remembered my first dinner with Charley and Ora.

Two years earlier, I had gone to western Maine to assist in the manhunt for my fugitive father. I'd been in a state of wild desperation back then, willing to sacrifice everything to prove my dad was innocent of murder. Out of unexpected and unwarranted kindness, the Stevenses had invited me to spend the night at their cozy cabin overlooking Flagstaff Pond. I'd drunk too much at the table and ended up sleeping it off in Stacey's childhood bed. I recalled seeing photographs of her as a girl, thin and tomboyish, with a natural confidence that leaped out at you from inside the picture frames. I never could have predicted that, one day, her physical presence would cause me such joy and misery.

Somehow we managed to steer clear of Morse's national park through the salad and entrée courses, although everyone wanted me to share what I knew about the moose shootings. Ora couldn't disguise her horror as I described the dead animals. Skillen put forth a new theory about the case; he suggested the massacre might have been an act of vengeance against the Warden Service for something we had done the previous week during the moose hunt.

"It's no secret you guys are disliked in Washington County," he said, refilling his and Stacey's glasses of wine while Charley

made coffee. "I've never understood it myself, but I guess it goes back to the history here. Have you ever read that book about the Down East Game War?"

"Yes, I have." In fact, I still had the borrowed copy I had forgotten to return to the veterinarian who'd loaned it to me.

"At the mill, guys are always bitching about how they got pinched for this or that infraction," Skillen said. "It seems to me like something a couple of pissed-off, drunk guys would do: drive around and kill stuff as a way of saying 'fuck you'—excuse me, Mrs. Stevens—to the local wardens."

"That's not what happened," I said. "This was all about Elizabeth Morse."

"Right," said Stacey, whose voice had grown a little wobbly after her second glass of wine. "Because there was that shoot-'em-up at Morse's house, too."

Skillen took a sip of wine. "Yes, but there's no way to know if the two incidents were even connected. It doesn't sound like they were. Or am I wrong about that, Mike?"

"Too soon to tell," I said. "We're still waiting for the ballistic evidence to come back from the state police lab."

"I can't imagine what makes a person so hateful," said Ora, turning her napkin in her hands.

"I don't know how you guys are ever going to solve this," Skillen said. Both he and Stacey had drunk a fair amount over dinner, but he showed no signs of being intoxicated, except that he had grown progressively more talkative.

"We will," said Charley, returning to the table with a tray of coffee.

Skillen set down his wineglass, spilling a little. "You talk like you're part of this investigation, Charley."

"Technically, I might not be," said my old friend. "But I'm going to keep looking for the murdering bastards who did

this, no matter how long it takes, and so is Warden Bowditch."

"*Murder* seems a bit extreme," said Skillen.

"You didn't see those animals," I said.

He nodded as if to cede the point. "From a legal perspective, I mean."

Ora passed plates of pie around the table while Charley distributed mugs of coffee. We ate in silence for a minute or two. It was early yet, but I was feeling an increasingly strong desire to wolf down my dessert and leave.

"It's because she's a woman," said Stacey out of nowhere. She leaned both of her elbows on the table. "If Elizabeth Morse was a man, people might disagree with her, but they wouldn't be attacking her this . . . violently."

I leaned back in my creaking chair. "I thought you didn't like her."

"I don't! I think she's nuts, but she's a strong woman, and strong women make insecure men feel weak. That's the story of my fucking life."

"Language," said her mother.

Skillen patted Stacey's hand, the one with the engagement ring. "I guess that means I'm not insecure."

She placed her free hand on his. "You have the opposite problem."

Ora looked at my half-finished plate. "Mike, would you like some more pie?"

"No, thank you," I said. "Can you excuse me for a second?"

I pushed my chair back from the table and went into the bathroom. The face in the mirror was fierce and uncompromising. I could stay here mooning over a woman I would never possess, or I could go back to work and find the men who murdered those moose. Maybe I wasn't cut out to be a game warden, and sooner or later I would need to make that

decision. But this wasn't the time to play Hamlet. I had a job to do, and Charley was right that this case would haunt me for the rest of my life unless I did my part to solve the crime.

Somewhere in Boston, my mother was lying in a hospital bed, her body racked by disease and flooded with strange and potent chemicals. In my gut, I knew she'd been thinking of me as the doctors inserted the needle, thinking about my future. It seemed important tonight for me to act like the man she'd always wanted me to be. I owed her that much.

I flushed the unused toilet, ran water in the sink, and returned to the dining-room table.

"I'm afraid I need to get going," I said.

"So soon?" said Ora.

"I got a text from Sergeant McQuarrie. He wants me to meet him."

Charley rose onto his overlarge feet. "Duty calls, then."

"Yes," I said.

Matt Skillen also stood up, but Stacey remained seated in her chair, studying me with an odd, confused expression. Her fiancé stuck out his arm, and we shook hands.

"It was a pleasure." For the first time, I heard the booze in his voice.

I smiled tightly but didn't speak. I kissed Ora on the cheek and thanked her for her hospitality, and she reached out to touch the side of my face. "You are always welcome in this home," she said.

"Good night," I said to the room.

Stacey didn't reply. She sat at the table, looking at her empty wineglass, while Charley walked me out the door and down the ramp. The wind was changing direction, swinging around from the north. The air seemed colder than it had since springtime.

"Keep me posted about the investigation," he said. "I depend on you to satisfy my boundless curiosity in these matters."

I told him I would and opened my truck door. Then I looked back, unable to stop myself from asking the question. "Do you know what was the matter with Stacey just now? Did I say something to offend her?"

"We don't have cell coverage at the house," he said, stroking his long chin. "Something about the hills around the lake. I'm sure she was puzzled how you could have gotten a text message in the bathroom. Stacey can be willful as all get-out, and she doesn't always see the light right away. But in the end, not much gets past that girl."

29

There were two ways back to my cabin. The longer one looped through Grand Lake Stream, acquiring a coating of asphalt along the way, turned east for eight miles to Indian Township, and then veered south again along Route 1 through Princeton and Woodland before it joined up with the highway that would carry me back into the familiar confines of District 58 and, eventually, the long dirt lane that led to my cabin.

Then there was the direct route. Unpaved and frequently blocked by toppled trees, it tunneled through the forest without passing a single secluded residence. A driver could break down on that remote logging road and wait twelve hours, or longer, for another vehicle to pass by. If he was lucky, the vehicle wouldn't be a truck full of pill smugglers.

I chose the road less taken because I needed to get my head together.

Charley and his daughter had seen through my fraudulent excuse for leaving. After I got over the initial embarrassment, I thought about her silent, sullen reaction. My presence hadn't even seemed to register with her over dinner, so why had my abrupt departure caused her to act that way?

The question didn't merit an answer. I'd just promised myself to stop obsessing over Matt Skillen's future wife. Instead, I needed to focus on the things that truly mattered

now: my mother's cancer and the investigation that might yet determine whether I would decide to leave my job with the Maine Warden Service.

By choosing the forest route, I had put myself out of the reach of cell phones for a solid hour. I wouldn't get a signal again until I intersected with Route 9 outside Wesley. In retrospect, this had been a dumb move, since I'd wanted to call Neil to check on my mom's condition. In researching chemotherapy online, I'd read that many people didn't experience any of the most-feared side effects—nausea, vomiting, fever—until twenty-four hours or more after their first injection. I found myself praying that my mother was sleeping soundly at the moment.

My lower legs were cold; I hadn't realized it until now. The heat wave didn't seem to be breaking so much as shattering like a sheet of dropped glass. I hadn't turned the heater on for months, and the vents gave off the musty odor of an abandoned nest.

A pair of yellow eyes flashed in my high beams, and I stepped hard on my brakes. A coyote—gray and reddish brown—bounded across the dirt road at the edge of the light. In Maine, they grew as big as wolves, and this one was as large as any I'd ever seen. I let my heart return to its normal rhythm before continuing on again.

My BlackBerry chimed as I was cresting the ridge above the Chain Lakes. I stopped the pickup in the center of the dark road and checked the phone's lighted display. I was still miles from civilization and couldn't imagine the possible vectors of radio waves that would have allowed a transmission to reach this spruce-blanketed hilltop.

I saw that I had received three missed calls from the same

number, my stepfather's, but Neil had not seen fit to leave a voice mail. He had, however, sent an e-mail message an hour ago:

> Mke—
> Tried your number a few times. I understand your work takes you out of cell coverage sometimes but had e xpected to hear from you before now. Your mother got through the procedure fine. The oncologist said it couldn't have gone any better ,although he said she had more questions about losing her hair than about anything else. You know how she is about her hair. She woke up nauseous a little while ago. So far no vomiting. This regimen is very aggressive , the doctor said. He e xpects significant side effects from the chemo ,and there is always the risk of infection in these cases from bacteria in the G tract. I'd appreciate a call when you get this. Day or night. Please.
> — Neil

I pushed redial on the last-received call. The phone started to ring and then the signal dropped. I tried a second time and got the same result. The single bar had disappeared, and the display now showed no coverage, even when I plugged the phone into the booster. Such were the vagaries of mobile communications in the Maine North Woods. I decided I would try him again once I hit the highway.

Fifteen minutes later, the phone rang again. I snatched it up without looking at the display and said, "Neil?"

"Mike?" The voice belonged to a woman.

"Briar?"

"I'm having trouble hearing you."

I raised my voice, as if that would somehow make a difference. "Briar, I'm here. Are you OK?"

"I can barely hear you. You sound like you're about to break up." The weakness of the transmission was distorting her voice, but I sensed a distinct note of panic in it. "Someone's chasing me again. I don't know where I am, Mike!"

I stopped the truck. "Are you in the woods?"

"I went for a drive again. The guard said to stay away from town, so I went—"

I turned off the engine to quiet the squealing belt. "Say again."

"Maybe the Stud Mill Road. I don't know!"

"Your car has a GPS, right?"

"It doesn't show logging roads!"

"That doesn't matter. What you want is the compass function. Head east."

"East?"

"You're either going to hit a bigger road or you'll come to one of the rivers or lakes. Most of them have roads that follow the shore. Turn north if you do. That will take you back in the direction of Grand Lake Stream."

"East and then north. What if I see that truck again, though?"

I didn't have an answer to that particular question, other than to hope that she didn't. "I'm going to head back toward Grand Lake Stream. In a minute, we're probably going to lose our signal, but I will keep trying your number."

"I didn't hear that."

"Just keep hitting redial!"

"Mike? Mike?"

Then she was gone. All I heard on the other end was a

drone. I restarted my engine and did a sharp three-point turn in the road, starting back north again toward Little Wabassus. I hadn't asked Briar if it was the same truck following her as before. Maybe when I came to that hilltop, I would get a signal again. I hoped to God I would. Finding her in these woods wouldn't be as easy as finding a needle in a haystack. It would be more like finding a single pine needle in a forest of pines.

30

Racing back along the logging road, worried about the very real possibilities of getting a flat tire or crashing into a moose, I tried to conjure the crazy map of logging roads between Grand Lake Stream and the Airline. My district crept into this wild country as far as the southernmost section of Morse's estate, and so I had learned the ins and outs of these particular woods over the course of the past year. I'd also familiarized myself with Cody Devoe's district to my west, which included a lengthy stretch of the Stud Mill Road. But the winding dirt lanes to the north belonged to Jeremy Bard, and he hadn't exactly hung out a welcome sign for me.

I paused for a few minutes at the top of the hill where I'd gotten Neil's e-mail earlier, hoping to see a bar or two on the BlackBerry display, but whatever genie had allowed a signal to reach me before had vanished in a puff of smoke. The best I could hope for was that Briar Morse would find her way safely out of the woods on her own. Why had she foolishly gone for a drive again after her last experience on these same logging roads? I was surprised that Jack Spense's guard had even let her through the gate, and I had no doubt that Betty would unleash holy hell on her new "threat-assessment specialist."

The wind blew fallen leaves into my windshield like kamikaze birds. I pushed my foot hard on the gas.

*

After what seemed like an eternity, I passed the road that led down to Little Wabassus and the Stevenses' house along the shore. I knew that if I could just get past the low hills to the west of the lake, I might find myself in range of the new cell tower outside Grand Lake Stream.

My phone chimed in the cradle of the signal booster. I grabbed at it and pressed it to my ear.

"Briar?"

"Mike," she said. "I've been trying you forever!"

"Where are you?"

"Outside Grand Lake Stream."

I let out a deep breath. "Great," I said. "So you can find your way back to your mother's north gate."

"No! You don't understand. I tried that, but there was a pickup truck waiting on the road to the gate."

My hand clenched the wheel. "Are you sure it was the same one? What did it look like?"

"I don't know! It snapped on its high beams as I came around the corner, like it was waiting for me."

"What did you do?"

"I got the fuck out of there." The signal was clear now, and I could hear how terrified she was. "You've got to rescue me!"

"Is the truck still following you?"

"Yes."

"Can you drive into town?"

"Yes, but I don't know where to go."

I tried to think of a safe haven, somewhere public where she could seek protection. But Grand Lake Stream was too small a village to maintain its own police force. A couple of times a day, a deputy sheriff or state trooper might swing through town, but most of the time, if the residents needed

the assistance of a law-enforcement officer, they would call the local game warden. Why did I have misgivings about sending her to Jeremy Bard's house?

I glanced at the clock on the dash. The Pine Tree Store would be closed now. There would be men fishing the stream this time of night, but the unlighted parking lot at the Dam Pool would hardly seem to Briar like a refuge. "Go to Weatherby's."

"The sporting camp?"

"You'll be safe with them, Briar. I promise. Honk on your horn if you need to wake people up. I'll meet you there as soon as I can. I'm going to call Jack Spense. He and his men might be able to get there before me. OK?"

"OK." She didn't sound assured.

"Everything will be fine," I said. "Just watch your driving, and everything will be fine."

After I hung up with Briar, I tried to key in the number for Moosehorn Lodge without crashing into a pine tree. There are good reasons so many states outlaw using a cell phone behind the wheel.

"Warden Bowditch?" said a man's voice.

"Mr. Spense?" I should have figured that he had installed some sort of caller-recognition device with my number in it. I'd certainly phoned the house enough at this point.

"What can we do for you?"

"Briar is in trouble," I said. "She went for a drive."

"What?"

"Someone must have let her through the gate. A pickup truck is chasing her again. She didn't get a good look at it, but I bet it's the same one. She tried going back home, but it was waiting to intercept her, so she turned around."

"Why didn't she call here?"

"It doesn't matter," I said. "I've told her to go to Weatherby's.

That's a sporting camp in town, on the left past the store. I told her to seek shelter there—the owners are good people—and wait for me to arrive."

The phone went dead, and not because the call had been dropped. The bastard had hung up on me. He must have realized the urgency of the situation and decided not to waste time with pleasantries. Either that or he realized the hit his reputation would take if his company failed to protect the daughter of one of the wealthiest women in America.

As I turned onto the Little River Road, I wondered if I should call Briar back to keep her talking. Would it be safer to have me on the line while she drove into town, or would it be better for her to focus on the road? The girl was such a speed demon. I worried that she would disregard my warnings about trying to outrace her pursuer on the winding woods road.

I was right to have worried.

I saw the red brake lights as I came around a sharp corner a few miles from the village. They stared at me out of the darkness like the eyes of a demonic creature. My high beams revealed the new skid marks in the gravel, and then they touched the bumper of the cherry-red BMW, angled off the road in a ditch. The front end of the vehicle was crushed against the trunk of an enormous white pine that the area loggers had let stand for unknown reasons, since they had already chopped down so many towering trees here. It was as if they had sensed that the pine had some other destiny than to be turned into a ship's mast, that it was fated to loom over this stretch of road for untold years until the moment when a young woman would drive her car into its trunk, snapping it finally in two.

The beams from my truck cast a white light around me as I approached the car. They projected my frantic shadow against the horrible backdrop. I tried both doors and found them

crushed permanently shut. Briar's headlights had gone out in the split second it had taken for the front end to hit the tree, pushing the engine back into the driver's compartment.

I might have called her name. I honestly don't remember. What lingers in my memory now is the brightness of the blood splattered across the air bag—as red as the car itself.

Maine game wardens are issued two flashlights. One is a small SureFire about the size of a quarter in diameter and not much longer than a pencil. It has a clip that fastens to your shirt pocket. The other is a black Maglite the length of a man's forearm. It is heavy enough to be used as a club and can be carried through a rubber loop on the back of your duty belt.

I used the Maglite to attack the already-spiderwebbed glass separating me from Briar. I had no illusions about what I would discover once I pulled back the useless air bag. I had seen my share of fatal crashes. But I had never looked into the open, lifeless eyes of a woman who had kissed me.

After I saw Briar's shattered face, I didn't want to see the rest of her. I could imagine what the damage might have done to her rib cage and pelvis, the possibility that her legs had been severed below the waist. I backed away from the vehicle, lost my footing in the ditch, and fell backward onto my rear end. The Maglite slipped from my hand and rolled into the standing water; its light continued to shine even though submerged.

I closed my eyes and sat there until the thundering of my pulse was no longer the only thing I could hear. Then I grabbed my wet flashlight from the ditch and returned to my truck to call 911 and await the arrival of Morse's ineffectual guards.

I didn't have long to wait. Jack Spense and another one of his men arrived in their black Suburban while I was still on the line with the state police dispatcher, telling her that a

young woman had been killed when a driver in an unidentified pickup had forced her car off the road and into a tree. I didn't know if this was literally true—Briar might have crashed on her own, without being tailgated—but there was a chance that the truck might yet be spotted if an alert went out to every cop within a fifty-mile radius.

The bodyguards didn't pause to talk with me. They threw open the doors of the SUV and ran directly to the crumpled roadster. Spense reached his muscular arm through the driver's side window, and I knew he was searching for a pulse he must have known he wouldn't find. The other man struggled in vain with the passenger door, just as I had, before he began to methodically break the window with his own tactical flashlight. They were both dressed in jeans and black T-shirts, and they both had shaved heads. I wasn't sure if the second man was the guard who had let me through the gate. In their informal uniforms, they all looked the same.

"Leave her alone," I said.

Spense spun away from the car, his right hand red with blood, spitting out curses. The other man stared at me for a moment and then looked at his employer. After a long pause, the second man decided to ignore my command and returned to work, trying to shatter the passenger's side window.

I raised my voice. "I said, 'Leave her alone.'"

When Spense finally looked up, his eyes were so full of rage that for an instant I wondered if he might attack me. His fingers had left blood on his face, which only made him seem more deranged. "What the fuck happened here?" he yelled at me.

"She called to say she was being chased again," I said, trying to temper my own anger through even breathing. "I don't know why you let her leave the property without a bodyguard after what happened before."

Spense turned his entire body to face the wreck again, where the other guard stood motionless. "You're fired! You're fucking fired!"

The second man gave him a beseeching look. "Jack . . ."

"Get the fuck out of my sight!"

The first officer to arrive, fifteen minutes later, was Trooper Belanger, who had been patrolling the desolate section of Route 1 between Indian Township and the Vanceboro border crossing. He was followed by two policemen and an ambulance from the Passamaquoddy reservation. Jeremy Bard lived closest to the crash site, but he had no explanation for his tardiness in responding, or if he did, he didn't share it with me. My fellow warden preferred to chat with the Passamaquoddies while I briefed Belanger on everything that had happened.

The scene needed to be preserved for the state police to map out the sequence of events leading to the fatality: how fast Briar had been going, whether another vehicle had been directly involved, when she had applied her brakes. The information would be needed if, by some stroke of luck, the driver of the mysterious pickup was ever identified. The district attorney might or might not decide to bring charges at that point; the decision would depend on the strength of the evidence and how well it would stand up in front of a jury. But in my mind, those distinctions were all meaningless technicalities.

The tall trooper peered at me from beneath the wide blue brim of his hat. "So you didn't see this truck force her off the road?"

"If I had, I sure as hell would have chased him." The night was getting downright cold, and I'd fetched my red warden's jacket from the backseat of my car.

"Then there's no proof she didn't drive into the tree on her own?"

"That's for you to determine. Her car might show signs of having been sideswiped." I stretched my arms out around me. "Maybe there's paint from another vehicle on one of these trees. You need to reconstruct the crash."

The trooper had eyes like shards of flint. "But you never saw the truck chasing her?"

"This is a homicide," I said.

I expected he'd give me the obvious rejoinder that the DA would require a higher standard of proof, but Belanger had looked into the car and seen Briar's mutilated face. And I think the trooper understood the rage I was doing my best to keep contained inside my chest.

"I need you and Bard to help me direct traffic until Zanadakis and the sheriff arrive," he said. "I'd like to keep the site as intact as I can. No one gets through except authorized personnel."

I'd had a few dustups with the state police, but Belanger struck me as a good cop: the kind who doesn't break the rules but is not averse to bending them in the service of a cause higher than the Maine Criminal Code.

Before I could move my truck, however, we saw headlights coming from the direction of Moosehorn Lodge. It was another one of Jack Spense's black SUVs. Three people got out quickly: the driver, whose impressive physique marked him unmistakably as another bodyguard; a bearded man in a floppy hat; and a middle-aged woman with a muscular build.

I rushed to intercept Elizabeth Morse before she could get close enough to Briar's car to see the damage. "Stop, Ms. Morse!"

"Let me through." Her voice was commanding. Her face, in the flashing blue and red lights of the emergency vehicles, appeared oddly empty of emotion, like a wax museum version of itself.

I spread out my arms to stop her, just as I had in the field on the morning we found the moose. "That's not a good idea."

She kept walking, even as I stepped in front of her. "I need to see her."

I grabbed her arm hard. "Not now."

She spun around on me, her eyes widening. "Let go of me!"

I shook my head no.

She tried shaking me loose. "I need to see my daughter."

I took hold of her other arm so that we were facing each other squarely. "Not like this."

"I need to see Briar." Her lip began to tremble.

"Ms. Morse," I said. "Betty."

She pushed herself into me, thrust her chest against mine, and pressed her head against my neck. She made no sound as she sobbed, but I could feel every muscle in her body shaking. I wrapped my arms around her, and she gave me a hug that nearly broke my ribs. I could smell the herbal shampoo in her hair. Then she collapsed. Her legs just went out from under her, and I found myself bending at the knees to ease the weight of her body gently to the earth. I held her like that for a while, huddled over her almost, as if to protect her from an airborne attack. She seemed like a small and boneless thing, unrecognizable as the powerful businesswoman I'd first met. She was a mother who had lost the only child she would ever have.

After a few moments, I felt someone tap me on the shoulder. Tears streamed down Leaf Woodwind's cheeks.

I let go of Elizabeth Morse and let him take my place. He tossed his hat to the ground and dropped to his knees. Then he wrapped himself around the woman he'd found by the roadside so many years ago.

31

The moon came up while I stood guard on the perimeter of the crash scene. I'd forgotten it was nearly full. Over the next few hours, I watched the white orb rise above the treetops and then climb steadily into the night sky, causing the stars about it to fade, eclipsed by its brilliance. It looked like a heavy stone that might drop unexpectedly from the heavens and smash the world to smithereens.

Elizabeth Morse and Leaf Woodwind packed into their black SUVs with their hired guards. The ambulance took away the lifeless body of Briar Morse, which had been removed from the wreck by using the Jaws of Life. A tow truck lifted the crushed roadster onto its flatbed. The Passamaquoddy policemen drifted away. I never did see Bard leave. Lieutenant Zanadakis and several other state police officers came and went, having taken my statement and begun mapping the accident scene. They would return in daylight to search for additional evidence of the fatal chase. Sheriff Roberta Rhine, who had arrived last, was also the last to leave—except for me.

"You should go home and get some sleep." Her breath shimmered as she spoke. She had her hands thrust into the pockets of a black windbreaker with a sheriff's star on the breast. Her long face had grown tight from the cold. "There's nothing more for us to do here."

"You know what's funny?"

"What?" she said.

"Belanger told me to direct traffic away from the accident scene, but there hasn't been a single car all night, except for the emergency vehicles."

She reached up to tug on a turquoise earring. "This is a deserted stretch of road even during the summer months."

The last words she said before I climbed into my truck were, "It looks like this is a murder investigation now."

It always was, I thought, remembering the sight of that dead moose in the grass.

When I got back to my cabin, I cleaned up after the squirrels and then, taking a deep breath, sat down to phone my stepfather. It was late, but I expected him to be awake. Instead, the call went directly to voice mail.

"Neil, it's me," I said with a faint stutter. "I'm sorry I missed you before. I was in the woods all day. I can't always get a signal up here. But I'm home now, so feel free to try me again. I'm glad Mom's chemo went OK. I promise to call tomorrow. Tell her I love her. I hope you're hanging in there, too."

It was only after I'd hung up that I realized I hadn't mentioned Briar. There hadn't seemed a point in it. She was just a name as far as he was concerned.

The phone rang just after I fell asleep. It was McQuarrie, wanting an update. He was driving back to Washington County after having been summoned away to help retrieve the corpse of a drunk boater from the lake where the man had crashed his boat. News of Briar Morse's death was spreading fast, Mack said. Reporters and state officials were demanding information. Rivard had already been feeling pressure over his failure to solve the high-profile crime. Now the daughter of the

most powerful woman in the state was dead, possibly killed by the same people who had slaughtered those moose. The meeting the lieutenant had scheduled for seven A.M. was going to be "a real shit show," Mack said.

"Be sure to wear your ballistic vest," my sergeant told me.

"I always do," I replied.

This time, no one brought doughnuts.

Rivard was running late, and the mood in the crowded IF&W field office was tense and irritable. The unspoken question hanging over every man in the room was: What if we had caught the men who killed the moose? Would Elizabeth Morse's daughter still be alive if we'd been faster in solving the first crime? The resident fishhead biologists had the good sense to skedaddle.

McQuarrie looked older than I'd ever remembered seeing him. "Didn't get much sleep," he admitted. "That poor girl. She was pretty, too. That always makes it harder, for some reason." He dug his thumb and forefinger into his bloodshot eyes. "This case might just be my swan song," he said.

Mine, too, I thought.

Rivard might as well have appeared in a puff of sulfurous smoke. He burst through the door, a crimson glow on his cheeks from either the cold wind blowing down from the north or too much blood pumping to his head. In his hand he held a newspaper, rolled up, as if he meant to swipe a naughty dog across the nose with it. Bilodeau slipped in behind him, looking as inscrutable as ever. Lieutenant Zanadakis came last, dressed to the nines in suit and tie, and eased the door shut behind him.

"I want to read you something," Rivard said without bothering to remove his red wool warden's coat or the olive

fedora that was part of our dress uniform. "This is from this morning's paper. The headline is 'Series of Missteps in Moose Massacre Causes Outrage.' It says here that 'game wardens are facing new questions about their handling of an investigation into the illegal shooting of ten moose on the property of entrepreneur and environmental activist Elizabeth Morse.'" When he glanced up, the sclera of his eyes were as scarlet as his coat. "There are quotes here from people accusing us of harassment because we detained them at a checkpoint and asked to see their guns. They say our conduct is improper because we entered private property to collect cigarette butts for DNA. You've got Karl Khristian—Karl Khristian!—bitching because Bilodeau dug up some bullets from outside his fence. We come across in this story like a bunch of circus clowns."

Rivard flung the newspaper away. Unrolling in flight, it struck Sullivan in the chest, causing the warden to leap back and nearly fall over a desk chair.

"That paper came out before Briar Morse died," Rivard said. "There's nothing in it about her driving into a tree last night. Imagine what's going to be in tomorrow's paper. Do you all want to see me crucified?" Before any of us could raise our hands, he continued: "The only way that's not going to happen is if we start getting some fucking results!"

I'm not sure why it surprised me that Rivard didn't ask for a moment of silence to remember the dead girl. Our lieutenant was unraveling in front of our eyes.

"Bilodeau, what can you tell us?" Rivard asked.

The warden investigator was wearing street clothes—fleece-lined denim jacket, flannel shirt, and dirty Carhartt pants—as if he intended to do some undercover work. "I've got a good feeling about those slugs from Khristian's driveway," he said. "Think we might be looking at a match there between them

and the ones we dug out of the walls of the Morse place. Should hear about those today."

"Anyone else got a lead here?" the lieutenant asked, setting his hat down on a desk.

Bard took half a step forward. "I've been sweating Chubby LeClair pretty good, and I think he might be on the verge of breaking."

"What the hell does that mean?" Rivard asked. It was the first time I'd heard him snap at one of his acolytes.

The lieutenant's response seemed to fluster Bard, too. "I, uh, think he, uh, might be our guy."

"What's that, your woman's intuition?"

Bard stared at the floor.

"The way you build a case is with *evidence*." The lieutenant unbuttoned his coat. "You want to impress me? Come back with a fucking confession." He tossed his jacket over the back of a chair. "I want everyone to tell me what the hell you've been doing for the past few days. You'd better not have been sitting around pulling each other's puds."

I didn't doubt that, at his core, Marc Rivard was a decent and dedicated public servant. For all my quarrels with my superiors, I'd never had cause to doubt they had solid reasons for making the decisions they did. But watching Rivard propped against the desk with his arms crossed, throwing insult after insult at the men he was supposed to be leading, it was hard to avoid the conclusion that they'd promoted him too far, too fast. Unlike me, a lot of guys in that room had never been on the receiving end of his anger. You didn't need a seismometer to sense the shock wave that rippled through their collective confidence.

By the time he got to me, I was braced for the worst. "Bowditch?" he said.

"Ms. Morse told me she didn't want a liaison anymore," I replied.

"So what have you been doing?"

"Regular patrol work."

McQuarrie stepped in front of me to take the bullet. "That was my decision, L.T."

"Lieutenant Zanadakis says you did everything you could to get that Morse girl to safety. He says you were helpful at the crash scene," Rivard said.

I didn't know how to respond, so I kept my lips locked.

"After this meeting, we're driving out to the Morse property to brief her. We'd like you to come with us."

I didn't have to look around the room to know that everyone was staring at me. Never before had Rivard singled me out for praise. Not a single person envied me, either.

32

A different guard let us through the gate this time. I wondered what had happened to the guy from the crash scene. Had Spense turned him out into the Maine wilderness to hitchhike his way back to civilization?

The three of us rode in separate vehicles: Rivard led the way in his black GMC, the state police lieutenant followed in his steel-blue Ford sedan, and I brought up the rear in my scratched and screeching old beater. The sky was as blue as a tarp. The brightness of the sun outside belied the cold wind blowing down from Canada. The treetops whipped back and forth like animate objects placed under an evil spell, and small storms of dust cycloned in the clearings where the dirt road left the shelter of the forest.

There were fewer vehicles parked outside the mansion than I had expected. If you didn't know better, though, you might've thought it was just another chilly autumn morning at Moosehorn Lodge. It was easy for me to imagine Briar shuffling sleepily down the stairs to the kitchen, where her mother would be making tea.

When I got out of the truck, I turned up the collar of my red warden's jacket against the gusts and shoved my hands deep into my pockets. Looking through the pillars of the trees, I saw whitecaps racing down Sixth Machias Lake. I would have

preferred to walk to the end of the dock and be alone with my riotous emotions: the grief I felt for Briar, the dread and regret I felt for my dying mother. But I had unfinished business inside the house that I couldn't avoid.

Jack Spense himself opened the door for us. As a concession to the sudden arrival of autumn, he had exchanged his black T-shirt for a black mock turtleneck. He'd had the night to regain his composure, and his hard, flat face was as unreadable as the day we'd met. I didn't want to shake his hand, but he went down the line with us as we entered, trying to crush our hands with his manly grip.

"How is she doing?" Zanadakis asked in a quiet voice.

"Better," said Spense. "She's a strong woman."

The security expert escorted us into the repaired great room to wait. There was a fire crackling in one of the two hearths, giving the air a pleasantly smoky scent, as if the logs had been especially chosen for their applewood aroma. The last time I'd visited the room, the windows had all been shattered, there'd been a shimmer of broken glass on the floors and furniture, and you could've played connect-the-dots with the bullet holes in the wall. The transformation was a testament to Morse's wealth. She had been intent on returning her home to normal as swiftly as possible. That would never happen now that Briar was gone.

Spense motioned for us to sit, but none of us did. Zanadakis wandered over to the wall and ran his forefinger over a place where one of the bullet holes had been. Rivard removed his fedora, smoothed his graying temples, and then returned the hat to his head.

"She sure fixed this place up fast," he whispered.

I didn't know what to make of Rivard's softened attitude toward me, other than to be wary of it. Maybe, in his desire

to save his job, the lieutenant was searching for whatever new allies he could charm. In his mind, I had a special rapport with Morse; she knew I'd found the moose on her land, and she knew I'd done my utmost to save her daughter.

Rivard thinks he needs me, I thought. The man is truly desperate.

Elizabeth Morse appeared a few minutes later. She had pulled on a fuzzy sweater made of unbleached wool, faded blue jeans, and rainbow-colored socks beneath her Birkenstocks. It was the first time I'd ever seen her in her hippie garb, and she looked like an impostor. She seemed to be making an effort with her appearance—she had washed her hair—but there were lavender shadows under her eyes that told the tale of the past twenty-four hours.

Behind her came Dexter Albee, who was dressed more formally: pressed button-down shirt, chinos, tasseled loafers. Put a necktie and blazer on him, and he would have been ready to testify in front of a legislative panel. Albee didn't seem to be holding up as well emotionally, though; the absence of color in his cheeks made it seem like he was coming down with the flu.

Jack Spense hung in the doorway, a square-shouldered silhouette, not fully in the room but close enough to eavesdrop on everything.

"Thank you for coming," Morse said in a slightly hoarse voice. "Please be seated." She gave me a special nod. "Good morning, Warden."

"Ms. Morse," I said.

"Before we get started, I would like to say something," said Rivard, emphasizing each word as if he'd practiced them before a mirror. "On behalf of the entire Maine Warden Service, I want to extend my deepest sympathies on the loss of your daughter."

She looked at him with that inscrutable catlike smile I'd gotten to know so well. "I didn't lose her, Lieutenant. She was taken from me. There's a considerable difference." Aside from a strangeness in her voice—as if the back of her jaw were wired shut and she was having trouble getting out her words—there was nothing in her body language that revealed her inner grief. "But I understand that you are trying to be kind, and I appreciate your sympathies. I am sure you have questions for me, and I have questions for you, so let's begin."

Zanadakis removed a notebook from his jacket and leaned forward on the couch where he had perched himself. "Briar told Warden Bowditch that she was being chased by a pickup truck last night. She had previously reported another incident like that several nights earlier. Do you have any idea who the driver might have been—any idea at all?"

"You've seen my file of death threats."

"I have," said the detective. "But I'm wondering if there were any unusual instances you can recall. Were you and Briar ever at a store or restaurant together and noticed someone looking at you in a menacing way?"

"Many times."

Zanadakis tried again. "Maybe there was a truck parked outside your property recently—on the road to Grand Lake Stream—and you assumed it belonged to a hiker? Sometimes people notice a detail that doesn't seem important at the time."

"Sorry. No."

"Is it possible that Briar was meeting someone outside the gate?"

"My daughter despised this place and the people here." She paused and flicked her eyes at me. "With the exception of a certain game warden."

I felt my face flush.

Zanadakis wrote something in his notebook. "According to Warden Bowditch, Briar could only describe the truck as 'dark'?"

"That describes half the vehicles you see around here. I take it no one was detained last night in such a vehicle."

"No, ma'am," said Zanadakis.

"What about physical evidence?" said Morse, clawing with several fingers at the fabric of her armchair. "Can't you take tire marks from the road?"

"The road there is gravel, so it doesn't show prints that are usable," he said. "We were able to determine that Briar did apply her brakes and she overcorrected as she lost control of her car. She was traveling at a high rate of speed."

"*Overcorrected,*" said Morse, almost to herself. "What is it with police officers and euphemisms?"

"There's nothing else?" said Dexter Albee, raising his voice suddenly. "You can't find any other evidence?"

Zanadakis flipped through his notebook, but he already knew the answers. "Her car shows no sign of having been sideswiped. There are no dents or scuff marks on it to indicate another vehicle actually pushed her off the road. I have some men out there this morning searching the foliage up and down the road. It's possible that the pickup might have scraped the trees and underbrush alongside the road. If so, we'd hope to find some paint we could match to the truck."

Elizabeth Morse stretched her arms along the top of the chair and planted her feet wide. It was very much the posture of a monarch on a throne. "There's really no reason for optimism, then."

"You shouldn't give up hope," said Rivard.

She glared at him with those handsome hazel eyes. "Warden

Bowditch can tell you how I feel about being patronized, Lieutenant."

Albee shot to his feet. "Well, what about the rest of this—the killing of those moose, and the attack on Elizabeth's house? Are you saying none of this is connected? Because it strikes me as the work of the same sick individual."

"We're investigating that possibility," said Zanadakis, looking up at him calmly. "At the very least, we have gathered some high-quality ballistic evidence that we can use to match the firearms to the two incidents."

"Those firearms are at the bottom of a lake," muttered Spense from the doorway.

Rivard frowned in his direction. "We don't know that."

The bodyguard didn't budge. "You won't find them."

"If there's one thing I've learned as a warden," Rivard said, "it's that criminals can't keep their mouths shut. Sooner or later, these guys are going to get drunk and start boasting about what they did. When they do, word will get back to us."

Elizabeth pushed her highlighted hair out of her face. "So the best-case scenario involves you hearing some drunken gossip in a bar and piecing together a case out of circumstantial evidence." Her eyes fixed on mine. "How reassuring would you find that approach if you were me, Warden Bowditch?"

"Not very reassuring, ma'am."

I felt Rivard's shoulders tense beside me.

Elizabeth gave me an affectionate smile. "My brave teller of truths. I have too few of those in my life. It's the price of being rich. People start telling you what they think you want to hear." She returned her attention to the arm of her chair, which seemed to require more scratching. "So what should I do now, then? Should I order Mr. Spense to continue fortifying

my bunker while I wait for some drunk in a bar to confess he killed my little girl?"

"Is there somewhere else you can go for a while?" asked Zanadakis.

She gave a snort. "Because my presence here is a provocation? I'm not the type to back down from a fight, Detective."

"Just temporarily," offered Rivard.

"It's what I have been advising, ma'am," said Jack Spense. "The first rule of conflict prevention is to do everything you can to avoid it."

"It's a little late for Sun Tzu, wouldn't you say, Mr. Spense?"

I had a feeling that Jack Spense's services would be discontinued very soon.

Dexter Albee circled around a coffee table until he was standing over his patron with his palms up in a beseeching gesture. "Betty, you can't let these bastards win! What you have planned for this national park is historic. It's your legacy. We've worked so hard and invested so much to make your vision a reality. I can't believe that Briar would have wanted—"

She raised a single index finger. "My daughter didn't give a shit about Maine, Dexter, and you know it. In fact, it would probably have given her pleasure to know her death made me give up on this godforsaken place."

"Betty, please, don't make a snap judgment you'll live to regret," said Albee.

She pushed herself up to her feet, using the arms of the chair for support. "I need to be alone. I need to think about what's important to me from now on."

The rest of us also rose. It was clear we were being dismissed.

But Elizabeth Morse wasn't done with me. She called to me at the door. "Warden Bowditch?"

"Yes, ma'am?"

"I hope we meet again."

"Me, too, ma'am."

Rivard decided to use this opening to make a case for himself again. "We're going to find the person who did this, Ms. Morse."

"Tell me something, Lieutenant," she said, her eyes flat and hard. "When I put up that reward for information about the killing of those moose, didn't you tell me then that criminals can't keep their mouths shut? I believe you said we'd get a flood of tips."

"And we did," Rivard said with more heat than he intended.

"None of which seem to have panned out. So if I offered twenty thousand dollars for those moose, how much do you suggest I put on my daughter's life?"

We found Leaf Woodwind waiting for us in the shady place where we had parked our vehicles. If Elizabeth Morse had internalized her grief, then her former partner was wearing his emotions for all the world to see. His hair was an uncombed mess, his eyes were raw, and there was gunk in his beard that had dribbled out of his nose and mouth. He looked like one of those mourners out of the Bible: a wild, wailing man on the verge of rending his tie-dyed garments.

"Well?" he screamed at us. "Have you found them? Have you found the fuckers?"

I had no doubt he had spent the night dosing himself with THC—the smell was baked into his skin—but the pot had done nothing to blunt his sharpened nerve endings.

Zanadakis and Rivard seemed taken aback by the display, so I stepped forward.

"Leaf," I said. "Please calm down."

He balled his hands into knotty fists. "Don't tell me to be

calm! That's all you've been saying ever since you got here. 'Be calm. Let us do our jobs.' And instead, everything's all gone to shit, man. You guys are fucking useless!"

Rivard's nose twitched, and I had a bad feeling that my lieutenant was going to arrest the man because he felt personally offended. "I think you need to go sleep off whatever magic carpet ride you're on, sir."

I positioned my body so that I was between Leaf and the other men. "Betty needs you, Leaf," I said.

"The fuck she does. She never has."

Whatever reconciliation they'd experienced last night hadn't survived the wee hours of the morning. "I think you should get some rest," I said.

"And I think you should get out of my face," he replied.

I'd always sensed an undercurrent of rage beneath that mellow smile and those glassy eyes. It seemed important to remember that this seemingly comical man was a former soldier; he had fought in a land where rice paddies contained hidden land mines and *punji* traps opened up under your feet. Back in Maine, a warden pilot had busted him for cultivating marijuana on his back forty. Out of desperation, he'd been forced to become the gopher to a cold woman who had shared nothing—neither her wealth nor their daughter's affections— with him. What did I really know of the darkness in Leaf Woodwind's heart?

"Get the hell off my land!" he said.

Zanadakis at least seemed to realize that we weren't accomplishing anything by further antagonizing the distraught man. My lieutenant, however, could never let any perceived insult go unanswered. The prick.

"It's not your land, sir," said Rivard through his truck window. "Never was."

"Fuck you, man."

As we drove off, I saw Leaf stoop for a handful of pebbles, which he hurled harmlessly into the bed of my truck. "Pigs!" he shouted.

I had been insulted hundreds of times in my job, but this blast from the past was a new one for me.

33

The lieutenant radioed me from his truck. The colonel had summoned him to Augusta for a briefing. He didn't say more than that, but I could guess what was happening behind the scenes. Powerful people inside and outside the government had begun asking questions about Marc Rivard and the investigation he'd been running for the past week. No doubt the national networks had begun calling, too, since Elizabeth had just made the rounds of morning TV shows. This story was exploding into a full-blown scandal. When you are a state employee, it is almost always a bad thing if your name begins to surface repeatedly in conversations. I knew this from personal experience.

If I knew Rivard as well as I thought I did, he would have already started searching for someone to blame. For once, that scapegoat wouldn't be Mike Bowditch. One advantage to being pushed to the periphery of the moose investigation was that no one could accuse me of having screwed it up. My suspicion was that the lieutenant intended to throw Bilodeau—or maybe McQuarrie—to the wolves. Being a political animal himself, Rivard would claw and bite to survive.

"What do you want me to do?" I asked him.

"Go with Zanadakis and see if you can help him reconstruct the crash scene," Rivard said. "He'll want to know where

Briar went after she left the property and where she saw the pickup."

"I already shared that information with him."

"Just do whatever you can to assist the Crash Reconstruction Unit. I promised them full cooperation."

Even over the radio, which tends to distort your voice in the worst way, he sounded like a man headed to the dentist's office—or the torture chamber.

"Good luck today, L.T.," I said, trying not to sound too phony.

"Ha," he said.

I followed Zanadakis back to the place where Briar had hit the tree. The road was still cordoned off, and a skinny Washington County deputy had been given the thankless task of detouring traffic around the lake. A team of state and local officers were already on the scene from the Forensic Mapping Unit. They'd done some of their analytical work the night before—as much as could be done in darkness using two-thousand-watt spotlights—but this morning they had brought along a Leica Total Station, a one-eyed contraption that looked like a surveyor's computer mounted atop a fluorescent yellow tripod. In a nearby garage, another team of police vehicle technicians and civilian mechanics from the Vehicle Autopsy Unit would be tearing apart the remains of Briar's roadster to inspect the brakes, suspension, and steering components for clues. And in Augusta, the medical examiner would be running a tox screen on her blood to determine whether she'd been drunk or drugged at the time of death.

Because district wardens are charged with reconstructing boat accidents and snowmobile collisions, we are taught the basics of crash reconstruction at the Maine Criminal Justice

Academy. We learn terms like *occupant kinematics* and *vehicle dynamics*. Our instructors quiz us on the three phases of a collision: precrash, at crash, and postcrash. We are trained to calculate approach vectors and determine velocity by using distance-based positioning analysis. We diagram fatalities using CAD software the same way architects design the contours of new patios.

The science of death is an awesome thing, I thought.

But what difference was technology going to make? All of these experts, all of this precise measuring equipment, and none of it was worth a damn thing compared to a single eyewitness to the event. Briar Morse had lost control of her car and driven into a pine tree. No computer in the world could tell me more than my own eyes.

"Everything will be fine," I had told her. "Just watch your driving, and everything will be fine."

Zanadakis did have questions for me. He wanted me to plot out on a topo map where I had been when I'd spoken with Briar: the first occasion, when I'd told her to head east toward Grand Lake Stream, and the second time, when we reestablished contact again. One of his officers would probably retrace my path to test the signals.

The detective seemed to sense my weariness. Maybe he shared my cynicism about the limits of technology to solve the mysteries that occur when neurons misfire in the brains of sociopaths. If there is one thing every cop learns, it is that humans are understandable and predictable constructs—until the moment they go completely haywire.

"So she couldn't tell you the color of the truck that was following her?" he asked me again.

"All she could see were its headlights. It could even have been an SUV."

He let out a sigh; his breath smelled of cinnamon chewing gum. "How about the size?"

"She said it seemed 'big.'"

"So more like an F150 than a Ranger?"

"I doubt Briar could have told the difference," I said. "I've gone over every word she used to describe it, and there's nothing to narrow it down."

He sighed again and scribbled something else into his notebook. Then he told me to wait while he conferred with his technicians.

My ex-girlfriend Sarah used to joke about my being a Luddite. She'd made fun of my ineptness using a computer or setting the time on the oven when the clocks fell back in the fall. I couldn't even program a special ringtone to play on my cell.

"You really are the second coming of Davy Crockett," she used to say with a laugh.

But it wasn't as if I was mechanically incompetent. I understood how my Bronco's engine worked. I could fix balky electrical wires in a wall without electrocuting myself. It was more that I had a deeply seated suspicion of miracles of all sorts, technological and otherwise. My mother had raised me as a Catholic, and she professed to be observant, but temperamentally, she had always been more a person of doubt than of faith. She had no more confidence that science was going to cure her cancer than I had confidence that science would lead us to Briar's murderer.

A brown creeper landed on the shattered pine and began working its way up the off-kilter trunk, investigating the cracks in the bark for insects. The little bird paid no attention to the uniformed men below with their high-tech gear. The fact that a young woman had collided with the tree and lost her life

was of no consequence to the creeper. All it cared about was finding the bugs. I found nature's indifference to my cares and concerns oddly consoling. If I ever started sinking into despair, I need only step outdoors and look around at the glorious green world.

I was leaning against my truck, thinking deep thoughts about the uselessness of science and the false promises of miracles, when Zanadakis returned with a big pearly smile. He carried his cell phone tucked into the palm of his hand. "You'll never believe this," he said. "Bilodeau just arrested Karl Khristian outside the Cigarette City in Calais."

"What?"

"Those shell casings he fished out of the lake matched cartridges he collected from Khristian's property. Not only that but the slugs he dug out of Morse's walls matched a round Khristian fired into the sand at that guy Cronk. The ballistics techs are sure they came from the same AR. That son of a bitch Bilodeau—he actually made a case."

My gaze drifted from the detective's beaming face back to the crash site. The creeper had flown off. I was having trouble registering the news. "Khristian just gave up without a fight?"

"Bilodeau showed up at the smoke shop with two wardens and three deputies. I guess one of Rhine's men had spotted his truck in the lot. Khristian came out of the store carrying a couple of bags. He must have figured he didn't have a chance to reach for his shoulder holster."

In my imagination I could picture the scene: the bald little man emerging from the tobacco shop, squint-eyed and sour-faced in the late-morning sunlight, to find himself staring down the barrels of half a dozen pistols and shotguns. For a moment, he must have wondered if he had time to drop the bags and draw the Colt 1911, or whatever death-dealing device he wore

strapped beneath his armpit. For years, Karl Khristian must have contemplated that eventuality—one final shoot-out with the socialists. How disappointed and impotent the sovereign citizen must have felt to be denied his rightful blaze of glory.

"Those rounds only mean that KKK was the one who shot up the mansion," I said.

"He also drives a Dodge Ram."

"So you think he was the one who forced Briar off the road?"

"My vehicle techs will go over every inch of his truck to find evidence that he was."

"Huh," I said.

Zanadakis's tanned face hardened. "You sound disappointed."

"Just surprised." I still couldn't reconcile the notion that Khristian had been the one who'd killed the moose, not least because he must have had a partner in crime that night.

The look the state police detective gave me might almost have been described as friendly. "Sometimes this is how it goes down," he said. "You kill yourself trying to solve a case, and then it breaks while you're busy doing something else, and you miss out on the takedown."

He flashed another chemically whitened grin and then went off to tell the officers from the Forensic Mapping Unit that he had an appointment with a nutcase at the Washington County Jail.

After a few minutes of watching the surveyors continuing with their measurements and waiting for that brown creeper to reappear, I decided that Khristian's arrest had freed up my own schedule. I found myself suddenly at loose ends for the first time in what seemed like weeks, which meant that I should be able to visit my mom. On the way back to my cabin, I would follow Zanadakis to Machias. If I hung around the county jail

and jawboned with the deputies, maybe this overwhelming sense of anticlimax I was feeling would wear off and I would come to accept that the monster I'd been searching for had been apprehended without my lifting a finger.

Unless the evidence techs could find a scratch of cherry-red paint on Khristian's truck, then the only hope of holding him accountable for Briar's death would be to get a confession. The wizened little man seemed like he would be a tough walnut to crack. And I sincerely doubted that Zanadakis would give me a chance to use my rubber hose. Hell, Rhine would probably bar me from the jail as a precaution against the two of us coming face-to-face.

I took the scenic route through the village of Grand Lake Stream because I needed gas again and figured a slice of pizza from the Pine Tree Store wouldn't hurt, either. There seemed to be fewer fishermen in town than the last time I'd passed through the village. The cold might have discouraged the fair-weather anglers from making the trip to what seemed like the ragged end of the earth. They didn't realize that spawning salmon grew more feisty as the temperature plunged. Maybe Charley and I could get together for one last evening on the water before the season closed at the end of the month.

Imagining my life returning to normal was a pleasant fantasy. My mother's illness would make such a thing impossible in any case. I checked my messages to see if I'd missed a call from Neil, but my stepfather must have taken my belated voice mail as an insufficient display of concern. If the investigation was winding down, and if Karl Khristian was indeed the guy, then I would request time off before deer season to spend with my mom. Not that a few days of hanging around her bedside would make up for years of freezing her out of my life.

And sooner or later, I would need to make a decision about

the Warden Service. I should have felt more of a sense of satisfaction at the thought of Bilodeau making his big arrest. No doubt Rivard had received the news with joy and relief. Knowing that the lieutenant might have just escaped an official ass whipping didn't make my future as a warden seem any brighter.

Then there was Stacey, whom I had resolved to forget. How easy would that be with us both working in the same state agency and assigned to the same wildlife division? Whether I wanted to or not, I was bound to run into her in the course of my patrols or over her parents' dinner table. Every time I passed Skillen's lumber mill, I was going to think of her sitting in the passenger seat of my truck. And it wasn't like Washington County, Maine—population twenty thousand or so—was the best place in the world for horny young men to go looking for new girlfriends. I had tried that before, to bad effect.

34

I had just crossed the bridge from Indian Township into Princeton, the one over the Grand Falls Flowage, when my police radio went wild.

"Shots fired! Shots fired! He's shooting at me!"

"Is there a unit calling radio?" the dispatcher asked.

"Twenty-two fifty-seven." Those were Bard's call numbers.

"What's your location, twenty-two fifty-seven?"

"Twenty-one Plantation. Near the corner of West and Pocomoonshine roads."

My mind didn't need to draw a map; I knew it was the half-cleared lot where Chubby LeClair had dumped his Airstream.

"I need units to the corner of West and Pocomoonshine Road in Twenty-one Plantation," the dispatcher said.

I grabbed the mic. "Twenty-two fifty-eight en route."

I hit my blue lights and pressed hard on the gas. A couple of kids jumped back from the side of the road outside the Princeton Food Mart as I went tearing down Route 1. Two other units—a county deputy and a state trooper—called in to say they were also on the way.

"I've been shot!" said Bard.

"Who shot you, fifty-seven?" the dispatcher asked.

"Chubby LeClair! He's shooting at me through the window of his camper."

"Bard," I asked, "how bad are you?"

There was a long pause. "I'm secure," he said. "But I need a medic."

"Ten-four," the dispatcher said. "Ambulance will be en route. All units be advised, suspect is armed and dangerous."

Washington County is a big and largely empty place, with a few clustered towns and isolated homesteads strung like beads along the paved highways. The sheriff's office keeps a grand total of eight deputies, working rotating shifts, in its patrol division. At any given hour, only three Maine state troopers are on duty. Seven district game wardens are assigned to the entire county. Add in the Passamaquoddy police, the DEA, and the border patrol, and you're left with only a dozen or so law-enforcement officers available to respond to an emergency in an area three times the size of Rhode Island.

Most of these officers had just assisted in the apprehension of Karl Khristian, forty-five minutes away in Machias. What this meant, I realized, was that Bard would be alone until I arrived. There was no one else to help him.

Even at top speed, it took me nearly fifteen minutes to cover the distance, bouncing along gravel roads. Bard stayed on the radio, so I knew he was still breathing. He reported that he had returned fire into the camper. No subsequent shots had been fired since the initial exchange, he said in a strained voice. That detail didn't sound good for Chubby LeClair. The Airstream had walls about as thick as a can of tuna and just as easily pierced.

What the hell had Bard done? Almost at the very moment that Bilodeau was arresting Karl Khristian on a felony terrorizing charge—when the case seemed finally on the verge of being solved and Rivard had reason to smile for the first

time in a week—Jeremy had gotten himself into a shoot-out.

The blood was pounding in my neck and my underarms were damp with perspiration as I arrived at the clearing. I stopped my truck far enough down the road so that I could survey the scene without coming under direct fire. Bard's patrol truck was parked directly across the road from the Airstream, which reminded me of a space capsule that had crashed to earth in the Maine woods. Chubby had chainsawed down a stand of paper birches to make room for it along the hillside, leaving foot-high stumps scattered about like crude pieces of sculpture. Among the amputated trees were other objects: a rusty bicycle, several scorched oil drums, a careless pyramid of wood scavenged from a rotting barn. I also saw a forest-green Toyota Tacoma parked at an abrupt angle to the door of the camper, as if its driver had arrived in haste or was planning a quick getaway.

I radioed the dispatcher to tell her I was on the scene and to see whether I could raise my fellow warden.

"Bard," I said, "where are you?"

"Bowditch? Is that you? I'm inside my truck."

"Are you OK?"

"The bullet grazed my fucking head. The blood keeps running into my eyes."

Head wounds tend to bleed heavily, so it didn't surprise me that Bard had panicked. I probably would have, too, if I'd been shot.

"Is Chubby still inside?" I asked, aware that if he had a police scanner—and most rural Mainers did, especially the inveterate lawbreakers—that he might be eavesdropping on our conversation.

"He hasn't come out the door, and there's no back way out of there."

I unfastened my shotgun from its holder. "Hang tight," I said. "I'm going to come up to your truck."

"Ten-four," he replied.

I pushed open my door and hopped out, keeping my body low to the ground, holding the heavy Mossberg with its sling around my wrist to steady my aim. Across the road from the camper, the hill fell steeply amid birches, beeches, and poplars. I figured I could circle around through the trees, using the embankment as cover.

I had to steady myself against tree trunks to keep from sliding on the fallen leaves down the hill. My torso was slick with perspiration beneath my ballistic vest, and I felt both hot and cold at the same time. Once I'd swung around below Bard's truck, I had to climb the hill again. The forest floor was wet from where the morning frost was melting away, and the leaves came off beneath my boots in layers. The air rising from the ground carried the nutty odor of decaying vegetation.

Eventually, I managed to pull myself out of the ditch beneath the passenger side of Bard's truck. I knocked at the door. It swung open suddenly from the pull of gravity, and I nearly toppled backward down the hillside to avoid being clipped in the shoulder. Bard thrust his bloody face at me. He was sprawled across both seats, his feet jammed beneath the steering wheel, and he had clamped a raincoat against his wounded skull. He looked like he'd spilled a can of red paint over his head.

"Took you long enough," he said, trying to blink the blood out of his eyes.

"How are you doing?"

"It stings like a motherfucker. But I'm all right, I guess."

"So what happened here?"

Bard rubbed at his eyes but succeeded only in rearranging

the smeared pattern on his face. "He shot me is what happened. Just opened fire out the window while I was sitting here. The glass exploded and the bullet clipped me in the head. Son of a bitch!"

The concept that LeClair had spontaneously started shooting didn't strike me as persuasive. There had to be more to the story. At the moment, I needed to focus on defusing the situation or at least stalling until backup arrived. "You said you returned fire?"

"Yeah, I emptied my magazine into the camper. He hasn't shot at me again, so maybe I got lucky."

So, if I understood what Bard was telling me, he had pulled his sidearm and fired blindly into the Airstream. Self-defense excuses a lot, but law-enforcement officers aren't supposed to discharge their weapons without knowing what else their bullets might strike. The attorney general had personally interrogated me when I'd shot a sociopath who'd cracked my head open with a crowbar. I'd barely escaped that interview with my badge.

"Stay here," I said, pulling away from the door.

"Where are you going?"

"To see if he's OK."

He twisted his mouth and blinked several times in quick succession. "What about me?"

I didn't answer that I expected him to live. I didn't say anything, in fact, because at that precise moment a shot sounded from the camper, and I dropped, face-first, to the ground.

"He's shooting again!" Bard said, as if I had somehow missed the news. He reached for his SIG, which he must have reloaded while he was waiting for me. Then he sat up and, with his bloody eyelids stuck together, shot at the camper through what was left of the driver's window.

"Stop it! Bard, stop it!"

He gave no indication of having heard me. He didn't stop shooting until the receiver ejected the fifteenth .357 cartridge from the magazine. One of the red-hot cases bounced off my leg, leaving a burn in the fabric.

A blue cloud of gunpowder smoke drifted over my head. "Goddamn it," I said. "He wasn't shooting at us."

Bard continued to stare up at the Airstream. "What?"

"That shot was muffled."

I rose from my knees and peered over the hood of the truck. Even from a distance, I could see the bullet holes in the metal skin of the Airstream. In his rage and blindness, Bard had mostly managed to miss the camper, but a few of his rounds had found their marks.

Holding the shotgun across my body, ready to bring the barrel up if need be, I darted around the front of the Sierra and ran in a straight line at the front door. If Chubby had been taking aim through one of the cracked windows, he could easily have ended my life with a single shot. But I was certain that the fat man wasn't pointing a gun at me.

"Bowditch!" I heard Bard shout. "Bowditch! What the fuck?"

I grabbed the metal handle of the door and gave it a twist. An odor spilled out in my face: a miasma of dirty dishes, stale marijuana smoke, and unwashed bed linens. I craned my neck to see inside. The interior was dim except for where the sunlight filtered in through the dusty windows.

I didn't recognize the Indian boy, although I found myself unsurprised to see him. There had been a reason Chubby didn't want to let Bard see what was happening inside his trailer. The boy's small body was propped against a blood-drenched cushion. He was naked except for his tight white underwear.

There was a bullet hole in his neck from where one of Bard's stray rounds had pierced the carotid artery.

Chubby lay on his back across the fixed table that occupied the center of the camper. He was wearing a stained T-shirt and denim coveralls, a strap loose over one shoulder. He was barefoot. His eyes were wide open. The gun he'd shot himself with had fallen from his burned mouth. I wouldn't have pegged LeClair for a suicide, didn't think he had it in him, but he must have known the torments that await child molesters in prison. In the end, the fat man had taken the easy way out.

35

The boy's name was Marky Parker. One of the Passamaquoddy officers who arrived at the scene knew him. He said Marky had gotten into some trouble on the rez for drugs and alcohol, but nothing serious. He was a good kid, the policeman said.

"I didn't know the boy was in there," Bard told Sergeant McQuarrie. "Honestly, Mack, I had no idea."

The paramedics had managed to staunch Bard's wound with a powdered clotting agent and a linen bandage wrapped tightly around the skull. They'd even managed to clean most of the dried blood off his pug-nosed face with alcohol swabs, although the process had tinted his skin orange in places. The EMTs made him lie flat in the back of the ambulance as a precaution. Bard had already fainted once when he'd attempted to look inside the camper himself.

The injured warden stared up at us with wide, imploring eyes that still had flecks of blood stuck in the lashes. He was such a muscular, energetic man, it was strange to see him in a posture of such helplessness. "There was no way for me to know that Chubby had a kid in there with him," he said. "You have to believe me."

McQuarrie wore the expression of a man who has just received a call from his oncologist. His broad shoulders seemed

bent, and his chin kept sinking against his barrel chest. He had a wad of chewing tobacco in his cheek, which made me think of a chipmunk carrying a nut.

Bard gave me a twitchy, uncertain smile. "Bowditch, you can back me up here."

I stared hard into his gray eyes; they reminded me at that moment of dirty nickels. But I didn't say a word.

"Let me just tell you what happened from the beginning," Bard said to McQuarrie.

The sergeant spat brown saliva onto the ground. "Stop talking, Jeremy."

"But I've got nothing to hide."

A vein began to pulse in my neck. "Listen to the sergeant, Bard."

In a hoarser-than-usual voice, McQuarrie said, "You'll have plenty of chances to tell it to the state cops and the AG's office. They're going to want a detailed statement on how this happened. I suggest you bring your lawyer to the interviews. In the meantime, my advice is to keep your trap shut."

From his back on the gurney, Bard gave us a defiant glare. "They're going to pay me while I'm suspended, though. I'm still going to get paid, right?"

"You'll get your money," I said.

Then I walked off to watch the activity around the camper.

Lieutenant Zanadakis had done a U-turn on his way to Machias and arrived shortly after the Passamaquoddy police. The deputy sheriff who had been directing traffic at Briar's crash scene had sped over, only to be given the same thankless job here. Wardens Bayley and Sullivan stood talking beside their patrol trucks at the periphery of the action. Every few minutes, another cruiser would arrive. The sheriff, I'd heard, was on her way, along with the district attorney and the

medical examiner. The attorney general would be sending one of his people, too.

I kept thinking about my last conversation with Chubby, how he'd called me in a panic, hoping I could persuade Bard to stop harassing him. It was hard for me to have much sympathy for a con man and drug dealer who had entertained half-naked kids in the privacy of his camper. LeClair probably deserved his violent end. The boy didn't, though. The image of his blood-soaked body was seared into my brain in a way that made me think I'd carry it around forever. The fact that Marky was a Passamaquoddy lent this shooting an awkward political dimension, given the tensions that always existed between the tribe and the state of Maine. I had a feeling that powerful forces would demand a sacrificial animal be thrown onto the pyre. Jeremy Bard was about to get his ass roasted.

"And I thought this was going to be a good day," Mack said in my ear. "First, Bilodeau gets those ballistic results. Then we arrest KKK without anyone firing a single shot. You'd think at my age I'd know better."

"Maybe this is just one of those cursed investigations," I said. "No matter what we do, it all turns to shit."

"Do you believe in curses, kid?"

"I'm starting to."

Mack let out a sigh that smelled of Skoal wintergreen. "So what do you think really happened here? Give it to me straight."

"There are black dents in the door of the Airstream," I said. "You can't see them because the door is open, but I noticed the scuff marks before when I approached the camper. I bet the dents match the bottom of Bard's boot. I think he came here trying to provoke Chub into doing something crazy. You heard the way Rivard laid into him this morning. Bard wanted to be

the hero. He caught Chubby fondling a half-naked kid and spooked LeClair into opening fire. We'll probably never know how it unfolded."

"You don't expect him to tell the truth?"

"Do you?"

I'd always had a cynical streak in me. It was just one of the emotional scars my father had inflicted on my character during my childhood. But my frequent bouts of pessimism had always been counterbalanced by a naive idealism: a belief that justice could be brought to the affairs of mankind, not in every case, but often enough to be worth the trouble. A sense of righteousness had led me to join the Warden Service. Now it seemed as if every sentence I uttered came barbed with sarcasm. And I didn't like what I heard.

Once again, the state police would need to get a formal statement from me: the second in less than twenty-four hours. The deaths of Chubby LeClair and Marky Parker had pushed Briar out of my thoughts for a short while, but when I closed my eyes, I found myself returned instantly to the bend in the road where her car had gone airborne. Her broken body was another image I realized I would never exorcise from my haunted head.

The sky was growing dark and the trees had taken on silhouettes that reminded me of deformed men by the time Zanadakis finally gave me permission to leave. I'd already told my story three times: once to the detective, once to an assistant attorney general, and once to Sheriff Rhine. I'd probably need to tell the tale a fourth time when the Warden Service conducted its own internal affairs investigation into Jeremy Bard's actions on this cold day in October.

On the drive home, I checked my messages and found a

text from my former sergeant, Kathy Frost: "I heard the news today. Oh boy."

I wasn't sure what news she meant: Briar's death, Karl Khristian's arrest, or the shootings in Plantation No. 21. Probably all of the above. I missed Kathy's wicked sense of humor. Her jokes had brought me back from many dark places in my rookie years, and it was probably no coincidence that my misgivings about the Warden Service had escalated after I'd been transferred from her squad. That was one of the reasons I'd been avoiding her. I didn't want reminders of a time when I'd worked for supervisors I liked and respected. Better not to think about those days.

There was nothing at all on the phone from my stepfather—no texts, no e-mails, no voice mail. I needed to see my mom. I decided I would try Neil again after I'd microwaved a couple of burritos back at the hacienda.

Whatever plans I was making flew away like so many scared birds when I pulled up to my cabin and my headlights showed Billy Cronk sitting on my porch steps. He was wearing his camouflage hunting jacket, blue jeans, and heavy boots, and his golden hair was loose about his shoulders. He leaned forward, with his shoulders hunched, resting his forearms on his knees in a contemplative pose. On the pine needles at his feet, five pint-size Budweiser cans lay scattered.

I hadn't left the porch light on, so when I shut off the truck, he disappeared back into the shadows. I reached for the SureFire I wore on my belt and shined it at his tanned face.

"What the hell, Billy?"

He squinted into the light. "I saved one for you." He raised the last beer in the six-pack as if it were a peace offering.

"Thanks but no thanks. What are you doing here?"

"I came to apologize for being a turd the other day."

I glanced around my dooryard, realizing for the first time that the only other vehicle present besides my patrol truck was the Bronco. "Wait a minute. Where's your pickup?"

"I walked here."

"You live seven miles away!"

"Needed to think about a few things."

I snapped off the light, plunging us both into darkness. "But you decided to stop for beers?"

"Figured you could use a few pops. But I've been waiting here a while. Expected you to be home sooner." He spoke in his usual decibel range, without slurring his words. I'd seen Billy drink prodigious quantities of alcohol on occasion, but he never displayed a hint of intoxication. When I didn't accept the can from him, he popped the top and took a sip. "I heard about Briar."

I reached down to collect the five empty cans. I arranged them in a row along the edge of the porch. "What did you hear?"

"She ran her sports car into a tree. Folks say someone was chasing her."

I think he expected me to sit down next to him, but I remained on my feet. "Folks are right."

"That fucking sucks."

"Yes, it does." I gave up and sat down beside him on the plank steps. "Is that why you decided to get wasted tonight?"

"It takes more than a few beers for that to happen," he said. "It's a shame about Briar. She was a crazy girl. She came on to me the first night we met at the lodge, but I didn't do nothing, on account of Aimee. After that, she was kind of bitchy, to tell the truth. She bossed me around worse than her mom. I don't think she was used to men telling her to keep her pants on."

He took a long drink of beer. "Do you know who it was who chased her?"

"Bilodeau thinks it was your buddy Karl Khristian."

"Yeah, I heard you guys arrested him."

I was always amazed at how quickly news traveled in the Maine woods. People might live miles apart, but when a barn went up in flames or a car skidded off the road, everyone seemed to know about it within a matter of minutes.

I rubbed my bare hands together against the cold. "It looks like your hunch about KKK was right."

"Looks like it," he said. "So I guess that means there's no more reward."

The thought of Betty Morse's twenty thousand dollars hadn't crossed my mind since my last conversation with Billy, but it was clear that my friend had been thinking of little else.

"There's ballistic evidence linking Khristian to the shooting at Morse's house, but I don't think Bilodeau has anything yet linking him to those moose. Technically, I suppose that means there's still a reward."

He finished the beer and crushed the can in his big hand. Then he flung it away into the darkness.

I jumped after it. The half-frozen leaves crackled beneath my feet. "Come on, Billy, this is my yard."

"Oh fuck," he said. "I'm sorry, Mike. I'm not thinking straight these days. My head feels like it's full of spiders."

I held on to the crushed can. "When I feel that way, it usually means I have a guilty conscience."

He rose slowly to his feet and towered over me. In the moonlight, his face had the hardness of welded metal. "What do you mean?"

I wasn't sure what I meant, other than that my friend was continuing to behave in odd ways, and I wanted to let him

know that I'd taken notice. "If you walked here, you probably didn't hear the news that Chubby LeClair killed himself."

His response was to grunt. "Fucking child molester."

I waited for him to say more. When he didn't, I continued. "There was a Passamaquoddy kid named Marky Parker with him in his camper. The boy is dead, too."

"Did Chub kill him?"

"I don't know," I said. "There was a shoot-out at the camper, and the boy was injured."

"What kind of shoot-out?"

"Jeremy Bard says Chubby fired at him from the Airstream. The boy was probably caught in the cross fire."

"Bard?" Billy gathered his pale hair in one big fist and twisted it into a knot. "Now that's interesting."

"What do you mean?"

He smiled at me; I could actually see his teeth shining in the moonlight. "Did anyone ever tell you that you're a suspicious motherfucker?"

I leaned forward, trying to catch his eyes. "What do you know, Billy?"

He turned his shoulder and took a step away from me. "I know it's time for me to go home to my wife and family."

"Let me give you a ride," I said.

"No thanks. I can find my way."

"It's seven miles," I couldn't help repeating.

"Yeah, but it's a beautiful night."

"I'm going to call Aimee and tell her where you are." My tone sounded more threatening than I'd intended.

He paused at the edge of the clearing. I could barely make out his looming shape in the blackness beneath the evergreens. "If you do, you'll only worry her. She's used to me going off like this when there's something on my mind. She calls them

my 'walkabouts.' Says it's an Australian word for walking and thinking. I'm sorry I drank the last beer, Mike."

And with that, Billy Cronk melted as quietly as a deer into the forest.

36

Whoever had built my cabin had used logs from the same spruce and fir trees that stood as sentinels around it. Sometimes I fancied that I lived in a house of bones. Tonight was one of those occasions.

Cluster flies buzzed along the dusty sills. I would open the window to let one swarm out and then discover that another swarm had appeared on the inside of the glass the next morning. I had no clue where the big gray insects came from or how they got in, but their incessant buzzing was like static inside my brain.

I dumped the empty beer cans into a milk crate I used for recycling and sat down at the table with a glass of milk. Of all the mysteries in my life at the moment, Billy Cronk had to be the most frustrating. I'd convinced myself that the hardened face he showed the world was just a mask he'd forged during tours of duty in distant war zones. I would watch him play with his ragamuffin kids or stare adoringly at his sweet wife, and I would decide that he really was a kind and gentle man, someone with whom I could be friends. Then he would look at me with those frost-colored eyes, and I would have a vision of him manning an observation post in Afghanistan, firing M240 machine-gun rounds into the bodies of advancing Taliban fighters, and I would begin to distrust my instincts.

Time after time in my life, I'd come to the conclusion that human beings are essentially unknowable. I'd been betrayed enough that I should have stopped trying to figure other people out and accept them for the enigmas they were. And yet, some stubborn, foolish part of me refused to go through life that way. I wanted to believe in Billy. More than that, I needed to.

After I'd eaten my usual unhealthy dinner—burritos that went mushy in the microwave and were made palatable only with a slathering of Tabasco—I checked in on my mother's progress.

"Hello, Michael," my stepfather said when I reached him on his cell.

"Hey, Neil," I said. "I just wanted to check in and see how she was doing."

"Fine, fine." He sounded distracted. "She's sleeping again."

Despite the autumnal darkness, it was still pretty early. My mom seemed to be sleeping a great deal, but for all I knew, fatigue was a side effect of the chemotherapy. I figured having your bloodstream filled with tumor-killing chemicals must be exhausting.

"Is everything all right down there?" I asked.

"Well, this is new territory for the both of us. We haven't been sure what to expect and—I'm actually waiting to speak with the oncologist now."

He said this in an offhand way, but the muscles in my stomach tightened. "What's wrong?"

"Just trying to sort out the side effects."

"What side effects?"

"She has a bit of a temperature, but nothing alarming. The doctor told us that mild fever was to be expected." He paused, as if something had caught his attention. "I have another call, and it may be the oncologist. Can I call you right back?"

"Sure," I said. "Absolutely."

I sat at the table for half an hour, waiting for my cell to ring again, but it never did. After a while, I got up and cleaned my greasy dish in the sink and lay down on the bed in my full uniform. I fell asleep in minutes.

When I awoke, the room seemed overly bright. Sunlight was poking in through the south-facing window of the cabin, but not hard enough to account for the intense illumination before me. It took a moment to realize I'd left the overhead lights blazing. And a new swarm of cluster flies was bouncing off the windowpanes.

I shaved in the shower and found the last clean undershirt in my bureau. One of these days, I'd need to drive into Machias with my Bronco loaded with bags of laundry. I could only get by for so long hand-washing underwear and T-shirts in the sink and hanging them on the line I'd strung between the pines. The owner of the Wash-O-Mat didn't like cops. He didn't have the guts to bar me from his establishment, but he treated my every visit as if it were an incitement, which to some degree it was. Living in a small community, you didn't have the luxury of avoiding your enemies.

Or your friends.

Unless McQuarrie had need of me this morning—and there were no messages from him saying that he did—I decided to make my first stop of the day Billy Cronk's house. I wanted to see whether he'd ever returned from his "walkabout." Our conversation had left me unsettled, and while I could have checked in with him over the phone, I preferred to see his expression when I asked him again what information he was hiding from me.

"He's come and gone," said Aimee Cronk. She stood in the

doorway of her home with the youngest of their straw-haired children tucked under her arm. The baby was red-faced from bawling, but his mother paid the noise no attention.

A chill wind was blowing at my back. There had been a coating of hoarfrost on my truck thick enough that I'd needed to scrape the windshield before setting out. "Gone where?"

With her free hand, she readjusted the scrunchie holding her ginger-red hair in place. "He told me this is the day he finds a job again."

"Do you know where he went?"

"Skillen's."

"The mill just laid off a bunch of guys. Why would Billy think they were hiring?"

"Why does he think any of the things he thinks?" She phrased the sentence less like a question with an answer and more like a declaration of her husband's essential naïveté.

Once again, I found myself envying Billy. No matter how often he fell ass-first into trouble, he still had a loyal wife at home who could see into his heart as if it were sculpted out of glass. I couldn't imagine what it was like to be *known* like that by another person.

"I heard about that Morse girl," Aimee said. "Billy said you liked her. I'm sorry for your loss."

"Thanks."

"You're going to go looking for him today, ain't you?"

This unschooled woman's ability to make deductions was far better than that of half the law officers I knew.

"I thought I might."

"Tell him supper is at five o'clock sharp," she said before she closed the door.

I knew she was really telling me to make sure he got home. We were both worried about him, I realized.

*

There wasn't a cloud in the sky this morning, but a wind was gusting out of the northwest, and the sun seemed unable to generate any real heat, as if it were spent after burning too bright for too long. I remembered the old couple my mom and I had met in the parking lot near Massacre Pond on our way to Scarborough Beach. The man had used a particular phrase to describe weather like this. "A bluebird day," he'd called it.

The only birds I saw were my two ravens. They might not have been the same ones, probably weren't, in fact. But watching them coast over the leafless treetops, riding the wind the way surfers negotiate a crashing wave, I experienced a sense of déjà vu that sent my thoughts spinning back to the Morse estate on the morning we'd found the dead moose.

What is Billy up to? I wondered.

He might have been desperate enough to apply for a job at Skillen's, knowing the odds were against him. Or he might have been lying to Aimee about his intended destination for the day. In spite of everything, I preferred to give him the benefit of the doubt. When I reached the main road, I turned the wheel in the direction of Skillen's lumber mill.

The phone rang. "You're never going to believe this," McQuarrie said in a voice that told me he was smiling.

Considering his sour mood the last time I'd seen him, I didn't know what to make of this metamorphosis. "Try me."

"The MDEA asked Devoe to bring Tomahawk to LeClair's place this morning," he said. "They wanted the dog to nose around the property. They figured Chubby might have kept his stash somewhere within reach. Probably not on his own land—Chub was stupid, but not that stupid—but close enough that he could fill an order if some junkie showed up at his door in the middle of the night wanting a kick in the noggin."

Like most of the veteran wardens in the service, Mack liked nothing better than to spin a yarn. I'd learned to shut up and let the old guys tell their stories. It was faster than interrupting them with questions.

"So Devoe and the K-9 are roaming around the joint," he continued in his hoarse, happy voice. "Tommie's not a drug dog, but if you give her a whiff of Mary Jane, she knows what you're after. Anyway, they're poking around every tree stump on that hillside, when the dog goes crazy. She practically pulls Devoe out of his boots. She races to this big pile of leaves and starts digging. Guess what was buried underneath it."

"I have no idea," I said.

"A trash bag with two rifles in it," he said.

"Twenty-twos?"

"Yeah. A Marlin 780 and a Browning SA-22."

He waited for me to leap to the natural conclusion: "So Chubby and an accomplice—maybe the Indian boy—drove out to Morse's land, somehow found their way through one of the locked gates, expertly executed a bunch of moose, and then drove back to his Airstream, where they then carelessly hid the rifles in a plastic bag in the backyard."

"The point is, we found the fucking twenty-twos." Mack no longer sounded like he was wearing a ten-karat grin.

"So you think Bard was right about Chubby?"

"It sure as hell looks that way."

"But it doesn't change the fact that he shot that boy."

"Jeremy's still in deep shit," my sergeant said. "He's going to have a hard time selling self-defense to the AG, but now at least there's something to back him up about LeClair. Those rifles give him extenuating circumstances."

"Come on, Mack," I said. "He recklessly discharged his weapon, and a fourteen-year-old kid died."

"He fucked up. But maybe his career isn't totally in the shitter."

I had a hard time summoning any good feelings toward Bard, who deserved to lose his badge in my opinion, although I was hardly one to pass judgment on a fellow warden accused of carelessness. "Have you talked to him?"

"I tried his place. His girlfriend said he went out. Didn't take his phone."

I nearly swerved off the road. "What? He just got shot in the head!"

"It was just a scratch. You know how heavy a cut on the head bleeds. The ER docs sent him home last night in record time."

So now Bard had gone off on a walkabout as well. When he returned home, he was going to find he'd won the lottery. And he wasn't the only big winner this morning.

"Rivard must be relieved," I said.

"Yeah, well, he's still got half of Augusta calling for his ass on a platter. But you've got to figure this news has definitely brightened his day."

"Has it occurred to anyone that the guns might have been dumped there last night?" I said.

"What do you mean?"

"If the ballistic techs can match those guns to the bullets we dug out of the moose, then it's case closed. Pretty convenient. Wouldn't you say?"

"I'm still not following you, kid."

"Everyone in the county must have heard about Chubby and that Indian kid. If you had shot those moose and were hanging on to those rifles, could you have come up with a better place to get rid of them than in the woods behind that camper?"

Mack disappeared into silence for half a minute. When he returned, it was with a caustic laugh. "You really do have an overactive imagination. People have been telling me you're all into riddles and conspiracies. I hate to tell you, Mikey, but sometimes life ain't that complicated. Your number-one suspect is usually the one who did it."

Dead leaves tumbled across the asphalt in front of my truck. "So I guess this means I'm free, then."

"Free?"

"You don't need my help with the investigation anymore."

"Not unless Zanadakis needs you for something," Mack said. "Why? Have you got other plans?"

A row of pines appeared alongside the road. All of the trees were the same height and sharply pointed, and together they reminded me of a turreted green wall. A wide lane led through a gap in the trees to a distant, unseen smokestack from which a column of white vapor was billowing into the cloudless sky. A sign loomed ahead: SKILLEN LUMBER COMPANY: SINCE 1879.

"I might," I said.

I stopped at the gate and rolled down my window, letting in a blast of bitter air. An old guy with bifocals was perched atop a stool inside the gatehouse, doing crosswords. "Morning, Warden," he said. "What seems to be the trouble?"

It was the same greeting he'd given me the last time I'd come here with Stacey.

I flashed a harmless smile. "I'm looking for Billy Cronk. His wife told me he had a job interview here this morning."

"Can't say I know the feller," the gatekeeper said. "He's not on my list anyway. And Mr. Skillen isn't hiring at the moment. Are you sure you've got the right place?"

"This is where his wife said he'd be."

He showed teeth that were heavily stained from coffee and cigarettes. "You don't think he might have fibbed to the missus?"

"Is Mr. Skillen around today? Maybe he can shed some light on this."

"I can call him, I guess." The old man's fingers hovered over the phone.

"Tell him it's Warden Mike Bowditch," I said.

He shrugged and made the call. With the window down, I could smell the familiar odor of the mill. The friction from the spinning blades chewing through logs caused the sawdust to give off the harsh smell of burning wood.

"He's gonna come down," the gatekeeper said, pointing at the lot. "Pull up over there next to that silver Tundra."

He pushed a button and the gate rolled open on its wheels, sliding back into the tall mesh fence. I wasn't sure why I'd asked to see Matt Skillen after vowing to avoid the man for the foreseeable future. He and Stacey were clearly in love, and the best thing I could do was wish them well. I would send a card when they got married in Bar Harbor or Bermuda or whatever fancy place they chose for the wedding. And then, hopefully, I would never see them again.

I had my head down and was checking the messages on my BlackBerry—nothing more from Neil—when a face appeared at my window. When I'd asked for "Mr. Skillen," it hadn't occurred to me that the gatekeeper might think I meant Merritt Skillen and not his son. I'd been under the impression that the father didn't spend much time at the mill now that it had fallen on hard times, and yet here he was in all his kingly silver-haired eminence.

"What can I do for you, Warden?" he asked in a voice that was considerably deeper than his son's. Everything about him, in fact, seemed more substantial than Matt. He was taller and bigger boned, with large, calloused hands, and he carried himself with none of his son's natural looseness. His noble face was wrinkled around the mouth and eyes, as if he'd spent many years worrying over important matters.

"I'm sorry, Mr. Skillen," I said. "I was expecting your son."

"Matt's not here today. Is there something I can do for you?"

I removed my sunglasses to be polite. "I'm looking for a man named Billy Cronk. His wife told me he came here for a job interview."

"If he had, Earl would have just sent him on his way. We have no openings at present." He peered in at me a bit

closer, pursing his lips. "Do you and I know each other, young man?"

I saw no point in reminding him that I'd been the warden who'd asked Jeff Jordan for a .22 round that day at the checkpoint. "No, sir. I'm the warden in the next district over."

"Is there anything else?"

I glanced around the crowded parking lot and saw quite a few pickups but no black Nissans.

"You wouldn't be able to tell me if two of your employees are working today? A Todd Pelkey and a Lewis Beam? You must have a lot of people who work for you, so maybe you don't know each of them personally."

"I know *all* of my employees," he said with a hint of offense. "What do you want with them?"

"They have information for me about some possible poaching activity," I said with a deadpan expression.

He reached for a cell phone clipped to his belt. "I'll find out for you." He turned his broad back so I couldn't overhear the whispered conversation. Unlike his son, the elder Skillen looked like a guy who had personally chopped down a fair number of trees in his life. I'd never met Matt's mother, but from the evidence, I assumed she must be a slender, delicate-boned beauty. Merritt turned back to face me. "They've gone home sick, I'm afraid."

"Both of them?" Men who worked at lumber mills did not, as a rule, leave work during their shifts except on ambulance gurneys.

"It would seem so." He reattached the phone to his belt. "I trust you're being honest with me, and Todd and Lewis are not in some sort of trouble."

"I'd just like to talk with them," I said. "Thank you for your time, Mr. Skillen."

He stuck his hand through the open window. His palm was calloused, his grip like a vise. "Call me Merritt."

Billy had lied to Aimee when he'd told her he was applying for a job at the sawmill. Either that or he had been waylaid before arriving at the gate. The two men he had named as potential suspects in the moose shootings had mysteriously gone home sick—both of them, at the same time. I didn't know what to make of these coincidences except that they couldn't possibly be coincidences. Billy was up to something.

The drive north from the mill to the wild woods of Talmadge took forty minutes. Along the way, I passed the gravel road that led to Plantation No. 21 and Chubby LeClair's camper (assuming the state police hadn't hauled it away). Later, I crossed the new bridge from Princeton into Indian Township and felt the usual despair I experienced driving through the reservation. I passed the shuttered pizzeria and the seedy brick houses—each built according to the same soulless architectural plan—arranged along the shore of Lewey Lake. Most of the homes had satellite dishes and clusters of vehicles parked out front, but wadded paper blew through the yards, and white shirts waved like flags of surrender from the clotheslines. The Passamaquoddy reservation was the most depressed place I knew in Maine, and I knew all of them.

The sparkling blue waters of the lake and the distant line of evergreens along Peter Dana Point seemed fraudulent in their bright beauty. I had entered a hall of mirrors in which I could no longer distinguish what was real from what was false.

North of the rez, I took a left off Route 1 onto the tributary roads that would bring me, eventually, to the mobile home where Pelkey and Beam lived. The woods crowded closer and closer around me as I drove up into the hills.

I slowed the truck half a mile from the trailer. My loose belt was wailing like a banshee again, and I had the strong feeling it might be better not to announce my arrival in such strident terms. Better to scope out the scene first. I removed my orange safety vest and unearthed the camouflage coat I kept behind the seat, then swapped my black baseball cap for one with a Realtree pattern. I hung my new Nikon binoculars around my neck. For a minute, I considered taking the shotgun, too, but I didn't want to appear unduly provocative. Pelkey and Beam were already wary of me.

I closed the truck door until it clicked and started on foot up the dirt road. With most of the leaves down, I could see far into the gray-brown forest on either side of me. Whatever color that remained was near the ground now: yellow carpets of leaves beneath the maples, bloody sumacs turning to rust, the same way drying blood does. Of the hardwoods, only the oaks had retained their shabby foliage. It felt comforting to have so much visibility.

As I neared the mobile home and caught the first flash of metal, I raised my binoculars. I adjusted the dial on the top until a vehicle sprang into focus. It was a blue F150 pickup.

I knew, without having to read the plate, that the truck belonged to Billy Cronk.

I felt my lungs almost fully deflate. I had resisted the idea that I might find him here. Now the only remaining question was why.

I raised the binoculars again and zoomed in on the yard. Two identical Nissan Titans were parked on the other side of Billy's truck. I didn't see Tiffany's crappy little Cavalier. Evidently, she hadn't yet come down with her boyfriends' malady.

For a split second, I considered returning to my truck for the shotgun. I would have felt more confident having the pump-

action Mossberg in my hands, but I wasn't sure what I was even witnessing. No crime was being committed, not unless lying to your wife or playing hooky from your job had been reclassified as misdemeanors. My suspicion that Pelkey and Beam were very bad men didn't give me cause to go stomping onto their property loaded for bear.

Still, I needed to sort this out. I stepped off the road and began carefully picking my way through the naked trees. The openness in the forest understory now put me at a disadvantage. I had almost no cover, except to crouch behind the Christmas tree–size balsams or the trunks of the larger oaks. The curled and drying leaves under my boots turned every step into an overloud rustle. What had Charley told me? *Heel first and then toe.* I wished the expert woodsman was with me right now.

When you stalk a deer, the trick is to imagine the slowest you can move—and then force yourself to move even slower than that. Breathe evenly. Pause with every step. Will yourself to become invisible.

Foot by foot, I drew closer to the ancient trailer. It was roughly the shape and size of a boxcar. Over the years, the sun had faded the orange paint until it was the color of human skin. It might have taken me twenty minutes—maybe longer—to cover a hundred yards. I tried to approach from an angle that didn't put me in the line of sight of any of the windows or doors, so that only someone pressing their nose to the glass could have spotted me.

Pelkey and Beam had stacked about four cords of hardwood neatly behind the mobile home. The pile provided me with excellent cover when I was finally able to reach it. Peering over the logs, I saw one of those teardrop trailers you use to haul snowmobiles. Beside it, an overturned bass boat had been chained to a tree trunk to protect it from thieves. Two Polaris

ATVs sat under an elevated crossbeam the hunters utilized to hoist dead carcasses into the air so that the blood would run out onto the ground. Pelkey and Beam must have been saving their pennies to buy those new Nissans, I thought, because everything else on their property was a piece of shit.

There were blankets and towels over the windows of the trailer. The occupants were either too poor or too cheap to buy actual curtains. The place reminded me of a cave. The thought of two men living inside with a young girl turned my stomach. I wondered whether Bard's cousin Tiffany had chosen her role as their shared playmate or whether she had been cajoled by her boyfriend into sucking his buddy's cock and then one thing led to another.

I crawled forward on my elbows and knees until I could hide behind the snowmobile hauler. As I was sitting against it, with my legs drawn up to keep them from jutting into view, I noticed a white cigarette butt lying in the dirt beside me. I reached into a leather holster on my belt and removed a single latex glove. I slid it onto my right hand. The cigarette butt came from a Salem, the same brand we'd recovered from the kill sites on Morse's estate. I wrapped the glove carefully around the filter to protect whatever trace DNA might still be on it and slid the wad into my pocket.

If I poked around the grounds, what else was I likely to find? Some Starburst candy wrappers? An empty bottle of Miller Genuine Draft? I already knew where to find the .22 rifles.

A gunshot sounded in the distance, followed by three more.

The echoes told me that someone was firing in the gravel pit at the end of the road. Four shots usually meant target practice.

I darted from the snowmobile trailer back to the woodpile and ducked behind the peeling birch logs. In all likelihood, the

mobile home was unoccupied. Billy and the two creeps were firing guns together at the pit. But it seemed prudent to sneak out of the yard as quietly as I could.

I remembered what a mess the road to the pit was. Erosion had made it close to impassable. There was also the chance I would meet the armed men on their way back down the hill. I was willing to bet my life that Pelkey and Beam had been the men who'd slaughtered those moose. The lingering questions were why and what Billy's connection to them was. The best place to start searching for answers was the gravel pit. I plotted a cross-country course that would bring me to the rim of the excavated amphitheater. I wanted a balcony seat to watch the show from above.

Knowing where Pelkey and Beam presumably were, I could move faster now. I leaped over toppled trees and scratched my hands pushing through a tangle of raspberry bushes. Branches snapped beneath my feet. The binoculars bounced around on their strap and kept whacking me in the sternum. At one point, I surprised a grouse, which rocketed up from his covert and flapped heavily away through a cone of sunlight.

As I ran up the hill, I made a semicircle away from the road and then began to loop back, hoping I'd judged the distances right.

Three more shots sounded. My ears told me it was a high-powered rifle and not a shotgun or pistol.

I began to second-guess my decision not to return to my truck for the Mossberg.

The gunshots informed me that I'd gone too far, that I'd circled all the way around the pit and was now well above it. I slowed my pace to a steady walk and ducked my head. The last thing I needed was to find myself standing suddenly at the cliff's edge, in full view of the armed men below.

Up ahead, I saw a curtain of light where the trees abruptly ended and the ground fell away into the pit. I dropped to my hands and knees again and began to crawl like an animal through the forest. The dangling binoculars kept snagging on branches, so I removed them and left them on a flat, mossy stone where I could find them again. I'd run too fast up the hill and my pulse was overloud in my ears. I worried that my labored breathing might give me away. I paused, closed my eyes, and focused on my breath, trying to bring down my heart rate.

I could hear voices, laughter. I flattened myself against the dead leaves and wriggled behind a small boulder that was perched atop the rim of the gravel pit. I kept my head down and listened. They were standing at the far end of the pit, maybe thirty yards away, and I had to concentrate hard to piece together the conversation.

"You like it?" said the man I recognized as Pelkey.

"Reminds me of the M4s we had in Afghanistan." The voice was unmistakably Billy's.

"Those Colts are sweet guns," said Beam.

"Personally, I prefer these Noveskes," said Pelkey. "Nothing against the Colt ARs, but the craftsmanship here is just fucking superior."

"Three grand is pretty steep," said Billy.

"But that includes your optics and your flash suppressor and your magazines." Pelkey seemed to be the designated talker. "You can always build your own if you want to go low-budget—and we can help you with that, too. But my philosophy is, you get what you pay for. Now see, I can fire this Blackout all day without the barrel warping. You said you didn't currently own a black gun?"

"No."

"How's the recoil?" Beam asked. "Pretty gentle, right?"

"Firing one of these puppies makes it hard to go back to a bolt-action," said Pelkey. "My thirty-aught-six kicks like a fucking mule, and the two-forty-three ain't much better."

"What about twenty-twos?" said Billy. "You guys got any of those?"

"We've got everything, man," said Beam.

"I thought we were here to discuss ARs." Pelkey sounded suspicious. "On the phone you said you were looking for a black gun."

"I am."

"So why ask about twenty-twos? You want one of those, go to Wal-Mart. We took time away from work to come out here today." Pelkey's voice rose.

"I was just asking," said Billy. "I've been thinking about getting a twenty-two Mag, too."

Suddenly, I realized why my friend was here and what he was trying to do. He's not smart enough to pull it off, I thought. They're going to see right through him if he keeps asking questions.

Pelkey had already adopted a different, more brittle tone. "What are you planning to use a twenty-two for? Squirrels?"

"Coyotes. Maybe deer."

"You need to be a wicked good shot to bring down a buck with a twenty-two," said Pelkey. "Why not stick with a big-ass thirty-thirty?"

"I'm looking for something . . . quiet."

"Check it out, Lew. Billy here is a poacher."

"Takes one to know one."

Shut up, Billy. Stop talking, I ordered silently.

Out of nowhere, a song started to play, a few bars of music. Led Zeppelin's "Black Dog." A ringtone. "I gotta take this," Pelkey said.

"So are you interested in this Noveske or not?" Beam asked with some heat. "Because we're busy men."

"Maybe you should take it easy," Billy said.

"Maybe you should shut your mouth."

As formidable as Billy Cronk could be, two against one is never good odds, especially when one of your adversaries is armed with an assault rifle. I reached my right hand down and pressed the thumb lock, releasing the SIG Sauer from its holster. There were fifteen .357 SIG cartridges in the magazine. I pulled the hammer back into single-action mode.

I stuck my head around the rock and spied down into the pit. Billy and Beam were standing toe-to-toe. I'd forgotten what a hulking guy Beam was and how white his platinum-blond hair looked in the sunlight. From this angle and distance, he resembled an albino ogre. The black AR rifle hung on a sling over his shoulder.

Billy was wearing the same camo jacket I'd seen him in the night before, probably the same clothes. Except that he'd strapped his KA-BAR knife to his thigh.

Pelkey had paced away a few steps to have a private conversation. He was dressed in his mill clothes: canvas shirt and pants, a Carhartt carpenter's jacket. When he turned around again, there was a pistol in his hand. Aimed at Billy.

I rose to my knees, pointed the SIG into the pit using a two-handed grip, and shouted, "Police! Put the guns down!"

Then all hell broke loose.

Pelkey fired a shot, which caromed off the boulder beside me.

I squeezed off a round that must have clipped his jacket, because he raised his left arm as if to get a whiff of his deodorant.

Beam tried to swing the barrel of the Noveske up, but

Billy grabbed the rail with both of his big hands and drove his forehead into the other man's skull. It sounded like two rams knocking horns. As Beam fell over, he drove his boot into Billy's groin. My friend let out a howl but somehow kept hold of the rifle, and both men fell hard to the ground.

My pistol had drifted off target from the force of the recoil. I brought the barrel down again, blew out half the air in my lungs, as I'd been trained to do, held my breath, and took aim squarely at Todd Pelkey's center mass.

But he was a much faster and better shot than I was.

I saw the blur of his hand coming up and then felt a pain in my chest, as if someone had driven a sledgehammer into my ribs. I found myself staring up into an achingly blue sky that seemed to be getting farther and farther away, as if my body were dropping down a mine shaft. It's true that you don't hear the bullet that gets you.

Holy shit.

The wind had been driven from my lungs by the concussion.

I've been shot.

Barely able to breathe, I clutched at my chest and found a smoldering hole in my shirt, just inches from my heart. I held my fingers before my wobbly eyes, expecting to see blood, but there was none. The bullet had flattened itself against the ballistic vest I wore beneath my uniform. A little lead pancake fell loose as I rolled onto my side. I tried to gulp down air, but expanding my chest only made my ribs ache.

Through the pain, I heard a shot fired. Then another.

Billy.

Gasping, I found the SIG where I had dropped it and fired a wild shot into the air. I wanted them to know I was still alive, still a danger to them. I wanted to give Billy half a chance if he wasn't already dead.

321

Each breath I took burned my insides, as if I were inhaling air from a blast furnace. I rolled toward the edge of the pit again and tried to see down to the gravel floor. My vision was blurred. I could make out two dark shapes thrashing about: Beam and Billy. I rubbed my eyes frantically with the back of my hand, trying to clear them. I blinked and blinked again. The AR lay in the dirt about ten feet from where the men were wrestling with each other. Billy was trying to wrap his arms and legs around his opponent's neck and pelvis. Beam was gnawing on my friend's forearm while his bent fingers searched desperately behind him for an eye to gouge out.

Pelkey had disappeared.

I fired a shot into the gravel near the feet of the struggling men, hoping it would cause them to stop, but they just kept rolling around.

Beam's hand found a rock. He drove it against Billy's forehead again and again. Even from this distance, I could see the blood. To protect himself, my friend was forced to loosen his grip, and the other man squirmed free. Beam spun around and tried to drive the rock into Billy's nose in an uppercut motion. If he had connected, he would have sent splinters of bone into Billy's brain. But Billy caught his opponent's wrist with one hand and delivered a jab to the jaw that snapped Beam's head around.

Where was Pelkey? I scanned the far end of the pit, but there was no sign of him. I hoped to hell he had run off.

I brought my left hand up to my aching ribs, but the slightest pressure caused white-hot needles to jab into my heart. I propped myself against the boulder, trying to use it as a brace to steady my aim. If Beam and Billy separated themselves by a few feet, I might get a clean shot. Panting like this, with my eyes watering, I didn't have confidence in my marksmanship.

I saw movement out of the corner of my eye. It was just a brief impression of something blue. And then a shot echoed.

I ducked my head—as if I could actually have dodged a bullet—and brought the pistol around.

Pelkey was creeping along the edge of the gravel pit. He had scrambled up the other side and was moving from boulder to boulder. I fired and heard the round career off stone. Pelkey showed his face for an instant, and there was a smile on it. He leveled his pistol, and I flattened myself to the ground. He didn't bother firing this time, not wanting to waste a round.

He was getting closer and closer. I felt a bubble of fear rise in my stomach. At least one of my ribs was broken. My breath was ragged, and my hands were shaking. This man was an expert shooter. I wasn't sure I could stop him before he drew a bead on my head. If I rose to my feet to run to the nearest trees, he would easily knock me over again, even if he failed to hit my brain. After that, it would just be a matter of delivering the coup de grâce.

I peered around the boulder, but I didn't see him. Maybe he was circling into the pines, planning to come up behind me. No, there he was. Behind that stump. I let off a shot and saw splinters fly up where the round dug into the pulpy wood.

Pelkey took the opportunity to rise to his feet and lunge across the open space between the stump and a nearby boulder. He was almost across, almost safe again from my bullets, when there was a single sharp crack. I saw Pelkey straighten up. He had the oddest look on his face; his eyes were wide and his mouth was open. I think he was already dead when his body fell off the cliff. He tumbled down the steep gravel wall as if his bones were all loose inside the skin and not connected. His lifeless corpse came to rest in a cloud of dust beside the man-shaped target they'd been using to test the AR-15.

Billy lowered the black rifle and looked at me. One of his eye sockets was swollen and bleeding. His forehead looked like it had a red dent in the middle of it. His long hair had been torn loose of the braid. And his entire body was coated with gray dust.

He threw his head back and let out a scream like nothing I'd ever heard. I didn't know if he was back in Fallujah or Waziristan, but wherever it was, it was somewhere very far away from the warm home he shared with Aimee and his children. He spit a gout of blood on the ground and advanced on the broken man trying to crawl away from him through the weeds.

I had the impression that both of Beam's arms were broken. It was something about the way he was using his knees to lurch along. He would get himself into a kneeling position, like a man facing Mecca, and then he would flop forward with a whine. He used his shoulders to throw his arms ahead of him, but his wrists were curled in on themselves, and his hands were boneless things unable to assist his movement.

"No, Billy," I said. The words came out like a parrot squawk. "Billy, don't do it."

I watched helplessly as my friend unloaded a magazine into the back of Lewis Beam's head, reducing it to an unrecognizable mass of red jelly.

38

I gingerly removed my jacket and shirt, then loosened the Velcro straps holding my ballistic vest in place. There was a bruise the size of a paper plate on my chest. I traced the map of broken blood vessels with the tip of my finger. In a few days, when the skin turned green and yellow, I was going to look like a card-carrying member of the walking dead.

Billy had told me that his people came from the marshes of Holland, not the fiords of Scandinavia, but after having witnessed what I just had, I had a hard time believing the blood of berserkers didn't flow through his veins. After I'd gotten my voice back, I called 911. I told the dispatcher that there had been a shooting and that two men were dead and a third man was in custody, and then I went down into the pit to arrest my friend.

He sat motionless on a rock, his head bowed. His hair hung like a hood around his face, and the rifle rested on his knees.

"Billy?" My voice sounded wheezy from the injury to my ribs.

"Yeah?" he mumbled.

"Thank you," I said. "Thank you for saving my life."

He kept his blood-soaked head down. "I thought you were going to say something else."

I stood over the headless body of Lewis Beam. My mouth

went as dry as if I'd stuffed it full of cotton. "You came here for the reward," I said. "You thought they might sell you one of the twenty-twos they used to kill those moose. Or maybe you figured you could trick them into admitting what they'd done. That was your plan, wasn't it?"

He didn't answer.

Every word made my ribs hurt. "But you didn't know they'd already gotten rid of their guns. Last night, after they heard about Chubby LeClair, they dumped the rifles in a bag behind his camper. As long as the twenty-twos couldn't be traced back to them, they knew they were in the clear."

Billy raised his head and showed me his one good eye. The other was swollen and scratched, and he kept it clenched shut. I wondered how much lasting damage Beam had managed to do to it in that fight. "I guess I can forget about that reward," he said.

I wasn't sure if he'd meant it as a joke. "Why, Billy?"

"Why what?"

"From the moment we found those moose, you've acted like another person. I don't know who the hell you are anymore."

He brought his hand up to stroke his beard, as he often did, and found the hair matted. He stared at his bloodred fingers with his good eye. "I left the gate open."

"What?"

"The night of the shootings, I left it open. It wasn't the first time I forgot to lock it. I was thinking about the toy fishing rod I was going to buy Logan, how I needed to use the ATM in Machias to get cash first. I was worried about being late for his party. So this is all my fault for being stupid."

I wanted to tell him that he shouldn't blame himself, but I was in no position to offer him absolution. However this mess had begun—whatever Billy Cronk did or didn't do on

the night those animals were slaughtered—no longer mattered. What mattered were the corpses. Briar Morse, Chubby LeClair, Marky Parker, and now Todd Pelkey and Lewis Beam. The state would demand a reckoning for them all.

My gaze drifted to the body lying against the wall of the pit. Billy had taken out Pelkey with a well-placed shot to the head. Half-blind, clawed to pieces, with a chunk bitten out of his arm, he hadn't hesitated to save my life. The recognition made what I had to do next that much harder.

"You didn't have to kill Beam," I said. "He wasn't going anywhere after all the bones you'd broken."

"I know," he said.

"The state police are going to be here soon. They're going to see what happened to his head. There's no way you're going to be able to claim self-defense."

Lots of men would have played upon my emotions and asked me to lie. They would have pleaded with me to concoct some crazy story that explained how a man's head had been reduced to raspberry Jell-O. But not Billy Cronk. My friend just nodded and rose to his feet with a sigh. He handed me the AR, and I slung it over my good shoulder. He removed the KA-BAR from its sheath and set it on the rock behind him. Then he held out his wrists. "You'd better cuff me," he said.

"I'm not going to do that."

"Yes, you are," he said. "You know why? Because you're a good cop."

Wincing, I reached for the handcuffs I wore on my belt. The locks made a ratcheting sound as I adjusted them around his thick wrists.

"I'm going to testify on your behalf," I said.

He kept his arms outstretched. "Take care of Aimee for me while I'm away," he said.

"You know I will."

I led him to the entrance of the gravel pit to await the arrival of the police. As we stood there, side by side, I noticed a metal object lying in the trampled weeds. It took me a few seconds to register that it was Todd Pelkey's cell phone.

The next day, I paid a visit to the Crawford Lake Club at lunchtime. I'd swung by the mill first, and the helpful gatekeeper had told me that Matt Skillen was spending his day off with his fiancée. He even told me where to find them.

I would have preferred to speak my piece without Stacey present, but anger had kept me awake all night, despite the codeine the ER had prescribed for my broken ribs. I needed to drag the truth out into the light of day, even if I doubted it would make a difference.

As I drove east beneath low-hanging clouds, I looked out at a world that had seemingly grown old overnight. The hills had a grayish cast from the exposed trunks of the hardwoods, and the color was draining out of the fallen leaves at their feet. Where once there had been splashes of brightness along the forest floor—yellows and reds and oranges—now there were just varied shades of brown that would eventually darken into a uniform russet. Defoliation had swept across the land like a forest fire or a plague, stripping all but the oaks and beeches of their ragged leaves. In the hollows and along the riverbanks were dark islands of conifers, but even these seemed more black than green this morning. Soon it would be winter.

I had to remind myself that this was just a seasonal change and not a permanent transformation. The color and warmth would return in April, and the majesty of these woods would reannounce themselves to a doubting world. In the meantime,

I needed to keep faith, knowing that this seeming wasteland was the same beautiful place Elizabeth Morse believed must be preserved at all costs—if she even believed that anymore. Would she return to Moosehorn Lodge now that Briar was dead, or would the regret be too much to endure? There were other wild places she could save: forests and lakes that were not stamped with bad memories. I wondered if I would ever speak with her again.

The parking lot of the Crawford Lake Club was largely empty. Between the end of foliage season and the arrival of the first snowmobilers was a quiet period for the shoreside restaurant. The speedboats and jet skis were all gone from the marina, and the ice-fishing cabins the owner rented by the hour were just waiting for the lake to freeze before they could be hauled out again. The club was the only establishment serving decent food for miles in either direction. I should have known this was where Skillen would take Stacey on a lunch date.

I pulled into the space beside his newly washed and waxed GMC and got out.

The owner of the club had decorated the front porch with tall plastic palms. The whimsical trees were almost famous in the vicinity. Travelers would snap photos of one another with them, laughing and holding tropical drinks with miniature umbrellas. If the earth continued its crazy weather, I wondered how funny the joke would be in ten years.

I passed through the lounge to get to the hostess station. Someone had started a fire in the big fieldstone fireplace. A young girl with a handful of laminated menus asked me if I wanted to be seated, but I told her I was meeting people and pointed at a table against the window overlooking the lake, where two men and a woman were silhouetted against the natural light streaming into the room.

"Good morning, Warden," said Merritt Skillen. I hadn't expected the father to be dining with them.

"Mike, what are you doing here?" Stacey asked with a bemused smile.

"Hi, Stacey." I tried not to make eye contact with her. "I'm here to see Matt."

Matt Skillen leaned back from the lacquered table. "Me? What's this about, Mike?"

"Maybe we should talk outside." I could feel the other diners in the place watching us.

"That sounds ominous," Merritt said, pulling out an empty chair with his strong hand. "Why don't you have a seat?"

"I'd prefer to stand, sir."

Stacey knitted her brow. "Mike, you're acting really weird."

"How did you know where to find us?" Matt asked.

"Your gatekeeper told me. I really think it would be better if you and I continue this conversation in the parking lot."

His expression had darkened, as if he was beginning to guess what was about to happen. "You sound like you're asking me outside to have a fistfight."

"I would if I could."

"What is that supposed to mean, young man?" the father asked.

I kept my gaze locked on his son's dark eyes. "I know you paid Todd Pelkey and Lewis Beam to kill those moose."

"What?"

"Pelkey and Beam are dead, so we'll never get them to admit why they did it. Right now investigators are calling it a random act of violence against a woman who makes enemies easily. But there was nothing random about it. Elizabeth Morse once told me, 'In the end everything comes down to

money.' It was obvious from the beginning that the motive behind the shootings was to intimidate her into backing off her proposal. The mistake everyone made was in not seeing there was a bigger plan here. Lots of people don't want Morse to create a park, but your family is the one with the most to lose financially."

"That's an outrageous accusation," said Merritt, removing his napkin from his lap and resting it on the table.

I ignored him. "The first tip-off was that they worked for you. The second was their new trucks. I visited their property and saw what a dump it was. Those assholes didn't have two nickels to rub together, and yet somehow they both came up with the money recently to buy two thirty-thousand-dollar pickups?"

"Maybe they took out loans," said Matt in a neutral tone. His face was utterly empty of emotion, as if he was willing himself to remain calm.

I noticed out of the corner of my eye that Stacey was no longer looking at me; instead, she had her gaze fixed firmly on her fiancé.

"I'm sure the state police will determine that they bought those Nissans with cash," I said. "I'm also sure they won't be able to trace the money back to you—although I bet their mourning girlfriend, Tiffany Bard, might have a thing or two to say on the matter."

Merritt rose to his feet. "I think you should leave, Warden. You're causing a scene."

"Yes, sir. That is my intention."

"Hearsay doesn't amount to anything in a court of law," Matt said.

Stacey leaned across the table, reaching for her fiancé's wrist. "Matt?"

"That's true," I said. "But physical evidence counts for a great deal, even if it's only circumstantial."

A tubby, bespectacled man came up beside me. "Is everything all right here, Mr. Skillen?"

I ignored the proprietor. "I don't know if you heard everything that happened yesterday in that gravel pit," I told Matt. "You might not have heard that Todd Pelkey shot me. Fortunately, I was wearing a ballistic vest, or the bullet would have gone through my heart. So you can see why I am not in the mood to be diplomatic this morning."

"Warden, can you please keep your voice down?" the bespectacled man whispered.

Stacey's eyes were wide and darting.

"A minute before Pelkey pulled the gun, he received a call on his cell," I said. "Someone was alerting him to the fact that I'd been asking around after him and Beam. He realized Billy Cronk was trying to set him up. I picked up the phone and checked the number. The call came from your lumber mill."

Matt Skillen had grown quiet. I noticed his hand had closed around the butter knife.

"Anyone at the mill could have made that call," Merritt said, his resonant voice full of anger. "How do you know it didn't come from me? I was the one you asked about their whereabouts."

"You're right, Mr. Skillen," I said. "I don't know it was Matt who called them. Maybe it was you. But I do know it was Matt who chased Briar Morse to her death."

"What?" Stacey said, so softly that it was hard to hear.

Matt Skillen glared at me. "That's bullshit."

"Briar didn't get a good look at the truck that chased her both times. It was too dark. The only thing she noticed about it was that it made a strange noise. She said it sounded like it

had a whiny engine. It made me remember something Stacey told me when we were in my truck together. She said your pickup had a loose serpentine belt, too. But I expect you've had it fixed by now."

Merritt Skillen sat back down heavily in his chair. Stacey, I saw, was twirling her engagement ring around on her finger.

"Where were you the night Briar Morse died?" I asked Matt.

"You know where I was—with Stacey at her parents' house."

She shook her head. "You went home. After dinner, you went home. You said you had to film a commercial in Bangor in the morning. You left right after Mike."

"Stacey," Matt said. There was an unmistakable warning in his tone.

"Oh my God," she said, pushing herself back from the table so hard she nearly toppled over.

"It might all be circumstantial evidence," I said, finally letting the venom out. "And it might not be enough to convict you. But it's enough to destroy your reputation in this state—and whatever else happens, I am going to make sure it does."

"Fuck you." He was still seated, gripping the knife tightly, but he didn't have the guts to use it.

Stacey leaped to her feet. She was holding a hand over her mouth. Her entire body seemed to be quivering.

"Stacey," Matt said again, this time pleading.

She shook her head no.

"It was me," said the father.

The words caught us all off guard.

Matt Skillen whipped his head around, his mouth opening. "Dad?"

"I was the one who paid Pelkey and Beam to shoot those animals," Merritt Skillen said, rising to his feet. "I was the one who called to warn them yesterday. I followed Briar Morse in

my truck. I only meant to frighten her. I didn't mean for her to die. I take complete responsibility for everything. If you're going to arrest someone, arrest me."

Matt Skillen reached for his father's hand. "Dad, no! You don't have to do this. There's no proof."

Merritt squeezed his son's hand. His eyes gleamed with tears. "I'm not going to see your life destroyed, Matt."

"But you didn't do those things!"

"I love you, son." Then he raised his eyes to mine and said with all the dignity he could muster, "Warden, I am prepared to make a formal confession."

This was wrong. This wasn't what I wanted. Matt Skillen was the guilty one.

Merritt held his wrists out for me to cuff. I knew it was unnecessary; the old man posed no danger to me. But I wanted his son to see the consequences of his actions. I reached for the handcuffs on my belt, the ones I had used to restrain my good friend the day before.

As I did, I caught sight of Stacey disappearing through the door of the lounge. I didn't know where she was intending to go on foot, out here in the middle of nowhere. But I saw that she'd left her diamond engagement ring on the table.

39

The old man didn't speak to me on the long drive to the jail. He sat with his big cuffed hands folded in his lap, staring out at the miles of timber that had once been his family's feudal kingdom. I fancied he was asking himself again how he had managed to lose his birthright, just as he was now about to lose his reputation and, maybe, his freedom. There was only one thing of value remaining in Merritt Skillen's life, and whatever else happened, he had made the decision not to lose that as well. Despite my general dislike of the man, I couldn't help but admire his willingness to sacrifice himself for his son. My only worry was that he would be successful in his deception.

Matt Skillen followed us into Machias in his gleaming GMC, his newly repaired truck as silent as a shark.

The sheriff came down from her office in the courthouse to the ill-smelling booking area. A white-nosed golden retriever padded along behind her. "Can you explain to me what's going on here?" Roberta Rhine asked as she pulled me aside.

"He wants to confess," I said.

"To what?"

"To everything."

I laid out the whole story to her, including my certainty that the old man was taking the rap for his murderous son.

"Merritt wasn't driving his son's truck the night Briar died," I said. "But I can't prove that he wasn't the one who chased her, either."

She turned her head to watch one of her deputies taking the mill owner's fingerprints. "Do you think Zanadakis can persuade him to give up his boy?"

"No."

"Me, neither," she said.

The Washington County Jail was lit by cold fluorescent bulbs and smelled of the chlorine the inmates used to swab the floors. Somewhere behind the locked door that led deeper into the ancient prison, another door swung shut with a loud metallic clang. The sound seemed to echo in my heart. "Is Billy Cronk still here, or has he been transferred?"

"He's still here," she said, pulling on her long black braid. "The AG made the decision that we'd be the ones to hold him until his trial. He's asking the judge not to set bail, and after seeing what was left of Beam's melon, I expect the judge will agree. Billy's going down for manslaughter." She studied my eyes as if they were one-way mirrors she couldn't see through. "Would you like to see him?"

I reached down to scratch the neck of the old dog. My hand came away with a fistful of hair from the shedding animal.

"I have to go," I said, rising to my feet.

When I got back to the cabin, I found Kathy Frost waiting in the dooryard in her unmarked patrol truck. It was a new GMC with the same teal paint job as McQuarrie's. It made me wonder whether all the division sergeants were getting the same new Sierras.

"You don't call, you don't write," she said.

She was a fortysomething woman with a tall, athletic body

that she kept in shape by running triathlons and playing smash-mouth basketball with a men's team at the YMCA in Camden. She wore her hair in a sandy bob beneath her black baseball cap, and she was holding two large cups of coffee, one of which she offered me. Her grizzled coonhound, Pluto, lay asleep on the pine needles beneath her feet.

"What are you doing here?" I asked. She lived three hours away to the south, along the Maine midcoast.

"I heard about your showdown at the gravel pit. I want to see your bruise."

I thought she was joking, but she actually made me unbutton my shirt and remove my vest. My chest was wrapped with bandages to hold the broken bones steady, but my ribs ached every time I took a deep breath. Goose pimples rose along my neck and arms from the damp autumn breeze. Rain was coming.

She pressed the purple flesh above the bandage with two fingers. "That is truly disgusting, Grasshopper."

"Ow."

"What are you doing on duty? Shouldn't you be in bed, resting?"

McQuarrie had told me to place myself on sick leave, but I had decided to postpone my time off until I'd had it out with Matt Skillen. "I had one last thing to do today."

"I want to hear all about it." She peered up at a red squirrel that was perched at the apex of my cabin roof, watching us. "How about you let me inside so I can use the little girls' room. I've had three cups of coffee today, and I didn't want to pee in your yard."

"I appreciate it."

Kathy was one of only a handful of female wardens in the state and the lone sergeant. She had been a trailblazer in the

337

service, resented at first by the old-school chauvinists like McQuarrie, but she had demonstrated her mental and physical toughness over the course of two decades. She'd dedicated her life to arresting scumbag poachers who boosted their incomes selling oxycodone to middle schoolers. She'd located the dead bodies of more raped and murdered women than anyone should ever be forced to see. And she'd shot a three-hundred-pound wife beater to death in self-defense. I had decided long ago that if I ever heard one of my colleagues make a sexist crack about female wardens, I would pop him in the nose on Kathy's behalf.

Inside, I started a fire in the woodstove, and we sat down across from each other at the kitchen table. Pluto plopped his tired old body next to the heat and fell back asleep in seconds. Kathy and I looked at the dog as he started snoring, and then we smiled at each other. She picked up a squirrel pellet and made a comment about how at least I wasn't living alone anymore. She took a sip of coffee and put the cup down, and suddenly she was all business.

"So this Cronk guy saved your life?" she said.

"Yes, he did."

"That will count for something at sentencing. You must have had a few tense moments in that pit. I would have wet my undies."

"No, you wouldn't, Kathy."

She leaned forward and rested her forearms on the table. "You did good, Mike. While everyone else was patting each other on the back, you went out and found the guys we were looking for. Don't think that will go unnoticed."

I hadn't told her yet about Matt and Merritt Skillen. As glad as I was to see Kathy, I didn't seem to be in a talking mood. I kept picturing the diamond ring Stacey had left on that table.

It seemed like the one hopeful thing I could cling to at the moment.

"Rivard is going to be demoted," she said. "Word around Augusta is that the colonel is hanging him out to dry for everything that went wrong with the investigation. Queen Elizabeth has too much money and too many powerful friends. If Rivard had done his fucking job and not zeroed in so fast on Khristian and LeClair, there's a good chance her daughter would still be alive."

"It's nice to think so."

"You're having doubts about the Warden Service." She scratched her freckled nose. "I know you, Grasshopper. This whole fiasco has left you wondering whether you made the right choice. I fought hard for you those first two years when you were hell-bent on getting yourself fired, and I'm not going to watch you quit now."

"I don't know, Kathy," I said. "I just don't know."

"What if I try to pull some strings and get you reassigned?"

My cell phone rang on my belt. I reached for it and saw that the number belonged to Neil. His silence had been another blade hanging over my head.

"Excuse me a minute," I said.

I got up and walked into the bathroom and stood over the sink, looking at my gaunt reflection in the mirror. "Hi, Neil," I said. "How is she doing?"

"I'm sorry I didn't call you back, it's just that—"

"What's wrong?"

"Your mom has a fever and a low white blood cell count. *Febrile neutropenia* is the term the doctor used. They think she has an infection from the chemo. We're in the hospital in Portland. Is there any way you could come down here?" His voice cracked. "It would mean a lot to us."

"I'm on my way," I said.

Rain was pattering on the roof as I returned to the kitchen table.

"I need to go to Portland," I said. "My mom's in the hospital."

Kathy stood up. Her knee knocked the edge of the table, causing it to shake. "What's the matter?"

"She has ovarian cancer. Now they think she has an infection from the chemo."

"Jesus, Mike," she said. "Why didn't you tell me?"

I didn't know. My mother had told me that I'd shut her out of my life, and I'd heard the same thing from my girlfriend Sarah. It seemed to be a pattern I was doomed to repeat forever. "I've got to go."

She grabbed her coat from the back of the chair. "I'll go with you."

"It's a four-and-a-half-hour drive," I said. "Maybe five."

"So what?"

"You really don't have to do that, Kathy."

"I'm your friend." She reached out and touched my arm with an uncharacteristic gentleness. "Now stop being a stupid idiot and let me help you."

I felt something break inside me. I'd struggled so long to keep the cracks from showing, but suddenly the wall just gave way.

"Can you drive?" I said.

Author's Note

When an author bases a novel on real events, he faces a choice: either cover his tracks or come clean. I'm choosing to come clean.

Back in 1999, someone slaughtered at least nine moose and two deer in an unorganized township northwest of Moosehead Lake. The Soldiertown shootings were the worst recorded wildlife crime in Maine state history. For years, game wardens conducted an investigation into what became known as the "moose massacre." They chased countless leads and identified numerous suspects—all of whom were later exonerated. The case was closed and remains technically unsolved to this day.

My involvement in the story began when former investigative journalist Roberta Scruggs informed me that a district warden named Mike Favreau had continued searching for the culprits on his own initiative. Scruggs compiled a thousand-page notebook on the case, consisting of her own interviews with suspects and wardens, evidence reports obtained from the state through Freedom of Information requests, court documents, and transcripts. Although the statute of limitations has run out on the massacre, Scruggs is confident that the individuals who killed the animals have been identified (although they will never be imprisoned), thanks primarily to one warden's determination to uncover the truth.

When I began this book, my intention was to base it as closely as possible on the actual events, but I soon realized that the complicated case deserved a factual telling. Fiction can reveal deeper truths than reportage, but history demands a corrected record. And so I decided to depart from the realities of Soldiertown and let Roberta Scruggs tell the full story, which I hope she will do in print someday. While I based aspects of my novel on the real investigation—the use of .22s to kill the moose, for example—this is ultimately a work of fiction, and none of the characters or situations I depict are based upon persons living or dead. I am immensely grateful, however, for the research Roberta Scruggs provided me.

Another inspiration for *Massacre Pond* is the expansive Maine North Woods National Park, proposed originally by the group RESTORE: The North Woods and the entrepreneur and philanthropist Roxanne Quimby. For more than a decade before the concept was shelved, the park attracted national controversy. Environmentalists saw it as a much-needed sanctuary in the boreal forest; conservatives viewed it as the death knell of Maine's logging industry and its hunting and fishing heritage. Quimby (whom I have never met and who is not the model for "Queen Elizabeth" Morse) has been especially vilified in the press. My imagination began to wonder what a woman in her position must feel: what drove her to invest so much of her fortune into advocating a cause that has resulted in so many death threats. Novels often start with the question "what if," and so it was with *Massacre Pond*. Again, this is entirely a work of fiction—which is why I have moved my proposed park to eastern Maine, near the existing Moosehorn National Wildlife Refuge.

Whenever I finish writing a book, I find myself with a host of people to thank. As always, I am grateful to Bob Fernald

and my team at *Down East*. I owe a debt to Wayne Curtis for introducing me to the wonders—and wonderful people—of the Grand Lake Stream region, especially the staff of the Downeast Lakes Land Trust and the guides at Weatherby's. Thank you to the men and women of the Maine Warden Service for answering my many nitpicking questions and to the crew of "North Woods Law" for taking me behind the scenes. I am grateful to the readers of my early drafts: Monica Wood, Kimberly Bryan-Brown, Beth Anderson, and Erin Van Otterloo. At Minotaur Books I have had the good fortune to work with some of the best people in the business: editor Charlie Spicer; senior publicist Sarah Melnyk; and publisher Andrew Martin.

Thank you, Ann Rittenberg, for always having my back. You don't know how much I depend on your support.

Lastly I want to express my love and gratitude to my family—all you Doirons out there—and especially my wife, Kristen Lindquist, the best writer in our house.